TOUGH AT THE TOP

Nicky Edwards

Published in 1992 by Onlywomen Press Limited,
Radical Feminist Lesbian publishers,
71 Great Russell Street, London WC1B 3BN.

Typeset by Columns Design and Production Services
Limited, Reading, Berkshire, U.K.

Printed and bound by Loader Jackson Printers,
Bedfordshire, U.K.

British Library/Cataloguing-in-Publication Data.
A catalogue record for this book is available from the
British Library.

For Sasha

ONE

Black clouds hung in the Norfolk sky like boiling lead, waiting to pour on the head of any invader. Along the track between two vast hedgeless fields, bouncing from pothole to rut, drove Felicity Rouse in a ten year old Saab. She had come to claim the legacy of Great Aunt Rapunzel.

"Flat as the bottom of a bed-pan, and twice as insalubrious," Mr Longe, the executor of the bequest, had described the location. "Nobody has lived in the house since your aunt went abroad in '79." Lugubrious Mr Longe had brightened a fraction. "There has been an offer for the property." Reverting to type he added, "although I can't imagine why."

Nor could Felicity, when the track finally brought her to the gates of Hope Cottage. She sat in the car, while dusk gathered about her, with the beam of the headlights illuminating the dereliction of her new home. The roof had lost all but a few tiles and the end gable sagged alarmingly away from the other walls, as though sulking. The stucco had crumbled off the face of the house, revealing bricks of a fierce red clay. Elder saplings flourished at the window sills, eating out the mortar with their roots. Every pane of glass was broken, and a sheet of corrugated iron had been nailed across the front doorway.

The garden, which Felicity had remembered from her only visit, twenty years ago, as a riot of apple blossom, was full of debris, not all of which could have come from the decaying house. Rapunzel had never owned a twin-tub washing machine or a Fordson Super Major tractor, yet the remains of both had come to rest by the gate. The fruit trees, ancient and naked, creaked arthritically in the easterly wind. They would have fallen to the ground, if they could only find room among the rubbish in which to lay their weary branches. A defunct agricultural implement, possibly a harrow, sprawled on its back with its claws in the air, like a defeated dinosaur.

The windbreak of evergreens, which enclosed Hope Cottage and a patch of waste ground beyond the garden boundary, crowded in on Felicity, shutting out any last glimmer of daylight. Bats flitted happily among the rafters. Deciding to leave exploring for the morning, Felicity started the car. She was not a coward, but there were more comfortable places to spend the night, and she hoped the White Stag Hotel in the nearby village of Orfton-Saint-Scabious might be one of them. Rather than reverse half a mile up the track back to the road, she began a ten-point turn. By the seventh point she had broken through the icy crust of earth, and by the tenth she was stuck fast in the gluey ruts. Bogged down more thoroughly with every manoeuvre, Felicity resigned herself to a night in the car, retrieved her sleeping bag from the boot (she never travelled without it) and settled down to sleep.

The sun had been up for an hour when she awoke, although its rays had not yet penetrated the dense screen of yew, holly, spruce and hawthorn which surrounded her. An insistent rapping on the car window invaded, shaped and finally dispelled her dreams. Ungumming her eyelids, Felicity beheld a man with a flat red face peering in at her. Behind him, the tractor from which he had dismounted chundered away to itself in the drive.

"S'pose you'll be wantin' a tow, then?" said the man, muffled through the glass.

"Jogalong, jogalong," chattered the diesel engine.

Felicity yawned and wound down the window. "Would you mind?" she asked. "I seem to have got stuck."

"Thought you would," grunted the visitor. "Saw you come down this old track last night. Said to the wife, 'Shirley, there's some chap drivin' up to Hope Cottage.' And she says, 'It's terrible sticky up the far end, they'll most likely get bogged down.' And here you are." He beamed.

"Too kind of you to have thought of me," Felicity said, slithering out of her sleeping bag. She felt at a disadvantage, cocooned.

"Well, I'd had to 'ave moved you anyway, you're

blocking my road to the Forty Acre," confessed the farmer, unabashed.

"I didn't realise it was a thoroughfare."

"It's not, by rights. But I can get in the bottom of the Forty Acre this way, it saves me going all round by the road. You can't come up here though, it's not public."

"Oh can't I?" Felicity was cross and rumpled, with a full bladder and a stiff neck.

"What you doing, anyway?" enquired the man, removing his checked cap to scratch his balding scalp.

"Looking at the cottage."

"You one of them property speculators?" His eyes, under their unruly overhanging grey brows, shone with interest.

"No." said Felicity shortly. "Now Mr. . .?"

"Bruton." He extended a hand the colour of his muck-encrusted boiler suit through the window. Felicity shook it gingerly, and announced her name.

The rescue operation was simple enough. In a cloud of diesel fumes, Marina the car was dragged out of the mire and set back on the firmer path, into the worst pot holes of which the odd load of hard core had been thrown. Farmer Bruton rehitched the muck-spreader behind his tractor and admonished Felicity about the folly of girls sleeping in their cars in lonely rural spots ('though I took you for a chap and so did the wife. Can't tell these days, can you?'). With a last curious look he drove off, leaving, as a parting gift, a solid brown lump of organic matter which flew off the back of the muck-spreader and struck Marina in the middle of her windscreen.

"And off in a cloud of cow-shit rode Sir Galahad," Felicity said to herself, walking back towards the cottage in search of a bush behind which to relieve her discomfort. This pressing problem resolved, she embarked on an inspection of her new domain.

The windbreak sheltered the cottage and about an acre of land. Beyond the garden was the rough patch on which Felicity had been trapped overnight. A decayed brick pigsty, overgrown with brambles, and the ruin of a wheeled wooden hen-house adorned this area. The remains of a stoat, somehow mummified, lay on the floor of the hen-house. The property boasted a small pond, scummy, green and sunless, with the promise of mosquitoes in the summer and damp all the year round. Willow trees inched out from the banks, reclaiming the water for land.

Within the erratic garden boundary (a sagging line of chestnut paling leaning on a patchy hedge) the dead stalks of last year's nettles rattled at Felicity's elbows as she picked a path gingerly across the lawn. Between the nettles and the giant dandelions, the cow parsley and rosebay willow herbs, the lawn was fairly notional. By summer, she imagined, it would be impossible to cross from the gate to the house without a scythe. Soothing dock leaves flourished under the hedge, and from what might once have been the vegetable garden she had a pungent whiff of garlic gone wild.

Felicity stood in front of her house and regarded it close up. Even intact, it would have been an ugly building, square and squat, a hundred and fifty years old, or therabouts. The walls were thick and the windows small, suggesting dark and stuffy rooms inside. There were no picturesque details or period features and the charm of the flint and brick Norfolk vernacular had not featured in the design of this agricultural dwelling. Not, thought Felicity critically, noticing the inappropriate proportions and asymmetrical face of the house, that there had been any design involved. Somebody had obviously just come along and built the thing one summer when Victoria was still a girl.

The back of the house faced north. The remaining plaster was covered with a slimy green algae. Behind a couple of ramshackle sheds ran a clogged and stinking ditch. The back door stood open, and Felicity cautiously stepped over the threshold.

She found herself in a scullery, small and damp, with a hand pump and a copper in the corner for boiling water. Old ashes still lay in the grate. Cobwebs filled the empty window frames. The air in the house was cold and close, none of the thin March sunshine had found its way in. The floor was of red tiles, laid, she suspected by their uneveness and wet gleam, directly onto compacted clay. The trails of busy molluscs crisscrossed the rubicund squares.

In the kitchen next door, the ceiling had fallen in. Plaster hung from the laths and was heaped onto every horizontal surface like powder snow. A Rayburn covered in bird droppings sat in the fireplace and several generations of wallpaper flapped sadly off the wall. Crunching across the rubble in her sensible boots, Felicity found a small parlour. The room was dark, the only window being covered by a wistaria that was growing into the house. In the gloom, fantastic fungi glowed pink and green from the soaking wall. A small overstuffed sofa, with the horsehair insides exposed, suddenly emitted a ping, as though something had tweaked one of the springs. A pair of red eyes appeared from the sofa's innards and stared at Felicity. She backed quickly out into the main room.

Opening off the back of this was the door to the bathroom. Felicity made her way cautiously to the door and peered into the lean-to. There was a toilet with no cistern, and a bath with no taps. Unable to fathom the meaning of this, she turned her attention to the enclosed staircase. Hoping that, if the treads were rotten, the handrail wasn't, and that their breaking strain was greater than ten stone, she proceeded to climb.

The staircase was so steep and narrow, it might better be described as a ladder with walls. It went straight up and emerged through a hole in the floor above. The lack of a roof at least gave light by which to see. There had been two bedrooms, or was it three? The partition walls were on the floor, in a welter of timber, plaster and tiles. The two chimneys still stood, without their pots. Not trusting the floorboards, Felicity stayed at the top of the stairs for her survey, then retreated cautiously backwards.

Once out of the house, having shut the back door carefully behind her, Felicity completed her circum-navigation of the exterior, and discovered a 1960's touring caravan by the compost heap. It was an off-white, bubble-shaped holiday home, which Great Aunt Rapunzel had towed behind her old tank of a Volvo on her yearly explorations of the seasides of Europe. The caravan was old and slightly foxed in appearance, but the door was locked, and inside it looked intact.

Felicity fished in her pocket for the bunch of keys which the sepulchral Mr Longe, of Messrs Longe, Waite and Highbill, family solicitors, had bestowed upon her after the reading of the will. As she opened the door, a brown rat (cousin of the occupant of the sofa?) stood on the sill of the caravan, as though to usher her into his home. The two creatures stared at each other for a moment, then Felicity seized a rusty star picket which was lying in the grass and smote the rat on the head, caving in its skull. She was a vegetarian and a pacifist, but there were limits to her benevolence. Removing the corpse with the pointed end of the fencing post, she climbed up into the caravan.

As the the blocks under the nose of the little vehicle had collapsed, she felt like a diver exploring a sunken ship. The floor listed crazily to port, and she had to hang on to the door frame. Although the air smelt damp and rather fertile, the foldaway bed, formica table, kitchenette and gas lamps were all in place. The rat had been a visitor rather than a resident, there was no sign of a nest; he was not a family rat.

Felicity was sitting with her elbows on the table thinking about breakfast, when she saw a small round hole appear in the picture window of the caravan, heard a flat crack, and realised that she was being shot at. Seizing once again her rat-dispatcher, she climbed against the gradient out of the caravan and charged without pause for reflection towards the hawthorn tree behind which she could see the gunman lurking.

Hurdling the ramshackle fence, she arrived in three bounding strides at the gnarled trunk, close to the old pigsty, which gave the sniper cover. Taken by surprise, he had only begun to scramble to his feet when Felicity was upon him, her condensed exhalations steaming dragon-like from her nostrils. Brandishing her own weapon with one hand, and seizing the air-rifle from her assailant's startled grasp with the other, she turned and marched away, with the boy following, protesting and trying to regain his property. He was about twelve years old, dressed in combat trousers and a racing driver's paddock jacket. His features looked as though they had been picked at random from a police artist's sketch book. His ears matched neither each other nor his head, but protruded at crazy angles through his cropped hair, which was the colour of wet sand. His eyes, one blue, one brown, also took an independent line. A pustulent eruption at the corner of his mouth heralded the onset of puberty, and one of his front incisors was missing.

"You wanna give us that back, or I'll tell my dad," he whined,

Unmoved, Felicity paused at the edge of the pond and hurled the rifle firmly into the water. "If you want it, fetch it," she said.

Disconsolately the boy watched the sluggish ripples spreading on the glutinous surface of the pond. The green and unreflective skin of the water composed itself as though never disturbed. The pond looked like the primeval swamp, from which the first amino acid was struck, galvanised by wild electrical storms into the long evolutionary haul.

"I can't go in there," he complained.

"I don't imagine it is very deep," said Felicity, heartlessly.

"Water's not deep, it's the clay. Last time I went in our pond, they had to call the fire brigade. Stuck half a day, I was."

"Then you must reconcile yourself to your loss."

"'That'll teach you, Don," said a girl who had rattled up on a brightly coloured bicycle during the course of this exchange. She was smaller than the boy, but, since her jacket bore the logo of the same tobacco company as did his (obviously an offer from the local petrol station), Felicity assumed a relationship.

"Shut up, Feeble," snarled the boy, rounding on his new tormentor.

11

"Both of you are trespassing, I'm sure you know. Why don't you go away and fight each other somewhere else?"

"'s not true, anyway," the girl returned with certainty. "No-one lives up here. It don't belong to anyone."

"It do," argued her brother. "That old woman what lived here. She went away the year I was born. Dad said."

"She must've known what you were going to be like then, if she left the country." The girl dodged a karate chop aimed at her head and returned her attention to Felicity. "So if anyone owns it, she do, and you've got no business telling us to go. What you doing here anyway, Felicity Rouse?"

"You have the advantage of me." The children looked up at her uncomprehending. "How do you know my name?"

"Our Dad give you a tow. He said."

"There's a man with a lot to answer for."

"You should be grateful," reproved the girl. "He done you a favour."

"That's not what I meant."

"What a silly name, is it foreign?" asked the girl.

"German," the boy said, dropping to his knees and pointing an imaginary rifle at his prisoners. "Raus! Schnell! Like in the old films."

"No, it isn't. Who are you then, apart from the minor Brutons?"

"I'm Don," announced the elder. "And this is Feeble Phoebe."

"People who live in glass houses," chirped the girl, "shouldn't throw stones. His proper name's Adonis."

"What was your mother thinking of?" asked Felicity.

"Civilisation," replied Phoebe, matter-of-factly. "She watched every episode, *and* got the book out the library. Don was going to be called Clark, but Dad said no."

"Didn't want everyone thinking she got me off some Yank up at Lakenheath," added her brother.

"Though she said we was the children of the gods, so I don't know who she was holdin' responsible."

"Stupid kid, you don't know nothin' about anythin'.'" Phoebe had obviously upset her brother. "Dad wouldn't of kept us, if he didn't think we was his."

"Then Mum buggered off to Lowestoft with some trawlerman," confided Phoebe.

"Called Poseidon, no doubt," murmured Felicity.

"What you tellin' her for?" raged Don at his sister. "She's no business round here." His fury reminded him of his original grievance. "When I tell Dad she stole my gun, he'll call the police. Come on, out of it," he cuffed Phoebe round the ear. "She'll be one of 'em child-molesters, I reckon. Get on home or I'll tell Dad you been talkin' to strangers."

"Don't hit your sister, or I'll throw you in the pond," said Felicity mildly.

"He's got a yellow belt in karate," warned Phoebe. Her square, open face, with it's high forehead crossed by freckles made her look deceptively innocent. With her mouth full of orthodontal ironmongery and heavy plaits either side of her head, she looked more like the product of an american serviceman's indiscretion than her brother.

"Shut up, Feeb," counselled this sage, pulling his own BMX bike, a larger and newer version of the one which his sister was riding, out from the windbreak where he had hidden it.

"Shut up yourself, Adenoids," she retorted happily.

"And you," her protector turned to Felicity, "Just you wait 'til I tell my Dad. You'll get wrong from him and the police. Better clear out now."

"Oh, get off my land, the pair of you," snapped Felicity, loosing patience. Phoebe, who was growing bored, had already started wobbling up the track towards the road. Adonis followed, pausing to throw a last sulphurous glance over his shoulder.

Felicity walked back towards the house, surprised at herself. She had sounded positively feudal. That phrase 'my land' had risen unbidden, but so easily, to her lips. She looked around her acre of overgrown garden, orchard and scrub, her crumbling buildings and encroaching trees. The place was clearly impossible, and Felicity had only come to view it for sentimental reasons before putting it up for sale. Even the famously hardy Great Aunt Rapunzel, pioneering spirit that she was, had been happy to exchange mid-Norfolk winters, with the wind blowing constantly from the Urals, for the more salutiferous airs of Menton.

She patted Marina on her blue metal flank, to encourage the car to start. Climbing into the driver's seat, she looked at the cottage, imagining how it would be when some developer had turned it into holiday flats. Or perhaps, since there was no natural attraction or beauty for miles in any direction, not holiday flats but a commuter's country retreat. Not that you could really commute from here to anywhere. A weekend cottage then. Refuge for Londoners sorely oppressed by the grime and noise of their vibrant but filthy city. It need not concern her, the use to which it was put. Closing the window, to exclude the sour and claustrophobic air which had settled within the sheltering trees, she set off.

Halfway up the drive, she found her way blocked by an old estate car, coming from the road. Its driver was a round, permed and practical-looking woman with the snub-nose and slyly set eyebrows of an older pixie. Her blonde, greying hair was managed by a headscarf with the Royal Castles depicted upon it, but her manner was far from regal. As Felicity braked to a halt, her visitor bounced out of her own car and advanced down the track at a bustle in her sheepskin boots.

"Mrs Bruton, the farmer's wife," sighed Felicity to herself, getting out of her own car. "Happy Families."

"Did you threaten to throw my boy in your pond?" demanded the new arrival, pugnaciously.

"Possibly"

"Don't get clever with me, madam. Did you, or did you not, say you would lay hands on my son?"

"Well, I've only promised to throw one boy in the pond today, but I don't know if he was your son."

"I'm Mrs. Bruton."

"Back from Lowestoft?" inquired Felicity.

"The second Mrs. Bruton," her visitor said, repressively

"That's the one then."

"You've no right to be threatening a child. And he tells me you chased him off with a great old iron bar."

"Did he tell you why?"

"For trespassing, indeed. If he's done wrong, I'm the first to tell him so. But no-one else has the right to raise their hand to my children, let me tell you. I won't have him bullied."

"And I won't be shot at. Frankly, Mrs Bruton, if you can't control your son. I don't see why I should sit quietly and let him use me for target practice."

"He was after pigeons. He said it was an accident."

"Do pigeons live in caravans?"

"It still don't give you the right to do what you did."

"Isn't the custom to send the father to make the threats in these cases? If your husband would care to stop round, I'll happily throw him into the pond, if you must assert your familial right to trespass with deadly weapons upon my privacy."

"Don't talk silly."

"Well then," Felicity, tired of the Brutons, concluded the interview by getting back into her car, "I'll be going. If you would be so kind as to get out of my way."

TWO

"When is a motorway not a motorway?" asked the lorry driver who tried to pick Felicity up in the Red Lodge cafe on her way home. She soused her chips in non-brewed condiment and ignored him.

"When it's the M11," he answered himself. "Terrible road that is. You going up to London?" Felicity grunted and hid behind a Sunday magazine.

"You got a good healthy appetite," continued her interlocutor relentlessly. "I don't like all these young girls on diets. Nothing to get hold of. You should have some bacon though. Get some protein on your plate."

"I'm a vegetarian," volunteered Felicity, spearing a well-lubricated mushroom on the end of her fork.

"That can't be good for you," reproved the trucker, who looked as much like a Michelin man as any professional traveller has a right to do. His lorry was loaded with mechanically recovered turkey meat slurry.

Felicity progressed through a meal calculated to send any driver to sleep at the wheel, and then cushion the subsequent impact, giving her full attention to a stoutly constructed crumble and a large mug of coffee as antidote. The attention of the knight of the road who had settled across the red-checked table cloth from her was fortunately claimed by the fruit machine. His fellows, men in the coloured dungarees and short polyester uniform jackets of their trade, eyed Felicity with muted curiosity as they queued for the 'phone, to call their depots and wives. A pair of salesmen carried on a perfectly audible and highly derogatory conversation about the age and depreciatedness of Felicity's car, which could be seen cowering in the untarmaced lorry park, dwarfed by the big rigs of the carcass hauliers. She could have gone to the Happy Eater next door, and braved the portion control, but even the name depressed her.

Once on the road again, she reflected that the lorry driver had been right about one thing, at least. The M11, when she reached it, was the worst sort of joke.

She had been on more progressive 'A' roads. Its rumbling, concrete-block surface reminded her of the older german autobahns, the ones which had been built to facilitate the speedy passage of tanks. Dodging the shreds of tyres shed by heavy goods vehicles, and negotiating a velodrome-sharp bend, she wondered why anyone would contemplate making this journey every week-end for the sake of two days in their Norfolk cottage retreat. Helpful signs informed her that there were no services on the motorway, and she was glad she had availed herself of the bracing outdoor privy at the transport cafe.

London was, after all, far more convenient, she mused, crawling in the Sunday afternoon traffic from Redbridge through the East End. Her neighbours in NW5 might, for all she knew, be as odd as the Brutons, but as she had never met, let alone been shot at, or towed out of a bog by, most of them, she was able to ignore their possible eccentricities.

Felicity's home on Dartmouth Park Hill might not offer her an acre of space, or anywhere to keep a pig, as did Hope Cottage, but nor was it a ruin. If the flat had been falling down, then surely the scaffolding which permanently bedecked one or other house in the terrace would serve as a sheet anchor. Victoriana could go on for ever, after all, if rejuvenated by teams of builders at regular intervals.

As she let herself into the flat, Felicity could hear the plummy tones of her landlady talking on the telephone in the living room.

"...I had an unemployed lodger once," she was saying. "It was terrible. Moping round the house all day, keeping the heating on, depressing the visitors. And of course they can't help but envy those who are still working for a living. Then of course, they start expecting you to subsidise them. Won't split the bills fifty/fifty. Which of course, considering they're the ones who run up all the electricity, sitting around the whole time, watching the tv..."

Felicity smiled. She could not imagine that Eilona McFadden, millionaire socialist, Labour parliamentary hopeful and daughter of a family which had won wealth and enoblement as successful slum landlords in Glasgow, had been troubled by that lodger for long.

". . .and they will tell the dole people that they're paying rent, so of course it gets back to the Inland Revenue. My accountant was furious," continued Eilona to her caller. "They hang about like albatrosses, trying to make you feel guilty for being solvent, and the worst thing of all, is they have no conversation. Nothing to talk about at all. I had a terrible time with her."

Felicity went to her room and unpacked her rucksack. Something emerged from the thick piled carpet and bit her ankle. She realised that Ming, Eilona's spoiled cat had reinfested the flat with fleas. She would have to get the pest-spray man round when Eilona was out. As Eilona refused to admit that vermin could be found in any but poor and dirty dwellings (which thanks to inherited wealth and a good daily woman, hers was not) the eradication of Ming's frequent visitors had to be conducted in secret.

"Hi, Fliss," said Eilona, looking self-conscious, as Felicity walked into the living room. Her 'phone call was apparently over. "I didn't expect you back so soon."

"I only went to take a look at it. Sentiment really."

"How is the inheritance?"

"An ancestral ruin, without the battlements."

"What fun," enthused Eilona, picturing one of her father's smaller baronial estates.

"Not really. It's only a farmworker's cottage, and pretty derelict."

"Oh well, you'll be selling it anyway, I suppose." Eilona dismissed Felicity's broken roof-tree with a shrug, which her grandfather's tenants would have recognised. "Dennis rang. He wants you to call him."

"Was that him on the 'phone just now?"

"No," Eilona looked even more uncomfortable. "That was someone else."

"Oh." Felicity wondered what had come over her normally self-possessed (not to say supremely arrogant) landlady. "Well I suppose it's about work, and I'll see him tomorrow in the office, so it can wait."

"He did seem to think it was rather urgent," insisted Eilona.

"Let him wait," repeated Felicity. "Has Ming been sick in here?"

"Does it smell?" Eilona looked behind the sofa. "I did spray it. I forgot to put the camembert away last night, and she ate nearly all of it, poor darling. I do hope she doesn't get listeriosis."

"I don't think cats do," ventured Felicity.

"I did ring Maria, and asked her to come round and deal with the carpet. You know what I'm like with things like that, only make a worse mess. She wouldn't come though, and it's just round the corner. So it must wait until tomorrow. Give it another blast of Arpeges if it's bothering you."

"This one's called Constanzia, actually. Maria was the last but three."

"Is she? I must try to remember. I wish I had more time for home-making. But I do think she might have turned out, just this once. It wasn't much to ask, and you think she would be glad of the money."

"Maybe she has things to do on Sundays."

"I suppose she must," agreed Eilona. "Catholics do, don't they?"

"So I gather."

"Anyway, I have to dash," said Eilona, scooping a mess of papers off the coffee table into her briefcase. "I promised I'd go to some ghastly meeting that the trots on the District Committee have organised. You can tell they don't have a social life."

"Why go?" asked Felicity, not really wanting to know, but feeling guilty about how glad she was not to have to spend an evening with the other woman.

"Every vote counts. Even those of young men with fake Liverpool accents and overactive sebaceous glands. Politics is hell."

"Well, if you can convince them you're the people's tribune you deserve the nomination," conceeded Felicity. "See you later."

"Don't forget to ring Dennis," commanded Eilona as she swept out of the room. Felicity smiled non-committally, already reaching for the tv guide.

* * * * * * * * * *

Dennis was, inevitably, waiting for her at ten o'clock
the next morning, hovering anxiously by her desk. She
had left the cheap plywood surface clear on Friday,
now a brown envelope bearing her name sat ominously
next to the filing tray.

"What's this, Dennis?" she asked, picking up the
envelope. "Did I forget my own birthday?"

"It's your notice," he writhed with embarrassment.
"I'm sorry. You know we didn't get the Trust funding
renewed. The executive council meeting this weekend
voted to, erm," he faltered.

"Give me the sack?"

"Let you go," he amended

"I wasn't straining at the leash." she observed,
sourly. The envelope contained a letter informing her
that her services were no longer required, and
expressing every confidence in her future success.
Stapled to it was a cheque.

"What's this?" she held the green slip up for
Dennis's inspection.

"Actually, it's a month's pay. In lieu of notice. I
thought you wouldn't want to hang around."

"Is that what you told them?"

"As your line manager," he twisted the ends of his
moustache, "I was called in to advise. But of course,
the decision was theirs."

"And you want me to clear my desk today?"
Felicity felt as she did at the dentist's after an
injection, numbed but aware that something nasty was
going on.

"If you could." Dennis avoided looking at her. "Of
course we'll have a leaving party for you, as soon as
we can arrange it. It's all been a bit sudden."

"Spare me," she snapped.

"All of us are feeling the pinch, Felicity." complained Dennis. "There's no need to take it personally.
None of us are getting an increment this year, and
they're putting a bar on the external telephone line."

"My heart bleeds."

"The fact is," he confided, "they can't even afford

to have you sitting at your desk for the next month. They need the space for the new clerical trainee."

"You're getting a YTS kid in to do the filing? What about Dawn?"

"She decided not to come back from maternity leave," said Dennis.

"Oh did she? How very convenient."

"Plus, of course," continued her manager, "employees under notice tend not to be very productive, and can be quite expensive. Not," he added hurriedly, "that I am suggesting you would.."

"Make personal calls to Australia and sabotage the computer system?" asked Felicity.

"Nothing of the sort. It's since we sent the treasurer on that management course. She picked up some very strange modern ideas. And the Chairman is so impressionable.."

"And you, dear Dennis," interrupted Felicity, "are a worm. And since I'm sure you would happily throw every one in this office out of work if it secured your own position, please don't bother to make a speech about how sad you are to see me go."

"There's no need to be like that."

"Why? Because I'll need you as a reference? Well you know what you can do with it."

"I'll be in my office if you want to say goodbye," Dennis retreated quickly.

"No way," she shouted after him. "Toady! Sycophant!" Heads of colleagues appeared in the corridor. "Never," she lectured them, "work for an employment rights charity and expect to have any of the damn things yourself." Returning to her desk, she flung her coffee mug, pot plant, and the historical novel she had been reading, into a carrier bag, searched her drawers fruitlessly for any other sign of her two year personal occupancy and was out of the building for good by eleven forty five.

****

It was soon borne in upon Felicity that by losing her job, she had committed a grave error of taste. She was

21

not aware of the process by which all her friends had drifted into salaried employment over the past five years, for at one time they had been as representative a sample of the unwaged as was to be found. However, mysteriously, the change had happened. Her peers had cut, or grown their hair (as the case required), stopped dressing from Laurence Corner, and ceased to pretend that they didn't have an honours degree apiece.

For these formerly politically aware women, who had been lulled into the comfortable state of feeling good about feeling good, Felicity's fall from grace sent a frisson of apprehension up their regularly shiatsu-ed spines. While between jobs, Felicity recognised that she was the spectre at everybody's feast. Bosom buddies, who had once called her up twice a week for inconsequential chats, were not heard from. No-one knew what to say to her. Once they had asked 'how's the job hunting going?' the subject was quickly changed.

To that formulaic enquiry, Felicity was tempted to respond 'How do you think?'. The market for unemployed unemployment researchers was not buoyant. Official policy on unemployment was that it would go away if ignored and the charitable industry which investigated the condition of the jobless found it hard to raise money. It was not a sexy issue, as Felicity's ex-line manager had often complained.

She began to avoid social gatherings where she knew the conversation would revolve around houses (owner occupied), holidays (foreign), builders (fecklessness of) and most of all, jobs. After two years in which her only acquaintance with the Department of Social Security had been at briefing-paper's length, she rediscovered the long queue, the lost application, the incorrectly filed form, the supplementary enquiry and the delayed giro.

"How's the job hunting going?" asked Eilona McFadden, en route to a Red Rose conference in Strasbourg. Felicity gritted her teeth. "Because if you haven't found anything by the time I get back from this Eurosoc jamboree, I think we should have a serious talk about whether you will want to go on living here."

"Don't you mean whether you want to get another lodger?" asked Felicity.

"No, I don't," said Eilona, peevishly. "Where is that taxi? If it doesn't come in five minutes I'm going to have to ask you to be a love and run me to Heathrow. I'll give you some petrol money, of course," she concluded, generously.

"Eilona, I'm not a pauper," exploded Felicity. "I haven't been to work for a week, so what? There have been times when I was home for longer than that with 'flu. I don't know if you've noticed, but I haven't started eating baked beans out of the tin and watching the daytime racing yet."

"Darling, do stop yelling," commanded Eilona irritably. "It's you I'm thinking of. Perhaps it would be better for you not to be living somewhere so. . ." she looked around the expensively furnished living room for inspiration, "so cushioned. I think it will undermine your motivation to get another job. Honestly, it would be better for you to go."

"The only thing that cushions this flat is cat turds," shouted Felicity, furiously. "It consoles me to think that when I move out, that incontinent fleabag Ming will starve to death, because you'll never remember to feed the bastard animal."

"I must go," complained Eilona. "I'll have to get the tube. This really is too bad, Felicity."

"Yes, too bad."

"I'll see you when I get back."

"You hope not."

"Perhaps if you were to find somewhere else in the meantime, it would be for the best," conceded Eilona, shifting her baggage out into the hall. "I won't hold you to the rest of this month's rent."

"I'm underwhelmed."

Eilona made an expression halfway between a placatory smile and a business-like nod, and left.

The telephone rang. Felicity picked herself up from the armchair into which she had collapsed and answered it. Mr Longe, the solicitor, desired an audience with her. His secretary wondered if Ms Rouse would be available after lunch. Ms Rouse intimated that she would be, put down the receiver and devoted the rest of the morning to wondering where on earth she was going to live. Grand gestures were all very fine, but she had only a week in which to make this one a reality.

The solicitor's office was in a labyrinthine old building in Bedford Row. Mr Longe's room had no windows and was as gloomy as the man himself. Apart from a desk and two underpadded chairs, it contained rows of filing cabinets which looked as though they were charged with dismal secrets.

"Will you be selling Hope Cottage?" enquired Mr Longe, after a brief exchange of pleasantries.

"I suppose I'll have to," said Felicity. "I lost my job last week."

"Oh dear me," tutted the lawyer. "Most unfortunate. Are you seeking another one?" Felicity gave him a repressive look. "Well," he shuffled papers on his desk, "then perhaps an expeditious sale of the property will be an advantage."

"Who has made an offer?"

"A solicitor in East Dereham. Acting on behalf of a client."

"Is that what you wanted to see me about?"

"Not primarily," said Mr Longe, leaning back in his chair and steepling his fingers. "If you recall, at the reading of the will, there was some mention of a parcel of shares, left to you by your Great Aunt."

"The Ventura Steamship Company?"

"Indeed."

"Sounds like Rapunzel's South Sea Bubble."

"As you know, we could not, at the time, trace the share certificates. Your late relative became our client in 1959, and we have all her business documents from then until her death. But as there was no record of this particular holding, we concluded that it must have been obtained prior to her favouring us with her instructions."

"Did you find them?"

"The shares have been traced," announced Mr

24

Longe, with a small smile. "They were in a deed box in the office of her previous solicitor. I have them here for you." He passed over a stiff brown envelope containing a bundle of certificates.

"Good oh," Felicity leafed through them. "Aren't they ornate?" She marvelled at the forest of curlicues snaking across the face of each yellowing leaf. "Even if they're worthless, they're pretty."

"The Ventura Steamship Company," said Mr Longe, unpursing his lips, "is now part of the Worldwide Container Group. A thriving concern."

"You mean they are worth something?"

"About fifteen thousand pounds."

"What?" Felicity sat bolt upright.

"Aproximately," the solicitor reaffirmed, stroking his waistcoat. "Congratulations."

"Thank you," Felicity looked stunned. An answer to her problems struck her with sudden clarity, like the first night of the Blackpool illuminations. She stood up abruptly. "I must be going now," she said. Mr Longe rose gracefully to his feet in accompaniment. "You've been most helpful."

"My pleasure," purred her host. "Shall I proceed with the sale of Hope Cottage?"

"No," said Felicity at the door.

"Perhaps you have your own solicitor?" Mr Longe looked hurt.

"No, I'm not going to accept the offer."

"But I thought. . ."

"I changed my mind," interrupted Felicity.

"May I ask what you do propose to do with the place?"

Felicity paused at the door. "Live in it," she announced, and left Mr Longe shaking his head in wonder at her imprudence.

THREE

How does a woman whose largest ever construction job has been the fixing of a bookshelf decide to rebuild an entire house on her own? Felicity did not know where the impulse came from, but from the moment she told the solicitor that she would live at Hope Cottage, she was convinced both of the rightness of such a project, and the necessity of carrying it out herself.

Thus it was, on a bitterly cold day, at the beginning of the third week in April, Felicity Rouse returned to Norfolk. Tugged along, at Marina's rear bumper, came a two-wheeled trailer, rolling about like an uncoordinated puppy. Through Thetford Chase she drove, where the regimented ranks of conifers, marching to the roadside in dark green rows, swallowed up the daylight. Emerging from the long silvine tunnel, a ragged gale caught at the trailer and shook it from side to side, like a wagging tail.

In a young snowstorm which made the morning dusk, she passed through Orfton-Saint-Scabious and took the slurry-dotted lane towards Hope Cottage. A low flying jet fighter buzzed her as she turned cautiously onto the track leading to the cottage, and dashed away, dodging the low-slung storm clouds, trailing its noise behind it. Reaching the belt of trees which encircled the house, she slowed to a crawl and peered over the steering wheel at the unmarked track. She had no intention of veering off into the slough a second time.

A pair of rooks rose angrily from the naked rafters as she got out of the car; screaming their protests at her incursion they flew off, almost parting her hair with their claws. Across the whitening garden she fought her way to the caravan, her arms full of a gas cylinder. In five journeys she unloaded the car, staggering through the thistles with cooking pots and bedding. She unhitched the trailer, without lifting the tarpaulin which covered it, and pushed it onto the waste ground beside the pigsty. Locking the car by habit, she wondered what car thieves might be wandering the by-ways of East Anglia on a day like this.

A gust of wind drove her into the caravan and slammed the door behind her in a flurry of snowflakes. Struggling to connect the gas bottle to the cooker, Felicity could feel a crop of chilblains sprouting on her numbed fingers. Clumsy with the attachment, she finally got the oven alight, and left the door open for the warmth to dissipate. There was no other source of heating in the summertime tourer. Cursing, that she had forgotten to do it before, she ventured out into the storm again to rearrange the props under the little caravan's drooping nose. The fallen breeze blocks were tangled with weeds, wet and slippery. As she tugged the unwieldy grey slabs into place, disturbed worms and centipedes crawled angrily away. Batting the snow from her eyelashes, she constructed a small podium, hauled the caravan up on to it and fled back inside, promising to do the job properly when it was warmer.

The heat from the stove had brought out the smell of fungal spores and covered the walls with a thin film of condensation, but had not made a noticeable dent in the chill. Pulling the bedding around her shoulders, she sidled on to the settee, access to which was severely restricted by the pull-down dining table. With her sleeve, she wiped clear a patch of the misted-over window and peered out at the world. There was a gap in the trees, inconveniently situated at the north-easternmost point of the windbreak, through which she could see the dirty white expanse of a flat and featureless field. This, she presumed, was Farmer Bruton's short cut to his Forty Acres. The screen of trees was also pierced by the track at the south-westerly side, giving the rushing, snow-laden wind a clear passage across her land. The caravan settled precariously on its blocks, rocking with the more violent gusts which lashed it. So long as everything remained relatively level, Felicity had no intention of going out again to improve the stability of her shelter.

It was dark in the caravan, as well as cold. Loth

though she was to move, Felicity shuffled out once more from her perch, blankets draped about her shoulders, and searched among her boxes and bags for candles. When lit, they cheered the appearance of the interior, and excluded the storm from the now black windows. Heartened, she decided to arrange her sleeping quarters while she was up. At the back of the caravan were two single bunks which, with the addition of a piece of hardboard placed between them, became an almost orthopaedic double bed base. The smell of mouldering foam rubber which rose from the thin mattreses determined their fate. Felicity seized them in two armfuls and flung them out into the snow. After all, if everybody else could throw their rubbish in the garden, why not her? With great difficulty she unrolled the futon which was her largest domestic possesion, and which she had lugged all the way from London, simply because she could not bear to leave her ex-landlady anything which she valued. It fitted snugly in the bed space, adding a cosmopolitan air to the caravan. A thin orange curtain was strung across the rear window on an elasticated line, and she left it in place for privacy, although it clashed horribly with her red blankets. The twelve and a half tog duvet she kept as a shawl. Returning in two steps to the living room, she extracted a bottle of rum and a tin mug from her essential stores and sat down again.

It was a long afternoon, and though the temperature rose by slow degrees, Felicity never unhuddled. By the faltering light of her draught-afflicted candles, she read her way through 'Restoring Country Cottages' by G.P. Turvey, an instructive work which she had borrowed from the library in Kentish Town on Eilona McFadden's ticket. It was a small act of revenge; she had no intention of returning the book. She had wanted something entitled 'How to rebuild a derelict hovel in Norfolk, when you don't know a pipe bender from a plumb bob; or an idiot's guide to everything in construction', but G.P. Turvey, who sounded like a reassuringly practical chap, had won her attention with his colour plates of dry rot eating a house, and other disasters. She liked to know the enemy. To wash down the dry rot, she had half a bottle of rum (abstracted from Eilona's antique tantalus, whose lock yielded to a hairgrip) and was, by evening time, feeling rather maudlin.

'Here I am,' she thought, self-pityingly, 'thirty years old, redundant, careerless, proposing to rebuild a ruined house that looks like it should be rendered in gingerbread, in the middle of nowhere, in the depths of winter, in a part of the world that seems to be peopled solely by congenital lunatics.' She lumbered unsteadily to her feet and made a hot water bottle. 'Why couldn't I have stayed in London, placated Eilona, got a job, and continued to be able to plug in an electric blanket on nights like this?' Deciding that her teeth could be cleaned in the morning, and that she was mad, Felicity crawled into bed and, for the first time since she had failed to win the third-year form-prefect election, cried herself to sleep.

The morning rewarded her with a jewel of sparkling warmth. The sun blazed down on rapidly melting snow, clinging to the ridges left by the plough in the fields. Every dead thistle and naked branch shone with drops of light-refracting water. A blackbird twittered from the empty window of the house and a gentle breeze brought her the warm sweet smell of cows from a nearby farm. Light tufts of cloud scudded cheerfully across an innocent blue sky. It was as if she was being persuaded to stay.

Felicity, mother of a thundering hangover, inspected the chemical toilet in the caravan, realised it was unusable, and stumbled out of the door. Jumbled footsteps in the sheltered snow on the ground, leading to a yellowed patch some yards away, showed her that she had come on the same errand the previous night, but she had no memory of it. She wanted to throw a brick at the blackbird, whose liquid notes shrilled in her aching brain, and winced as the bright sunlight struck her sensitive eyeballs.

Blearily, Felicity looked at her inheritance. Hope Cottage twinkled back at her, catching the sun with every melting icicle and sodden creeper leaf. "What a charming old ruin," said Felicity. The face of the house grew smug, as though it could say the same about her. Ignoring her desire to lean feebly against a wall of the cottage, which might, or might not, support her, and wait for the horizon to stop rotating, Felicity decided that pissing in the snow was all very well, but she must dig herself an earth closet if this outdoor life was to continue. In one of the cranky old sheds at the back of the house, she remembered seeing a rusty mattock. Struggling through the brambles, which embraced her boots, she retrieved the implement, picked a spot and began digging. The earth was wet and matted with coarse grass roots, and she was soon sweating profusely into her down-filled jacket. She hacked at the ground, half expecting to find decomposing domestic pets in shallow graves, it was that sort of a garden, and as she picked up each loosened sod with her hands, her skin crawled in anticipation. But her trepidation was groundless, nothing more sinister than a centipede was revealed by her excavations.

Equipped with a respectable pit, sheltered by a small hollybush, in which to do her business, Felicity rested on the shaft of the mattock and considered her raging thirst. Water mains, like sewers, had never ventured out this far, and unless she wanted to be carrying jerry cans to and from the car forever, she would have to get the pump in the scullery working.

Inside the house the air was cold and clammy, all the sounds of birds and distant tractors seemed to be blotted out by the thick, streaming walls. Felicity seized the handle of the pump, a smooth wooden baton which reminded her of friendly beer dispensers in her local pub, and worked it from side to side. She produced a fearful screeching and a disgruntled spider, but not a drop of water. Pulling and pushing furiously, the only moisture resulting was the sweat of her own brow. Felicity stilled her inadequate brawn and racked her brain for the fifteen-year-old rudiments of 'O' level physics. Pumps need priming. What with? Water. She didn't have any water until the pump worked.

"Don't be a dolt, Felicity," she reproached herself aloud. "There's a bottle of Evian in the car." She fetched the precious liquid, resisting the temptation to pour it all down her blotting-paper throat, and donated it generously to the gaping mouth at the top of the pump. Once more, she threw her weight against the handle. Terrible noises, like the death by strangulation of a dozen chickens, split her head, but she kept swinging the lever through its ninety degree arc. When she had almost decided that the well was dry, with a cough and a belch, water began to pour from the mouth of the pump and splash onto the tiles. Felicity had forgotten to bring a receptacle in which to catch the flow. Not wanting to waste her achievement, she stuck her head under the pump and soused her hair and face. The water was icy, but welcome. The drops which ran off her lips into her mouth tasted fresh, even if the groundwater was full of agrochemicals. She hadn't lived in London all these years, just to turn up her nose at the odd nitrate. Messily she refilled the Evian bottle and drank from it.

"Eau, dear, what can the matter be?" she sang cheerfully, returning to the caravan. Her saliva glands, woken from their parched torpor, filled her mouth with bitter-tasting secretions.

"I haven't got a flush lavatory", she warbled, putting the kettle on to boil.

"Dear, dear, what a catastrophe,

I have to teach myself plumbing."

A purr of appreciation came at the end of the song. Felicity, who had thought she was alone, looked around. A small tabby cat sat basking on her doorstep. Every possible shade of brown was represented in her shining coat. She looked like a wool merchant's sample card.

"Did Kaffe Fassett, who made the embroidery kits, make thee?" enquired Felicity. The cat yawned in her face, rolling a pink tongue, then set to chewing a bramble out from between the pads of her paw. Felicity, accepting the inevitable, reconstituted some powdered milk and filled a saucer for the visitor, who sniffed disdaindfully at the offering, before condescending to drink it.

"Have you come to live with me, cat?" asked the

animal's host.''You will make me sneeze, but I don't suppose you care for that. Will you chase away the rats?'' The cat squinted up at her from the saucer. ''Of course you won't. You'll hide behind me when you see a rodent and wait for me to deal with it. Oh well, I would have preferred a team of burly manual trades-women, but as company I suppose you'll do.''

Unimpressed, the cat finished her milk and stalked into the caravan. Having inspected its possibilities, she plumped for the futon, pummelling the duvet into a nest with her paws.

''Quite comfortable are we?'' The cat combed her whiskers and purred. ''Good. I'm going to Dereham to hire a skip and some scaffolding.'' The cat closed one eye, slowly. ''And, obviously, a tin of disgusting slaughtered whale offal. Yes, I thought that would interest you. And some real milk you say? Not skimmed. Certainly. And you might like to know that I have to demolish half that cottage over there, before I can rebuild it. See the way the end gable sags away? And demolition is the most dangerous area of building work, according to G. P. Turvey, who knows about such things. So I will feed you the sad remains of endangered species, on condition that you will run for help, like Lassie would have done, should I get buried under a falling wall or collapsing scaffold. Is that a deal?''

The cat wrapped her paws around her muzzle and went to sleep, her sides heaving as she breathed. The saucer of milk, meagre though it was, had distended her stomach fully. Felicity observed that the little animal was young and undernourished, the healthy gloss of her coat had been a trick of the light. Taking out her list-making notebook, she started with Cat food, cod-liver oil, worming tablets and flea powder, and continued, adding various items of building plant and, as an afterthought, food for herself. The cat was still asleep and snoring gently when Felicity shut the caravan door and set off on the first of many trips to the builders' merchant.

* * * * * * * * * *

I don't understand this woman who has come to disturb me. What is she doing? She asks herself that. And she seems afraid. If her enemies are coming, why doesn't she hide? If she has no enemies, why does she dither about, shedding sour drops of indecision? It's no great thing to build a shelter. I could have it done by sundown. In fact, I would have made a point of it. Darkness, now there is something to worry about. Who knows what it might hide? Why does she bother with that big, crumbling house? What a liability. An undefended home should not be seen. Anything but invisibility is asking for trouble. When I came here to hide, I had more sense than to announce my presence with two stories. No, I don't think she has enemies. No wolves will come to her door. So why does she smell of fear? She can't fear building her own house. Even a beetle can make itself shelter. Even men can manage that. Why should she worry about a spot of construction? It would be like fearing to breathe or eat. Every animal knows how to make a nest. What's the big deal? I tell you, I don't understand this woman at all.

FOUR

Stay here with me. You want to follow her to
Dereham? Why? What's so interesting about a woman
at a builders' merchant? She's being patronised by the
boy at the plant hire counter. You know the story. He
talks a technical patois; 'load levelling' and 'firm
footings'. She must bluff, or he will take advantage
and fob her off with rubbish. She has memorised her
list of requirements, so she does not have to consult
the book, out of which she has cribbed the trade terms.
But he knows, her smooth white hands give her away.
She may order a cement mixer, but he can tell she has
never lifted a shovel in anger.

She is very smooth, isn't she? And so pale. But a
giant of a woman, seventeen handsbreadths tall, at
least. OK, five foot eight, I translate, but don't expect
metric, alright? And red hair. I never knew anyone
with a red pelt before, except The Man with the Soft
Axe. But he came from another place altogether. I
thought she had the mange, at first. So little hair. Red
curls down to her shoulders behind, but her face so
naked, barely enough on her brows to catch the sweat.
On her arms, a little sprinkling of golden down, like
the underside of a plucked fowl.

She says she is thirty summers old. She talks aloud
to herself, cries in the night. Well, I can understand
that. But she doesn't look thirty to me. She has the
body of a young woman. Full grown breasts, yes, but
never dragged down by the weight of milk. And all her
teeth. Despite that, she still eats pap, like a toothless
elder, though I'm sure she could grind her own grain
with those molars, if she had to. She has wrinkles, but
no scars; a knowing face and the body of one who has
never had to do a hand's turn.

I was not old, when I came here. Full of strength,
and, more to the point, cunning. That's what you
need, after all. A bison is strong, but it won't save his
life. Not when the hunters have learned to stop
running after him and dig pits instead, dropping

stones on his head when he falls in. Then what use is all his muscle, apart from to be eaten by the hunters?

I was in my prime, if a bit bedraggled by events. Strong and stocky, with a good covering of black hair (not like that poor moulted woman with her naked limbs). All my family who lived to be weaned had the same look about them, but none had my sharp wits. Nor did any of them have my skill. A craftswoman, that's me.

What was my craft, you ask? What made this part of the world rich. Flint of course, flint was my fortune. Oh, not those clumsily split lumps they put in the walls of houses. Very pretty, but it's hardly an art. And why waste good tools on a building? Homes are places from which you flee, not worth more than one day's labour. I don't understand this passion for structural solidity. These angry red houses that draw up the damp, and funnel in the wind, and crack instead of bending in the face of a frosty gale. What is the point? Have you seen these people? They build their houses, then straightaway, they have to start putting them back together again. Tiles fall off the roof, insects eat the timbers, water unlaces the walls. That's in the nature of things, decay is unstoppable. Why not accept it? Like this poor woman, worrying over her tumbledown cottage. There are plenty of branches, and clay and moss. She could make a hut, nicely hidden and quite snug. But no, even now she bears the humiliation of pretending to a trade that is not her own, in order to do something that daunts her. And for what? She'll move on as soon as it's finished. A home is a necessity, like food, but there's no more a permanent home than there is an everlasting meal. Silly to suppose otherwise.

This spot is bleak. It was better when there were more trees and bushes. These great expanses of ploughland remind me of her poor hairless arms. Naked and un-natural. When I came, it was a scrubby area, but not forest, you understand. I've never really been a forest woman. I like to be able to run away, and you can't do that among the tree roots. This is where I built, when it was my home. Yes, on this very spot.

One of the pathways that you feel, but don't see, runs through it. That must be why people keep building here, the pull of the line. It's an inconvenient hole, in other respects.

Here she comes again. The red-haired giantess. The racket she makes, thump, clatter, rumble. An enemy too blind to follow her tracks would just put his ear to the ground and know her direction. I can't see that vehicle of hers lasting. She should get a pack animal. She thinks this is her land now. No sense of territory, these people. How can you own land? Such an idea. She has no defences. How does she propose to protect herself against those who might wish to drive her away? This one has a lot to learn.

* * * * * * * * * *

Felicity climbed out of the car and stretched the tension from her shoulders. She would rather rebuild Notre Dame by hand than do that again, but she supposed she would have to grow accustomed to the sneering adolescents with pencils behind their ears and their gratuitous (un)helpfulness. 'What's your max bore, forty mil?' they would ask, maliciously. Maybe she should have her hair cropped and buy a donkey jacket, then they would mistake her for a builder's lad? There were plenty of them around, helping to shoe-horn impossible baulks of timber into the overloaded rear of their master's Transit; in the no names, no tax, no guarantees, end of the business.

Would the light down on the edge of her jaws pass as pre-shaving fluff? She thought not. And could she button up a donkey jacket tight enough to conceal her protuberant chest? It seemed unlikely. Although she was of a light and wiry build, her breasts were large enough to impede the swing of a bit and brace. What worried her most was not the pantomime possibilities of disguising herself as a boy, but the inevitability of having made some crashing and obvious mistake in what she had ordered, so that nothing could be used because she had forgotten the horse-shoe-nail of building equipment. But then, she soothed herself, mistakes are inevitable when the boss appears for the express, spiteful purpose of suggesting a vibratory rammer as an essential item of equipment.

Felicity had abandoned her reverie, and was pacing out the site of a putative cesspit, when, through the south-westerly gap in the wind-break, across a field of winter wheat, she saw a sudden plume of smoke shoot into the air. Consigning her ground plan, on the back of the paper bag in which her breakfast sticky bun came, to her pocket, she walked a short way into the field to look. With two shrilling blasts on its whistle, a steam train advanced towards her. She blinked. There was no railway here. Why should a stray steam engine be driving itself about a wheat field? Could it run on the ruts, instead of tracks? She may have been hungover this morning, but this apparition was in the pink elephant class.

The train, having advanced a short distance towards her now paused, as though for thought, and eventually started retreating slowly, back the way it had come. Felicity began to jog towards it, but the claggy earth dragged at her boots, forcing her to slow to a walk. The train sat puffing and steaming behind a clump of evergreen trees half a mile distant, set back from the road as was her own similar copse.

At last she reached the train, hurrying and breathless like any commuter. It sat, black and shining, looking so like a childhood toy that she half expected to find a giant key sticking out of the side. There was, as she knew there must be, no railway line, but instead, a short length of track lying on the edge of the field at the back of the trees. Buffers at either end of the track delineated the extent of this train's world. The engine rested its nose against the nearest bumper, huffing to itself. Peering through the smoke, Felicity could see on the footplate, preoccupied with his valves and gauges, an elderly man in blue overalls and a greasy cotton cap. A dirty rag hung out of his back pocket, and his greying forearms were covered with oil.

"Good afternoon," Felicity shouted over the hissing

and creaking of the engine. The man looked around. Finally he spied Felicity.

"Afternoon," he shouted cheerfully, "come to have a look at the Spirit of Private Endeavour?"

"It's a very fine train," admired Felicity.

"Hop up then, youngster. I might let you blow the whistle."

Clambering up onto the footplate, she realised that the old man had, unlike the builders' merchant, mistaken her for a youth.

"She's a 1951 Class '5' 4-6-0," proclaimed the enthusiast. "With Caprotti valve gear, roller bearings, double blastpipe and chimney. Bought her from a scrapyard in a terrible state. I've restored her myself."

"You've done a very good job," said Felicity, politely.

"Hard work and attention to detail, that's what it takes," said the engineer. "Just what you won't find in a nationalised industry like BR. The only things those chaps treat with tender loving care are their tea-breaks, and time and a half."

Felicity studied a pressure gauge intently, and avoided being lured into a discussion of the iniquities of unionised labour.

"Let's take her for a stretch," shouted the man, tapping dials and twisting stop-cocks which released great gouts of hot, sooty air into the cab. Peering back over his shoulder he reversed to the end of the track, where he paused to twist, pull and tap more of the welter of controls.

"Throw on a shovelful of coal," commanded the driver, flinging open the firebox door. She felt the raw, red glow engulf her, and quickly shovelled fuel from behind her into the hot and gaping mouth. Inside her winter clothes, she was sticky with sweat.

"Ready, Assistant Fireman?"

"Fine," she assented.

The train moved forward again, chuffing slowly across the field.

"Four hundred and forty yards of track," informed the man. "Salvaged from the Orfton to Norwich line. Beechinged, of course. This was all I had room for. Of course, I wanted a circuit round the house, but it would have taken the whole of Bruton's wheat field. My engineering skills aren't up to tight bends. Here we are." He braked, as they reached the end of the line. "All stations for Maybe Halt."

"As in Maybe Not Halt?" enquired Felicity. "Don't you trust the brakes?"

"The brakes are first class," the driver repudiated the slur on his engine. "Overhauled them last week. It's a pun. Archibald Maybe. That's my name. And who are you, young man?"

Felicity was peeved. A boyish figure was all very well, not that she thought she had one, unless the basic design had changed considerably. But did so many youths in Norfolk have shoulder length red curls? Reviewing with her mind's eye the assembled loutery of Dereham, as seen in the market square, she concluded that shoulder-length curls were probably de rigueur. How sickening to think that she looked like a minor professional footballer, without the gold chain or cropped sidewalls.

"Felicity Rouse," she announced tartly.

"Oh my goodness," the old man flustered. "How terribly silly of me. You must forgive me, Miss Rouse, my spectacles are rather grimy." He wiped his filthy hand on the oily rag and offered it to Felicity. She shook it gingerly. "How do you do."

A woman was coming through the trees, bearing a steaming enamelled mug and wearing an apron. "Elspeth, dear," called out Archibald Maybe. "We have a visitor."

Elspeth arrived at the footplate and looked up at them, with her head on one side, like a bird considering a worm.

"This is Felicity Rouse," he continued. "She came to look at the 'Spirit'. Felicity, this is my wife, Elspeth."

Felicity jumped down from the locomotive and shook hands with the woman. The Maybes were as unlike one another as could be. He was tall, cadaverous and stringy, with tendons standing out on his mottled neck, and wispy grey hair escaping from under his cap. She was round in every detail. She had a short round body, plumply rounded limbs and a perfectly circular face with a little button of a nose. Her small dark eyes were like raisins set in gingerbread. Felicity found herself being shepherded away for a cup of tea.

Elspeth Maybe led her visitor back through the trees from which she had just emerged and onto the lawn of a small, aggressively neat garden. Symmetrical beds, over the edges of which not a blade of grass crept, showed a brave display of daffodils, and every sign of having been cleared for the winter at the appropriate time. Dotted about the lawn was a strange crop of railway signs. A station name-plate pronounced the rose bed Llangollen. The raspberry canes would, in season, be netted over Haltwhistle. Warnings against trespassing on the line and littering the platform sprouted among the vegetable patches. In one corner of the garden was a full sized signalling gantry, complete with semaphore arm and hooped iron ladder.

The house itself was an ugly pebble-dashed bungalow, with browning paint, which looked as though it had been splattered with rabbit droppings. At the front was a verandah containing an assortment of waiting room benches, and a metal sign hanging over the front door announced 'Maybe Halt'. Elspeth, having wiped her shoes on the bootscraper and the doormat, ushered Felicity into the lounge. Here the riot of railway memorabilia was, if anything, more intense. 'No Smoking' signs bedecked the window, and a first class antimacassar hung over the armchair by the electric fire. One display cabinet was filled with scale model locomotives, and the record collection seemed to consist entirely of albums of steam train noises and Bulgarian folk choirs. A notice by the settee rather cryptically requested Gentlemen not to Loiter At This End Of The Carriage. Felicity felt sure that in the toilet she would find that Gentlemen Raise The Seat.

Mrs Maybe returned from the kitchen with a pot of industrial strength tea, of the sort that used to be served on trains before the advent of Maxpax. Felicity gasped at the first mouthful, but it cleared the remaining sludge from her alcohol-abused tongue.

"You must be the new woman at Hope Cottage," announced Elspeth Maybe, arranging herself on the settee.

"Yes," agreed Felicity through a mouthful of scone. "How did you know?"

"Shirley Bruton told me that you were around."

"We had words last time I was down," agreed Felicity, cautiously.

"So she tells me. I wouldn't worry about her," said Elspeth, comfortably, "Her bark is worse than her bite. She has a lot to put up with."

"Oh. Well, her bark was fairly fierce."

"They are like that round here. They don't take to strangers at all. We've been here ten years, and I've only just persuaded Jean at the post-office to stock my favourite sort of washing powder. She says it's not worth getting things in for visitors, they only go off and leave you with boxes of unsaleable exotica."

"Visitors?"

"Quite. I've even been on the parish council, but it doesn't seem to make any difference. The worst ones, of course, are those who arrived the day before you did. They have to try so hard, you see, to prove that they're more local than the locals. The worm farmers are like that. Very unfriendly. Or at least he is. She went to the other extreme, rushed round joining everything," Elspeth snorted. "Even the Women's Institute, though she didn't spell it like that. Well, I didn't want my consciousness raised, thank you very much, and nor did anyone else. They needn't think we're peasants, just because you can't get the Guardian delivered round here. Although I find the EDP quite adequate for my needs, and Archibald has his magazines posted. Anyway, she's left now, thank goodness, with her Paisley skirts and her headscarves. He's got a very sensible new girlfriend, I believe, a local lass, much younger than him, of course, and I don't think the parents are very happy with it, but anyway, much more suited to life on a farm."

"Should I have waited ten years before coming

round then?" asked Felicity when her hostess paused for breath.

"Not at all, dear, I told you, I don't hold with being stand-offish. We came from Acton. Archibald was deputy head of a boys' school in Ealing. He took early retirement so we could live in the country, we had always planned it, and then we got a very good offer on the house. But I don't think it's true what they say, do you, about London being so impersonal? I always found people much more friendly and welcoming in Acton. Of course, I know it's only a suburb, but I wouldn't have thought twice about popping in on a neighbour, even if we weren't particularly friends. Here, you're quite likely to be chased across the cattle-grid at shot-gun point. Are you from London?"

"I was," admitted Felicity. "Dartmouth Park Hill. Handy for Highgate Cemetery and the Heath."

"Was? You don't mean you're going to live down here now?"

"Yes."

"That is a surprise," marvelled Elspeth. "You don't really look like the back-to-nature type. I suppose you'll be getting the builders in? They say Hope Cottage is a terrible ruin, not that I've been up there since Scotty ran away, and we thought he might be ratting."

"I'm going to be rebuilding it myself, actually."

"My goodness! Are you really?"

"Yes," said Felicity, staunchly.

"Your cup's empty. Do let me top you up," Elspeth stretched out a plump little hand for the tea-pot. "Have you done this sort of thing before? If you don't mind me asking."

"No. It will be a first."

"Isn't it funny, how people like to do it themselves these days? When I was young it would have been considered very odd to labour yourself when you could afford to pay workmen."

"I don't think I could, even if I wanted to. Great Aunt Rapunzel left me some money, as well as the cottage, but not enough to join the idle rich."

"Oh dear, I am sorry," Elspeth blushed a rosy pink.

"You must think me terribly rude. I wasn't meaning to pry into your business."

"That's alright," Felicity soothed, quite sure that Elspeth loved a good pry as much as the next woman. "Isn't there meant to be a bush telegraph in the countryside, whereby everyone knows all about you down to your sock size within five minutes of crossing the county boundary?"

"It's true, they do manage to know an amazing amount about one's affairs, without seeming even to acknowledge that one exists. But I'm not sure that I'm privy to its inner workings. I often have the feeling that the darkest secrets are still hidden from me, even though most of the old inhabitants will just about admit to knowing my name now, and the post-man doesn't call in Special Branch any more every time Archibald gets his Bulgarian Folk Music Newsletter, although, of course, a lot of his fellow-enthusiasts do have rather peculiar political views, so I suppose that they have to be vigilant, but Archibald isn't a mole, he just likes the tunes. I know the cold war's supposed to be over, but they're suspicious of change round here. I'll ask Shirley, she's rather a friend of mine, and a native born and bred. It's a shame you two didn't hit it off. I'm sure she'd be very impressed if she knew you were going to rebuild that house all by yourself. I do think you're terribly brave. But they say women can do anything they like these days, don't they? "

"So I've heard," answered Felicity, drily. "Thanks for the tea, Mrs Maybe,"

"Call me Elspeth, do. And I shall call you Felicity, if you don't shorten it to something, though I can't think what. Anyway, there's no point standing on ceremony, not with us being neighbours. Drop in any time, I'm always glad of a visitor."

"You must come and see the building site. I can at least manage a cup of tea, if not much else in the way of hospitality. I must go now, so that I can be there when they don't deliver my cement mixer, portable generator etcetera, etcetera. In fact, as I've been out for an hour, they've probably been already, so that they could miss me."

"Oh no, there hasn't been a lorry down your lane, I would have noticed," said Elspeth, comfortably. She ushered Felicity out, pretending not to mind the crumbs of mud her visitor's boots had left on the pristine biscuit-coloured carpet.

Felicity strode up the drive to the road, deciding it would be a quicker way home, if further than the field. In the carport, she saw the Maybe's other transport, an ancient, but obviously low-mileage Allegro. Did all Deputy Heads drive them, she wondered, was it part of the job?

At the end of the drive, she turned left along the made-up road and strode into the teeth of a playful easterly wind, pulling her scarf up round her face. From the road, neither Hope Cottage, nor Maybe Halt were visible behind their windbreaks. On the opposite side of the road she passed a singularly naked house, thatched and peach-painted, but without so much as a hedge behind which to shelter. The pinky-orange walls did nothing to give an impression of warmth. Gathered round the yard was an assortment of Nissen huts, rusting under their camouflage paint and various long, low sheds with asbestos roofing. Faded MoD signs announcing 'Fragile Roof, Use Crawling Boards,' suggested that these farm buildings too had been purchased in a job lot at the end of the war and shifted from the nearby aerodrome. A creaking sign at the gate announced 'Sourwell Farm-Vermicular Productions'. The sign had been beautifully lettered on a hanging board, but was old and rather faded. Propped against the gate-post was a more recent announcement, executed in marker pen on a piece of scrap wood. 'Bait' it said coyly. Felicity peered into the yard and wondered how one grew worms, and which of the low buildings contained the maggot hatchery. She imagined she could hear a suppressed buzz from the nearest Nissen hut, and with a shudder of revulsion hurried on her way.

FIVE

Clank, bump, rumble. What does a flat-back truck full
of scaffolding sound like driving down a rutted track?
Like a tank. Yes, I've heard those going by here in my
time. Crash, jingle; unloading, hurling poles and
planks onto the ground; two of them, scaffold erectors,
it sounds like a species. Now they're setting up, clink,
thud, 'up-your-end, to-me, pass-the-wrench, soddit.'
Noisy bastards, men. Some things don't change in
three millennia. Careful, metal-worshipers, that the
legs of your construction don't sink into this boggy
ground and topple over. The crust of earth is not solid;
like the boundary between past and present, some
things may slip through.

She stands and watches her two hirelings with
their arses hanging out of their jeans. She should make
a proper scaffold, branches lashed together with
twine, but she doesn't know she is able. I don't think
you should work with tools in which none of your
spirit is invested. But she is trying to do it by the book.
If this is progress, I don't think much of it.

There has been a lot of clatter lately. Crunch, jingle,
slam. A skip, suspended off a lorry by chains is
dropped in the spot where I had my shelter. Rumble,
thunk. A cement-mixer is towed to the place where
my midden was and sits, open mouthed, demanding
sacrifice, waiting to belch out fumes and vomit
cement. Screech, clatter. Ladders are unloaded close
by where I killed the wild boar that saved me from
starvation, and got a tusk in the thigh as its dying gift.
So much metal clanging about the place. All it needs
now is for the wicked man with the red face to tow his
chain harrow up the path, and I think I'll go mad with
the racket.

You notice, I don't say desecration. I'm not old
fashioned about the-stone-which-is-not-a-stone, also
called that-which-rings-when-struck, or shining-stone-
which-bends. There are fourteen words in my language to describe different grades of flint, but when
the Man with the Soft Axe came peddling his

45

blasphemous wares, there was no word for metal. Perhaps if we had named it, we would have had the power over it. But his people were quicker off the mark, and the rest is history.

There are many superstitions about naming. I myself am variously Third-Liveborn-of-the-Lefthanded-Wisewoman, Came-with-the-Midwinter-Fullmoon, Goddess-Maker and She-Who-Lives-Alone. Quite a mouthful, eh? And those are just my proper names. You should hear some of the things I've been called in my time.

The Goddesses I made were mostly for the mines. Full bellied, splay legged, tits lapping over the smooth-stretched stomach, a face to frighten fools. Perhaps the proportions were a bit off sometimes, but that's divine inspiration for you. The great thing about sculpting deities is that one is spared the opinions of the village art-critics. No one dared suggest that the finished product was less than beautiful, for fear of being struck down.

Once it was done, I would climb down the notched spar to the bottom of the shaft carrying the Goddess while the miners howled and drooled around the pitmouth. There, standing on the chalky floor of the workings, thirty feet below ground would be the wisest woman. Actually, my mother, but for ceremonial purposes, we were not related. The air was thick with the smoke and stench of sheep fat dips, their flames casting moving shadows over the white walls. (Not the shadows of our ancestors, as the idiots above ground supposed).

It would be a new working, of course, but a few galleries would already have been driven out from the central shaft, high enough to accommodate a man lying on his side, at the level of the good, hard, weapon-making flint. Enough to know that this was a workable digging, that all those tons of earth, chalk and rubbish flint had not been shifted in vain. There was no point going to all the trouble and expense of a ceremony if the site was going to be unproductive, after all.

The wise woman would set the Goddess on her

pedestal, while the rest of us sang the sacred chants. No-one knew the words, of course, but that sort of thing you can make up as you go along. Seven of us would be down there, each with a fancier ceremonial title than the last. We had all been duly elected; any member of the spirit world was eligible to vote. My mother interpreted the signs by which the electorate made known their wishes. Turnout varied, but the results were amazingly predictable.

The Goddess established on her niche would bring luck and protection to the miners, as they crawled on their bellies into the galleries, scraping away with their red-deer antler picks. It is a skill, knowing how much of the chalk you can eat away to find the flint, how much must be left to hold up the roof above your head. When greed or desperation drove a miner, and just that bit too much was nibbled from the supporting walls – well, we didn't have to bury him. You can see why the miners needed the Goddess to sit in the shaft watching for them. Frankly, you wouldn't have got me at that job, with or without divine protection. But then, menial work is best left to the men.

When the wise woman had finished mumbling to the Goddess, she would pass round the rotten-grain water for which she was famous. I often wonder how any of us managed to climb back up the ladder after a few draughts of it. They do say my mother had to be hauled up from one of her first ceremonies in the bucket-hoist in which they bring up the flint; but no-one thought any the worse of her for that. The seven of us howled and shrieked a bit, so the watchers up above would feel awed, as they should. Every now and then, a hairy, anxious face would peer down from the lip of the shaft, but mostly they thought it best not to see too much of the sacred mysteries. My mother burnt a handful of the herbs whose smoke is sweet and makes it hard to walk in a straight line. Then we would crawl away into the galleries together, for there is nothing like pleasure to make a Goddess feel at home. Fortunately, since custom had decreed an odd number be present at these ceremonies, my mother preferred to stay by the statue and welcome the

47

Goddess in her own way. I wouldn't have liked to think of her being left out.

The next day, none of us would want to wake up for work, but time to lie around nursing thick heads and smelling the sweat a lover had left on your body was a luxury not afforded to us. Out, into the fever-bringing fogs of dawn we had to go, picking our way round the dozens of open shafts, worked out, collapsed and infilled diggings, past the great waste piles of flint sheared off by the women who roughed out the tools on the working floors, close by the pit heads. I had done that once, and, what's more, could strike a finished blade for axe head, spear or knife. Mostly though, we traded the tools in the roughly worked form; people like to finish their own implements, just so, back in their own homelands. Not that our finished item wouldn't have been as sharp, or durable, but it wouldn't have been so personal, and as I said before, you must put some of your own spirit into your tools, if they are not to work against you. This was our marketing strategy.

Don't wince like that. Everybody in the village used to have the same reaction, when I tried to introduce a bit of economic theory into their lives. It's all very well, I would tell them, knapping flint because it's the craft and trade of your forebears, but business is business. The laws of supply and demand should be as well-known to us as the time of solstice, or the rotation of the planets. That's why they put me in charge of trading. My talents were wasted on the stone-working floor.

I had to put up with a lot of the 'what was good enough for our mothers ought to be good enough for us' nonsense, of course. Traditions are not lightly changed. But after one particularly disastrous exchange, in which the elders made a deal to take the coming crop from a faraway corn patch, for three sackloads of our finest quality rough axes, things had to change. We never saw a grain of that corn, of course; eaten by weevils, or carried away by a dragon, I can't remember the story our debtors told, but who was to say that the crop had ever been planted? And what were we to do?

Go and raze their village? Round up their cattle and burn their huts? Please, be realistic. We lost seven days production in the deal, were we to loose another seven traipsing about the country seeking vengeance? I had warned them about dabbling in futures, and they were glad enough to take my advice when it was too late. After that, I took charge, and there was strictly no credit. Of course, being in the right is not always popular, but on the whole they were pleased to be spared the old system of taking these pots for those flints. How many pots can a village use, I asked, even when they have pretty scratch markings and rope-press patterns? From then on, I set the tariff, and if what we needed was hides or salt, you can be sure that's what I traded our flints for, not useless gee-gaws.

Every day, in the travelling seasons, strangers would be brought to my hut to boast about the strength of the ropes or the sharpness of the antlers they wished to barter. No see, no sale was always my motto. I must confess, I loved the haggling. There's a look in a man's eyes when he has reached the point at which greed is overcome by need, and then you have to make the deal. I could smell how much they meant to give, and then extract just a little bit more. But it was a risky business. You can't push it too far, or you find some trader who's walked thirty days to reach you breaking his staff over your head because he thinks he's not going to get what he wants. Lucky I was strong. But mostly it's in the eyes, and in the smell, and in the voice in your head which tells you 'This much I can take from him, and this little give him, but not more or less.'

Business was good for two, three summers, after I took over the dealing. They came from so far away, I didn't know the world was that big. Our fame was widespread. Sometimes, when the larders were full, I would accept beautiful things with no practical use, but not often, I was prudent. Then the Man with the Soft Axe came, with his crude bronze and his knowledge of the future. After that, nothing was the same, although it seemed to be at first. Our problem was that of any one-industry village whose technology is outstripped. Like a steel town in the rust-belt. There's an irony for you. But that's a story I might tell you another day. For now I'm thankful the scaffolding is up, the lorry is gone and there is a bit of piece and quiet again. I'm sure it won't last.

****

Felicity stood atop her scaffold, carefully dismantling the sagging west gable end of her house. Brick by brick, she unbuilt the wall, whistling, shirtsleeved in the sunshine. The small tabby cat sat beside her on the wooden planks that made a path around the cottage at roof level, playing with the loose-hanging rope of the hoist with which Felicity lowered the removed bricks to the ground. With her paw she batted at the dangling rope end, leaning perilously out over a twenty foot drop.

"Do be careful, dear cat," warned Felicity. "I'm sure it would use up at least two lives, falling off here. And goodness knows how many you expended in the course of whatever disgraceful wanderings brought you to my door." The cat rubbed one of her healing flea-bite sores against Felicity's shin. Woman and cat worked on, the latter in a supervisory role.

The view from Felicity's perch was extensive. Spring suggested itself all over the landscape: clothing the chestnut trees up by the roads; sprinkling new shoots around the few remaining hedges; dusting the wheat field next to Hope Cottage with a sprouting crop, like mustard and cress grown on a giant flannel. She saw the worm farmer drive up at great speed, swerve into his yard and jump out of his van. Could there be such urgency in vermiculture, she wondered? Further along, on the other side of the road, the roof of the Brutons' more substantial farm house was visible above the trees, chimneys smoking. A flight of geese rose from the Bruton's pond and Felicity meanly hoped that they would decide to transfer their residence to the scummy green water of her own pond, but the skein rushed by, honking. She had met a similar reaction from the Bruton's straying bantam hens, when she tried to entice them to come and scratch in her burgeoning jungle of a garden, and deliver to her small, rich, salmonella-free eggs. But they had merely used the old pigsty as a maternity ward, hatching out their chicks when they went broody, then leading the resulting family proudly back to Mrs Bruton, who had started out with five bantams, nominally the childrens', and now had at least fifty to feed and keep out of her garden. She wished she knew where the hens sneaked off to, as she was always destroying nests where she found them. Mr Bruton, who had no time for sentiment, accounted for at least half of every crop of fluffy little chicks under the wheels of his Rover.

Looking in the other direction, Felicity could see the gleaming flanks of the steam train at Maybe Halt, and hear the clang of dropped wrenches as Archibald regreased the bearings on the love of his life. Beyond that, at the far end of the the two mile long, dead-straight road which ran past their respective homes, was the flat sprawl of the airfield, its hangars long taken over by an agrochemical supply company; but still with a runway, a dirty orange windsock flapping in the breeze, and the occasional take-off or landing. As she lowered another bucket of bricks to the ground, Felicity watched a light airplane gallop impertinently down the runway from which Hurricanes and Spitfires had once hurled themselves into the sky. The little 'plane unpeeled its wheels from the concrete, climbed into the sky with its propeller whisking the air and flew towards Hope Cottage. Felicity could see the pilot staring down at her from the cockpit, and waved, as people have always done to small machines which fly like a confidence trick played upon nature.

Unnoticed by Felicity, a small figure was stumping up the garden path in sensible brogues. Mrs Maybe, tightly buttoned into a purplish tweed overcoat, rolled to a stop at the bottom of the ladder and called out to the woman on the scaffolding.

"Coo ee!"

"Hullo Elspeth," Felicity called down. "I didn't know I was expecting visitors."

"I thought I would come and see how you're getting on. Is it inconvenient?"

"Not at all." The cat jumped into the bucket on the end of the hoist and indicated that she wished to be let down. Felicity lowered her gently to the ground, where she disembarked to inspect the hem of Mrs Maybe's garment.

"How sweet," cooed the visitor. The cat turned up her nose and stalked off into a patch of sunshine by the front door. Felicity laughed.

"I apologise for her manners."

"She can probably smell Scotty on my coat. What a good thing I didn't bring him."

Disdaining the ladder, Felicity slid and scrambled down the scaffolding pole. "Would you like the guided tour?" she offered.

"That would be interesting. But not if you're busy."

"It's time for a break anyway." Felicity took the yellow plastic helmet off her own head and placed it on the other woman's sausage-shaped curls. "Beware of falling masonry."

"How exciting. I must say, you do look the part. Clanking about with that great belt full of tools."

"It keeps the hands free," Felicity said gruffly, not sure if she was being laughed at. She began to show her visitor around, and there was no mistaking Elspeth's interest. She peered into every corner, and tutted over the state of things. Her eyes grew rounder as she glimpsed the inside of the building.

"My goodness," she observed, "you have taken on a herculean task. How on earth do you know where to begin?"

"It was either at the top and work down, or at the bottom and work up," Felicity explained, wiping her sweating brow with a red handkerchief. "So I'm demolishing the roof."

"I hope you will be careful."

"Very. Would you like a cup of tea?"

"Yes, please." Elspeth's face lit up, "If it's no trouble. Can I see your caravan?"

"Of course," laughed Felicity leading the way.

"I've always wanted a caravan," chattered Elspeth, practically skipping through the weeds. "So snug and miniature. I liked playing house as a girl, and I suppose I've never grown out of it."

"How come you never had one?" asked Felicity, opening the door of the caravan and ushering in her guest, and the cat, who was waiting.

"Oh well," Elspeth settled herself with difficulty on the settee, squeezing round the table, "our holidays have always been tours of steam rallies. Bed and breakfast, usually. And we've been putting money aside for Archibald's engine for as long as I can remember, so there wasn't much to spare for fripperies. This is cosy, isn't it?" She admired the interior, which had been much improved by Felicity during several snowbound days when she had nothing better to do than brighten up her living quarters. "Is that your bedroom I can see at the end?"

"The cat's actually; she lets me crawl into a corner if she's in a very good mood. Milk and sugar?"

The two women sat companionably drinking their tea, and Felicity felt pleased that her home was fit for visitors. Elspeth tirelessly enumerated the good features of Hope Cottage and its situation, even though they were more potential than actual. Hers was the eye of faith. It was, she confessed wistfully, going to be much more her idea of a country cottage, when it was finished, than Maybe Halt.

"Of course," she confided, "a bungalow is very convenient, it would be silly for us to have taken on a rambling old place at our age. But when Archibald said we were going to retire to Norfolk, I did rather picture one of those sweet little cottages with flint walls and a thatch. And honeysuckle growing round the door." She pulled herself together. "Now, you've got honeysuckle, but no front door to speak of. It will be lovely in the summer, but it needs a bit of tidying up."

"I think I'll get a roof on before I start worrying about the decorative features,"

Elspeth looked thoughtful. "My garden," she announced, "is very well in hand at the moment."

Felicity murmured polite assent, unsure what this had to do with anything. "I was planning to build a rockery, but it can wait." She stood up. "I'll just go home for my gardening gloves and wellingtons and a pair of slacks. Those nettles of yours are getting rather lively, aren't they?"

"Riotous," agreed Felicity.

"Do you have a bill hook?"

"I believe there's one in the shed. But honestly, you don't have to. . ."

"Just a bit of tidying up," interrupted Elspeth, firmly. "I can't bear to see weeds getting the upper hand like this. It's such a waste." Her vehemence surprised Felicity. "This must have been a lovely cottage garden once."

"It's very kind of you, but. . ."

"But me no buts," commanded Elspeth. "I shall regard it as a challenge." The scent of battle was in her nostrils, and her face glowed with anticipation. Leaving her second cup of tea half drunk, she bustled off, returning within half an hour, re-equipped with trousers, gauntlets and a leather jerkin. The martial light in her eye had not dimmed.

"I popped a shepherd's pie in the oven for Archibald's lunch," she shouted up at Felicity, who had regained the scaffolding and was knocking out bricks with a lump hammer, "so I shall be able to make a proper start on these weeds." She swished the bill hook with lethal precision at a clump of nettles, felling them cleanly at a stroke.

"Great," said Felicity weakly, bowing before an irresistible force.

"Those bricks you're taking out of the wall," called Elspeth, entering the lists against a heavily armed thistle, "what will you do with them?" She tilted at her adversary and laid it low.

"I was going to rebuild this wall with them," replied Felicity, "but they're not in very good nick. I'll have to use new ones. The skins of these aren't weatherproof anymore."

"You do know a lot about it," admired Elspeth, poking gingerly at a plastic bag full of rotting magazines that had nested in the cow-parsley. "Where shall I put the rubbish?"

"I read a book," confessed Felicity. "In the skip, if it's non-biodegradable. Otherwise, on the waste ground, by the pigsty. I think we'll have a bonfire."

"What fun this is," beamed Elspeth, spearing an old mattress on the end of her fork and tossing it expertly into the skip. "I was thinking of salvaging the bricks for a raised bed. Down by the ditch, where I can see from the way the rosebay willow herb flourishes, that the soil doesn't drain very well."

"Elspeth," Felicity leaned down from her perch, looking worried, "it's lovely that you're clearing up, and I do appreciate your help, but I can't ask you to re-landscape the entire garden."

"You haven't asked me," giggled Elspeth, like a naughty schoolgirl. "In fact, I'm amazed at my own pushiness. But I seem to have taken you, or rather your garden on, as a project. You see," she said, earnestly, "my garden, you must have noticed, is very small, and rather established. It doesn't offer me any scope. I've always longed for a real jungle to tame."

"Well, this certainly qualifies," Felicity looked at the weed-choked, rubbish-infested, acre of garden. "But it hardly seems fair."

"If you want to make your own garden, I shall understand perfectly," said Elspeth nobly. "In fact, it was very thoughtless of me to have torn into it like this. You must be looking forward to doing it." Felicity disclaimed any desire to paint her environs with a palette of flowers. "Well then, if you don't feel I'm poaching on your pleasures, I intend to explore the possibilities of this wilderness. It would be very kind of you to lend me your garden. You needn't worry that I shall start getting all possessive about it," she reassured, improbably.

"Please, do what you like to it," Felicity was embarrassed. Part of her was jealous. Of course she had pictured herself creating a haven of fruit and flower. Then she eyed the gaping roof, and reminded herself that if anyone worked on the garden this year, it wasn't going to be her. Summoning up what grace she could, she gave Elspeth, who was anxiously watching her deliberate, a free hand in the garden. After all, she reflected, the woman must be in her fifties. She would probably potter about among the weeds for a few hours, and then go back to her knitting. "It's all yours," she announced, trying to mean it. "But please don't feel you have to."

"Oh, thank you," enthused᷈ Elspeth. "You don't realise what a treat it will be to do a bit of real garden pioneering. And not have to organise everything around tons of railway scrap."

When it was time for Archibald's tea, Elspeth departed, leaving her gardening gloves in the shed. Felicity thought this was an ominous sign. The novelty of company had been quite gratifying, scraps of Elspeth's conversation about mulches and tubers had floated up to her on the scaffolding, as the other woman rummaged in the hedge, or marvelled at the persistence of dandelions. But she wasn't sure if she liked the idea of having her solitude disturbed on a regular basis.

Deciding to call it a day, Felicity slid down the scaffold, with the cat perched nonchalantly on her shoulder, and retired to her caravan. A bath would have been nice, for her muscles ached with the unaccustomed labour, but a basin of water from the kettle and a soapy flannel served the purposes of hygiene as well. Having opened a tin of spaghetti for herself, and a tin of something unspeakable for the cat, she curled up with the thoughts of G.P. Turvey on roof pitching, to do her homework, solaced by Brahms on the portable stereo.

SIX

Early the next morning, Felicity was stacking slates, removed from the roof, on what had once been, and might be again, the front lawn, when the rumbling chug of a tractor coming up the drive caught her attention. Farmer Bruton, once more desiring passage to his Forty Acre, was stopped by the obstruction of Marina the car. Even at this hour of the day, his face was alcohol-tinged red.

Flinging open the door of the cab, he shouted "That old car of yours is blocking my way again."

"Oh dear," replied Felicity politely, strolling over to lean on the garden gate, but not too heavily, in case it fell off its rusty hinges.

"Are you going to move it then?" enquired the farmer, impatiently.

"I quite like it where it is."

"How am I s'posed to get to my field, then?" he demanded.

"You could try using the road," suggested Felicity. "This isn't actually a public highway."

"That's right out of my way," shouted Bruton, over the noise of his engine. "Why put two miles on a journey when I can pop through here? I always do."

"Did Great Aunt Rapunzel let you drive through here, when she was alive?" asked Felicity, innocently.

"Yes,"

"Really?"

"Well, I got some damn letter from her solicitor once, tellin' me not to, but I don't mind that."

"But I do. I must respect my relative's wishes after all. Go by the road."

Farmer Bruton leaned out of his cab and snarled at the woman by the gate."There's no point antagonising your neighbours," he said, menacingly.

"Quite right, Mr Bruton." Felicity straightened up and spat out the grass stalk which she had been chewing. "I think you should bear that in mind. Good day." She nodded, dismissively.

Bruton slammed shut his door and threw the

tractor into reverse, his wheels churning up pebbles from the water-logged pot-holes. Felicity went back to her salvage work.

The next arrival was much politer. Elspeth Maybe, in the family saloon, nosed her way cautiously to a halt on the very spot where Farmer Bruton had been repulsed.

"Morning, dear," she greeted Felicity. "Your drive is in a bit of a state."

"It'll be better when it isn't being used as a rat run for tractors."

"I've brought some of my gardening tools," said Elspeth, unloading the car, "I think I'll be needing them up here more than at home, and it's silly to keep running back to fetch the very thing you want. I'll keep them in the shed at the back, they won't be in your way. And some Marks and Sparks digestive biscuits. I do particularly like them with my tea. Oh, and they haven't got animal fat, I read the label, so you'll be able to eat them. They're rather a treat, we can only get them from Norwich, but I prefer them somehow."

And so Elspeth set-to. For a week, she came every morning, hacked and hoed, trimmed and weeded, up-rooted and scythed. She filled one skip with junk, and Felicity had to order another one. The cottage began to emerge from its surroundings like a boil in a newly shaved armpit. Surprising things were found under the weeds, some recognisable, others not, but Elspeth, ladylike, refused to acknowledge the worst horrors socially, while carting them efficiently to the bonfire which burned between the pigsty and the hen house.

Felicity's contribution to the blaze was the spectacularly rotten roof beams, home to every species of pest and fungus. She had tried with the aid of G.P. Turvey's twelve colour plates to identify all the parasites which she was depriving of a home, but she gave up after wet rot, dry rot, wood-boring weevil and house longhorn beetle. Under the eaves, she found a particularly picturesque colony of weeping sporophores, which at first she thought was snow left over from the day she arrived, so white and fluffy did it look. Her method of demolition was not scientific, she simply hacked the rotten wood into manageable baulks, lowered them to the ground on the hoist, and, with (she grudgingly admitted to herself) the valuable help of Elspeth Maybe, dragged them to the bonfire.

One bright spring morning, with a gentle breeze rustling in the newly clad fields, and a peewit falling about laughing high overhead, a delivery lorry loaded with bricks and breeze blocks bumped its way down to the cottage. The driver, operating a mechanical grabbing arm that elbowed up from the lorry's bed like a penny arcade game, delivered a plastic wrapped pallate of bricks neatly to the ground at Felicity's feet. They were of a nasty red colour which matched the originals in a perfection of ugliness.

"'That's unusual for a girl, buildin' a house," the driver remarked, as he did every time he brought a load of material, which was often. He was a shifty young man, whose looks spoke of ancestors who had had no truck with genetic diversity. Felicity coughed non-committally and signed the delivery note. He stared at her, and the scene of her eccentricity, with frank curiosity.

She looked a very different woman from the one who had ventured from London a few weeks before. The sun, which had broken out intermittently since the end of April, had given her skin not a tan but freckles and an all over pinkness of health. Newly developed muscles bulked in her shoulders and arms, for there is nothing like demolishing a roof by hand to build up the physique. She could have paid hundreds of pounds to join a gym and simulated the exercises with machines. Running up and down a ladder all day had put a spring in her step, and her hair was a wild tangle of red curls, with the odd grey hair set off by sun-bleached streaks. Going to bed by ten o'clock every night, because she was tired and no other entertainment offered itself, had removed the puffy purplish bags from under her eyes. The eyes themselves, variable of colour according to Felicity's state, were more often green these days than murky brown, or hazel with yellow flecks.

She stood, on her recently scythed lawn, loading bricks into a hod, her arms and neck bare to the sun, while the delivery driver loitered as long as he could, fussing with his dockets in between staring at her. Felicity swung the loaded hod to her shoulder and stepped smoothly up the ladder; he could find no further excuse to linger and took himself off.

"In the merry month of May," sang Felicity, returning for another load, "and in six weeks time the nights start drawing in."

"Let's not rush on our fate, shall we?" said Elspeth Maybe, appearing from the caravan with two mugs of tea. She was wearing a small scarf knotted round her neck, which made her look even more like the Pilsbury doughboy. To Felicity, it seemed that she never simply arrived, she always appeared to pop out of nowhere, and should have been accompanied by a puff of smoke or a round of applause.

"Thanks," Felicity took the steaming mug and wrapped her calloused hands around it.

"Has that nice boy who brought the bricks gone? I was going to offer him a cup too."

"He had to dash off," lied Felicity.

"I must say, he always seems very friendly and interested. Not at all what I'd expected from your tales of the timber yard."

"Oh, I never said they weren't affable," she began deftly reloading the hod.

"Anyone would think you had been born on a building site," marvelled Elspeth, "to see you rush about so confidently with a ton of bricks over your shoulder."

"Actually," admitted Felicity, "I've never carried so much as a wooden playbrick before. I just had to fill my first ever hod, under the critical gaze of a lorry driver."

"No one could tell," Elspeth assured her. "You look as though you know what you're doing."

"I do think that's the secret. It's all very logical, being about arrangements. If you put one thing on top of another in a certain order, voila, a house. All the component tasks of building seem to be susceptible to the same treatment."

"All of them?"

"Except the times where you just have to hit something with a wrecking bar and yell at it. That works too."

"Yes, I thought I'd witnessed a few incidents recently which looked like the triumph of matter over mind."

"There's always brute force, for occasions like that. But there's a logic to the point at which you apply the said brute force."

"I'm very impressed, anyway, that you have such an appearance of competence. It's more than the builders who did my kitchen could manage."

"I spent a year and a half staring out of the window at work at the men building an office block across the road. It's amazing how much you pick up without realising it."

"Like how to fill a hod?"

"And how to bullshit the delivery driver."

"Not the sort of thing they teach you at school," commented Elspeth.

"Unfortunately."

"Although I thought the younger generation were all doing metalwork for girls and cookery for boys, these days."

"The younger generation might be," snorted Felicity, "but I left school in 1977. Virtually pre-metric. And anyway, if sexual equality was raging through the curriculum, I'm sure Chelmsford Girls' High School could have kept it at bay."

"Didn't you like school?"

"I loved it, actually. Hundreds of very brainy girls, surging their way through public exams. When I was ten, I thought god was the president of the drama club. She was one of those sixth-form Oxbridge entrants, and you could hear her cerebellum throb, even in repose." Felicity sighed, fondly. "I was a dreadful little tory."

"You?" Elspeth was incredulous. "I find that rather hard to believe."

"It's true. I used to read the Daily Telegraph and worry about inflation, like other children scan the Beano. I was one of those middle-aged preteens. Then in the fourth year, I became best friends with a Fabian, and I've been getting pinker and pinker ever since."

"Don't let Archibald hear you say that. He's got rather a down on lefties. Personally, I think it would be much nicer if we could do without all the party political business. When the County Council elections come around, I get so fed up with all the posters in the hedges, Labour this and Conservative that. Why don't they just say they want to represent local people, and never mind the colour of their rosette?"

"But they'd still have axes to grind, wouldn't they?" reasoned Felicity. "Isn't it better to know who's going to side with the farmers, when it comes to a vote, and who would put the rates up? If they didn't admit to party labels, the manifestoes would be identical, a white man, claiming to be more local than the coypu, with a picture of his wife and kids to prove how normal he is."

"I suppose so," Elspeth sighed. "Politics can be so depressing. People do get heated. Chelmsford's a lovely town," she changed the subject, "did you like living there?"

"No, I hated it," Felicity chewed at a split fingernail.

"Oh dear," Elspeth, who had thought she was shifting the conversation onto non-contentious ground, looked dismayed.

"It was the worst of all worlds. Small and provincial, without being properly in the country. And the more they speeded up the trains, the more of a commuter suburb of London it became. Mum used to get the train up to town every day, along with all the other lemmings."

"What on earth for?"

"She was a consultant neurologist at one of the teaching hospitals."

Elspeth's mouth formed an O of surprise. "That's very," she searched for the word "high-powered."

"Yes," Felicity said, wearily, as one who was used to this reaction. "And Dad was the local GP, just like his father, and his father before him, all the way back to witch-doctors. That's why the family stayed in Chelmsford, it's where the ancestral practice was. And now they've both retired, they grumble about how the town has changed, and talk about getting a house in the country, but they never will."

"Excuse me asking, but who looked after you, if your mother was always away?"

Felicity pondered the question. "The usual arrangement, I suppose. Mum was meant to do everything when she got home from work, while Dad sat and read The Lancet. Once I was at the big school, I more or less fended for myself. I was a latch-key kid."

"How terrible!" Elspeth was shocked, as Felicity had known she would be.

"I survived," she laughed. "I was a self-reliant child. I pitied the girls who had full-time housewife mummies. They had much less scope for getting up to no good."

"Oh dear."

"The worst thing about being the child of doctors is that they're such dreadful hypochondriacs themselves, they'd be doing blood tests for Lassa fever every time I had a temperature, and forget to give me an asprin for the 'flu, which was what I really had."

"I'm surprised you didn't become a doctor yourself," observed Elspeth. "Lots of doctors' children do, don't they?"

"It's practically compulsory. My adolescent rebellion took the form of doing Arts 'A' levels instead of Sciences. Not very wild, eh? Actually, I think I was secretly frightened I wouldn't be able to get the grades, even if I'd set my heart on medicine, so it was quite a relief not to have to try. I was one of those gloomy teenagers, all long hair and unrequited love."

"I dimly remember hopeless passion," said Elspeth, nostalgically. "He was an inspector from the bus depot in Acton, a very fine-looking man. We never spoke, and I worshipped him from afar."

"Mine was the Captain of Swimming," said Felicity

with a sly sideways glance, "and I worshipped her from as near as possible, but to no avail."

"Oh, well," Elspeth flustered, "that sort of thing does happen between schoolgirls, I hardly meant. . ." she trailed off, discomfited.

"And so I left the little town of Chelmsford, as soon as ever I could," continued Felicity, smiling to herself, "and took myself to a big city."

"London?" enquired Elspeth, still avoiding Felicity's eye.

"Manchester."

"What was it like?"

"It rained. For three years. I lived in one of those deck access flats in Hulme, which was chronically infested with cockroaches, and went on a lot of demonstrations, because that was the cheapest way to get a coach to London. By that time, I had realised that if one must live in a filthy, noisy, ugly city, there's no point settling for second-worst. Why not go the whole hog and live in the biggest and noisiest? Which is how I came to move to London."

"There's a sort of logic in that."

"And now, I must move up that ladder. Elspeth, you are a dreadful encouragement to me to sit around and chat. There's work to be done!"

As Felicity finished her tea and prepared to re-climb the ladder, a horrible electronic honking split the still morning air, and Phoebe Bruton shot into sight, pedalling furiously, hotly pursued by her brother, also on his bike and with one hand jammed on the button of the Sonic Laser mounted on the handlebars. Phoebe, standing up on the pedals, skidded her back wheel sideways across a puddle, throwing up a sheet of muddy water which splashed Elspeth's gumboots. Adonis, triumphant, with a last ear-shattering squawk, dismounted his bike and tackled Phoebe to the ground before she could come out of her sliding turn.

"Let go of me, Donny," she squealed, as he pushed her inexorably towards the puddle.

With a sigh, Felicity rested her hod against the brick stack, walked over and grasped Adonis by the collar and hauled him off his struggling sister. She looked down at the indignant, mud-bespattered girl.

"To the rescue again," she commented.

"Adonis Bruton," said Elspeth in tones sterner than Felicity had ever heard her use. "Behave yourself."

The boy stopped struggling in Felicity's grasp and looked sullen. "I wasn't doin' nothin'," he complained.

"You let him go," commanded Phoebe unexpectedly switching enemies. "My dad said he'd thump you, if you laid a finger on Don again."

"'That's right," confirmed her brother. "He will too."

"Why aren't you children at school?" enquired Elspeth.

"We're off sick," they chorused.

"You look pretty healthy to me," observed Felicity. "Why aren't you in bed?"

"We're not that sick," explained Phoebe.

"What are you doing down here, anyway," asked Felicity. "I didn't exactly put the welcome mat out for you."

"Ask Feeble," sniffed her brother. "She's the one what come tearing down here. I was just tryin' to stop her." He looked virtuous. "Mum said we wasn't to come near the place."

"I thought you might chuck my bike in the pond," explained Phoebe. Felicity and Elspeth looked at each other with blank incomprehension. "Dad went out an' bought Don a new rifle, after you slung his old one in the pond. I reckoned it might work the same with my bike. It's a heap of junk."

Elspeth continued to look puzzled. Felicity burst out laughing. "Very ingenious," she said, "But I only disposed of your brother's gun because he was shooting at me. I don't make a habit of stealing children's toys."

"Was not a toy," pouted Adonis. "Dad says you're one of them yuppies, come to do up the house and sell it, so none of us local kids'll get anywhere to live when we grow up."

"He said a lot worse than that," added Phoebe,

looking slyly at Felicity. "You should hear some of the things he calls you."

"Which we don't want to, thank you very much," reproved Elspeth. "And you have a very nice house to live in, much bigger than Hope Cottage, so I don't think you should begrudge Felicity her home."

"Just tellin' you what dad said," Phoebe assumed an air of injured innocence.

"You took the roof off!" exclaimed Adonis, noticing the altered state of the cottage. "Who'd'you get to do that, then?"

"She did it herself," said Elspeth, proudly.

"Dad says," began Adonis, in a way that made Felicity's heart sink, "it's not right, you doin' it yourself. You should've got in one of the local blokes. You're doin' some contractor out of work to save money. Anyways, I don't s'pose you done it all by yourself, did you?"

"With my own fair hands," confirmed Felicity.

"Can we go up the ladder?" asked Phoebe.

"Certainly not," said Elspeth, sharply. "It's very dangerous."

"Oh, please, Mrs Maybe," they chorused.

"Absolutely not," reiterated Elspeth. "Anyway, isn't that your mother's car coming down the drive? I daresay she's on her way to fetch you back to your sick-beds."

The children looked at each other. "Don't tell her you saw us," commanded Phoebe. "Promise?" She looked at Felicity, then took to her pedals and dashed after her brother who was already heading up the track, away from the road, presumably to hide in the Forty Acre.

"Good morning, Ms Rouse," said Shirley Bruton, getting out of her car. "Hullo Elspeth."

"You know Felicity?" said Elspeth brightly.

"We have met," Felicity and Shirley acknowledged each other stiffly. Elspeth was covered in confusion, as she remembered the story of their previous encounter. "Are my children here?"

"Shouldn't they be at school?" enquired Felicity, playing for time.

"They should be," agreed Shirley, crossly. "I been in to Jean's, and she says they never left their bikes there this morning, or got on the school bus. She thought they must be poorly. Playin' truant again, that's what they're doin'. Have you seen 'em?"

"This puts me in a very difficult position," said Felicity. "One the one hand, if someone asks you not to divulge their whereabouts, you should respect the confidence. On the other hand I think you're entitled to know where the little monsters are. You see my dilemma?"

"She means they went heading off that way five minutes ago," explained Elspeth, indicating the escape route.

"They'll be goin' home by the back road then. Varmints. I'll drive round the other way and meet 'em."

"Poor Shirley, what a worry for you," said Elspeth.

"I blame their dad. Fillin' their heads with stories about when he was a lad. I tell him, it was all very well for you, country weren't full of people goin' to run you over, or kidnap you, them days. It's different now. He don't listen, though, and they do, that's the trouble. You can't tell kids school's for cissies and expect them to go."

"I think they're hiding behind that oak tree by the field gate," said Felicity. "I caught a glimpse of Phoebe out of the corner of my eye."

"They must be waiting for you to go, Shirley," suggested Elspeth, taking a discreet look at the hiding place. One of the bikes' tyres protruded beyond the tree trunk. "They'll probably come back when they hear your car go and start pestering Felicity to be allowed up on the scaffolding again."

"Is that what they come for?" asked Shirley.

"No, apparently Phoebe hoped I would dispose of her bicycle for her, so that you would buy her a new one."

Shirley snorted. "She'll be lucky."

"It seems my way with her brother's air-gun impressed her."

"Yes, well," Shirley looked uncomfortable. "I've

been meaning to speak to you about that. Perhaps I was a bit sharp with you."

"I got the impression you thought I had wronged your son," agreed Felicity.

"Well, you hadn't, and I apologise," said Shirley, with something of an effort. "If he'd done that to me, I most likely would've had the same reaction. He was irresponsible with that gun, and he's worse with the new one. His dad wants to give him a shot-gun for his thirteenth, god help us."

"I don't seem to have made a very good start with your family," said Felicity, ruefully.

"Well, you won't get my husband to like you now, not even if you save his life. He's set against you, and he's a stubborn man in his dislikes. The kids just need to mind their manners a bit. As for me, live 'n let live, I say."

"Shirley, I think you should go and climb up on the scaffolding," suggested Elspeth suddenly.

"Why's that then?"

"Just an idea I've had."

Obedient, but puzzled, Shirley mounted the ladder and walked round the platform, inspecting the cottage. "My mum was a carpenter during the war, you know," she informed the two women on the ground. "She's built the odd roof in her time."

Elspeth was watching the oak tree and, sure enough, the children emerged from hiding.

"Mum," cried Phoebe, "What you doin' up there?"

"It's not fair," complained Adonis, elbowing his sister aside. "We weren't allowed on the roof." Elspeth smiled with pleasure at the success of her stratagem. Shirley descended from on high with surprising speed and collared her errant brood.

"I'm takin' you two into school myself," she announced. "And you can think yourselves lucky if I don't take you home for a beltin' from you dad instead."

"Oh mum," protested the boy, "there's no point goin' now. Day's half over."

"And we can't leave our bikes here," pointed out Phoebe.

"Half over is half begun." said their mother, firmly. "Put your bikes in the car. No arguin'."

Recognising a non-negotiable position when they met one, the children dragged their bikes reluctantly into the back of the estate car. Shirley winked at the others, in a conspiracy of adulthood.

"I might come and have a proper look round, one day when I haven't got the kids to worry about," she said, "if that's alright with you?"

"Do." Felicity was surprised, but pleased. "You'd be welcome."

"You doin' her garden for her, Elspeth?."

"Just tidying up a bit."

"You wanna watch her," Shirley said to Felicity. "She'll have you in 'Homes and Gardens' before you know it." With a cheerful wave, she pushed her protesting children into the car and set off to deliver them to school.

SEVEN

Warm, heavy drops of rain spatter on the viscid surface of the pond and fall sizzling in the embers of the bonfire. It has been a good spring, not too cold, not too dry, and this is a real plant-refreshing shower. She re-covers the cement bag she was about to open and waves to the old crone, who is doing some religious ritual with pigs' blood, dead fish, and ground-up animal bones under the hedge. What a stench. I don't think she can have told Felicity, but then priestesses are often sly.

They retire to the caravan. With the cat, of course, pampered beast. Why does she take a wild animal into her home? Into her bed, even? If a marten came to my home, I wouldn't welcome it. I'd rather lie down with a wolf. Those small creatures with sharp teeth and cunning, they eat your heart if you give them the chance. This one disdains even to combat the rats who scamper about so freely in the night. She feeds it, grooms it, does everything for it that its mother would, and it is full grown already! Very strange.

It was just such a day as this when Soft Axe first came to my village. Fat raindrops hurtled down the shafts of the old workings to explode in the still pools on the bottom. Two-Tooth's son, leaning over the lip of an old shaft to watch the ripples as the rain hit, lost his balance and tumbled into the puddle at the bottom. Aged five he should have had more sense. He squealed like a rabbit being gutted, the fuss, you wouldn't believe. He wasn't badly hurt, but the way Two-Tooth was carrying on, you would think the whole village was being razed. By the time someone had clambered down and retrieved the child (none too gently, I suspect), and Two-Tooth was alternately beating him and weeping over him, half the flint-knappers in the village were gathered around, grinning all over their faces. In the furore, it was hardly surprising that nobody noticed the arrival of Soft Axe.

He was a fox of a man. Red hair all over, matted and curly. It was darkened and dampened by the rain to a dirty brown, otherwise he must have been remarked upon sooner. We were a black-haired people. He was sharp; pointed ears like a dog-fox raiding a bird's nest, twitching back and forwards. He had angled eyebrows that never stayed still and a nose like an arrow.

He stood at the back of the crowd of flint-knappers as they jeered at Two-Tooth and made ribald suggestions about the true parentage of her son, who was, it must be said, a very silly and troublesome boy. Eventually someone noticed the stranger, and pushed and dragged him to the front of the throng. They were in an excitable mood, and might have killed him on the spot, for he didn't answer their questions, not speaking our language. But he seemed to understand what was going on, and calmly indicated, by gestures, that he had come to trade.

I wished I could tell them all to go back to work and let me get on with it. If it had been the miners, I could have, but the women wouldn't be told. So they stood about, passing comment on his strange appearance for a few minutes more, until they were good and ready to return to the flint-knapping floors. I took him to my hut then, and left him outside while I boiled some herbs for us to drink.

When I came out again with two steaming beakers, I found him squatting comfortably on his heels, leaning his back against the wall. The rain collected in his hair, glistening on the grease and the prominence of his ribs spoke of a long journey with little time to hunt on the way, but he seemed perfectly at ease. I asked him where he came from and he indicated the far west, tallying up the days he had walked with a stick in the earth.

I can't say I wasted much hospitality on him at first. He didn't look like a good proposition. Serious business comes in larger groups, carrying packs of worthwhile barter. He had only one small bag, slung over his shoulder. I wondered whether I should have let the girl who I was training to my work deal with him. But I didn't yet trust her ability to resist charming, useless trinkets, and ten ox-hides to a rat turd, this man was just such a trickster as would claim to have dragons' teeth, or the root of the life-tree to offer.

He was very sure of himself, though. He drank his drink and looked about him, as if it mattered not at all whether he went away with one scraping knife, or a pack load of best axe heads. I didn't like him, I must say. There is something wrong about a trader who walks so far to make a deal, and then appears not to value that which he has come to obtain. I spread before him on the ground some samples of our flints, raw, roughly worked; and one finished axe, which I kept for trade demonstrations and would never have used, or parted with. It was a beautiful piece, sharp edged, well balanced, it sang in my hand. He picked it up respectfully enough, and hefted it on his leathery palm, but still he said nothing.

I sat back and waited. I was puzzled. Why come so far to trade with us, if he wasn't interested in our flints? Travel is a risky business, and not to be undertaken lightly. To have come so far alone he was either mad or lucky. To all my questions about his family and village, or any companions he might have had on the journey, he smiled and shook his head. His teeth were sharp and pointed too, like a fox's.

Perhaps there was a band of them waiting in the woods. This man could have come merely to size my people up for an attack, before returning to report to his comrades. If I did not soon find out what he wanted, I decided I would have to kill him. Carefully, I removed the beautiful axe from his reach and grasped it in my own hand, casually, as though to expound on its merits.

He knew what I was thinking. It is disconcerting when you look into somebody's mind and find they are reading yours. I am not accustomed to discover in men the skill of talking without words, but it was a skill which he had, and was using to eavesdrop. I looked at him sharply. He was slight of build, and even forewarned by his intuition, he would not leave this place alive unless I chose.

Without hurry, he unrolled his pack and drew from

it an object wrapped in deerskin. I was curious to find the point of this visit, but I hid my impatience, and watched with a blank face as he unwrapped the precious bundle and produced an axe. He laid it on the ground between us for my inspection. Laying to rest my own weapon, carefully behind me, I picked up the strangest blade I had ever seen in my life.

It was not made of stone, carved in wood or moulded from clay. Sea salt was not in its making, although it glinted as if full of crystals and had a greenish tinge. The working of the cutting edge had not left shell-shaped depressions where the bluntness is chipped away with the stone. Although it had been beaten, no flakes had been sheared off it to obtain a fine blade.

I sniffed the axe. It had a sour tang, like poisoned bait. The head was bound with thongs to a normal wooden haft, but its weight was less than it should have been for its size. I chopped at a dry stick with the strange tool, and it whittled away at the wood in a satisfactory manner, though not, to my admittedly partial and expert eye, as well as a properly-shaped flint would have done.

Finally, I took the blade into my mouth and tested it between my teeth. Its give was more than stone, less than wood. It lay sour and heavy on my tongue, like a dead thing. I took it from my mouth and regarded it. There, faint but visible, were the marks of my teeth. I tossed the axe to the ground. What use is a weapon that is no stronger than my teeth? Will it fell trees or slay a raging boar? All this I communicated to the man in a few abrupt gestures, and throwing my own precious axe to him, I motioned him to try and mark a real axe with his teeth. He declined the challenge.

Instead he retrieved his strange possesion, wrapped it in its skin and sat with it on his lap, sometimes stroking it, or holding it to his cheek and humming to it. The man was mad. He began to tell me the story of how it was made. I would have had him driven from the village, if it had been later in the season and there had been real dealing to do. But he was the only visitor that day, and besides, who knows what wayward spirit had inhabited him to make him mad? I didn't want it decanting itself into some poor miner, as it might, if I killed the stranger within the bounds of our own homes.

He told me how this axe had come from under ground, or been found in the beds of streams hidden in rock. I could understand that. I haven't dealt in stone all my life not to know of the bright spirits that sometimes hide in it, spoiling its purity. That is why we value flint, for its freedom from such mischievous contamination by shining ones. Then he showed stones being crushed to yield their non-stoneness. After that, he indicated fire to make the non-stone malleable, like a river. This struck me as blasphemy. The earth makes fire in her belly, from which she belches non-stone; soft rock that hardens, and the foul gasses of her indigestion. No, I had never seen it myself, but it was known. And here was an impious man, claiming to mimic the working of the earth's own body. The very idea! I shifted a little further from him, in case the anger of the Goddess took the form of the ground opening up and swallowing him.

Unabashed, he continued with his nonsense, show-ing how the non-stone was cooled in water (great hissings and swishings here) and beaten into shape. Ah-ha, yes, I thought as much, real stones were needed for this. Without good striking flints with which to beat a blade, this axe would have been a lump of cleverness with no practical use. But why go to all that trouble, I asked him, to produce something that wasn't half as good as what could be dug out of the earth ready to shape, and with far less effort?

He couldn't answer that, of course. so he sat there, smiling foolishly at his treasure, and crooning a wordless song to himself. What a dreamer! I know men love things for their newness, and all to the good it is, or we would never have progressed from mammoth tusks to shaped axes, and I'd be out of a job. But this did seem like a lot of sweat to expend on something that was never going to be more than a curiosity. How many trees did they have to burn in order to melt one little non-stone blade? Enough to cook three bison on, I'm sure. If his tribe had time to go bison hunting, which no doubt they didn't, spending all their days grubbing around for flawed stones with the soft and gleaming impurities.

And why had he come here? What did he want from us? I asked again. He shrugged and suggested maybe a few perfectly round flints for beating their stupid non-stone tools into shape. He must have known I wouldn't let him have the gleanings from our spoil heap for anything he had to offer, but he didn't seem to mind. I sensed some other purpose in his journey.

The cooking fires were being lit, and I realised that we would have to offer this strange visitor hospitality. His nose twitched at the smell of food and when I invited him to eat with us, he positively drooled, saliva dripping off his yellow fangs and into his beard. He looked expectantly into my hut, as though waiting to be ushered across the hearth. It would be a long wait, for I had never permitted a man in my home, and wasn't about to make an exception for an errant lunatic. I took him over to where the brothers SameBirth were making themselves comfortable for the night and left him in their care. They were pleased, as I knew they would be, and fussed around him, exclaiming at his rufous pelt and barbaric tongue.

He stayed three days, lounging about and making a complete nuisance of himself. He diverted the miners from their work, entrancing them with tall stories and songs which they could not understand, but seemed to pick up. Neither Elder nor Younger SameBirth showed any inclination to leave their visitor in the morning and go down the shaft, they had to be dragged out of their hut by the other miners, with much cheerful and vulgar abuse. He ate vast quantities, but nobody seemed to mind, drank potsfull of rotten-grain water and never fell down an old working in the dark, and was generally the life and soul of the village, displaying no inclination to go home.

Then he showed them the axe. He must have been drunk, or feeling that he owed the SameBirth brothers something for their hospitality, because on the fourth night, while they were sitting about the fire, singing salacious songs in a foreign tongue, he pulled out his treasure and began to tell them the story of how it was made. The miners were used to his stories, and cheered him on regardless, being too far gone in drink to tell that this was not one of his fables. But some of the flint-knappers were present at that fire, and they were not the easily charmed wastrels to whom the stranger had grown accustomed. Seizing the axe, they examined it as I had done, and, when they found that they could leave the marks of their teeth upon it, you couldn't have quenched their scorn with a whole salt sea. They ran through the village, calling to the other women, and to the sober miners to come and see the wonderful axe about which the stranger had been boasting.

From mouth to mouth the axe was passed, and with the impression of every pair of teeth that savaged it, the hilarity grew. The whole village was astir in the dark, adults howling with derision, children just howling. The drunks, feeling the mood of their fellows, joined in the chorus of jeers against the man who had, a few minutes before, been the best fellow ever to up-end a drinking pot with them. The stranger himself darted about trying to retrieve his axe. Mockingly, the crowd passed it from hand to hand, keeping it out of his reach. The firelight glinted on his red hair as he danced from one tormentor to another, now smiling, now glaring, cajoling and threatening for the return of his axe.

The oldest of the flint-knappers had it now. She bit it contemptuously with her still-strong teeth, and flung it at the feet of the stranger. It landed in the ground between his legs, the handle quivering with the impact. Suddenly the mob was quiet. I don't know how those things go, but it was at that moment that his life was in danger. Picking up the axe, he wrapped it quickly in its skin and thrust it inside his own clothing. Knowing better than to turn his back on his opponents, he walked away slowly, feeling the ground behind him with his foot before taking a step backwards. In front of him were the glittering eyes of a score of people who were now his enemies, red in the firelight. Step by dangerous step, he made his way out of the centre of the village and into the darkness beyond the ring of huts. Then he turned and ran, with the villagers baying at his heels.

Where was I when all this was going on? What a question to ask a woman with a new lover. I was in my hut, all my senses filled with the joys of discovery. All but my sense of danger, that is, which never got the evening off. But even a howling riot racing towards my dwelling took a few minutes to impinge upon my consciousness. Stumbling from an embrace that would have melted a mountain, I arrived at the door of my hut at the same moment as the stranger collapsed upon the threshold. I was tempted to break his neck myself, as you can well imagine.

My neighbours stood panting around the fallen man. One or two had torches, by the flickering light of which I could see the desperation in the stranger's face and the blood lust in the villagers'. They were a wild, rough-house mob, but they hesitated to butcher the man at my hearth. I was glad that no-one bore me a grudge and wished to unleash bad spirits in my home. The stranger grovelled his way to his knees, and squatted on his haunches, looking up at me. He did not plead, he did not speak, but I heard his intrusive voice in my head, demanding my protection.

"Soft Axe!" spat the oldest flint-knapper, who was a natural ring-leader. "He mocks our craft with his blasphemous creation. These fools listened to his stories, but some of us left our teeth marks in his magical blade. What a Weak Tool!" Her contempt aroused the crowd, who began jeering again, where before they had fallen silent. A stone, thrown from the back of the crowd hit him on the shoulder and he flinched.

"I invited him to stay here," I said, summoning all the authority I could to my voice and gesture. I looked the oldest flint-knapper directly in her sceptical face and addressed myself to her. There had been many things between us over the years, and we were wary of one another. "I will get rid of him."

The people howled with disappointment, because their blood was up and they wanted a killing. But I knew their soft-bellied ways; to run screeching through the dark to the execution of the stranger was one thing, to wield the knife themselves was not such an entertainment.

"He must not be killed in the village," I said. My mother has taught me many useful skills, not the least of which is how to make up ancient lore on the spot, as the need arises. "Or his spirit will stay to trouble us and strike our crops barren. I welcomed him, I must remove him. Alone" I added as an afterthought, but they were convinced it was all part of the ritual.

"Come, Soft Axe," I commanded in a terrible voice, kicking him in the ribs for effect. While he scrambled to his feet, I stuck my head inside the hut, and explained to my rumpled bed-mate that I had to go off into the forest for a short while. I can't blame her for being angry, but when she said I needn't expect to find her waiting upon my return, it did nothing to improve my mood, and with authentic savagery, I drove the shivering man before me towards trees.

A few of the children trailed after me, but their mothers restrained them. The miners, slightly sobered by all this, muttered whatever spells they thought appropriate to the occasion and slunk off back to their fires. It is lucky that we are a superstitious lot, but I hoped this wouldn't set a precedent for dealing with other enemies. I didn't want to find myself trotting off into the forest for hand-to-hand combat with a genuine mortal foe.

Soft Axe wailed very convincingly, and the last of the public, satisfied that the doomed man was suitably terrified, went about their business. I drove him into the forest, with kicks and curses, and the odd blow from a stave which someone had thoughtfully pressed into my hand. When we were well away from the village, I stopped and made him face me. He saw in my eyes that I was not going to kill him and began to smile. I was exasperated by the whole ridiculous business, and cracked him round the shins with my staff, to teach him not to be too smug in the face of danger. More staidly, he opened his pack and showed me the flints which he had collected during his stay. He had a good eye for striking stones, I will say that for him, I couldn't have picked out a better selection of rough-worked pieces myself. Grateful for his life, he offered to return the stolen goods, but I would have given a sackful of flints to be rid of him, and told him to repack them in his bundle.

Having done this without any great show of gratitude, he extracted a cloth-wrapped object, smaller than his notorious axe, and held it up. Bared of its coverings, it was revealed as a knife, made of the same non-stone which had earned his expulsion from the village. Wondering if he meant to cut my throat, I made as if to strike, and he dropped the blade, gesturing me to pick it up. It was a gift.

A poisoned gift, as it turned out. Oh, not in that way. No snakes' juice had been squeezed onto its handle. I did not fall to the ground, choked by my own blackened and protuberant tongue, with popping eyes, simply because I had taken the knife in my hand. It was a more subtle poison, perhaps an enchantment, which worked on me slowly, as the best poisons will, before it brought me here.

I tucked the knife into my belt, it seemed such a small thing, and commanded Soft Axe to be on his way. He was bidding me farewell until we should meet again, but I intended this parting to be final. Cutting his valediction short, I bundled him onto the path into the heart of the forest with an abruptness that enabled even him to get the hint. As his next meeting would most likely be with a wolf, I did not envy him the journey, but nor did I intend to waste the rest of the night waiting for him to go. Correctly interpreting the direction of my thoughts, which were firmly back in the bed from which I had been roused, he gave me a lubricious smile and, squaring his bony shoulders against the weight of his pack, strode off into the darkness.

I hurried home. Of course, good as her word, she had gone by the time I returned, leaving a pleasant disorder and an air of pique. I lay on my bed, with the moonlight flooding through the doorway, looking at Soft Axe's parting gift. The knife lay lightly in my hand and had a good edge. A design had been engraved on the blade near the handle, which looked like the newborn sun, although it could equally well have been the Mother's pregnant belly or an accidental scratch. I bit the blade, but my teeth made no impression, it seemed to be harder than the axe head. I amused myself by throwing the knife at the roof tree. It was perfectly balanced, and landed point foremost, embedded in the wood. In spite of myself, I was impressed.

We had a good trading season that year, and entered the winter with our stores full of grain. Soft Axe's visit quickly passed into folklore. I carried my knife, but hidden, I didn't want the villagers accusing me of dishonouring that which provided our living. As chief negotiator of our trade, I could hardly walk around advertising a rival product in my belt.

At mid-winter, my mother, always keen to test the extent of public gullibility, announced that the Goddess had intimated to her that our traditional solstice festival was too tame. In future she required that all the women devote themselves fully to her rites for the entire ten day period, undisturbed by domestic burdens. When the men sullenly demanded to know what these rites where, that they should have to wait on the women for such a long time, my mother withered them with a look. The impiety of even asking about a sacred mystery, she managed to imply, might be enough to bring an angry Goddess to their door. Hastily the miners went about their arduous tasks, consoled only by an extra allowance of my mother's best rotten-grain brew.

What a wild time we had, I hope the Goddess enjoyed herself as much as we did. The death of a fat hog, which ran into the village and impaled itself on the stake of a half-built hut, was taken as an indication of the Goddess's pleasure at the new arrangements. Generously, we allowed the men to share in the resulting feast, my mother revealing that this was the will of her mistress. We spent ten days in festive riot, and as many nights again to clear our bleary heads and thickened blood. My mother, of course, had it coming and going, for in her role as medicine woman, it was she who administered the herbs which mitigated the excesses which she, as priestess had ordained. I had heard that in the west some tribes allowed men to conduct religious ceremonies, but I could not imagine that their rituals were half as acceptable as ours. I didn't think it would catch on.

When the days lengthened once again, the trickle of traders coming to my door increased to a flood. Our fame was at its height, although I didn't realise it then, the success and wealth of my village that year was the last bright flare of a star that was dying in the sky. Of course, human affairs jog along through times that appear never-ending and it is only later that we may look back and say, ah, yes, those were the golden days; that was the glorious past. At the time we did not know that we were living in what would soon become the stuff of nostalgia.

I don't know how rumours get around the world, but they do. One or two of my visitors that summer, the second since the banishment of Soft Axe, asked me if I had any of the new tools, the ones that were light and could be made into any shape, and sang when you struck them with a flint. They asked in low voices, or small gestures, and they asked when we were alone, for they knew the treachery of what they were suggesting. No-one seemed to know who made such implements, but the news of their existence was out.

Although, as I have said, business was good that year, the best it had ever been (or, had we known it, was to be again), there was a disturbing undercurrent. One of the tribes which came every year from the west, where the holy plain stretches out, covered in old and awful sites, did not appear. Usually, their visit was a highly profitable one, they were a large and successful tribe, who never brought less than twenty people to carry all their bartered goods. Although we could afford to lose their business, it worried me. I asked other groups from that area whether they had been wiped out in a war, but I could get no word of them.

Neighbours of this tribe arrived at the very end of the summer to trade as usual, although they brought a smaller quantity of grain and pots than they had last year, and drove a harder bargain. For the sake of their old custom, and because I wanted news, I allowed them to make a deal that would have shocked my apprentice, had I not sent her out. When the business was almost concluded, the elder, who represented her tribe, asked me if I had heard of the marvellous weapons, made, it was said, by the spirits under the earth.

I told her angrily that our flints were made by the spirits under the earth, had been from time immemorial, and more to the point, you couldn't chew them like an old sheep's loin. The elder rocked back on her heels and smiled gummily. "So," she said, "you have seen the non-stone blades?"

I was cross with myself, because I had walked right into her trap, like a stupid ox, blundering into the hunters' pit. There, in the half-light of my hut, I showed her my knife, and asked if she had ever seen anything like it before. She sucked her hollow tooth noisily, and shook her head. "But," she said, "people are talking in my country of such things." It appeared that the reason her neighbouring tribe had not come to trade that year was because they had gone off west to hunt for the new non-stone weapons. If they had not perished in their foolhardy search (for they only had the vaguest rumour to guide them), then next year all the young hotheads from the holy plain would want to go and get the new blades. The elders might counsel caution, and stick to the old ways, but we all know in which direction that river runs.

I knew I must find out for myself how serious was the threat to our livelihood. When I discussed it with the oldest flint-knapper, grey now, and just as wary of me, she was of the opinion that quality would prevail over fashion. Soft Axe's wares had not impressed her, she couldn't see people flocking to buy non-stone axes that would bend in a season, just because they had pretty runes on the side. I was not convinced. The sort of men who are in love with the new, as Soft Axe had been, will never give up until they have improved and changed and tampered with a thing. Maybe they had made their blades harder, perhaps they were better at shaping them now, or why did the rumours whisper of metal pots and jewels? Soft Axe had been right about one thing, which I had not expected. I was going to have to see him again. And so, at the season's change, that summer-end, with the whole village turned out to bewail my folly in embarking on a journey that would be the death of me, I set out with my pack, and my staff and my non-stone knife for company, on the long and dangerous walk to the west, where the sun dies in the sea.

My mother, in her role as fortune-teller, displeased, but not as hysterical as the other villagers, agreed that the expedition would imperil my life, but not immediately, that I would return safely and suffer the consequences. She was having one of her gnomic days, I preferred her routine predictions, of the 'you will be unlucky at gambling and meet a woman with lop-sided ears' variety. Still, one can't question what the Goddess sends, even when it is incomprehensible. Having kissed every woman in the village, and half the children, I left, promising to be back by spring at the latest, ready for next season's trading.

EIGHT

With the handle of her trowel Felicity tapped the last brick into place to complete the rebuilding of the gable end. She allowed herself a moment of quiet satisfaction. It was a bright, blustery day, and her fingers were chapped and blue with cold, but she felt that her bricklaying would pass muster with the most discerning of cowboy builders. Admittedly, her first attempts at a wall had been taken down as often as they were put up, in a welter of tangled level-lines and the sullen stiffening of cement that has gone off. The finished wall, however, if not beautiful was certainly regular and functional. If the odd gobbet of mortar, squeezed from a join, had set hard on the face of the wall, who was to say that she might not have got the same result a great deal more expensively from one of the local handymen who so resented her refusal to employ them?

As an afterthought, she applied her spirit level to the last brick, and found that it was unevenly laid. Gentle tapping to one side or the other did not remedy the situation, and she was forced to remove the obstinate block, scoop up the mortar on her trowel, and re-lay it. Finally satisfied, she gathered up her tools and descended to the ground. Elspeth approached with a cup of tea as she was washing down her trowel in a bucket of water drawn noisily from the pump in the scullery, from which no amount of penetrating oil could remove the squeak.

If Elspeth had not made herself useful restoring the garden to order, which she was well on the way to doing, Felicity would have found her invaluable company for her habit of brewing up every hour, on the hour. It was not possible, Felicity had found, to labour out of doors, even on seemingly clement days such as this one, without having a hot drink at least every fifty minutes. Gratefully, she wrapped her cold and lumpy hands around a half-pint mug. Her initial resentment of Elspeth's invasion of her solitude was long gone, even if the other woman did seem to have staked a strong territorial claim to her garden. Elspeth's tools filled one shed, and the pigsty housed a range of horticultural treatments and potions which Felicity did not care to investigate closely, and which Elspeth applied in the slightly furtive manner of one doing magic in a rational age.

Elspeth was looking very well on her labours, and, Felicity was surprised to realise, increasingly happy. Her round, smooth face was rosy with health, and she no longer bothered to powder her nose when coming to Hope Cottage, 'as it's only us girls' she explained, 'although Archibald doesn't like to see a woman with a naked face.' She was prone to sudden unexpected bouts of singing as she dug. One day, she brought her radio, tentatively, hoping that Felicity wouldn't mind. Now, despite Felicity's initial reluctance, it sat on the wobbly gate post belting out Radio Three for as long as they both could stand it. Sometimes, when Elspeth had to go into town to do her shopping, or have her hair done, or run some errand for her husband, who could not get away from his steam engine, Felicity would listen to pop radio, until the hook lines of all the current chart hits were firmly embedded in her brain, and she found herself singing them, mindless macho lyrics and all.

"Your hedge," announced Elspeth, who still maintained the polite fiction that the garden belonged to Felicity, "I've been thinking about it."

"Uh huh?" Felicity dunked a biscuit in her tea. They were taking their ease on top of a timber stack. She slipped off her steel toe-capped wellingtons, which Elspeth had taken her into Dereham to buy, horrified at the trainers in which she was working, and wiggled her sweaty toes in the breeze.

"I think we are past the danger of frost, although, of course, you never can tell; but by my calculations, it's time for a good hard trim, if we're going to get the poor thing into shape for the summer. It has gone rather wild."

"I know how it feels," said Felicity, trying to run her fingers through her impossibly tangled curls.

Elspeth's hair was contained under a tweedy head-scarf.

"Then there's the question of the dog roses."

"Is there?"

"The hedge is full of them. They're choking it in places. Would you mind if I took them out?"

"They are rather pretty, aren't they?"

"If you like little pink things," said Elspeth, scornfully. She had a taste for strong colours and large blossoms. "They are weeds. And the hedge is filled with briars."

"Isn't a weed a flower in the wrong place?"

"No," joked Elspeth, "a weed is something that thrives on being dug up, chopped down or choked off. A flower dies if you threaten it with a spade."

"Could you not leave some of the dog roses? I remember that hedge with flowers in it from when I was a child, and I'm sure most of them were in the wrong place."

"I suppose so," sighed Elspeth. "It is very hard, gardening by compromise."

"I hope I'm not cramping your style."

"I must remember that it is, after all, your garden. It's quite tempting to run wild."

"Like the dog-roses?"

"They shall stay. In moderation. You know, that hedge is older than the cottage. Probably about three hundred years old. I don't suppose this is the first building that there has ever been on this site."

"It's a funny place to put a house, isn't it? In the middle of a field."

"Norfolk people seem to like their privacy. Once I've licked the hedge into shape, I shall have to root up all those self-seeded sycamores. Unless you want to live in an arboretum."

"I'd be happy with the fruit trees alone," said Felicity, "not that I suppose it's fair to expect them to produce, at their age." A hoary apple tree groaned against its supporting stake, as if in agreement.

"We shall see. I might try root pruning them. You shouldn't give up on them because they're old and creaky. Apart from that diseased pear tree, which I was thinking of having down. Did you bring a chain saw, in that Aladdin's Cave of tools?" Elspeth indicated the trailer, in which Felicity had conveyed her tool chest, fruit of a delicious morning in Tyzaks with a long-suffering credit card.

"No, but we can hire one, if you are determined to be a lumberjack."

"Absolutely," said Elspeth, looking at the encroaching trees. "This is a very secluded place. Don't you worry about being lonely?"

"I do get scared sometimes," admitted Felicity. "The lack of continuous background noise makes every stray sound suspicious, when you're feeling jumpy, especially in the night. I suppose I'll get used to it."

"I felt so terribly isolated, when we first moved here, although it was what we had always wanted and planned for. It was a frightful shock to go for a whole day without speaking to anyone. Apart from Archibald, of course, but not to meet anyone from the outside world. It wasn't what I was used to."

"I know that feeling. When I get like that, I drive into Orfton-Saint-Scabious and go into a shop, just for the excuse to have a conversation. I've bought boxes of matches, although I don't smoke, and gallons of petrol, when the tank was half full already, solely for the exchange of spoken words such purchases bring. It's a good thing you decided to take the garden in hand, or I'd be barking mad by now."

"Don't you miss your friends? I found it a dreadful wrench, parting from people I'd known all my life. Even if I didn't like them very much."

"That's the thing, isn't it?" Felicity agreed. "You acquire friends by chance, because you work together, or live near each other, or because they know someone you know. In London, I always had to arrange a dinner engagement a month in advance, my social schedule was so busy. But I don't find that I miss most of them. You know how it is, any number of acquaintances, not very many bosom-buddies."

"It wasn't like that in Acton," confessed Elspeth. "But then the suburbs are different."

"When I first moved down from Manchester, and I didn't have a job, which my family considered an inevitable consequence of doing a History degree, but was, in fact, a choice which many young feminists made in those days, I had a very close-knit circle of friends." She laughed, "that sounds like a soft-furnishing doesn't it?"

"It sounds very nice," said Elspeth, stoutly.

"It was, actually. We all did lots of splendid ILEA classes, for 50p a term, and used our UB40s to get into plays and concerts like we use our credit cards nowadays. We had plenty of time for each other, and for meetings, and causes and plots."

"Wasn't it a bit precarious?" said Elspeth. "As a way of life."

"It was alright."

"And what became of your circle of friends?"

"We woke up to the fact that all around us, people were doing very nicely, thank you, out of some kind of right wing New Deal. One by one, we got jobs, at first directly connected with our political causes, then less so, until finally nobody asked 'what do you do?' anymore, because the key question was 'what do you earn?' Of course, as with anybody who jumps on a bandwagon late, and with reservations, we didn't become very rich, like the young people who go straight into accountancy from college, but we were a reasonably affluent bunch."

"It all sounds like growing up, to me," said Elspeth, tartly. "You can't expect the state to subsidise you forever."

"Perhaps not," Felicity agreed, sadly. "But I don't find that the friendships built on a weekly game of squash and a shared salary grade have been very durable. No doubt, when Hope Cottage is fully restored and modern conveniences are installed, there'll be a traffic jam of little urban hatchbacks in the drive every weekend. All Londoners dream of having a friend with a cottage in the country, upon whom they can descend in their leisure time."

"Will you be hospitable?"

"No doubt, I'll be very pleased to have visitors. A

girl must exercise her social faculties, after all. But even if I have felt lonely, since I came here, I can't say that I've missed many of my former friends as individuals, any more than I suppose that they've missed me. It's more the feeling of moving in a homogeneous crowd, being part of a network, having a full address book and being able to say to someone who wants to fix a social engagement with you 'I'm free this Thursday fortnight'. That shows how popular you are, you see."

"It sounds rather sad, to me."

"I suppose it is. I drifted into friendships with women as easily as I drifted into my various jobs, because I wasn't qualified to do anything else. The friendships were profoundly superficial, and as for the jobs. . ."

"But you were made redundant from the last one," protested Elspeth, "you can't have wanted to leave."

"Getting the push was the best thing that could have happened," said Felicity. "Otherwise, I'd be there still, drifting along, like plankton in the sea of capitalism. I'm better off without the job, and without friends who are really only acquaintances. Us latch-key kids, you know, do alright on our own."

"I must confess, I am very fond of my own company," said Elspeth.

"Good thing too, living out here."

"In moderation, though."

"Naturally."

"I don't like crowds, but one or two close friends are essential to happiness, I think."

"You've got Shirley."

"Yes," Elspeth brightened.

"And Archibald."

"Of course. Excuse me," she stood up, "I must go and spend a penny."

"As euphemisms go," said Felicity, "that's better than 'powdering your nose'".

Elspeth smiled and retired behind the holly bush to the shit pit, which she had improved with the addition of a colourful seaside windbreak as a screen, and a tupperware box full of soft toilet paper. The orange and green canvas flapped noisily in the breeze, but it increased the privacy of the amenities. Felicity had intended to revitalise the chemical toilet in the caravan, but being three miles from the nearest main drain meant long trips in the car with a bucket full of sewage to be emptied, a prospect at which she baulked. The toilet in the cottage, she had discovered by simple experiment, vented straight into the ditch behind the house. A cesspit went up and down her list of priorities, depending on the severity of the weather.

Happy with a blow torch, she went around the inside walls of the upper storey of the cottage, exterminating any lurking spores of dry rot. Ancient cobwebs looked suspiciously like the fungus, so she torched them as well, hoping that the spiders had long since moved out. The floors of the bedrooms, once the fallen rubble had been cleared painstakingly away, were revealed as sound in joist, if not in floorboards, capable of supporting her light step as she had worked her way along the walls. Now she played the flame to and fro, scorching away the traces of rot, her hands warm for once and her mind occupied with the problem of putting up the new roof. When the gas canister expired, she climbed out onto the platform around the upper storey and considered her problem.

With the aid of G.P. Turvey, dim memories of the Pythagorean theorem and much scratching of the head, she had worked out the angle at which the roof should be pitched. She had ordered the timber, which now lay, neatly stacked, in the garden. She was reasonably confident that she understood the layout of the top plate on which the rafters would rest, and that she could woman-handle the joists into position on her own. But she saw no way that she could single-handedly raise the roof. G.P. Turvey, writing in the days when labour was cheap, recommended that three men be employed in hoisting the rafters into position, or at least two carpenters and a lad. Felicity thought two people might manage, but there was only one of her.

Felicity looked down to where Elspeth, straight backed, elbows out, was subduing the unruly hedge.

Although she could garden all day, with endless reserves of stamina, Elspeth was not a carpenter, or even a lad. She was a short, middle aged housewife, and even though she had taken to the cement mixer with surprising ease, and kept Felicity supplied with mortar for her bricklaying, she could not be expected to skip along the rafters carrying a length of two by six. Felicity resigned herself, with great and surprising regret, to the inevitable. She would have to get help in. She knew that builders, once employed, would not see themselves as help. They would expect her to pay up and keep out of their way. They would disparage the work she had already done, advising her that it would be best if they tore it all down and re-did it properly. When it rained, they would expect to shelter in her caravan, and they would probably tell her that Hope Cottage wasn't worth saving anyway, and why didn't she let them demolish it and start again?

Knowing all this sank Felicity into a gloom, but she could not see any way out. In order to postpone the dreadful day, when she would hand over her project, her home, to careless strangers, she got on with those parts of the roofing that she could do herself. In grim silences, punctured only by curses when she dropped tools to the ground, or crushed her thumb with an injudicious hammer blow, she crawled about the roof, fixing plates and hammering joists into position. She took fewer breaks, and made more mistakes through exhaustion and depression. Her hands were full of splinters, which, because the timbers were treated with toxic chemicals, festered. She found the only way to remove the more obstinate pieces of wood was to slice her skin open with a well-sharpened chisel, the fibrous splinters fragmenting in the face of attack by needle and tweezers. One afternoon, when she had hauled a joist up to the top of the house, only to discover that she had somehow, inexplicably, cut it six inches short and rendered it useless, she perched on the scaffolding and wept tears of bitter frustration. Elspeth scuttled up the ladder to proffer a clean handkerchief, but otherwise she stayed well out of the way during this period of depression.

After a week of hardly speaking, even to the cat, who slunk about the fields and appeared only for meals and sleeping, Felicity found herself huddled over a length of timber with a roofing square, setting out her first rafter, the one which was to be a pattern for all the others. This was the point at which she should stop and hand over to the professionals. Wilfully, she continued stepping off from the centre line of the ridge to the tail cut. She cut the birdsmouth notch which would fit over the plate on the wall. Although the task was pointless, she took endless pains over it. When she had finished, she laid another timber on top of her pattern and marked out the angles she had cut in the first piece of wood onto the second, with the sharp pencil that lived behind her ear. Her stomach rumbled that it was tea-time, and she knew that she must stop this folly and find a builder, but still she continued, marking out and cutting the second rafter into shape.

Elspeth approached quietly and coughed to attract her attention. She had been scything the grass in the orchard and the heavy sweet smell of pollen filled the air. The dog-roses, grateful for their reprieve, bloomed in a riot of delicate pink at the garden's boundary. Birds, attracted by the feast of worms and grubs revealed by Elspeth's constant digging, sang from the trees. The air was still, and a calm enormous sky rested the thin, clear light of a May evening over their heads. Ungrateful for these many blessings, Felicity worked on, miserably absorbed. Elspeth coughed once more.

"I must be going home," she said, "It's nearly suppertime and I can't think what I'm going to make. Shopping day tomorrow."

Felicity grunted absently, without looking up.

"Are you alright, dear?" asked Elspeth, boldly for one who venerated privacy above all others virtues, although (sinner that she was) her nature was curious and gossipy.

Felicity put down her saw and sat back on her heels. The bags under her eyes had returned, dark and puffy, for she had not been sleeping well. On recent moonlit nights, the cat had preferred to go out hunting field mice and nestlings, rather than share her restless bed. Her skin was roughened beyond the capacity of a gallon of Aloe Vera lotion to repair and she had begun to forget about meals. She was a woman in the grip of an unhappy obsession.

"It's this roof," she confessed to Elspeth. "I will have to get some men in, and that's the last thing I want to do."

"Is it so terrible?" asked Elspeth. "Couldn't they do the roof and go away? It's not as if they would take over the whole building."

"It would feel as though they did. Can't you imagine how patronising real builders would be about all this?" she indicated the cottage, half-dismantled, surrounded by stacks of material, encumbered with its scaffolding, like a child with its teeth in braces.

"But you've done so much," protested Elspeth. "Anyone would be proud of what you've achieved."

"It will all be different if I have to hand it over to bloody experts," mumbled Felicity, disconsolately. "How would you feel if you had to get a contractor to lay out your garden, while you were left to trim round the edges and pick up after them?"

Elspeth was struck by this argument. She wrinkled her brow in thought and ignored the dictates of her conscience, which was nagging about Mr Maybe's supper. "I wish there was something I could do," she said, "I've been so worried about you, this last week. You've seemed so unhappy, and I'm sure you're not eating properly."

"I'm sorry, Elspeth, I know I am a complete pain at the moment. It can't be much fun for you."

"Don't worry,dear," Elspeth patted her arm, "I'm used to those around me being in moods. I've got the garden to keep me cheerful. Don't you think it's looking promising?"

"Beautiful," said Felicity politely. "You've got more things growing than I ever imagined were here, lurking under the weeds."

"I wish I could think of a way out of your predicament."

"There isn't one." Felicity stood up and stretched her aching back. "Tonight I shall go down to the White Stag, which is where I gather the horny-handed sons of toil forgather, and invite some jobbing builder to come and raise my roof. And after he's finished knocking the place about for money, I don't suppose I'll feel the same about doing it for love, but it can't be helped."

"Oh dear," said Elspeth. "I really must be going. I'll be over late tomorrow, I'm going in to Norwich to do a big shop. Do take care of yourself."

"Yes. See you tomorrow."

"And have something hot to eat before you go out." Two shrill blasts on a steam whistle, which indicated that Archibald was growing impatient for her return, set Elspeth trotting back to Maybe Halt.

Felicity dragged a comb painfully through her hair, splashed her face clean in a bucket of cold water and put on her least ragged pair of jeans. All her jumpers were redolent of the building site, because she never cared to risk them in the automatic, on her weekly visit to Elspeth's house to use the washing machine. This ritual had developed to coincide with Archibald's regular trip to the library, which allowed Felicity to sit around in her underwear while her meagre store of garments was cleaned. Somewhere in London, in the cupboard of a friend, she had left a suitcase full of smart clothes for which she had no use in the country, or space in the caravan. The best thing about her outings to Maybe Halt was the hot bath, for her new muscles had as many knots as they had bulges. However, it was now several days since her last exposure to hot water, and sniffing her armpits to make sure that she wasn't too much in a state of nature, she set off for the pub.

Orfton-Saint-Scabious was a pretty little village, clustered around a triangular green, and adorned by an early perpendicular church of great charm. A small terrace of Georgian cottages facing the green was empty, because it was a weekday, and the old vicarage was for sale again. These were the only signs of the foreign take-over of the county, and locals congratulated themselves on living in such a splendidly dull and ugly part of Norfolk, so obscure that most week-enders would not even notice passing it by on their dash for the coast and genuine period features.

The spire of the church of Saint Nicholas was crooked, knocked askew by a bomb in 1944. It was an American bomb, dumped from a Liberator in difficulties after take-off, but as the people of Orfton-Saint-Scabious were less than enthusiastic about their gallant allies, the blow which knocked the spire askew, and caused the weather-vane to give misleading directions ever after, was fairly regarded as enemy action. The second largest building in the village was the White Stag Hotel. Although it had ten bedrooms, and ran to three separate entrances at the front, few visitors ever stayed the night, except for the odd agricultural salesman. Ducks from the pond on the green perched on the slats of the wooden benches placed outside the pub for the use of customers in warm weather, splattering the greening seats with their droppings. A life-size plaster model of a white stag perched on the roof of the porch as an aide to those too drunk to read the sign. One of its antlers had been broken off by a live-in barman, climbing out of his bedroom window after locking-up time, with the day's takings in his pocket.

Felicity walked in through the front door and found herself in a hall, with doors to right and left. Feeling like Alice, she chose the door to the left and stepped into the Lounge Bar. Rough carpet tiles on the floor, and the disapproving glare of a man with a gin and tonic at the bar, informed her that this was the preserve of the cavalry twill and tweeds brigade, not unkempt women in muddy boots. She retreated. The door to the right was marked 'Public', and she hoped it would be athrong with resting builders. Cautiously, she looked round the door. Bare floorboards and formica table-tops confirmed that she was in the right social milieu, but only one old man sat in a corner, sipping a barley wine. If he had ever built anything, it was probably St. Nick's.

Leaving by the front door, Felicity walked along the

street and re-entered the hotel by a less imposing door. This hall contained a pay-phone and an overweight spaniel, who lay wheezing under the coat rack. She was again offered the choice of two doors, one of which must be the rear entrance to the Public Bar, and another, on her right, which bore no name, but from behind which the sound of many voices came.

Taking a deep breath, Felicity threw open the door and walked in. Fifteen men, standing round a pool table looked up as one and stared at her with bovine hostility. They were all young, dressed much as she was, and each was equipped with a pint of lager. A juke box in the corner belted out a particularly inane song about the faithlessnes of women, which Felicity recognised from her secret radio days. No-one spoke. At the far end of the room, the man at the dart board had swivelled round to look at her, as had all the others. He still held a dart in his hand, and Felicity felt as if it was aimed at her heart. The pool player was the first to turn away, making a break with more strength than skill. Balls crashed against the cushions and ricocheted around the table. Felicity beat a strategic retreat.

The Public Bar, with its solitary occupant, seemed cosy and welcoming by comparison. Behind the bar, the landlord stood, watching her suspiciously. She considered abandoning the project, but stubbornness drove her on.

"Yes, young man," said the landlord, with false geniality, "what can I get you?"

"You can get yourself a new pair of glasses," snapped Felicity.

"Oh, I do beg your pardon, miss," he gave the last word an unpleasant emphasis.

She ordered a pint of IPA and he went to the pump to pull it. His way was barred by the sudden appearance of a large woman, with a mountain of bleached and back-combed hair that added nearly a foot to her height. The landlord patted her rump and got out of her way. She pulled the beer and brought it over to Felicity.

"Excuse me," said Felicity, surveying the small glass tankard, "but I asked for a pint."

Wordlessly, the landlady returned to the pump and pulled another half, which she set down on the counter in front of Felicity with a snap.

"Do you think I could have both halves in the same glass?"

"I don't like to see ladies drinking out of pint mugs," pronounced the gorgon. Behind her back her husband smirked.

"But I'm not a lady, so you needn't worry about that."

"I can see," said the landlady, icily. "A lady wouldn't come out dressed like a cowherd. It's an insult to the men, who've taken the trouble to clean themselves up and put on suits."

Felicity looked at the only other customer, the ancient in the corner. It was true he was wearing a suit, but it was obviously the one in which he had been demobbed, possibly from the Boer War, and the trousers were held up with bailer twine. He chortled to himself and blew bubbles in his barley wine.

The landlady retreated to the nether regions, from which a waft of stale scampi and other tired basket meals floated through the door. Felicity sipped thoughtfully at first one glass and then the other. The beer was good, but the glasses had not been rinsed in hot water, and a crust of tea-towel fluff was gathered around the rim of each. The landlord perched on a tall stool behind the bar reading the Eastern Daily Press, and taking sly glances at his customer over the top of the paper. Gales of raucous laughter came from the games room, and every few minutes one of the burly young men would appear through the door with empty glasses to be refilled, or demanding change for the pool table. They stared at Felicity, but she was determined not to leave before she had finished her drink. It occurred to her that she should restock her own drinks cupboard.

"I want to buy a bottle of rum to take away," she said to the landlord.

"Jug and Bottle," he returned from the corner of his mouth, without lifting his eyes from the paper.

"I beg your pardon?"

"Off sales in the Jug and Bottle, out the front, down the side-street on your right, it's the green door."

"Thanks," she murmured, setting off. The Jug and Bottle was a tiny room, more of a cubicle, with brown wood-panelled walls and a counter, behind which were displayed boxes of crisps, dusty beer bottles and cigars wrapped in cellophane. There was no-one there to serve her. She waited a moment, then rapped on the counter. There was no response. Minutes passed. She shouted 'shop!' tentatively at first, and then louder. Eventually the landlord appeared behind the counter, which obviously ran uninterrupted through every bar in the pub.

"There's no need to shout," he reproached her. "Now, what's your fancy?"

"The same as it was ten minutes ago when you sent me on this wild-goose chase. A bottle of rum."

"A whole bottle," he marvelled, "for a girl who lives on her own. That's most unusual, I must say. Unless you have a lot of gentlemen callers. Would that be the case? Your great aunt used to drink gin, they say. Now that's a proper lady's drink." He turned to walk away.

"Hey, where are you going?"

"Oh, I don't keep bottles of spirits down here. They might get stolen. I'll pop back to the public and fetch you one. Don't go away." Eventually he re-appeared with a grimy bottle, whose seal he hid with his hand. Felicity strongly suspected he had been watering it. With a conjurer's dexterity, he wrapped the bottle in green tissue paper which looked as though it had been recycled from a vegetable shop.

"That'll be fifteen ninety nine, thank you very much."

"You're joking!" Felicity was aghast.

"That's the price. You've got to think of my profit margins."

"Keep it," snapped Felicity, slamming out of the hotel. She got the message.

Leaning against the passenger door of her car, like the cat when she was waiting to be let in, was the old man from the Public Bar. Between the support of the car and a stout knobbled walking stick, he was upright, but only just.

"Yugoin'bac'a'Ho'eCo'age?" he slurred. "'ucangimmealif' home."

"What?" struggled Felicity. He had the most impenetrable accent she had yet encountered. She was surprised that the fumes he was breathing on Marina weren't blistering the poor car's paint.

"'a'sonyurway," reasoned the old man. He had a face like a hazelnut, dark and shiny, with unexplained bumps. Helplessly, Felicity opened the door for her uninvited travelling companion and held his stick while he clambered unsteadily in.

"Where do you live?" she asked, driving round the village green and onto the lane that led home.

"Th'olecouncil'ouse onth'bend o'th'road. Wher'th' ladsa'ways go offa th'road comin' back fro'th'pub. I seen some crashes."

"I bet you have," said Felicity, trying not to inhale too deeply, lest she became intoxicated by her passenger's alcoholic breath.

"'a's very good o'you to fetch us home," he said, obviously speaking slowly and carefully for her benefit. "I'm Chalky Whi'e."

"Nice to meet you, Mr White," Felicity braked to avoid a pheasant that was standing in the road, staring at her headlights. "I'm Felicity Rouse."

"Oh, I know 'oo you are, a'right."

"Does everyone in the village know about me?"

"'a's righ'," agreed her companion. "'ere we are, on the righ'." He indicated a small semidetached house, set on a ninety degree bend in the narrow lane. Felicity could see the potential for accidents. The headlights picked out a concrete plaque on the front of the house, which announced the date of their building to be 1922. "Home fit for 'eroes," said Chalky, struggling with the child-proof lock. Felicity got out and helped him, lending him the support of her arm to the front door. The top of his head barely reached her shoulder.

"I use' to do Miss Rapunzel's garden," he said. "Won' you come in an' have cocoa?"

"No really," she replied, helping him into his kitchen, "I must be getting home."

"Won' be a minute," he ignored her protestations and reached unsteadily for a milk pan, leaning the hip of his gammy leg on the edge of the table for stability. Rejecting all her offers of help, Chalky shuffled around fetching mugs and spoons, while keeping half a bleary eye on the milk-pan. Feeling that she could not refuse something which cost so much effort to make, she accepted the hot sweet drink, although it cloyed.

"She were a nice lady, your grea' aunt," he said, when he was settled comfortably in a chair. "Weren' liked by mos', they said she was stand-offish. I never foun' her so. Bu' then, newcomers do have a hard time."

"But she lived here for years!" protested Felicity.

"Weren' born local, though, was she?"

"Does it matter so much?"

Chalky rolled a bleary eye at her and did not answer.

"What did you do when she left Hope Cottage?" asked Felicity, changing the subject.

"I was cowman at Bruton's farm."

"Are you retired now?"

Chalky cackled. He had a few teeth left, and appeared to disdain the use of dentures. "Got my leg squasht by a heifer," he said, slapping the afflicted limb. "Tha' ol' cow retired me, a'righ'. Save' Bruton the trouble o' doin' it. 'Course, they don' keep cows no more, so 'e would've got rid o' me sooner or la'er."

"That's too bad."

"Wha' was you doin' down the White Stag, anyways? Di'n't look like you was havin' much fun."

"I was looking for some men to fix my roof," sighed Felicity.

"I though' you're doin' it yourself? 'a's what they say."

"Well I am, but I can't raise the rafters on my own."

"You don' wanna get any of them blokes tha' was in tonigh' workin' on your house. Buncha bloody cowboys. Now, if you'd'a' asked me, twenty year ago, I coul've given you a hand."

"That's very kind of you."

"No, you don' wanna encourage those lads. They're turned right against you. You see that nasty lookin' boy come in the bar with 'is pool cue in a little case," Felicity nodded. "'e's Bruton's tractor driver. You should 'ear wha' names 'e call you."

"I rather get the impression that my neighbour doesn't like me."

"Well, 'e's a bad man to cross." Chalky rubbed his bristly chin. "But I reckon the lads'd be set against you anyways, on account of you bein' a girl, an' doin' them outta work an' all."

"Do none of them have jobs? I can't be held responsible for depriving the entire population of a livelihood. I'm not the parish relief."

"They gets work, here an' there," conceded Chalky. "Mostly. But they don' like you doin' your own buildin'."

"Can't I work on my own house?"

"I shoul' say so. Don' take no notice 'a them. Bunch of kids. Get a proper builder out from Dereham, if you need help. Though I wouldn' trust any of 'em, myself."

"Thanks a lot."

"You'll be a'righ'," said Chalky, cheerily. "Now, I'm goin' to bed, an' you better get along home to your caravan, else people will talk."

Dismissed, Felicity took her leave, no nearer to solving the problem of her roof, but consoled by the idea that she was at least on speaking terms with a man so deeply rooted in the neighbourhood that his ancestors had probably looked down their noses at the Iceni as a bunch of incoming foreigners with flashy chariots and a disinclination to shop local.

NINE

Felicity was restless the next morning, pottering about starting one small job and leaving it unfinished to begin tidying something else away. The cat rolled on the lawn, taking a dew-bath, then came to dry itself against her legs.

"Cats hate getting their fur wet, did nobody tell you?" said Felicity. The cat, who, if she had a name, had not yet revealed it, made no answer. Rubbing herself blissfully about the captive legs of her human, she left a trail of damp tabby fur around the top of Felicity's boots. "I need powdered chalk for my chalk-box," continued the woman. "Pink or blue? Pink, I think. For a girl. And some more nails. Where do all the nails go, cat? Do you eat them? I seem to drop as many as I ever hammer in, and then I never see them again. And you've finished your last tin of kangaroo offal, haven't you, disgusting monster?" The cat purred. "Do you think all that justifies a trip to Dereham? I don't seem to be able to settle to anything. I think I've got enough excuses to go into town. Isn't it funny, dear cat, I've completely ignored Elspeth all week, but as soon as she isn't here, the place seems empty? No offence to you." The cat was chasing a slow-flying bumble bee and took no notice.

Felicity climbed into the car and bumped down the drive, slightly more passable now that it had had a few days of sunshine and drying breezes across its soggy surface. At the end, on a wooden post, stood the little container which looked like a birds' nesting box, and in which the postman deposited her letters. Stretching an arm out of the window, she unhooked the box at the back and extracted her mail. Receiving a letter made her day. So isolated was she, even circulars were welcomed. She particularly relished the badly personalised prize draw letters with which her motoring organisation favoured her. 'Imagine the faces of your neighbours,' one such effort had read, 'when you walk into the bank at (different typeface) Orfton-Saint-Scabious with a cheque for seventeen thousand pounds.' Orfton, of course, did not boast a bank, but the computer which had Mailmerged the letter was not to know that.

In Dereham, having done the supermarket and the hardware store and obtained a few fancies from the bakery (Elspeth was very partial to a Bath bun with her tea) she bought a local paper and found a quiet pub in which to treat herself to lunch. Although the other customers looked at her sideways when she walked in, nobody bothered her while she sat in a corner, with a pint, all in one glass, and a sandwich, scouring the trade ads for builders. There were several, all offering free estimates, references and membership of any number of master-craftmen's associations. It seemed to Felicity, as she scanned the closely printed advertisements, that there was a federation dedicated to promoting the image of every possible building task. Plumbing, heating, gas installation, new building, thermal insulation, timber preservation, the list was endless, and each with an elaborate logo. Some general builders' adverts seemed to consist of little else but membership badges. She drew asterisks against the ones she should telephone, in a halfhearted way, and soon turned to the crossword.

The mid-day rush came and went, which meant that an extra six people passed through the bar. Still Felicity sat at her table, drinking her beer and dreaming the impossible. It had been a pure whim, in the offices of Longe, Waite and Highbill that had prompted her to announce that she would be keeping Hope Cottage, and she didn't know how rebuilding it herself had become a fixation. She had no reason to suppose that she could even begin to achieve such a thing. The nearest she had previously got to an enthusiasm for DIY was the 'renew his interest in carpentry – saw his head off' postcard, which her friend Melissa had sent her, and which she had displayed over her desk at work.

Feeling that she had played truant long enough, Felicity dragged herself out of the pub and into the market square. She should ring the builders and

103

arrange for them to come and estimate the job, she told herself. In the 'phone box, she called the first three numbers, and was so relieved when one was engaged, the second didn't answer and the third had gone bankrupt, that she realised that she didn't want to be doing this at all, and went home.

Elspeth was nowhere to be seen when she arrived, although a still-warm mug on the timber stack proclaimed her recent presence. Two warm mugs, in fact, and a cigarette end on the ground. It was hard to imagine Elspeth indulging in such an unladylike vice, Felicity wondered whether Archibald Maybe had come with his wife to inspect the works.

"Coo ee," called Elspeth, as a voice from the clouds, "we're up here."

Felicity looked up and saw Elspeth clambering about the roof accompanied by Shirley Bruton. Looking rather like a pair of schoolchildren caught scrumping, they descended to the lawn. Walking round the wood-stack to meet them, Felicity tripped over an old brown holdall full of what felt to her protesting shins like solid metal objects.

"Careful," called Elspeth, hurrying to help her up.

"Thanks." Felicity regained her balance. "Nice to see you again Mrs Bruton."

"Shirley," said the other woman, gruffly.

"I've been thinking," said Elspeth, with a conspiratorial twinkle, "and while we were in Norwich this morning doing the shopping, I had a chat with Shirley."

"In the freezer centre," her friend added.

"And it seemed like such a good idea, we even stopped at that new patisserie for coffee to discuss it further."

"You see," explained Shirley, "I used to have the cows."

"Did you?" asked Felicity, mystified.

"I did. It was my dairy, I done all the managing. Kept me busy, that did."

"Then what?"

"Mr Bruton decided to rationalise," put in Elspeth.

"He sold the milk quota," said Shirley, not without

a trace of bitterness. "Only had the ten, Jerseys they were, He said it weren't viable. But I loved those cows. It wasn't just a hobby, you know."

"And since then, of course, although a farmer's wife is always busy, Shirley's had a bit of time on her hands. Especially now the children are at school."

"He don't like me to drive a tractor, since I rolled one that time, and on such a little old hill too. And he's got a girl in to do the office and keep the accounts. Well, I don't understand the computer, anyway."

"So here she is," announced Elspeth proudly, with the air of one producing a rabbit out of a hat.

"I brung my mum's old tool kit," Shirley indicated the bag over which Felicity had tripped. "We were poor farmers, my family, I reckon I've helped patch up enough barns 'n things, before I was wed."

"Have you?" Felicity felt she was being very slow to see the point.

"She's come to help with the roof," said Elspeth, impatiently.

"That's right," agreed Shirley. "I reckon we should be able to do it, between us."

"Well," Felicity looked from one to the other, "I'm gobsmacked. What can I say?"

"Say yes," advised Elspeth.

"Bruton won't like it," said Shirley, "but women done all this sort of thing in the war. Don't see why you shouldn't get a bit of help from your neighbours."

"I'd be very grateful."

"Let's get on with it then. You cut out the rafters yet?"

* * * * * * * * * *

Dear me, would you look at that? Two old crones and the red-headed giantess planning to raise the roof. They all come here, don't they? Every disaffected hag in the neighbourhood, drawn here as if by magic. Maybe it is. But my Felicity, she isn't sure she wants them here at all.

Look at her now, if you don't believe me. All smiles. Personally, if someone bared their teeth at me like that, I would suppose they were about to go for the jugular, and leg it. She's thrilled, of course, not to have to call in the men. I never hesitated to put a team of miners to work, when they could be useful, but then I was more or less the head-woman of the village. They didn't manage very well when I was gone, but that's another story. So, thrilled she may be, but, perversely, she isn't sure that she wants this new-comer around. Oh, she is so jealous of her building. By now, she is almost reconciled to Elspeth and her chattering. Shirley is harder to take. She won't defer to Felicity's superior building skills, that's for sure. Felicity stalks around her, wary and bristling. You don't notice her neck hairs standing, do you? I am alert to these signs.

She wants Shirley to be a good builder, but not too good. In reality, she knows she must have help with her wretched roof (why build above the height of a woman's reach, if it causes so much grief?). In her dream-world, which is very real to her, she sees herself creating and transforming the entire house on her own. Magically, without sweat or splinters, without the mistakes and broken thumbnails, freed from the experience of toiling all morning to assemble a joint, only to find that she got the measurements wrong in the first place. In her failures, she would rather be alone, to rage at the misfit wood and cry with vexation. Elspeth has become adept at knowing when to leave her alone, but will the presence of this new one demand that she appears competent at all times? What a terrible strain.

I do approve of the credence she gives to her dreams and desires. Reality is all very well in its place, but to dream is to make possible. Felicity has powerful dreams, but not so strong as to raise the roof-tree, unsupported by human hand, to the top of the house. Even my mother, who had the power to be still and let things move around her, had to grind her own maize. Magic seems to draw the line at domestic chores. So, my red-headed giant must welcome the newcomer, knowing that she needs her, but hoping that she does not need her too much.

Do you think I sound proprietorial? If Felicity is not mine, then to whom does she belong? In the long evenings when she paces around her building, muttering about her plans, who else but me is there to hear her? The time she spends, sitting and looking at that house! It must be an essential part of the job, but I don't understand these methods.

Now she has two helpers, Elspeth who is a disappointed woman, and her friend, the farmer's wife, who is an angry one. How can I tell, when they are so smiling and polite? Not that that will last, once Felicity starts giving orders. I learned to look beyond smiles. A snake will smile, as it bares its venom-filled fangs. Elspeth is disappointed because she has reached an elder's years without ever having done other than what was expected of her. She feels like an impostor because she has never earned respect. Shirley is angry because she has fought, but not quite hard enough, for what she wants. Her cold blue eyes are full of the fury of a thousand small surrenders. I am glad I have never kept slaves.

And my giant? My freckle-faced, hoarse-voiced dreamer, what of her? She may be angry, she may be disappointed, but that is in the past, or the future. At the moment, she has an obsession, to build her home, that has filled her up and left no room for other emotions. Her obsession makes it more likely that she will get what she wants, but less likely that she will realise when she has it. Some tribes, I hear, worship one god only (the blasphemy!), and him a man. They believe that getting what you asked for is the ultimate punishment with which their deity disciplines hubris. With the Goddess, it is more simple. If you say, when you are out on a hunt and parched with thirst, 'Goddess, I want water to drink,' she won't send you a poisoned pool, to teach you a lesson. I'm not saying that she always gives you everything you want, but at least she doesn't mess you around. Of course, if you say 'Goddess, I want water,' she might send a rainstorm, but how is she to know what you meant? Clarity is the thing, one should know what one wants.

* * * * * * * * * *

'Oh God,' thought Felicity, 'this woman is like a ramrod, unbending in every plane.' She was confabulating with Shirley Bruton on the roof, aided by a spring-loaded tape measure. Although supposedly joined in a common purpose, the two women were wary of each other, and circled the scene of operations with snarls of excess politeness, like dogs about to fight. Elspeth maintained a helpful commentary from the ground.

"We should get the first two rafters up here," said Felicity, glad that she had mugged up the procedure in G.P. Turvey, "and check that I've cut them to the right shape. If we hold them in position, we can see if the angles are correct."

"Walls'll need a bit of patchin' up," commented Shirley, inspecting the tracks of Felicity's blow torch around the inside surfaces. "You've lost a fair bit of the lump."

"Have I?"

"See the pond?" Shirley pointed to the sheen of water, lurking behind a splendid willow, "that's the walls of your house."

"Uh huh," grunted Felicity, unwilling to admit ignorance.

"Nowadays, they'd use breeze blocks, with a brick claddin', so the outside would look much the same. But then, they just dug a big hole in the ground, carted all the muck to the building and slapped it on in handfuls. They call it clay lump, this sort of building. That's why the walls're so thick, and they never dry out. Keep drawing moisture up; well, if they dry out, they crumble down in no time. It's why these houses are always damp,"

"Yes, naturally."

"And of course," continued her informant, relentlessly, "You never get a real flat surface, not with a clay lump wall, so it's hell when you're trying to hang cupboards, or put up shelves."

"I wasn't planning on a fitted kitchen."

"Fitted anything, you'd be lucky. But you can get some nice old cupboards up at Wymondham auction, on a Thursday. Solid oak, that's what you need, and a dresser that'll stand on its own four feet."

"I'll worry about the furniture and fittings later."

"She's right, you know," said Elspeth, popping up like an anxious chaperone. "That's what reconciled me to living in a modern house, even if it isn't very pretty. At least we can have proper shelves and kitchen units on the wall. Otherwise it would be such a clutter.

"I suppose it gives you somewhere to hang the station nameplate from LlanFair PG," said Felicity, waspishly.

Elspeth's eyes glazed over. "The longest station name in the British Isles," she said, as though in trance. "Archibald would have sold his grandmother for that sign, but he never got it. If he did, it would have to go in the garden, it would be too big for our living room. I expect he would build a special shed for it."

"Anyway, these walls need patching," asserted Shirley.

"Do you know," chirped Elspeth, "when I first came here, I thought all the houses had ponds beside them because they were keen to protect wildfowl? I didn't realise that they'd been built out of clay dug on the site, and the ponds were the holes they'd made. Isn't that silly?"

"Shirley's been telling me all about it," said Felicity.

"Shall we get on?" suggested her tormentor. "I'm meetin' the kids off of the school bus; little monkeys, can't trust them to be on it, if I let them go to the stop on their bikes."

"Sure," agreed Felicity ungraciously. She knew she was being childish, and that this was ten times better than having a firm of builders in, but she felt she was being instructed and organised. The more Elspeth marvelled at how lucky it was that Shirley could help out, the more Felicity sulked. Even the cat had taken to the new arrival, and bounded out of a recovering herbaceous border to greet her as she stepped off the bottom of the ladder. Felicity, following her grumpily down to the ground, felt betrayed.

TEN

They are putting up the rafters. Even Elspeth lends a hand, she leaves the garden to its colourful devices and scurries about the skyline like a mouse herding cattle. The other two hammer and haul, puzzle and confer, consult the runes on the roofing square and generally carry on like any two women bluffing their way through something of which they are not quite sure. Because, it turns out, Shirley is not as expert as Felicity feared. She is good enough, but not too good.

Sometimes, often, she even seems to be enjoying it, the sulks abated. They laugh together, the three of them, and eat enormous lunches, like children at a party. When things go wrong, there are curses and tantrums and stormings off, but Elspeth placates them, trotting diligently from one thunderous corner of the house to the other. Actually, I think it is rather nice for the pair of them to have someone else to blame for any difficulties with the roof.

It has shape now, a wedge of rafters atop the building, like the ribs of a cleanly-stripped carcase, pointing skywards. It becomes easier, too, as their confidence grows, the two women with hammers begin to work almost as a team. Of course, they do not know each others minds, as those who work together should, so they waste time in talk and consultation. But they begin to have an inkling. As they are more sure of what they are doing, they begin to make mistakes of carelessness, rather than of ignorance, so we are never quite free of arguments here. The angry newcomer with the slate-blue eyes smiles more often, and Felicity accepts her presence, with only occasional outbursts of resentment. Then Shirley and Elspeth go shopping, and leave her to her moods.

It is warm now. Almost summer. The garden is heavy with the scent of flowers which Elspeth has persuaded to grow. Roses have emerged from their ruthless pruning into flamboyant colour. There was a fine crop of poppies and cornflowers, nodding red and blue the other side of the hedge, but a drift of poisonous spray from the great field saw to them. Elspeth and Felicity were angry, but Shirley knew better than to protest. The fruit trees blossomed miraculously, although they are really too old to be anything but sweet-smelling firewood. The blossom fell, disguising the piles of sand and wood chips. Now, a further miracle, it seems that some fruit has set. It is never quiet during the day, even when they are not hammering and crashing and cursing on the roof, for the garden is full of the buzz and hum of gluttonous insects, gorging themselves on fruit, flower and vegetable. Elspeth supplements the efforts of the predatory ladybirds with secret applications of a noxious substance, with which she anoints the plants while pretending to water them. If the others notice the dead insects, they say nothing.

They eye each other's tools. Felicity has such a dazzling array, in that cart of hers, all new and gleaming, with paint barely scratched by recent use. For every different task, she has an implement, even if she has to discover their uses by trial and error. Shirley has her mother's tool-kit, small but sufficient. They are properly crafted things, made to last, or so she says, the wooden handles, venerably dark, worn smooth by the polish of many sweaty palms. Each secretly suspects the other of coveting her tools, and furtively they check, at the end of the day, to see that all is returned to its rightful place.

They are happy, working in the sun, seeing the whole emerge from the chaos. That is not to say that Shirley is not still angry, that Elspeth is no longer disappointed, or that Felicity has lost her obsession. Life does not change because of a few days of enjoyment.

When she is alone, in the hot late-afternoon sun, when the other two have gone back to serve their husbands' meals, she strips to the waist and works at her saw-horse, sweat gleaming on the rolling muscles of her back, and dropping from her obstinate chin to fall in the sawdust. Later and later she works, as though in a frenzy to complete the roof. Does she have a vision of this work completed, that drives her so? How strange, to think of a home as a finished thing, rather than one which requires constant nourishment and care. When the light begins to go, she washes the sweat from her body and sits on the grass, with the cat for company, and dreams of her home as it will be. The cat dreams of pilchards, for all I know, but its presence is not intrusive.

Sometimes, as she sits there, she starts at noises from the fields, and is afraid. She lives with fear in the background. She does not fear her inability to complete the building, as she once did (except at those times when everything that can go wrong does so). This country has not welcomed her, although she has two friends, a familiar cat and a home that grows before her eyes. Still, when it is quiet, she jumps at the call of a hunting owl, or the scream of a rabbit dying in the jaws of a fox. When she meets people other than Elspeth and Shirley, she stares them down and watches them all the way out of sight, to make sure they really have left.

What does she know of danger? My journey from the village at the end of the trading season, to find Soft Axe and his people, that was dangerous. Felicity's life is tame in comparison. Perhaps my neighbours were right to think me mad. I set off at the autumn equinox, with winds tugging in five directions at once and ragged clouds chasing each other across the face of the sun. My mother, angry that I wouldn't stay to lend a hand with the equinox rites, remained sulking in her hut. I had her predictions to take with me, and a mixed comfort they were. The miners turned out to bid me safe journey, and press little charms into my hand, but they love a diversion. Simple as they were, I didn't believe that they would be able to remember me once I had gone more than a moon-set.

The girl to whom I had been teaching my craft stood a little to one side of the gaggle of people, blubbering noisily. Personally, I thought she was overdoing it a bit. Behind her lurked the Man-Killer. He was a low-browed malcontent, who had once murdered a visiting trader for looking at him the

113

wrong way. That's not how to do business, and Man-Killer was sentenced to leave the village and never return, but somehow, his friends, the most loutish of the miners, made such an agitation that he had been allowed to stay. He had festered in the village like a poisoned thorn ever since.

My apprentice, Little Stone-Dealer, wept and wailed, wringing her hands and making such a fuss that my suspicions would have been aroused, had I not been preoccupied. She was a quick-witted girl, which was why I had chosen her, and not overawed by her elders. She was a slightly built thing, always darting around the village running errands for me, or collecting gossip (for herself). Her nose was never clean of other people's business, but I have been guilty of that myself.

Although it was the end of summer, the day was not cold, yet Little Stone-Dealer, unlike anyone else, had provided herself with a cloak, which she kept pulled around her. Under her sharp little face, her chin had begun to swell, like a rodent at harvest time, whose pouches are full of grain. I would like to think I wondered what the voluminous cloak concealed, perhaps the first thrusting bump of her previously flat stomach, but I was not so prescient. I merely thought it a shame that such a bright young woman should have taken up with the most malodorous oaf in the village. I allowed her to kiss me farewell, although she was not the sort whose familiarities I would normally encourage, and then I was off.

In my small pack I had dried fruits, some grain, twine for making snares and some deer meat, pounded flat, rolled into a stick and dried until it was tough as an old tree root. It was black and pungent, but weighed next to nothing. It took a lot of chewing, but was more use to me than a whole herd of fresh-killed hinds. I raided the larders of the tree-rats, and filled my pack with sweet, fat nuts when I found their stores. Berries and mushrooms were plentiful at that time of year, and what I could not eat, I carried away.

I slept in the branches of oaks and hornbeams, where I could, but even so, my nights were often broken by the howling of wolves. During the day, I carried a big stick and gave attention to the tracks and smells, in case a pack was waiting for me over the next rise.

The leaves turned from green to yellow and fell in great rustling waves about me. My feet crunched and shuffled in the dead drifts, and the path was sometimes obscured. Fortunately the road to the West was well-trodden, so I had little worry of getting lost. The nights became clear and frosty; I would wake in the morning with stiff, aching bones and ice on my outer garments. Oftener still, I could not sleep for the cold, and if there was a moon, walked through the night, sleeping in the morning. I was forced to abandon the shelter of the trees, as the trunks were too frozen and slippery to climb. I took to building nests of leaves and branches, scooping a hollow in the earth for hip and shoulder.

Once (but only once) I made the mistake of entering a cave for the night. It was so inviting; small and rockbound, with a warm sandy floor. I should have known that such a desirable residence would have attracted other occupants. Luckily, I smelt the bear before she smelt me, and got out in time. Maybe she was glutted from her autumn gorging, or maybe the first sleep of hibernation made her slow, for she should have been able to catch me. After that, I returned to my sodden burrows and thought the aching chill of the ground a small price to pay for not being eaten.

I was lucky the season was dry, to start with. The path I was on was a summer road for most travellers, firm under foot when the spring heads had dried up. Even in a rainless autumn, I was up to my knees in water, fording streams and rivers, oftener than I cared for. Blue with cold I would pick my way across the river bed, bruising my feet on the rocks and hoping not to trip into a pot-hole and be swept away. I was glad to reach the downs and move onto the high ground.

On I plodded, day after day, becoming stringy on my sparse provisions and hollow-eyed with sleeplessness. I probably was mad, at the time, staggering along, talking to myself, pouncing on a colony of grubs or a handful of berries like a starving rat. I wasn't starving, quite, but food was my sole excitement and comfort. I crossed huge open plains, on which I seemed to be the only thing moving, like an ant crawling across a rock. In one swampy lowland, I caught a marsh fever and lay for two days in the shelter of a tree's roots, sweating and shivering. In the end I decided that I had either to get up or to die and leave my bones to be picked by the birds who were already perched in the branches above, eyeing my succulent parts. So I got up. One makes these decisions. My mother's knowledge of herbs saved me from many ills. I did not realise I had absorbed so much of her skill, but some learning must stick even in the head of a rather wild girl such as I had been.

Travel is a great thing, I decided after all. I had always pitied the scrawny traders who straggled into our village, unkempt, their skin torn and blistered, withered by too much sun and too little water. But there is something to be said for having been further than a day's walk from the place of one's birth. How smugly we used to despise them, the travellers, with their hollow faces, and a few fly-clouded animals to carry their loads or feed them upon the way. They may have great knowledge of the world, my people would say of those who wander the long roads, but they are cursed by their knowledge, which makes them dissatisfied with the small pleasures of the hearth.

The stone circle was new, when I first saw it. I topped what I thought was a rise, and found myself standing on the great bank beside the ditch they had dug. I don't know who 'they' were, for one generation of builders succeeds another at these places. Beyond the ditch, the circle of standing stones had been raised; so recently that the root-holes of the posts against which the ropes had strained to haul the great slabs into place were not yet filled. Interested though I was in the mechanics of the construction, it was not the place to indulge idle curiosity. I edged away, along a path which I hoped would take me quickly from the scene. In fact, the path itself was part of the sacred site, and my footsteps were led to another, smaller circle.

I was travelling at night, by the light of a blood-red moon, with a faint mist swirling about the plain, which is how I came to blunder into a holy place, which I would have avoided had I known. Trembling with cold, and fear (I admit it), my hair standing on end and bedewed by the fog, I sank down against one of the stones of the sanctuary and peered at the strange landscape. To my right, the great circle from which I had fled; to my left a round hill, rising abruptly from the plain. I wondered how a hill so smooth and conical had grown in this unhilly region. Do you think I was a fool to set off and climb it? In that bad light, in mortal danger of being discovered trespassing on a sacred site, when I should have been slinking away into the night? Perhaps you are right, but cautious people die, just like the rest of us. Even if they never took a risk in their lives.

The hill sang to me, as I clambered up it in the mist, a low, throaty hum. I pulled myself up to the top, and lay listening to the rumbling of a giant stomach. Lying on the short, rabbit-cropped turf of the hill's crown, I knew I was in great danger, yet I felt safe. That is not to say that I was no longer terrified, for of course I was; I pressed my face to the ground, the mist completely covering me and blotting out the light of the moon. With a piece of chalk, I drew a circle about me, for protection, and within its security, went to sleep.

I can tell you are thinking, by this time, I was definitely crazy. No-one in her right mind, goes to sleep in a strange country, surrounded by who-knows-how-many enemies and predators, on top of a precious and holy hill. And all because the Goddess sings a lullaby and the mist provides a bed-cover. What can I say? Terror is a tiring emotion, and I would not have missed the dreams I had on that hill for a lifetime of guaranteed safety. And if I was mad, what of the madness that had made them, scrabbling with their picks and shovels, build such a hill? Because of

117

course, it was built, not thrown up by any chance force of the earth's movement. In a place so full of divine madness, sanity is hardly a virtue.

That night, I was slept like a child and dreamt like a baby, secure in the knowledge that all life revolves around it. I would say that I saw the future, except there is no future in dreams, only truth. When the sun rose, dispelling the vapours of the night and revealing the two stone circles below the hill, I did not rise with it.

I regained consciousness two mornings later, in a strange hut, having suffered a recurrence of the marsh fever. Weak as a new-born infant, I lay, dazed, listening to strange voices raised in argument. Luckily, I had been brought to the hut of the old woman with whom I had discussed the stories of non-stone axes, when she came as elder of her tribe to trade with me. Had it been anyone else, I would undoubtedly have been put to death on the spot for blasphemous trespass. Fortunately, the hardships of my journey had not changed me beyond recognition, and the old woman knew me, when I was carried, delirious with fever, into her camp.

All the time I had lain unconscious, a dispute had raged about what was to be done with me. In the end my host persuaded the head man that I was obviously in the keeping of the Goddess, and it would be sacrilege to slaughter me. As no-one had seen me arrive, she was able to spin them some story about how I had been borne in from the sky, flying on a bed of mist. The people were quite prepared to believe in this mode of transport, but it did not make me popular. However, the device saved my life, and I had no objection to being an object of awe and mystery until I was well enough to leave.

The old woman's daughter overcame her superstitious dread sufficiently to nurse me (and very pleasant it was to be in her hands), but she could not bring herself to look me in the eye, and fled from the hut if ever I spoke. When I was strong enough to stand, her mother appeared to look me over. She gave me the impression that my life might be sacrosanct at the moment, but that she was having a hard time holding the line with the head-man. In other words, I should clear off as quickly as possible, and not push my luck. I sipped the disgusting fortifying broth which she had brought me, and enquired about the success of the neighbours who had gone off to search for the new, improved weapons.

Squatting down in the dust beside me, she told me the story. The young bucks of that tribe had ventured off, abandoning tradition and precedent, in search of the magical bronze. The elders had tutted and deplored their waywardness, but were powerless to stop them. I must say, I don't understand why the men in these parts are allowed to do as they please so much. I could easily picture a party of youths, exactly the sort of people who should be sent down a mine to keep them out of mischief, charging about the countryside, looking for excitement. Anyway, they had returned, much to everyone's surprise, armed with as many of the new-fangled axes, knives and scrapers as they had been able to trade and carry.

Of course it was a craze. The youngsters who had not gone on the trip were wild with jealousy, and immediately planned to get up another party to obtain more of the precious new implements. The elders forbade it, and fights broke out. The original group formed themselves into a gang and began lording it over their fellows who were only equipped with good honest stone. Tormented with envy, the stay-at-home lads broke into the winter grain pit one night, stole half the village's harvest store, and set off to trade for metal axes, which would render them once again equals in their own village. In the morning, when it was discovered, the new gang set off in pursuit, joyfully brandishing their weapons, which could now be blooded. And blood was shed. The miscreants were caught, and a battle fought in which a man would happily spill the intestines of his brother if the two were in different parties. The runaways were brought back to the village, defeated and humiliated. Most of the grain was spilled in the fight and trampled in the blood-soaked earth, but none of the combatants worried greatly about that.

This episode confirmed the status of the men with the metal weapons. The other youths were no longer their peers, but their servants, and the elders, who had been so ineffectual, were disregarded from then on. The victory of the new gang was ascribed to the magical properties of their weapons, and fear of magic had probably stayed the arm of their opponents in that crucial first moment when you must strike or be struck down. Personally, I did not believe it. My own bronze knife, which bumped at my side as I walked, was lighter than a good stone, and endowed my arm with a little extra speed because of its lack of weight. There is no magic in that. Nor in the fact that the lads who had set off first to try their luck in pursuit of the weapons were probably the boldest in the village, which is why they had won the fight. Whatever the truth, the new weapons were firmly believed by all who heard the story to be magic, and the craze was spreading to other tribes on the plain.

My host pulled a face eloquent of disgust and amusement. I gathered she was not impressed by the novelties. Even in her own camp, where my life was so precariously protected, the news of the exploits of their neighbours had unsettled things. The young men were all raring to go on some crazy expedition, although they had all the tools and weapons they needed, and had nothing with which to trade, apart from their grain harvest and the recently slaughtered cattle which could not be fed through the winter. The elders, frightened that they might be cast aside, tried to restrain the youths, and the harder the tried, the more evident their lack of power became. The women, young and old, bemused by this mania for things which were not needed, looked on.

The young men's argument was boosted by the recent activity of the Beaker People, who took their name from a fashion they have in pottery working. I thought this a pretty thin excuse, myself, for the Beaker People had been coming for as long as anyone can remember. In my village, we called them the Flat Headed Ones From Overseas. Up the Wash they would sail, from Goddess knows where across the mist-covered sea in the North. We had been raided by them from time to time; but mostly they pressed on south and west, along the paths by which I myself had travelled, to reach these rich lands. We had even traded with them, which I think was a wise move, and one that had preserved us from having to fight them more often. They knew the value of keeping well in with a weapons supplier, and if they had killed us all, there would have been no-one to knap the flints, for slaves brought from across the water do not have the necessary skill.

Every year, these bandy little men, with their guttural speech and insatiable appetite for other people's property, jumped out of their ships and swarmed down the long road across the country, their eyes agleam with the fabled wealth of the South Western lands. Every year, they killed cattle, slew a few villagers, burned some houses and stole the crops. Some of them would stay through the winter and try to hold the land from which they have driven the people, but in spring the lure of booty usually enticed them away on further raids, for why be a farmer and grow that which, with far less expenditure of effort, may be stolen?

The depredations of these foreigners, their annual recurrence, was like a crop blight; these things are a fact of life. Now they had camps and villages of their own, we would never be rid of them. They had mixed their blood with that of the people of the plain; even playing around the hut of my rescuer, I had seen more than one child with the square head and bowed legs of the invaders. Of course, living in the middle of the Southern plain, the old woman was more concerned by the Beaker People's activities than I was. Perhaps she knew that I had supplied them with the weapons? A businesswoman herself, I hoped she wouldn't hold it against me. Her people clung on to their rich lands, ever vigilant, not trusting their grazing cattle to the care of an unarmed cowherd. They put their faith in the holiness of the hill and circles by which they sheltered and spent their time preparing for battle.

My head ached, and my throat hurt, for the old woman had been perched beside me telling stories half the day, and I was barely over my fever. All I wanted was some idea of the location of the tribe who had provided the controversial metal weapons to her neighbours, and I would be on my way. Still the old hag fixed me with her glittering, sardonic eye and rambled on about the hardships of living in a battleground. Did she hold me responsible? I may have provided weapons to murderers, but it wasn't the weapons that made them murder, it was what their hearts told them. In the case of the Beaker People, I believe it was economic necessity, since their own land would not support them; or a preference for easy pickings and excitement over honest toil and annual profit. Either way, it was not my responsibility. Nor did I wish to be involved in the dispute between the young men who believed that modernising their weapons would give them an advantage against the invaders, and those who don't. Personally, I thought that trying to stop the tides of foreigners coming down from the North was like trying to stop a river flowing. One must adapt to change, or be swept away by it. "Believe me," I told the old woman, "the Beaker People are here to stay. They will not destroy us, because then they would have no-one to rob next year. In time, we will assimilate them and they will turn to trade instead of plunder."

The old woman sucked her hollow tooth and spat on the floor. "Not with you, they won't trade," she said, "with your old-fashioned flint axes. When they don't need you they will kill you, and all you can assimilate then is their water as they piss on your burial place."

I know when I've worn out my welcome. This whole business of new technology and social change was obviously putting the old woman under a great deal of stress. Her position among her own people was threatened, I could see. As the young men arrogated the right to run the camp, having decided that military emergencies called for active leadership, the older men were being displaced. It seemed inevitable that they would try and take over the religious functions of the wise old women and relegate them to pot-scourers and herb-wives. I couldn't see the Goddess being pleased at her ceremonies being conducted by a gaggle of self-important old men (she wants joy in her worship, passion and pleasure, not dreariness and mumbled curses). Perhaps they would decide to retire the Goddess too? I joke, of course.

I slunk away that afternoon, when the men were having one of their endless councils of war, brangling over whether or not to re-arm with bronze axes. My head spun as I stepped out into the daylight, and every joint in my body ached from the fever, but better sick on the road than dead in bed; so I directed my tottering footsteps around the great ditch that encircled the standing stones and back onto the road to the West. The old woman's daughter set me on my way, still afraid to look me in the eye. At the edge of the camp, she scampered back to the safety of her own hut, casting fearful backward glances at me. In my view, she would have done better to fear the young man with whom she shared her hut who (so her mother told me) was emerging as a leader of the new-axe party, and had taken to saying that defeat in battle was a consequence of letting women meddle in the affairs of the tribe.

Her problems did not concern me long. My own village would not be so quick to throw off the old ways, nor so foolish as to imagine that the wisest heads sat on the broadest shoulders. Women had always been the leaders of my tribe, and we had prospered under this arrangement. No wonder the Goddess's hill had groaned as I lay upon it, if she had all this nonsense to contend with amongst those who were supposed to be guardians of her sacred site. Weak though I was, it was no sorrow to me to quit that place, and by nightfall I was far down the road, away from the old woman's camp.

ELEVEN

Not all journeys involve movement. My red-headed giant travels towards her home while rooted to this small place in which she and her friends work. Or friend, should I say, for now the rafters are safely raised, Shirley does not come every day. Perhaps she has been reminded of her duties elsewhere? The two of them joined together to lay out the roofing felt, like a pair of housewives hanging up a recalcitrant sheet on a gusty wash day, and now all is safely battened down, Shirley has gone back to her farm and her children.

* * * * * * * * * *

Elspeth and Shirley sat side by side in the hairdresser's salon, basking in the warmth of a cluster of infra-red lamps, which waved about their heads on stalks, like the monstrous eyes of a hung-over martian. Elspeth's drying curls were styled in her usual fashion; Shirley had, for the first time, had her grey hairs tinted out.

"We haven't seen you at Hope Cottage for a while," said Elspeth. "No trouble, I hope?"

"Bruton thought I weren't home enough," said Shirley, gruffly. "How's it coming on?"

"Things went quicker when there were two of you working on the house. Felicity misses your help."

Shirley grinned sideways at her friend, "She'd rather do it on her own, though, wouldn't she? A bit solitary, by nature, that one."

"She does seem to be very fond of her own company."

"You reckon she's going to turn into one of them batty old people as lives on their own, and never has visitors?"

"I don't think she's quite dead to all the social graces yet," protested Elspeth, "although I can easily picture her as a cantankerous recluse in later years."

"Like her Great Aunt."

"She's a bit young to be a dedicated eccentric."

Shirley blew smoke rings at her reflection in the mirror. Elspeth hated the smell of tobacco clinging to her clean hair, but said nothing. Something in her expression must have alerted Shirley, who stubbed the cigarette out.

"Do she ever talk about friends to you?" she asked.

"I don't think she has anyone very close," Elspeth sighed. "And she doesn't seem to miss the people she used to know, before she moved down here. I get the impression she has rather cut herself off. It does seem strange, she's such an attractive girl, I'm sure there's no need for her to be such a hermit."

"It's most peculiar. Maybe she had a bust up with some chap?" suggested Shirley, slyly.

"I've never heard her mention a boyfriend," worried Elspeth.

"No, nor did I." The eyes of the two women met in the mirror for a pregnant moment, and then, by mutual, but unspoken agreement, they changed the subject.

Elspeth's happy nature soon banished speculation about Felicity's oddities, and she returned next day to the garden, thinking of nothing but horticulture. She hummed along to the lunchtime concert, which happened to be the Four Seasons, and was content. Unlike her husband, who had been collecting his Bulgarian folk albums for years before anyone had even thought of World Music, she did not value obscurity for its own sake. Archibald did not know whether to be flattered to have anticipated a fashion of which he was now presumably at the forefront, or to be nauseated that young club-goers had besmirched his discovery with their transient interest. His wife, although she was broad-mindedly always prepared to give difficult or experimental works a hearing, however Slavic and modern they might be, frankly preferred the canon of established classics. Elspeth was proud to be middle brow; if she had not thought her tastes shared by a million others, she would have felt isolated.

The radio, perched in its usual place on the gatepost, warbled out Primavera, while Elspeth hummed an accompaniment. She was working on the vegetable garden, happy as a pig rooting for acorns. In the face of a patch of weather so benign it might almost be called a heatwave, she had adopted a floppy sunhat that made her look like a dissolute umpire at a village cricket match. Her bare arms, emerging from an old tennis shirt, were as generously freckled as Felicity's, although with larger and more faded patches of brown.

Elspeth forked another load of wet and rotting brown stable manure onto the French beans. Much to Felicity's disgust, she had appropriated the trailer, turning out all the tools, in order to fetch the smelly load from the riding school beyond Orfton-Saint-Scabious. The trailer had returned with a dark brown liquor dribbling from every crack, and would never be the same again, but Elspeth was happy. She could almost hear the undernourished soil soaking up the goodness of this feast of muck. Next year, she was determined, this vegetable patch would feed an army, and Felicity would no longer eat exclusively out of tins.

She trundled the wheelbarrow, which she had also commandeered from the building site, to the trailer to fork in another load of the gorgeous sludge. The straw was so well rotted down that no single stalk could be distinguished in the matted heap. Bestowing a few forkfuls of bounty upon the herbaceous border which, surprisingly, had survived in the wild, and a few more as a mulch around the roses, she congratulated herself on having made quite a good start on the garden. The roses bloomed, shed their petals and bloomed again and the rock garden was beginning to take shape. The front of the house was covered by heavy-scented honeysuckle and in the small vegetable patch, which she had hurriedly cleared back in the spring, a few potatoes and carrots were swelling to acceptable maturity. Baby lettuces sheltered under cloches made from sawn-in-half plastic beer bottles and the nettles, thistles and cow parsley, after many hard-fought engagements, had beaten a tactical retreat to the far side of the garden hedge. The front lawn was of course hopeless, while it was being used as a builder's yard, but next year, she would re-seed it. At least Felicity's brick stacks and timber piles were doing a good job of flattening out the bumps and discouraging moles.

Elspeth leaned on the fork and planned the garden's future in her mind's eye. With the end of a ball of Nutscene trailing out of her pocket and slurry on her gum-boots, she looked like a scarecrow. This afternoon, she would plant radishes, dibbling in the warm crumbling earth with her bare fingers, like a child at the sea-side. Maybe Felicity could be persuaded to regard radishes as a convenience food. Tomorrow, she would do something about the ivy that was eating the mortar from between the bricks at the back of the house. A pretty red creeper, or an ivy with delicate yellow and green leaves might have been permitted such a destructive liberty, but not this plain dark green growth, no more distinguished than that which trailed its leaves from a thousand office plant pots.

The peck of hammer blows from the roof ceased, and a shrill whistle split the air. Elspeth trotted obediently round to the front of the house in response to the summons. Felicity took her fingers out of her mouth and grinned. She looked, despite her thirty years and scattering of grey hairs, a complete urchin.

"Could you send up some more tiles, please?" she asked. Elspeth gathered an armful of the red slabs from the pallet on the lawn and took them over to the hoist. "You are getting through them fast," she remarked, arranging the load. "Don't you think it's time for a break?"

"Has the news been on yet?"

"Ages ago. It's nearly two o'clock."

Felicity finished stacking the slates on the platform of the scaffolding, and slid down a pole, like a child on a climbing frame. "Alright then, let's stop for a bit. Do you fancy baked beans for lunch?"

"If you haven't got scurvy by the time this house is finished," sighed Elspeth, "I'll be amazed. When did you last look a fresh vegetable in the eye?"

"Last time you were worrying about my health. Which was about three days ago. I looked that lettuce which you bought at Jean's in the eye, and the lettuce, being rather bug-ridden, looked me right back."

"She only gets deliveries once a week," said Elspeth, defensively.

"I'm all in favour of supporting the local shop. And the local wildlife. I only wish that doing the former didn't involve eating the latter."

"Anyway, I'm going to put some radishes in this afternoon, so you'll be able to nibble them when you get peckish."

"You make me feel like Peter Rabbit."

"Does that make me Mr MacGregor?" asked Elspeth.

"Now you come to mention it, there is a certain similarity. Toast?"

They sat in the shade of an apple tree eating in silence. Felicity gazed ruminatively at her house, and Elspeth at her garden. Each was planning the next task but three. Their silences had the comfort of familiar preoccupations. A wood pigeon crooned with pleasant monotony, ignoring, as did all other living things, the regular blasts of the bird-scaring machine in the wheat field.

"Shirley hasn't been here for ages," remarked Felicity eventually.

"You don't need her help, do you, now that the roof is up?"

"It's not that I can't manage on my own," Felicity sprawled against the mossy trunk, pulling up a long grass to chew. "I love tiling. It's like doing a jigsaw with all the pieces the same shape. Perhaps I shall take up as a jobbing roofer, when I need to earn some money."

"Well then."

"It's a bit odd, that's all. One minute Shirley's over here every day, the next thing we know, she's vanished."

"She did only offer to come because the roof-raising was a two woman job."

"But I thought she liked being here. I suppose I thought that when the rafters were fixed, she would still pop over and see us every now and then. She seemed so interested in the whole business."

"I'm sure she is."

"Have you seen her lately?"

"I met her in Dereham yesterday afternoon."

"You didn't say."

Elspeth looked uncomfortable. "Didn't I?"

"No. Is there something going on?"

"What could be going on?"

"It's not like you to be evasive Elspeth. I wondered if, for some reason, Shirley was avoiding us. Or, since she's obviously talking to you, avoiding me."

"Marriages sometimes involve compromise," said Elspeth sagely.

"We're not married."

"Don't be flippant, you know what I mean. You know Bruton doesn't like you, for whatever silly reason. He wasn't happy about Shirley being over here so much."

"Isn't her time her own?"

"Of course it is. But Shirley isn't a single woman. She can't gallivant about the place doing as she pleases, like you can. She has responsibilities. She has other people's feelings to take into account."

"It doesn't sound like much of a compromise to me. He says 'don't go to Hope Cottage,' so she stops coming."

"I'm sure she will come and visit again."

"When she's allowed to?"

"It isn't like that," protested Elspeth.

"Or when he's gone off to market to get drunk with his cronies in the NFU?"

"This is a building project, not a secret affair," said Elspeth, tartly. "A sensible woman doesn't always insist on getting her own way, not if it is going to make her husband unhappy and cause family friction. You can afford to be selfish, the rest of us can't."

"Do you think I am selfish?"

"Anyone who has got to your age without being married must be."

"I thought marriage was something you did because you wanted to?"

"Well nobody ever left me a house and thousands of pounds to play with. Perhaps I would rather have been independent. The choice didn't arise."

"But Elspeth," protested Felicity, "I was well settled into spinsterhood before Great Aunt Rapunzel left me the cottage."

"When I was your age," said Elspeth, with a quiver of disapproval, "that word would not have been used so lightly. It would have been considered unnatural to embrace what we were taught to believe a misfortune."

"Times change."

"Indeed they do. Not always for the better."

"Shirley's mother was allowed to muck about on a building site, but Shirley isn't."

"That was different. There was a war on."

"Does Archibald mind you being over here so much?"

"He doesn't notice, he's playing with his train all day. And I'm always home to get him his tea. More to the point, you and he aren't sworn enemies, as appears to be the case between you and Mr Bruton."

"If your husband forbade you to come here, what would you do?"

Elspeth looked around the burgeoning garden which she had rescued from the wild. Some parts of it she could even be said to have created. Superimposed upon the picture before her was the image of next year's flowers, and those of a summer in ten years time.

"It wouldn't arise. Archibald is not autocratic."

"And Farmer Bruton is?"

"He has the reputation for being a rather abrasive and headstrong character."

"A bully, in other words."

"But Shirley is a sensible woman."

"And she's made her bed and must lie on it?" added Felicity, sourly.

"If we all consulted our own desires and nobody else's, what would become of the world?" asked Elspeth, as a clincher.

"There would be fewer wives and mothers."

"I'm sorry if you despise me," Elspeth stood up, indignant. "I personally happen to think it an achievement to have made a family which has stayed together for thirty-five years. Some of us think building a home more important than building a house, you know."

"Elspeth, I'm sorry, I didn't mean to offend you. Please don't go." Elspeth sat down, huffily. "I don't despise you for being married. I only wish that Shirley didn't feel she had to stop coming to see us. It seemed to give her pleasure. What's wrong with that?"

"I'm not saying that Bruton's right," she said, stiffly. "In fact I think he's a nasty tempered, unreasonable and selfish man. Not like Archibald, who, whatever his faults, has never tried to stop me doing what I wanted."

"As a gardener, I would have thought you were pretty unstoppable."

"We all have our consuming interests. I only wish that a bit more credit was given to women like me and Shirley, who stay with our husbands, even when they're unbearably tiresome, and work at our marriages. It's so easy for women just to walk out when the going gets difficult, like the first Mrs Bruton. That's all you ever hear about, broken homes, no-fault divorce, support the single mums. What about the ones who stay, I say?"

It was the most impassioned speech which Felicity had ever heard Elspeth make, and she was at a loss for a suitable response. "Isn't it a matter of choice?" she said, feebly.

"Not for me, it wasn't. I was brought up to believe that spinsterhood was an affliction to be pitied and divorce a disgrace that befell others. Even if I had ever wanted to leave Archibald, which of course I haven't, although he can be very trying, and leaving aside the question of where on earth I would go because homelessness and poverty aren't very appealing at my age; but never mind the practicalities, I could no more choose to break up a marriage than I could dance naked on the village green. And," she continued, "don't talk to me about choice. What about the one who is left? They don't have much choice. The first

Mrs Bruton didn't give her husband much choice about being divorced; she upped and offed as the fancy took her."

"Presumably he had the choice of whether to behave like a pig to her or not, which I imagine he must have done, unless she was swept away by the superior charms of her lifeboatman."

"Wasn't he a trawlerman?"

"Whatever he was, I don't imagine the young Neptune of Lowestoft could have wooed her away, if Bruton himself hadn't been providing a major disincentive to stay."

"Shirley manages to stick with him," Elspeth pointed out, "perhaps she is made of sterner stuff?"

"Or maybe she reckons that if all the bread in the shop is stale, she might as well have the piece that is buttered on the affluent yeoman farmer side."

"Bruton isn't rich. He only has seven hundred acres, and terrible cash flow problems, so I gather."

"Poor boy. Spare your sympathy, Elspeth, haven't you looked into his yard in passing? It's like the John Deere stand at the Royal Norfolk Show. He may be a miser with the soft and foldies, but he's got capital like we have greenfly, and he obviously doesn't stint himself when it comes to new toys."

"Agricultural machinery can't really be classed as an indulgence."

"Oh no?" Felicity raised a sceptical eyebrow. "Bigger, faster, louder, shiny new tractors. Parp! Vroom! Haven't you ever seen little boys playing with their Tonka trucks?"

"No," said Elspeth tartly, "and I don't need you to remind me that I'm childless."

"Oh, god, you're so sensitive today. How do I keep putting my foot in it?"

"It seems to come quite naturally to you."

"Don't be cross, Elspeth, you know I didn't mean to have a go at you. How should a dried up old spinster like me be critical of someone who doesn't want to sign on for twenty years or so of motherhood?"

"Now you are being silly. Sometimes, you're such a bull in a china shop." It was true, Felicity, with her red hair and curious nature might well have been a Jersey heifer, in a previous life. "You should recognise that it is a touchy subject. You have all the delicacy of a garden roller."

"Did you want children?"

"No."

"So why the big fuss?"

Elspeth sighed. "We are having a trample on the social conventions today, aren't we? If you marry, but have no children, everyone either assumes that you've tried and failed, in which case they pity you, or that you never wanted them, in which case you bear the stigma of being unnatural and selfish."

"Why this concern with public odium?"

"Because I'm a conventional sort."

"If you don't mind me saying, you and Archibald aren't exactly Mr and Mrs Average. Isn't one of the advantages of living in the middle of nowhere that you can flout convention? There aren't exactly hordes of people waiting to pass judgement on what goes on at Maybe Halt. In fact, only you, me and the postman ever go there, so who's to know how wacky your family life might be?"

"Were you this heedless when you lived in London?"

"I suppose so," said Felicity, wrinkling her brow, "I don't remember ever having been much concerned with the good opinion of the neighbours."

"It's all very well for you free spirits, but the rest of us must make our way through the world with one eye out for its prejudices."

"I do that alright. Only I try to dodge them, instead of conforming."

"I think Archibald has paternal feelings for his trains," said Elspeth, unexpectedly.

"You sound wistful."

"We decided early on not to have children. I can, believe me, walk past pramsful of cooing, suckling infants, without feeling my withered womb reproach me for its emptiness. When I see young women in public toilets changing their babies, trying to find somewhere in their holdalls for the little plastic bag

133

full of dirty nappy that they don't seem to like to put in litter bins, I don't feel desperately left out. But sometimes I try to imagine how different life would have been."

"They probably would have sniffed glue or gone to Stonehenge for a riot at midsummer, like anybody else's kids."

"I don't dislike children, which people assume one must, having voluntarily gone without them. I don't like to have my comfort disturbed, though, which seems to be the prime purpose of youngsters. I quite enjoy the company of Phoebe and Donny Bruton, although nobody would describe them as good children. I think I'm ready to be a grand-mother."

"What a shame you can't skip the in-between bit."

"Isn't it?" agreed Elspeth.

"I should be getting back to work," said Felicity, picking up their empty plates. As she was about to rise, a pointed canine face, the colour of a carrot appeared at her shoulder, the black lips drawn back to reveal at least a yard of sharp and yellow teeth. The dog growled and issued a blast of foetid dog-breath into Felicity's face. Her hackles rose. A long pink tongue flopped from the animal's jaws, flicking drops of slobber about. Elspeth, leaning against the other side of the apple tree, her hat pulled over her eyes for shade, was unaware of the new arrival.

"Elspeth," asked Felicity, "what sort of dog is orange and hairy, stands three foot six in its bare paws and has a face the shape of a Gerald Scarfe cartoon of the Prime Minister's nose?"

"Sounds like a lurcher to me, dear."

"Would that be a mixture of Irish wolfhound, red setter, greyhound and assorted other dips into the gene pool?"

"Could well be. Why do you ask?"

"There's one standing behind this tree, and it seems to have mistaken me for dinner." The dog opened its tremendous jaws, looked as though a flock of sheep would barely take the edge off its appetite and let out a deep-throated noise somewhere between a growl and a yawn. It also wagged its long and shaggy tail, but Felicity was not convinced of its good intentions. The cat, which had been asleep on Felicity's feet, had shot up the apple tree and stood on a branch, every hair upstanding, and spat defiance at the intruder. The dog, who was obviously after larger prey, ignored the furious ball of fur and fixed Felicity with a glittering stare. She stood up slowly, not wanting to antagonise the dog.

"Fluff!" scolded Elspeth, peering round the tree trunk. "Naughty boy! What are you doing here?" The hound prostrated himself before the voice of authority and thumped the ground with his tail.

"You know this creature?" Felicity was amazed.

"It's Chalky's dog. Bad boy!" growled Elspeth, although whether she was referring to the dog or its owner was not clear. The animal, having grovelled enough, leapt up and placed his forepaws on Felicity's shoulders. Staggering under the considerable weight, she found herself eyeball to eyeball with an adversary of uncertain intentions. The long, slathering tongue lashed across her chin, and she gathered that she was regarded as friend.

"Get down, Fluff!" commanded Elspeth, who had a way with dogs.

"Fluff?" Felicity wiped her face on the back of her sleeve. "Are you serious? I know people who aren't as big as that thing."

"You would have to ask Chalky how he came by such a name, but that's all I've ever heard him called, apart from Fluffy."

At that moment, Chalky himself heaved into view, picking his way up the drier bits of the drive, leaning heavily on his stick. Drunk or sober, he listed thirty degrees to port, and swung his right arm as a counter-balance. Despite the heat of the after-noon, he was wearing his antediluvian brown suit, the trousers turned up many times to accommodate his short legs. Under the jacket, he had on a collarless shirt, buttoned up to the throat, and his face, not surprisingly, shone with sweat. Every ten yards he paused, removed the cap from his head, and wiped his gleaming forehead dry with the back of his hand. Felicity, hoping that the dog would not interpret it as an assault on his master, went to lend Chalky a hand.

"How do?" Chalky greeted her, accepting the support of her hand under his elbow. "Tha' dog a mine 'int bin botherin' you?"

"Not at all," lied Felicity. "A charming animal. Won't you come into the garden and sit down?"

Elspeth hurried to unfold the deckchair, which she had retrieved from one of the cluttered store sheds. Its canvas was faded and frayed, but it held up as Chalky lowered himself carefully into it. The lurcher flung himself adoringly at Chalky's feet and panted as though he had run to fetch the chair himself. His master looked around, at the trays of stocks and asters waiting to be bedded out, at the newly cleared borders and freshly dug vegetable patch, from the emerging roof of the cottage to the jumble of builder's equipment and material on the front lawn.

"I come to see how you girls's gettin' on," he announced from his canvas throne, like King Canute at the seaside. "It looks to me like you doin' alrigh'."

TWELVE

Felicity could never work out how Chalky had decided that he would be welcome at Hope Cottage, but welcome he certainly made himself, settling comfortably into the old deck chair, his disreputable dog at his feet. Having seen her visitor snugly ensconced, with a can of beer and a cheese and pickle sandwich, Felicity resumed her roofing. Elspeth and Chalky embarked on a long and highly technical discussion of the proper composition of a muck heap accompanied by the stertorous rumblings of the sleeping dog who was being allowed to lie.

The sun blazed down, soaking the new tiles with heat. Felicity, crawling shadeless across the roof, felt like a mollusc in a bake-oven. With every hammer blow, sweat splattered from her arm onto the porous clay and rapidly vanished. Above the airfield a team of biplanes tossed and tumbled in the cloudless sky, like fighting puppies, rehearsing for an air display. The noise of their engines came like a magnification of the voice of the slow moving bees who bumbled among the flowers. Elspeth had turned off the radio, the better to converse with Chalky, who was slightly deaf. He perched magisterially in his deck-chair, shouting to Elspeth across the vegetable patch, the peak of his cap pulled right down onto the bridge of his nose to shelter his face from the sun.

Fluff lay snoring, twitching his large floppy ears in sleep if a fly ventured too near his face. When Chalky hauled himself, with great difficulty, to his feet to observe where Elspeth was planting the radishes, Fluff reluctantly arose and accompanied his master on a tour of inspection of the vegetable beds. When Chalky resumed his chair, the dog continued to quarter the garden, poking his long face into every interesting smell and leaving his mark on the trunk of each aged tree. Felicity, watching from the roof, had a horrible vision of the havoc which those extensive jaws could wreak upon the half grown ducklings, who only a few weeks before had been led from nest to pond for their first swimming lesson, trailing behind their proud mother like a string of yellow pompoms.

"Chalky," she shouted.

"Eh?"

"Don't let Fluff eat the ducklings, will you? They're rather sweet and not very big."

"Don' worry," he shouted back, "even if he pick one up, he won' sink 'is teeth in. Good lurcher's trained no'a damage the game."

"Poor little ducklings. They'd die of fright."

"No, they won't. Like Jonah an' tha' whale."

"Can't you get him to chase the rats instead. He's welcome to puncture them with his teeth as much as he wants."

"He's a good ratter, tha' one. Fluff!" he commanded, "Where's th' rats?"

It was only by translating 'whizzrass?' from Norfolk into RP that Felicity was able to comprehend this instruction. "They're all over the place," she shouted helpfully. "They nest in the cottage furniture."

Fluff bounded about, obediently, sniffing at the plethora of rat trails. A rodent motorway passed between the front door of the cottage and the old pigsty. The cat, who had made her way down from the tree while her enemy slumbered, was now up on the roof with Felicity, pouring scorn on the proceedings and seeking reassurance that she was not being usurped by the loud-mouthed newcomer. Felicity stroked her soothingly and tripped over her every time she went to fetch another tile from the stack. With a yelp of martial enthusiasm, Fluff snuffled his way over to a corner of the garden behind the caravan, where, nose to the ground, he began to dig in a fury of flying clods. Chalky encouraged him with whistles and grunts, and the dog was soon elbow deep in the hole.

"Move him over a bit, Chalky, I want a border dug by that fence," called Elspeth, looking up from her planting.

"I was going to get a JCB to dig out the cesspit," shouted Felicity, "can I borrow your dog instead?"

Chalky grinned and waved his walking stick. Fluff

continued his excavations well beyond the depth at which any rats' nests would have been found, finally emerging, triumphant, with an ancient bone in his teeth. Ignoring Chalky's curses and Felicity's laughter, he trotted off to the shade of a pear tree with his prize, leaving a large hole and a scattering of topsoil on the lawn.

"Terriers is best for rats," explained Chalky, defiantly. Elspeth kindly changed the subject to sweet peas, and Felicity got back to work.

With a sheet of lead and a wooden mallet, she beat out the flashing that would fit around the kitchen chimney stack, like a collar around a sunday-school boy. She loved the malleable grey metal, which went where she bent it, like adult plasticine. If only all the other building materials were so tractable, she could simply shape her house with her bare hands, like a child playing on a wet-sand beach. Today was a Possible day. On Possible days, what she was doing seemed eminently reasonable, and every task, if not going exactly right, could be seen to be going wrong for comprehensible reasons. For the past week, she had known only Possible days, which filled her with euphoria, and a false sense of having got this building business finally licked. Felicity did not hurry to finish the roof. Now she felt confident of what she was doing (and tiling had come to her so easily), why rush on to some other part of the project, which might defeat her? She suspected that as soon as she left the roof and embarked on the plumbing or the floors, a series of Impossible days would ensue. Then her mind would go blank, the instructions of G.P. Turvey would mean nothing and the intractability of inanimate things would render her powerless. On days like that, she would rush into Orfton-Saint-Scabious to buy a Guardian and look for a proper job back in the smoke. Most likely there would not be a Guardian in the village, because, as nobody read it, naturally it always sold out before the other papers. She would not have been surprised to have been offered the suspect reading matter in a brown paper bag. When, having trailed from one village newsagent to the next, she finally found a copy, she always bought an EDP as well, to show willing, but they were never fooled, and knew her for an incomer.

On Impossible days, she sat in her caravan, not speaking to Elspeth, hunched over the newspaper, realising that the only sensible thing to do was to go back to London and get a job, abandoning the fantasy world in which she was playing house. On Possible days, it was London which seemed unreal, and she wondered what bad dream had kept her there for so many years, when here in Norfolk existed a world so much more vivid and alive than the one which she had left, a world in which, with the application of faith, common sense and brute optimism, anything could be accomplished.

So, on this most Possible of days, Felicity simultaneously sped through her work, because to work fast was a demonstration of her ability, and dawdled, not wishing this part of her project to be over. With the whole house, she alternately hurried on towards completion, wanting the successful outcome, and dallied, enjoying the means more than the end. No wonder she found happiness such a difficult state in which to be, always rushing on to the next thing, and never knowing what had been until after it was gone.

The biplanes buzzed past overhead, trailing great plumes of coloured smoke. Everyone at Hope Cottage looked up, as the streamers of red, white and blue looped and wriggled across the sky. When they looked down again, it was to find that Shirley Bruton had arrived with the children.

To her, who had not seen the building since the tiling began, the change was dramatic. She had left a naked house and returned to find it almost half-clothed. From one end-gable to the central chimney stack, the roof was now covered with neat overlapping rows of bright red tiles. Adonis and Phoebe, born within sight of the airfield, were blasé about biplanes, and barely gave the display team a glance as they droned above the trees. They made for the ladder directly, and swarmed up to pester Felicity with questions and demands to be allowed to have a go at fixing tiles. The mistress of the house looked ruefully down at Shirley, who indicated her consent to the children's activities with a wave.

"Don't get up, Chalky," she said to the little old man in the deck chair, who was trying to stand up to meet her. Relieved of the necessity, he took off his cap and wiped his forehead, in what could be interpreted as a salutation.

"Hullo, Shirley," Elspeth hurried across the garden, wiping earth from her hands. Although they had known each other for nine years, and been friends for the last five, still they hesitated over their greetings. They saw each other too often for the formality of a handshake yet neither of them felt able to signal a greater level of intimacy with a kiss on the cheek. Shirley kissed all her female relatives and the old friends with whom she had been at school, with a quick and mutually understood peck. Elspeth would have done, if she had ever had close family or old school friends, but her social circle was more restricted. So the two women compromised, as they usually did, approaching to within a foot of one another and expressing their pleasure in the meeting by each leaning her upper half towards the other, giving proximity without contact. As an addition to this ritual, Shirley patted Elspeth on the arm, just above the elbow. They had not met for several days, and really did rather miss each other.

"Hullo, Elspeth. I was fetching the kids back from the school bus, and thought I'd look in."

"Oh dear, are they still in disgrace for playing truant?"

"They're in disgrace, it's me as gets punished. No hardship to them to be driven to the bus and wait in the car for it, instead of standing out in the weather. Don't half cut up my day though."

"Still, it gives you a chance to visit. Isn't it all coming along splendidly? Felicity's been going at that roof like a young demon."

"It's looking good," Shirley conceded.

"Of course, she wouldn't have been able to get this far without your help," Elspeth added hastily.

"What's Chalky doing here?"

"I'm supervisin'" joked the old man, overhearing. "Every buildin' site needs someone to sit around doin' nothin'. Tha's me."

"Come and help me find the best place to put in the petunias," Elspeth steered her friend over to the border on which she had been working, once the radishes were safely put to bed. Although out of earshot of the others, she lowered her voice anyway and said "I hope it won't cause problems at home, you coming here?"

"He didn't forbid me to set foot in the place you know. We got a Queen called Elizabeth, not Victoria."

"He wasn't happy about you being here every day, was he."

"No," Shirley looked uncomfortable. "Maybe I was neglectin' the house a bit, while I was doing the roof over here. You can see his point. That's not to say I've been locked in a cellar since, mind."

"Nor was I suggesting it."

"Good."

"I wish there wasn't this unpleasantness though. We did have such fun, the three of us."

"When she wasn't in one of her moods," said Shirley, nodding towards the roof, where Felicity was trying to prevent Adonis throwing the cat off the scaffolding, to see if it would land on its feet.

"Or you in one of yours."

"Me?" Shirley was affronted. "Sweetness and light."

"I think I know you a little better than that," Elspeth smiled. "After all these years."

"It don't seem like yesterday, you were moving into that old bungalow. They didn't talk about nothin' else for weeks, you and that train of yours coming up the road on a low-loader in pieces. God, I weren't even married then."

"Tempis fugit, as Archibald says. We're none of us getting any younger."

"You're not a pensioner yet."

"I won't see fifty again."

"I will, soon enough," grumbled Shirley. "Not that

anyone will remember the day. And nothin' much to show for it, anyway. Half a century of what?"

"You've got the children."

"You can have 'em if you like. Special offer."

"It's a shame you don't have the dairy any more."

"I do miss my cows," Shirley confessed. "But farmers can't be sentimental."

"Much less farmer's wives?"

"It's a business, not a hobby."

"But you were making such a good thing of it," protested Elspeth.

"I was, wasn't I? Delicatessens in Norwich, fancy restaurants. All took my cream and butter, you couldn't buy anything like it in the shops. I had a market."

"It's a shame your husband's accountant didn't agree."

"He's a bulk man. Thinks in pounds and talks in units of production. Bruton thinks the sun shines out of his Psion."

"There's more to life than making money, surely?"

Shirley looked at her sideways. "Perhaps. But it was his money bought the cows in the first place, what could I say? The milk quota weren't mine to keep, it belonged to the farm. And the farm belongs to the company, and the company belongs to him. I never brought any money to the place when we married."

"Liz Taylor couldn't have brought more to a marriage than you did," said Elspeth heatedly.

"Is that meant to be a compliment?"

"Jackie Onassis, then."

"You don't half pick 'em."

"You know what I mean. Money isn't everything."

"It's true, I don't reckon there's many others would've taken on a man with a ready-made family and no inclination for any more kids. My family thought I'd done well for myself though. Him with no brothers to try and split the farm up when his dad popped his clogs. And he was on his last legs, the old man."

"Did your family understand that you wouldn't be having children of your own?" Elspeth knelt by the border with a polystyrene tray of bedding plants in front of her and a bucket of compost to hand. Having asked such a personal question, she avoided Shirley's eye, and busied herself digging little holes in which to plant the petunias.

"They do now, more or less. I told my mum, when we was engaged, that he'd said he wouldn't be wantin' any more, havin' the two of them already, and Phoebe no more than a baby then. That's why he was in such a rush to get spliced, he had his sister down from Bungay looking after the kids, and they couldn't stand each other, she thought she should've been left a share in the farm, and of course the old man had practically cut her off with a shilling, when she went RC. Though why such a godless old sod as Bruton's dad was should bother about the bells and smells brigade is beyond me."

"Didn't she believe you, your mum?"

"Well no, she didn't. She thought he'd been put off kids by having them dumped on him like that, and when they were properly looked after he'd forget what a nuisance they was. Plus, of course, everyone was thinkin' we'd get some of our own, to make a proper family of it."

"I'm sure no one could have been a better mother to Phoebe and Adonis than you have."

"If anyone was expecting more, they've been disappointed. I wasn't married 'till I was thirty-seven, which is a bit old to be startin' all that. And he reckons too many kids on a farm only leads to squabbles. It's true, I know brothers who've practically fought over their father's death bed for the biggest share of the farm. And they don't wait 'till the old farmer's dead, neither. Years of bickering, you get. Bruton don't hold with splitting up farms. One son to inherit and a daughter to keep house for the lad until he's married, that's his idea of a family. Now it's all mechanised. If you still needed ten kids for their labour, no doubt I'd be stretch marks from here to my ankles."

"He couldn't have known that Phoebe would be a girl."

"I don't suppose she would've dared to be anything else," joked Shirley. "He always gets his own way."

"What strange prejudices people hold."

"Owning land does funny things to you. Some of the family feuds I seen, you wouldn't believe. And Bruton's dad was obsessed with keeping the farm together, quite crazy about it he was. So it's no surprise he turned out like he has."

"Old people can get very fixed ideas. I hope I don't become so unreasonable in my dotage."

"He was a cantankerous old bugger to start with. Had good reason to know about farms being broken up, the old vulture, he'd caused it often enough himself."

"How?"

"In the thirties, or thenabouts, there was a terrible depression. Agricultural land weren't worth nothin', and there was mortgages being called in all over the place. Bruton's dad weren't even the eldest son, he'd been kicked off the farm by his brother, along of the land army girls, after the war. So off he goes to Canada and makes a nice little fortune running brothels up in the timber-country for the lumber jacks. Then home he comes, right at the bottom of the depression, with money in his pockets and starts buying up a field here and a small-holding there. They was wild to sell, some of those people, half a step ahead of the bailiffs. One-legged ex-officers who'd set up in chicken farming with their gratuities, that sort of thing. They was going down like flies, them days. On the side, he was lending money to desperate fools who thought he wouldn't foreclose on a neighbour, not like the banks. They soon found their mistake. And never being one to buy for a shilling what he could have for sixpence, he was in a ring too.

"A what?"

"There was precious few with cash to spare buying farm land, and fewer still who thought it worth their while. Him and a couple of others, who was buying up all the bankrupt little farms round here, got together in a ring. Meant they agreed which one of them was going to buy a certain lot at auction, so as they didn't run the price up against one another. Must've paid off the auctioneer, I reckon, 'cos everybody knew it was going on. Bargains for them and tough luck for the families who was selling up, but that's the way of the world."

"If he was the younger son, how did he come to inherit the farm?"

Shirley laughed. "He didn't, his brother did, and him left without so much as an acre. Mind, it was only a small farm in them days, but Bruton's grand-dad had fell out with his youngest boy over the brothel-keeping business, didn't hold with living off immoral earnings, so he cut him out of the will. Then Jake, that was the eldest, inherited the lot, found that it didn't amount to more'n a parcel of land and a mountain of debts and was forced to go begging to his little brother to help him out with a loan. Like old Esau, he was, 'cept it was all hard cash, no messing with pottage."

"And?" prompted Elspeth.

"Jake borrowed the money from Simon, that's his brother, and paid off the bank. Then, 'cos of having bought bad seed, trying to save a bit of money, he didn't get much of a crop that year, and what there was he lost to rust. Couldn't pay Simon the interest he owed him on the loan."

"Did Simon foreclose?"

"No, Jake deprived him of the pleasure. Took a twelve-bore out into the hayloft and blew his brains out. Left a note saying if Simon was to have the farm, he should pay inheritance tax on it. Of course, Simon had the last laugh, on account of getting the farm by default, rather than bequest, so he didn't even have any capital gains to pay. Cunning old sod. Rolled up the day after Jake's funeral, he did, and turned his own brother's widow out of doors, with a six-month old baby in her arms. That's Randolph, as lives next door to Chalky. No wonder he turned out so peculiar."

"I don't believe I've ever met him. In fact, I thought that house next to Chalky's was empty, there aren't any curtains up at the window."

"Not very sociable, Randolph. Named for Winston Churchill's dad, much good it done him. I took the

kids there to meet him once, he is their cousin, but he
didn't say much. You can't blame him for bearing a
grudge. The kids was scared of him, he's a giant of a
man, and mad as a march hare, but I've never heard
that he harmed anyone."

"I had no idea," said Elspeth, patting the earth firm
around a newly planted petunia, "that your family had
such a colourful past."

"Ain't my family," Shirley corrected her, "and you
can see why he don't like it talked about. By the time
old Simon'd finished buying and selling land round
here, the farm was twenty times bigger than it had
been when his brother topped himself. Of course, he
had the money to mechanise, and he saw there wasn't
no point having a dozen little fields too small to turn a
combine round in, so he never stopped trading and
dealing, trying to make the biggest fields he could. He
didn't do bad, though we're still a bit scattered about,
and you could've fitted Jake's entire holding into that
Forty Acre behind this house."

"Times change."

"The Bruton's, father and son, have ripped out
enough hedges from hereabouts to fence around a
national park."

"Is that the price of progress?"

"It's the price of success. Little farmers go bust, big
ones don't. We can't all be conservationists like the
worm-man," said Shirley, scornfully.

"Felicity tries to get me to be ecological in the
garden," Elspeth said, furtively sprinkling slug-pellets
on the earth.

"She don't know what's good for her."

"She didn't want to use treated timbers, in case it
poisoned the bats."

"She's not getting me up there every year to redo
the roof when it rots."

"Oh, she gave in on that one. But I would love to
have been there when she asked the timber merchant
in Dereham what was his policy on rainforest conser-
vation."

"Don't suppose he knew what she was talking
about."

"I don't imagine that he did."

"I must get those kids off home for tea, before they break their silly necks." She began walking towards the house, with Elspeth following. "You've got this garden looking a picture."

"I'm making a start, but there are so many things still to do."

"Donny, Phoebe," shouted Shirley, "come down off there. We're going home."

"Oh mum!" chorused the children from the roof.

"Now. I mean it."

Felicity gave Adonis a helpful shove in the direction of the ladder. She was sure that tiling made splendid educational play, but she would rather get on with it on her own. Phoebe hung off the edge of the platform at arms length until, releasing her grip, she fell into the flowerbed by the house. Because his sister had disdained to use the ladder, so naturally did Adonis, hurling himself from the scaffolding and landing with what he hoped was a parachutists roll on his bottom. Luckily Hope Cottage was a squat building, and the distance to the ground was not great.

"Come back soon," said Felicity, who had descended to the earth to say goodbye.

"Yes, it's so nice to see you here," added Elspeth.

"Maybe, when I can get away. Hurry up Donny, or you'll be late for karate."

"He failed his orange belt," confided Phoebe to Felicity.

"Shut up, Feeble," hissed her brother, red in the face.

"You kids," commanded Shirley, "in the car! Now. Honestly, chauffeur come parlour-maid, that's me. Fetch them from the bus. Take them home. Make tea. Drive Donny to Thetford."

"Why Thetford?" asked Elspeth.

"Don't ask me. There's a perfectly good karate class in Dereham, but it's Shotokan, so my Adonis won't have anything to do with it, too dead common for him. So off we go, all the way to Thetford, so as he can study IshinRyu, whatever that may be when it's at home."

"What's the difference?" enquired Felicity

"Don't ask me, I'm only his mother. Any class of children standing on one leg and shouting in Japanese looks very much like another to me. Storing up hernias, I don't doubt, poor little mites. It's not even that he's very good at it, from what I can make out. Still, his dad's keen that boy should do it, on account of having been mugged by some Korean bloke in Seoul, when he was doing his national service. He reckons he was overwhelmed by mysterious oriental martial arts, but I bet he was a pissed as a fart, and would've been a push-over for an arthritic rickshaw coolie. Anyway, it's me as has to take the boy, wait for him and fetch him back when he's finished."

"Come and help with the cement pour, if you get the time," offered Felicity. "I'll be down to the floor soon."

"We'll see. You want a lift home, Chalky?"

"You goin' that way?" he enquired, suspiciously.

"I got to pop in the house first and get Phoebe a bit of tea. Won't be ten minutes though."

"No ta."

"My husband won't be there."

"I'd rather walk."

"You're a stubborn old man."

"An' I don' s'pose you liked it any better than I did, when he got rid of the cows."

"I must be off," Shirley got in the car and turned it carefully around on the rough patch by the pigsty. They waved at the departing visitors, and Adonis stuck his tongue out.

"I'll run you home, Chalky," volunteered Felicity.

"Tha's good, I don' fancy the walk."

"Why didn't you go with Shirley then?"

"I'm not settin' foot in Bruton's house, after the way he treated me."

"Pride is a deadly sin," admonished Elspeth.

"An' charity's s'posed to be a great virtue," replied the old man. "If I got too much of th' one, Bruton ain't got none of th' other, you can be sure of tha'."

THIRTEEN

This used to be such a quiet place, before she came.
Now it's infested with people. Is the old man going to
become a fixture? I should say so, he has made himself
at home. At least he isn't a giant, there's that in his
favour. It is quite a relief to see someone around here
shorter than me. He wouldn't have looked out of place
in my own village, apart from being well past his sell-
by date, and with that leg, too. Maybe the flint-
knappers would have found him work sweeping up
the spoil, as they sometimes did for broken miners
who had survived roof-falls, if they were feeling kind.

The road I took that autumn was busy, crawling
with people like ants streaming to a broken food jar.
Yes, we're back to that story. Don't complain that I'm
giving it to you in pieces, blame Felicity and her
turbulent friends for interrupting. I don't understand
this mania for facts in a logical sequence, stripped of
inessential details. If we didn't tell stories, how would
we know anything? A story should grow like a bush,
with a bud here and a shoot there. I suppose you want
stories like nettles, that thrust straight up in one
direction, on one stalk, until they are tall enough to
sting you?

The road was busy, and the weather had turned
foul. It rained for seven days and nights with barely a
pause, and even on the well-drained uplands, the
going was almost impossible. Streams sprung across
the path, my feet slipped in the slithery, chalky mess.
I was white as a corpse from tumbling on the
uncertain surface, weak as I was after the fever. The
rain washed the grease out of my hair and left my poor
body exposed to the cold and wet. If I had been a fowl,
I would have sunk. In shivering misery I journeyed,
and if one day's travel only took me as far as I would
normally have walked in half a morning, I was glad to
put that distance between myself and the camp I had
left, where I had so narrowly escaped becoming a
sacrifice to the greater glory of some minor god.

The good thing about those dismal days, flounde-
ring along in the ankle-twisting mire, was that the

misery was equally divided. In better weather, the other travellers, who were mostly in bands, might well have decided that a woman on her own was easy prey. As we all slogged along that filthy path, heads down and faces dripping, the effort of pugnacity was beyond them.

I don't suppose I looked like much of a prize, for even the most weather-proof brigand. I was thin as an oversuckled nanny-goat, and twice as foul-tempered. Each night I set my snares, and found them empty in the morning. Every nut or berry that grew within easy reach of the path had been stripped away and eaten. I spent as much time foraging as I did walking towards my destination, making ever-wider casts away from the road. The rain rotted the fruit on the trees and produced a great crop of poisonous toadstools, which were of no use at all unless I felt like putting myself out of my misery, which (considerable though the misery was) I did not. Thin as a twig, filthy, cold and racked with feverish shivers, muttering to myself as I went, I can understand why no-one bothered me. I must have looked like the unburied dead, possessed by demons.

Eventually the rain stopped, but the bogs were over-full, and I nearly drowned any number of times as I picked my way across the last part of my journey to the West, where the road which had taken me so confidently from my own home to the old woman's camp petered out in a series of confusing tracks and trails. I fell in with a family who had traded with Soft Axe and knew where his people were. With their directions, I had no further trouble in finding the place, which turned out to be a hill-fort, close by the Western sea.

The hill commanded a view of the road, was gently rounded and had been cleared of trees. A rude fence and a staked ditch were the defences, but visitors were obviously not a rarity. So used to strangers were they, that nobody stopped what they were doing, or bothered to ask what I wanted, as I stepped through the gate and into the circle of huts.

I was wondering if anyone was going to offer me a

drink, when Soft Axe appeared and greeted me as though my arrival was expected, and not as if I had completed an improbable journey which no one in her right mind would have undertaken. He was the same foxy little man as I remembered, only sleeker and more poised than he had been when he arrived in my village. His red beard had been trimmed back and his hair recently untangled. I got the immediate impression that he was rather a swell among his people, which was, I am sure, what he wanted me to think. When they saw that I was known to the boss, the inhabitants of the fort, who had been staring at me carelessly, hurried to fetch food and invited me nearer to the fire to warm myself.

Soft Axe introduced me as a flint trader, although it must have been obvious from the smallness of my pack that I had brought nothing to trade. At the mention of flints, even though I could tell that Soft Axe was really boosting the excellence of my product, and my importance as a trader, I could see the people who were standing about look rather smug and superior. There was not a good stone weapon to be seen on any of them, the men wore metal knives at their belts, and certainly did not look as though they thought them magical or rare. The women had pins and clasps of polished bronze holding their garments together, or keeping their hair up. Soft Axe himself, who must have put on all his finery when he heard of my arrival, was wearing a great brooch, set with coloured stones. With smaller ornaments around his neck and on his hands, I can only describe him as flashy. Even his hair was tied back with a metal clasp which twinkled in the sunlight.

Soft Axe showed me to a hut, where I was to stay. I caught a number of knowing, and rather sceptical glances from the others at this, which I did not understand, but which put me on my guard. Although I was wary, I was also, for the first time in days, warm and dry, with a belly full of meat. I no sooner lay down on the bed of springy brooms covered with skins, than I fell asleep.

It was that sense of danger, without which one does

not live past childhood, that woke me. Darkness had fallen, but I knew there was someone else in the hut. Stealthily, I drew the knife from its wrapping, in the pack which I had used as a pillow. My nose told me that the intruder was a man, and I did not intend to waste time questioning his motives. As he clambered onto the bed, I got my hand round the nape of his neck, grasped his hair and pulled his head backwards, exposing the neck to the blade. Soft Axe can thank his taste for baubles that he survived that meeting, for I recognised him by the fancy hair clasp around which my hand closed.

He made apologetic noises, and fetched a tallow dip, so that I could see. It was his hut. I could have kicked myself for a fool. What sort of a place did I think I had come to, that they kept a house of such comfort solely for visitors? I indicated as plainly as I knew how that I was in his bed for the purposes of sleep alone, which he seemed to accept. I dozed with one eye open, as he climbed in beside me and wrapped himself in a tight separate bundle. On that night, and the ones which followed, he never laid a hand or a glance upon me, but I slept lightly, with my knife within easy reach.

For the first, and only time in my life, I was sharing a bed with a man. Although the arrangement was strictly chaste, it bothered me nonetheless. For Soft Axe's people naturally assumed that there was more to it than that, and I found myself being treated like his concubine. They were respectful and polite, I was welcomed and fed as long as I stayed, but to them I was only of interest as Soft Axe's unexpected woman. Thus they saw me, the woman who controlled the trade of the most successful flint mines in the world, who had walked unaccompanied across country in foul weather, who could run faster, fight dirtier and drink harder than any man ever weaned. To them, I was just a foreign floozy. It was very demoralising.

It was one of those depressing tribes which had drifted away from the worship of the Goddess, and was trying to muddle through with a collection of new and argumentative godlets. The men strutted about, full of themselves under this new order, busily appointing themselves lord high priest of this and that. Their rituals were a pitiful jumble of old and new, and they had somehow decided to venerate their pricks as the source of all fertility. Such nonsense. The women of the fort were increasingly confined to the chores of providing food and shelter, and to hear the men talk, you would think the only important part of making babies was the planting of the seed. The knives they crafted at their forge down in the valley grew longer and longer. I am sure with every extra handspan added to their weapons, they felt their magical pissing-spouts grow.

I was an anomaly, neither sitting round the cooking pots with the women, nor considered by the men. Under Soft Axe's protection I was allowed to stay, and this grated on me. I took advantage of my protected status, even while inwardly resenting it, to hang about the foundry, from which the other women were excluded, and learn what I could.

No wonder the ignoramuses of the great plain thought the new weapons miraculous, for garbled accounts had circulated of their production amidst leaping flames, great clouds of foul smelling smoke and the hissing frenzy of steam as the molten metal was cooled. Whatever their brand-new gods were called, it was obvious that metal and its making were their chiefest objects of reverence.

In the valley, overlooked by the fort was the place where they came to worship their new technology. The foundry was beside the river, which provided the cooling water, in what had once been a small clearing in the forest. As they felled the trees for charcoal, so the open patch grew larger and larger, too full of stumps to plant a crop on, and no longer home and shelter to the animals of the forest which could have fed them. Hunting ceased to provide any part of their sustenance, as they traded for much of their food and left the women to raise the rest. On days when the metal-workers were not busy at their craft, they would go into the woods and play at chasing the deer, with their shiny new weapons. I accompanied them once, but their ineptitude disgusted me. Crashing through the undergrowth with enough shouting and hullooing to make a dead pig run away, they seemed to have lost all their skill in the hunt, and any feeling for the ways of the wood. Why make a sport of a serious art? If they so much as caught sight of a lame calf, or an ageing stag, they were thrilled, but should some poor old animal cross its rotted hooves and trip in the hunters' path (which was the only way in which they ever made a kill) their joy knew no bounds. Usually, though, if their quarry had three legs to carry it, the beast would escape, then they would console them-selves with a drink and return to the camp, very pleased with themselves and hungry, to find what the patient women had cooked for them in their absence.

The women and children grew the crops and tended the cattle; to the men, the wealth of trade accrued. I hung around, disregarded by most, able to observe with a freedom which I would never have permitted to a commercial rival. Convinced as they were that the days of flint had passed, they did not think of me as such. I began to understand their language. I drifted along the river bank, watching the metal-making, from the crushing of the rock at the start, to the setting of the finished blade. In time I came to know the way it was worked better than those who did the working, for they each had one task and stuck to it, while I saw the whole process. The most skilled and dangerous part was the casting of the hot metal from the fires. This was the work of the powerful, and only Soft Axe had higher standing in the village than these men. They were ugly and scarred with the burns and scalds of molten splashes, with exaggerated muscles in their arms and back and fire-reddened faces, with eyes the colour of the setting sun. Of course, they were often maimed at their craft and I was puzzled to see so few cripples about the village, until I realised that a metal-worker too damaged to work would be put over the cliff, or driven out into the forest to starve, for they did not care to have the formerly powerful reduced to idle trouble-makers in their midst. This only makes sense when you realise that food and other desirables were divided unequally, according to status. Not only a man's pride, but also his stomach was hurt by a fall in standing.

Many things puzzled me about those people, at first. The men clattered about, their belts a-clank with knives and stabbing spikes, and none of them would so much as walk from fort to foundry without taking his knife-on-a-pole (a silly innovation of theirs, unweildy in combat, but big). It was a good advertisement for their craft, yet they were the most un-warlike people you could ever hope to meet. Fighting, like hunting, was something at which they only played. I shuddered to think how they might defend themselves from attack, until, that is, I met their Beaker People.

They were a surly lot, villainous, thuggish and brutal. At first, I thought they must be captive slaves, for they have been the invading enemy in this country for more generations than I can remember. In my part of the world, they were an occasional nuisance, who attacked only in passing, on their way to more rewarding targets, but here in the South-West was the land which they had come to raid, and were now beginning to covet for itself, not just the plunder it might yield. When I discovered that these people were allowed to maintain a camp only a stonesthrow from the hill-fort, I was amazed. There was a preponderance of young men in the Beaker People's settlement, and a gang of them were apparently free to strut their way, heavily armed and aggressive, around the area.

It was their arms that gave it away. Metal, of course. Provided by my hosts, Soft Axe's people, probably on his orders. The idea of hiring a gang of enemy hard-cases to do the fighting for a village which had better uses for its time than playing soldiers, was such a strange one, that it was difficult to believe the evidence of my own eyes. It was true; the Beaker People were given weapons and a proportion of the gains from trading, in return for protecting the metal-workers from the depredations of envious neighbours or jealous customers. Although the two groups should have been enemies, they co-existed to their great mutual benefit. That is not to say their was any love lost between them, for the metal-workers thought the Beaker People stupid foreigners, forced to hire out their brawn for the weapons they had not the skill to make, while the young mercenaries despised their hosts as etiolated half-men, who would rather build their wealth by trade than by plunder. So the two groups co-existed in mutual contempt and incomprehension, both sides convinced that they were getting the better of the bargain. The Beaker People women, meanwhile, got on with making a village out of their camp, building homes and planting crops. The warriors sat around, when they were drunk, singing outrageously depressing and home-sick songs, about their land across the fog-bound Northern sea, but you could tell how it would be. In ten years time, the thugs would suddenly find themselves old men, with grey in their beards and slack in their paunches, and a herd of thrusting grandchildren by their hearths. Then they would be the ones to rail against the uncouth ways of newly arrived foreigners, and they would never go home again. The mournful songs would no doubt remain, and be passed on to their grand-children as nostalgia for a time which they had never known, and a place where they would never be.

In the meantime, I avoided the gang of well-armed hoodlums who hung about the place. It seemed inconceivable to me that they would continue to accept the crumbs from the feasts of their masters, when, by the application of a little thought, they might discover the way of melting the crushed rock to make metal for themselves, and take over the whole business. Soft Axe's people could not have stopped a determined putsch by the hired muscle, but so long as the heavies felt themselves better off, by virtue of their possession of bulging arms and small heads, than the metal-workers, who merely had wealth and power, nothing would change.

Soft Axe became very gloomy, as the autumn wore on. As the man who set the price at which the worked metal was to be traded, he had great prestige, but at this season, little actual work to do. Even the most hot-headed youths from the great plains were beginning to think twice about making the trek west in search of the magic weapons. The old men cautioned the young that it was no time for travel, and the counsels of the old prevailed. In the spring, consoled the elders, an expedition should be made, and in the meantime the greybeards heaved a sigh of relief that the old order had not yet been overthrown. When the spring came, a dozen local wars came with it, and the tribes which had not equipped themselves with the new weapons were subjugated by those that had, whose warriors had spent the winter perfecting their use. Then it was too late for the timid youths who had heeded their elders to re-equip, and they were roundly defeated. Which shows that there is no use to be had from the new religion, which does not even seem to confer the grace of prediction upon its practitioners.

That is to get ahead of my story. The turbulent spring, and its aftermath, the consolidation by the Beaker People of their hold on the great plain, whose defenders were exhausted by inter-tribal strife, were still a hard winter away. In the meantime, I had to contend with Soft Axe, the only person in the hill fort who would talk to me without making the sign against bad spirits behind his back, increasingly sunk in silent gloom. In the evenings, when he had been in the habit of entertaining me with scurrilous gossip about his neighbours, which stories, as an unnoticed observer of life in the hill fort I could often cap, he now rolled himself in his bedding and lay staring at the ceiling of his hut. Whenever a visitor was spied approaching, he hurried to the gate to see who it might be, rather than waiting in dignified retreat to be informed of the arrival. Whole days he passed up on the cliffs, straining his eyes out to sea, as though expecting an arrival, although who he thought was going to pop up from beyond the end of the world, I don't know.

I did try to find out what was wrong with him, but I was not used to playing the soothing help-meet to a man burdened with cares, and I soon grew exasperated at his refusal to tell me his worries. Also, I must confess, I had cares of my own, although of a lighter nature. There was a woman (of course), Soft Axe's own sister, in fact, Green Eyes, the Grain Crusher. She had the red hair and sharp features, but if her brother looked like a fox, she was more of a squirrel. She was the only woman in the camp who did not appear to be attached to a man, perhaps the connection with Soft Axe, which I had found so useful, protected her too. Like me, she worked with stone, for there was no metal substitute for good rock when it came to grinding grain, which was her trade. I followed her on one of her trips to the hills, supposedly to search for the rocks hollowed by water that make such a good bowl in which to crush seed with a pestle. In fact the cave she took me to was the one in which she had made her drawings of the Goddess, and where she took her trances, for she had detected in me a lack of enthusiasm for the new religion. The Mother's worship has often led to a certain understanding arising between the celebrants, and we were no exception. I made her a Goddess figure from the local stone, having lost none of my skill, and we spent many afternoons exploring together, caves and other things. Among her own people, we gave no hint of our attachment, which was not how I was accustomed to conduct my affairs, but I understood her caution.

One day, when Green Eyes was, for form's sake, actually doing some work (which she had rather neglected of late), I strolled up to the headland and found Soft Axe, as usual, staring out to sea. Instead of the expression of fixed depression, to which I had grown accustomed, he wore a look of excitement, and could barely stand still. He pointed to a dark speck on the horizon, so small that no-one would have noticed it had not his inner voices been telling him where to look. Gradually the speck resolved itself as a sail, far away out to sea, but scudding nearer before a driving westerly.

"Where," I asked, "has that come from? Is it blown down from the North?"

"No," replied Soft Axe, never taking his eyes from the distant ship, "It comes from the West."

I told him not to be absurd, for I well knew that nothing lay to the West of us but the end of the world, where the sea broke into nothingness. He insisted that the ship came from the West, and I began to wonder if his modern gods had come to steal his spirit home in the craft, or whether he was simply raving mad.

"There is a land to the West," he said, as I backed a couple of paces away from him at the cliff's edge. "A rich island." He tore his gaze away from the approaching sail and showed me the brooch which held his cloak together. It was a fine ornament made of the gold metal, which his people seemed to prize above anything else. Only Soft-Axe and some of the metal workers possessed gold jewellery, and Soft-Axe's brooch, which was a heavy piece, set with stones, he wore as a badge of office, for it was larger and more ornate than that owned by any of the others.

Convinced that he had lost his wits, I admired the jewel, which I had seen countless times already, for he wore it every day. I did not share his taste for fancy drapes and knick-knacks.

"The gold comes from the land across the sea to the West," he explained patiently. "I am not mad. It is from the people of that land that we learnt the art of metal-making; from them that we get the gold." He turned back to his watch on the sea, as though he could not bear to miss a single minute of the ship's approach, although it would obviously take all day to reach the shore.

I am not a heartless woman, as some would say, and although I had little patience with Soft Axe's wilder affectations, I did not like to see him tormented with anxiety. To distract him, while we waited to see if the ship would come safely to land, I asked him questions to keep his mind busy. "Tell me the story," I said, "of how metal came from across the sea."

As a boy, Soft Axe told me, he had been wild. Although he seemed like a comfort-loving grandee now, ensconced in his own hill-fort, then he had been more like the lean and wily rogue I had first met, all those seasons ago. His father had been a great man in the village, by virtue of his skill as a hunter, which in those days the people took seriously.

His father, as a hard man will, naturally wanted a hard son, in his own image, and had managed to kill off half a dozen of his male children before they reached puberty, with various ridiculous quests and tests. One brother froze while being made to swim the river at mid-winter, another was gored to death by a stag he was supposed to be roping, and various others died of cold and exhaustion on hunting trips that would have taxed a hardy adult, let alone a half-grown child.

This business about sons was quite a new departure, and one which, I am thankful to say, had not yet reached my own people. I hoped it never would. Children have always been the property of the mother, and if we are to live on, it is because our spirits have a longer span than our bodies. It all comes back to religion, you see. Soft Axe's people had lost the old religion, in his father's day. Because their connection with the spirit world had been severed, the men had begun to think of living on through their sons, an absurd idea, but one which I could see would lead to a great deal of trouble.

It already had, for Soft Axe and his family. Having seen most of her children slaughtered on the altar of manliness (for the daughters also suffered from the father's obsessions), Soft Axe's mother exaggerated her youngest baby's sickly nature, so that the father would not bother himself with the boy. Soft Axe could not have been that much of a weakling, or he would not have survived infancy, but the ruse worked; with every childish fever and ailment talked-up by his mother, his father ignored the boy, convinced that he would soon die, and concentrated on getting another.

It came as a great shock to Killing Skull, as the father was known (for he had once head-butted a man to death with his unusually bony forehead) when Soft Axe reached thirteen, still alive and on the verge of manhood. True, he was rather scrawny, as his mother had not been able to secure full rations for him, but he was fast of foot and wits, and alive. Killing Skull (or Dead Head, to the disrespectful, who included his surviving children) set about belatedly trying to mould the son he had not expected to live into his own image.

Not surprisingly, he failed. The child who had not been thought worthy of notice, the puking, shivering, neglected infant could not be expected to show much interest in pleasing its heedless parent. Soft Axe had spent his childhood with the women, or playing on his own among the hills, anything to keep him from being noticed by his father. As a consequence, he had more wisdom than most boys, and was as tough as an old sandal. He knew the ways of nature and was not inclined to join with the old man in slaughtering every species of animal he had ever delighted in watching, simply for the exercise of blood-lust.

The quarrels grew more frequent and alarming, although Soft Axe, being the quicker witted, always managed to avoid the fight in which Dead Head would have crushed the life out of his still-scrawny frame. The new religion was the last straw, for Soft Axe did not care for it at all, while his father was an enthusiastic convert to the blasphemous idea of male gods (well, he would be, wouldn't he?). When his mother warned him that the high priest (a crony of Dead Head's) had suggested that the sacrifice of an eldest son would be particularly acceptable, Soft Axe did not wait to hear his father grinding an edge to his best flint hunting knife, but took the hint and left.

More practically, he took a small boat, most valuable possession of his family, built for fishing on the river. I know all rivers are called 'the river', because no-one ever thinks that there is a world beyond their home, which might contain other rivers. In the language of Soft Axe's people 'the river' was Sabrina, which can do as its name, to distinguish it from others. In your tongue, Sabrina becomes the Severn. That is by the by. Soft Axe stole the boat, and was swept inexorably out to sea, the broad Western sea, on which he had never sailed.

How the boy came to survive the journey, and fetch up more or less alive on the shore of the island to the West, I do not know, nor can he explain. His mother kept to the old religion, covertly, and she must have worked some pretty potent magic on his behalf. He was found on the shore of that island by a kindly people, who pulled him from the breakers, while his boat was smashed to pieces on the rocks. The occupation of these people was sifting gold from river beds, in the flakes and nuggets in which it occurred, for they were well advanced in metal craft. Because they were kind to him, and also because he had no means of returning home, had he wanted to, Soft Axe stayed with the Gold People and learned their ways. He was adopted by one of the elders, a man who had lost one family and never started another. When the people travelled, to trade their gleanings, or find new deposits, Soft Axe accompanied them, and in this way went a great deal about that island. Along the way, he learned the making of bronze, the inferior greenish brown metal that, although not so decorative as gold, had far more practical use.

For five summers he stayed, while the warm soft winds of the far Western sea, the other side of the island where the world really did end, breathed upon him. Then the Gold People, with whom he had made his home were hit by two successive years of crop failures, and all the civil commotion that ensues when one's neighbours are also hungry. It was decided to send a ship, with the precious metal and some of the ugly but useful tools to the land from which Soft Axe had come, hoping to trade them for grain.

Soft Axe's people, who in those days lived by the banks of the river Sabrina, had trouble grasping the concept of a foreign trade mission. They saw the ship approaching and prepared for battle. The Gold People were forced to take up the axes and daggers which they had brought for commercial purposes, and brandish them as weapons. The native people, gathered on the shore, led by Dead Head himself, saw the boat coming in from the West, filled with people in whose hands gleamed blades of fire. Actually, it was the sun striking a reflection off the metal, but they were not to know that. Convinced that this was an arrival of the gods, they fell on their faces, grovelling before the war-like deities. Another ill effect of the new religion, you observe, it distorts the judgement and allows men to be mistaken for gods; force confused with power.

Soft Axe was quite a politician, even then. He knew that what these men wanted, as they abased themselves on the shore, weapons cast from them, was a show of strength. If he had told them to be reasonable, stop making such fools of themselves and get up to arrange a deal, they would have killed him. They were prepared to be totally dominated, but not partially humiliated. Further, while they might believe him a supreme being at the moment, should his father ever recognise him as the runt of the litter, presumed drowned long ago, pride would prevent him bowing to his errant son.

In short, Soft Axe could see an image problem looming, and decided to forestall it with a measured use of force. This is how he described it to me, but I think there was also an element of revenge, on behalf of himself, and his poor siblings. Jumping from the boat, before his companions had time to formulate a plan, he strode over to where his father had prostrated himself on the ground, and struck off the old man's head with one blow of his shining metal axe. It was not only politically, but also commercially a success-ful stroke. Dead Head's fellows were cowed by the brutality, grateful it was him, not them who had suffered, and impressed by the technical excellence of the decapitating tool. Soft Axe was made.

The Gold People stayed until the harvest was gathered, and the cattle driven for slaughter, taking what they needed and loading it onto their ship. Nobody would have stopped them taking the food without any payment, but they left in exchange the tools and weapons which they had brought. Perhaps this was because they were also leaving Soft Axe, and the elder who had adopted him wanted him to have some advantages in his new chieftaincy.

For who could resist the sudden elevation to high status which had come to Soft Axe? He had told his people sternly that he was not a god, but they remained convinced that the Gold People were, and they had brought Soft Axe, so if not a god himself, he was obviously in cahoots with some pretty powerful beings. If Soft Axe stayed, he would be the head man. How could he refuse? Sadly, the Gold People departed, with the elder climbing last into the boat, having stayed to present Soft Axe with the great brooch from his own cloak, as a token of who knows what?

By his own account, Soft Axe made his new people hop, as retribution for his miserable childhood. He moved the camp from the banks of the estuary up to the hill fort where it has remained ever since. Although he could not risk reintroducing the old religion, he was a natural choice for high priest of the new, and took delight in decreeing ever more absurd rituals and observances, although he was careful to stay just within the bounds of what would be accepted. They were a stuffy lot, and would not have taken kindly to being teased by their religious leader. Dead Head's cronies were found, one by one, moribund in the morning, lying stiff and cold with foul smelling froth at their mouths, for Soft Axe had learned about plants and their powers during his wanderings. Here revenge combined once again with what was politic, for a few murders were enough to ensure the loyalty, if not the love, of the remaining villagers. Quite possibly, they were grateful, for the removal of the old bullies made space for new men to advance themselves.

I imagine Soft Axe was completely unbearable at this period, something that he did not himself deny. Tyrannical, calculating, vengeful and subjecting his bemused people to every variety of spiteful whimsy, he was humoured, venerated and indulged, He was also, until the women came back from the caves whence they had fled at the approach of the strange ship, friendless. Then he discovered his sister, who had somehow, miraculously, survived the regime of harsh neglect. That mellowed him somewhat, and he ceased his worst excesses of capriciousness, and settled down to the serious business of establishing his people as the only masters of metal-working this side of the Western sea.

FOURTEEN

The ship was a long time putting in to land, and I shared Soft Axe's watch, although not his anxiety. Whether it was for the ship's cargo, its crew, or the news it might bring that he was eager, I didn't know. The whole vessel was now clearly visible, its leather sail caked with salt crystals and torn with jagged gashes. When the boat reached the mouth of the estuary, we hurried down to the place on the river shore where it would anchor. We might as well have saved our hurry for close though the boat was, and clearly visible the steersman at his oar, it was still some time and tricky manoeuvring before they were able to land. We sat down by the water's edge to wait. Soft Axe, at a high pitch of nervous excitement, was paring his finger nails with a small knife, a dandy even under stress. I was worried about involuntary amputation, as his hand shook, and to divert him, I urged him to continue with his history. He did so, reluctantly, although he never took his eyes off the boat, as it inched its way towards us.

When he had settled down to his responsibilities as a big noise in the village and decided to set up a metal working industry from scratch, his people were willing to comply, since they regarded him as the next best thing to a god. Their enthusiasm did not compensate for their ignorance of the processes involved, many of the older ones preferring to believe that metal was the product of gods farting underwater, or dragons breathing on stone. Anything that released them from the possibility of having to make the damn stuff themselves.

On the island where the Gold People lived, the raw materials were plentiful and easily found. In his own country, Soft Axe was not only project manager and foundry designer, he was also chief prospector. To the South-West, where the land sticks out into the sea like the outstretched leg of a giant waiting to trip passing ships, all the crude components of bronze were to be found. The difficulty was in extracting the ores. Soft

Axe did not have enough people himself to dig or pan for the minerals he needed. Over many seasons of negotiation and coercion, he had persuaded the neighbouring tribes to augment their farming and raiding with metal-hunting, and now these supplies were established, coming to him along the coast in heavily laden boats, the miners being paid with finished goods.

At first, the only reward he could offer was thinly beaten plates of gold, and luckily this caught the fancy of the head-men and elders with whom he was dealing. They would accept the tokens and set their people to the unaccustomed work of mining and prospecting, but I still don't understand why they should, for pretty though it is, there really isn't much that one can usefully do with gold. As for the ordinary people, who had to do the work without even receiving the payment, I fail to understand why they didn't mutiny.

Meanwhile, Soft Axe had caused his foundry to be built, where they would smelt the bronze, and was teaching the more receptive of the men how to cast the moulds into which the burning liquid would be poured. Some of the older men, being stiff-necked, refused to mess their hands with clay and wax, making axehead, or knife-blade shapes, judging it fit employment for children. It was true, many of the children were more adept at making the moulds than their elders, being quicker of hand and imagination, but to the great indignation of the adults, Soft Axe decreed that the children should not be put to work in the foundry. This was regarded as subversive and unnatural, but I suppose the memories of his own childhood were too unpleasant. Disregarding the protests, he ordered the children to stay with the women, out of reach of the molten splashes and fierce heat.

The first productions of the new industry were laughable, misshapen, heated to the wrong temperature, poured carelessly into cracked moulds, or inefficiently hammered out by a beater who had ruined the blade's edge. Soft Axe wisely had this crop of failures destroyed, hurling them back into the fire to melt. He didn't want to ruin the reputation of his product at the outset. Word had spread of this new enterprise, and the other peoples of the area were waiting with keen interest to see if the new weapons would be as magical as the stories of the arrival of the Gold People had promised. Soft Axe's men had their properly made implements, traded from the visitors to show, and these excited the admiration and envy of all who saw them.

Gradually, the metal workers became more competent and goods fit to be traded were produced. They were still not of the quality found in the island to the West, but they were servicable. They were also fashionable, for the local young bloods had hit on the new weapons as a chic novelty. The market was buoyant. Soft Axe had not then established the reliability of supply of his raw materials, and sometimes used lead, a soft grey poisonous metal, as the second component of the alloy, instead of the more desirable tin. When the mixture was thus altered, the resulting metal was tender enough to take a toothprint, as had been the blade Soft Axe was carrying, when he came to my village.

"Why did you come?" I asked him. "Business was established at home, and starting to boom, your position was unquestioned. Why take on the hardships and dangers of a solitary journey to a distant country where the only thing on offer is a stone-craft that you intended to displace with your modern metal?"

Soft Axe stopped staring at the boat as it edged closer to the shore and looked at me for a moment. "Perhaps I came to find you," he said.

"Don't be ridiculous."

"Someone like you, then."

"In what respect?"

"Someone who was influential in the flint business, who might be persuaded that the time had come to change."

"You didn't persuade me," I pointed out. "Especially not with that half-baked sample you brought.

How did you expect to win any converts with a weapon that was easier to chew than some of the meals I've eaten?"

"I thought if I'd taken a sample of better quality than we could actually make, you would have been disappointed when you came to trade. Anyway, I was sure that axe would have been enough to impress you with."

"What a bunch of bumpkins you must have taken us for. It was rubbish."

"We make better ones now."

"Maybe you do, but I wasn't to know that."

"Yet you still made a journey of even greater danger and discomfort to come here and see for yourself," he pointed out.

"Market research."

"You accept the inevitable. Stone is on the way out."

"How do you grind your corn, crush your metal ore, beat out the edges of the blades?" I sneered.

"With stone."

"Well then, don't tell me it's a thing of the past. You still need it."

"Not as much as your people will need to abandon flint-knapping and become metal-workers, if you are not to be forgotten by history and swallowed up by the Beaker People."

"What if I took your crazy advice and turned a perfectly good, established business upside down, for the sake of a fad? We'd be rivals then."

"I don't fear a rival at the other end of the land," he said, staring out across the river again. "I stand to gain if you abandon stone-craft, because it will increase demand for metal. You must see that I have to ensure that these silly boys who have got a craze for metal weapons will never go back to the old ways."

"That's putting it bluntly."

"I can't force you to change, I can only present you with the idea and hope it takes root."

"And I can't subsidise three seasons of abject commercial failure with golden gratuities from the

Western island, while we learn metal-craft. My people wouldn't even recognise gold as valuable."

"I think they would," said Soft Axe, dreamily. "It seems to appeal to men's covetousness. Maybe it is magic."

"It doesn't do anything for me," I replied, tartly.

"You're just bloody-minded," he looked at me and smiled. "I've seen you, watching everything that goes on, down at the foundry. You could set up your own, back home, if you wanted to."

"If I did."

"Perhaps with a bit of technical support from me."

"You're not building a market, Soft Axe, it's an empire you're after. Why not settle for the good living you have here? Why go trying to meddle in the future of the flint-knappers?"

"Because if they have a future, metal-workers don't."

"Why should I help your grand plans?"

"Because you know it will come anyway," he suggested. "Because if you don't lead a change in the market, you have to follow it. And you know how unprofitable that can be."

"If it is all so inevitable, why try and chivvy my people into making the change now?"

"Of course it's inevitable," he sounded impatient. "It's inevitable that plants will grow in the summer. That doesn't mean you can't try and decide what grows where. I would rather have a crop of grain than a plain full of weeds."

"If I considered such a move, I wouldn't be doing it for your benefit."

"I know that. You will either ride this wave or be swept away by it. And I wouldn't be doing you any favours if I offered to help you get started. It would be to our mutual advantage."

"I'll think about it," I promised, "though I hope your miserable religion doesn't come with it."

He looked at me strangely, but said nothing, for other people from the fort came running up at that moment to watch the ship. Although I always spoke freely in front of Soft Axe, I had more sense than to pursue a conversation about the inadequacies of the local religion in public.

The people stood around chattering and pointing to the ship, exclaiming to themselves and speculating on the success of the journey. The steersman had brought the vessel to the edge of her depth, and had sent a boy ashore with a line, so that she could be hauled above the tide-mark. You know how it is with arrivals and departures, the one who waits stands foolishly poised with a smile and a wave that is finally abandoned because nothing has finished happening yet. A child was sent running back to the foundry to fetch spare men to help pull the boat in, and with their assistance the heavily laden craft was finally brought to ground.

The crew came ashore on infirm legs, a ragged, emaciated bunch with salt-caked hair. I gathered they had made a difficult voyage. Last to emerge over the side was a young man clutching a deerskin bag to his chest. He staggered up to Soft Axe and laid the bag at his feet. Soft Axe released the drawstring at its neck, and revealed, to the interested audience, a man's weight in gold. The crowed oohed and aahed and craned their necks to see the nuggets that lay at their leader's feet. Other, smaller bags, containing flakes of the same metal, were unloaded and laid in a pile on the ground. Soft Axe beamed.

"Is this why you were so anxious for the return of the ship?" I asked, amid the general hullabaloo.

"It bore a very precious cargo," he said, acknowledging the cheers of the populace. Not only were they suddenly rich, they were also getting a half-holiday from work, and everyone was in a carnival mood. The young man who had brought the first bag of treasure ashore looked pleased with himself; despite his dishevelment, he was obviously the leader of the crew. He received Soft Axe's congratulatory hug with a modest smile, and was carried up to the hill fort on the shoulders of two hefty metal-workers. Others carried the bags of gold in equal state, and with far more care. The whole procession wound its way up from the river, singing and shouting, which was as good a way as any of letting the women know that they should kill a pig or two and get a feast underway.

It was a good feast, even if the pork could have done with a bit of hanging, and everybody got agreeably (or argumentatively) drunk. Even the lads from the Beaker People's camp, who had come running up to see what the fuss was about, were allowed to share the food, although they took it away to eat somewhere else, to everybody's great social relief. The bard, a sodden rogue, began composing an epic song about the voyage. He was a tiresome old party, wrinkled and evil-minded, and had only survived being dropped off a cliff all these years because he had the dirt on everyone in the camp and could make scurrilous songs even about the powerful. Through his interminable, and inevitably scatological, verses. I learned the story of the expedition which had just returned, covered in such glory.

The young man who was the voyage-master was called Gull, because he crossed the seas. So did all the other men in the boat, I thought, but for some reason they had to make do with perfectly ordinary names. Perhaps they merely hauled on ropes and oars, while he alone could read the stars and the wind and know where they were going. Personally, I wouldn't go on any journey in a party of which only one member knew the way. What if he fell overboard? Anyway, Gull had been dispatched at the end of last winter with his boat and crew, to the Western Island to barter for more gold, which was rapidly becoming accepted as currency, this side of the water. Because the people of the Western Island were a great deal richer and more sophisticated than their visitors, they were not much impressed by the goods they were offered in trade. The elder of the Gold People, out of his goodwill for Soft Axe, accepted their proffered wares in exchange for some nuggets, only a few, but more than anyone else would have given them. He also had the kindness to suggest to Gull that his efforts would be better spent in prospecting for his own sources of gold.

The suggestion, although kindly made, came with a clear hint that the visitors would be foolish to tread on any local toes. Indeed, they had more sense than to start panning in any of the rivers of the Western Island for flakes of the treasure, for the gold-bearing streams were well known, and in the territory of jealous metal-hunters, the chief amongst which were their hosts. Then the helpful elder mentioned that he had heard that the land across the sea, on the mainland but to the North of the great river beside which Soft Axe's people lived, was rich in metals. Indeed, his own brother had once visited there, and swore that the hills were full of gold.

Now, at this point, I would have stopped to ask why the elder was being so damn helpful? If the mountains across the sea were indeed laced with gold, why was he not over there himself? It sounded to me as though he wanted to be rid of Gull, and hesitated, for some reason, to have the lad slain on the spot. Perhaps because Gull had brought greetings from Soft Axe, he thought it would be rather low. I wouldn't hesitate to have killed someone who announced their intention of setting up a flint mine to rival that of my own people, but we all have our own business ethics.

So Gull, of whose intelligence I did not, by this time, have a very good opinion, obediently jumped in his boat and headed east. To be fair, they could hardly have stayed in that country after such a hint. They were lucky that they had not suffered a more permanent warning-off. A sensible trader would have counted himself fortunate to have got anything out of the journey, and come home with a modicum of gold and his life. But there was a bravado about Gull and his companions, which made them point their prow at the mainland across the sea from the Western Island, and take their hunt up into the hills.

Even in my part of the world, I had heard of the Blue Stone people who lived in that country north of the river Sabrina. They picked their stones from the screes at the mountain foot and neither dug nor delved for them. I had even seen one of their axes once, not to be compared to a well-set flint, but good enough. I imagined that they would be about as receptive to the new metal age as my own people.

The men who had been on the trip had the best

places at the fire, and all, apart from Gull, who had vanished, were trying to tell the story at once, for the umpteenth time, as the bard spun his song. The babble of drunken voices, bragging and contradicting one another did not make for clarity, but they were the heroes of the hour, widely indulged, and the gist came through. The children crept near to the fire and listened open-mouthed, the ones who weren't asleep, their bellies stretched smooth with the unaccustomed feast, or being sick in the ditch.

Through the land of the Blue Stone People, the party had blundered (I put my own gloss on this) politely asking all and sundry if there was a hill of shining yellow metal in the vicinity. After a few of them got their heads broken for this blasphemous impertinence, they wised up a bit, and approached the matter more stealthily. Luckily for them, the country is thinly populated, and they managed to avoid further encounters with the Blue Stone People. In the middle of the mountains, they did indeed find a stream which washed over a rich seam of the precious metal, bearing pieces large and small which our heroes could easily recover. They stayed the whole summer, adding to their store, and unwilling to tear themselves away. Previously, they had had to get this valuable commodity at the charity of the Gold People. Now they had their own supply, for nothing (if you can call two seasons' hard labour nothing), ready to be plucked out of the earth. They felt very clever, and always stayed just one more day, in the hope of finding the nugget that would really make the people back home take notice.

The weather broke while they were still in the hills, and autumn set in with a vengeance, that same bitter weather through which I had struggled along the road. Encumbered by their heavy burden of metal, they slogged back towards the coast, without even any oxen to carry their loads. The Blue Stone People, who were backward, but not stupid, were waiting for them. If you must go looking for treasure in a strange land, you should at least have the sense to keep your mission quiet, and these boys had not. As a result of

174

the encounter, half the men of the party were killed or captured, and more than half the gold was lost. The survivors scrambled back to the cove where they had hidden their boat and put to sea, with their pursuers hot on their heels.

In their hurry, they failed to overhaul the boat as they should have done, having left it so long on the beach. It was only when they were well off the shore, with leaks springing here, and ropes parting there, that they realised their predicament. They had also failed to re-provision the craft, and were adrift with neither food nor water. Luckily the absence of their dead comrades compensated for the extra weight of the metal, but even so, the ship wallowed low in the water and waves broke over her side. To add to their miseries, a storm blew up and swept them all the way back to the Western Island. Their landfall was in the country of the Gold People, where they hid, in fear of their lives, trying to repair their vessel and waiting for the storm to abate. They might have been allowed to go once, but if they were found, skulking with a load of the gold in the very homeland of the chief producers of that substance there is no doubt what course commercial rivalry would have taken.

Eventually they managed to get afloat again, staying that way only with constant bailing, and the whole miserable, bedraggled crew strained to bring the boat home. They had been two full moons hiding on the coast of the Western Island. Three times they were swept by storms past the mouth of the sea channel into which the river Sabrina debouched. On one occasion, they were so close they could even see the smoke from the hill fort, but to no avail. If Soft Axe had been brooding at the look-out point that day, he must have thought them drowned, for they were swept north before a raging sea.

Painfully they worked their way back, losing two ship-mates en route and casting their bodies into the sea, for want of anywhere else to bury them. If I had had as little food on board as they did, I would have kept the bodies. Maybe they did. Then one day, when the autumn storms were past, a favourable winter wind blew them into the mouth of the channel and the rest you know already.

The people cheered the end of the story, and slapped the semi-comatose survivors on the back. I thought it a sorry tale of muddle and incompetence. While the men around me congratulated themselves that they were now masters of gold,and would soon make the Western Island look like a poverty-stricken backwater, I brooded. They were busy planning the ornaments they would make with their share of the treasure, the armbands and necklaces they would award themselves, and voting ever higher rewards to the returned sailors, none of which would be remembered in the morning. I thought of the Blue Stone People, in whose land this bounty lay. They may not have valued the precious metal before, but now they knew it was important enough to die for, they would reassess its worth. What was to stop them scooping up the harvest of the river bed and hillside, so that, by the time another foraging party bumbled into their land next summer, they would find an industry already established and a people ready to defend it? The Blue Stone people didn't even need to know about smelting, the gold was so soft it could be beaten into shape with their good stone tools. When the last carouser fell face forwards into the embers of the fire snoring, and his woman covered him with a rug and doused the cinders that were scorching the hair off his scalp, I took myself thoughtfully to bed.

I stumbled into the hut, my head full of business, and found Soft Axe closeted with Gull. I elbowed him aside and sat down heavily on my side of the bed.

"I'm debriefing Gull," said Soft Axe, at his most pompous and chieftainly.

"He went, he came back, what's to talk about?" I said grumpily. I must confess, I was a little fuddled. Not hog-snoring drunk, like the metal-workers and sailors, but my wits weren't fully about me.

"We're busy," insisted Soft Axe. Gull looked embarrassed.

"Go and be busy somewhere else then," I said, ungraciously.

"It is my hut," protested Soft Axe. "You might show a bit of respect."

"Try that on your pigeon-witted people," I grunted, rolling myself in my bed clothes.

"Please," Soft Axe changed his tone and wheedled. "Why don't you take a walk?"

"It's nearly dawn and I don't need the exercise."

"You could always stay in my sister's hut," he suggested, slyly.

"What?" I sat bolt upright "Are you proposing..?"

"I'm not stupid."

"People would talk."

"They wouldn't know what there was to talk about," he said. "Some things are so unmentionable, they become unimaginable. Go on, do me a favour. I want to talk to Gull." The young man blushed. Now he had tidied himself up a bit, I could see that he might be quite presentable if he weren't half starved. He looked, for my taste, rather too like a startled faun, with his big brown eyes, and shock of soft hair, but he was pretty, if you like that sort of thing.

"I'm not going to make a habit of it," I grumbled, trailing out of the hut with my bedding wrapped around me. "It's too dangerous."

"Thanks," Soft Axe held aside the door curtain for me, relieved. "Only this one night. And you don't have to tell anyone about it."

"I won't if you don't," I muttered, hoping that no-one else was awake to observe these goings on. "I don't have a fancy for being stoned to death, and I hope you don't either."

"Don't worry," he hitched the trailing blanket around my shoulders and sent me off with a pat on the back. "Discretion is the word."

FIFTEEN

Felicity woke with a start. The call of a hunting owl sounded close by the caravan, but it was not that which had woken her. She lay, snug under the duvet, with the silver light of a half-moon coming through the flimsy curtains, listening. The cat, curled up in a ball on top of the covers, pinned the bedclothes tightly against her side. Felicity strained her ears against the resumption of silence. She could hear nothing sinister, but her heart would not stop pounding. Perhaps she had woken herself with a vivid dream?

Climbing out of bed without disturbing the sleeping cat, she pulled on a sweatshirt, jeans and her boots with the steel toecaps, just in case. Stealthily she opened the door of the caravan and slipped out into the shadow of the cottage. Deeply though she had been asleep, it was not late, a few minutes past midnight, and the night air was still warm. Insects scraped, and from the pond came the croak of a frog. She brushed against the honeysuckle which draped the front of the house and its scent poured over her. As she was about to convince herself that she had been woken by a dream, she heard a crash from inside the house, and someone moving about rapidly on the ground floor. Without giving herself time to think, she strode round to the side door and into the scullery. "Who's there?" she called. Someone coughed. Wishing she had a torch, she advanced into the main room, her hand outstretched before her in the dark. Her searching fingers met a warm body and she jumped back with a suppressed shriek. The body pursued her out into the open, where it was revealed as belonging to Chalky's lurcher.

"Fluff!" she yelped. "What are you doing here?"

The dog sat on the lawn thumping the earth with his tail and grinning at her, shamefacedly.

"Stupid animal, what am I to do with you? I suppose you jumped out of the window while Chalky was at the pub. Why come here to do your ratting, wretched beast? Come on," she grabbed his broad leather collar, "we'd better get you home." With a spare length of rope from her building supplies, she improvised a lead, with which she dragged the errant hound to her car and opened the door for him. Fluffy firmly refused to get in so unnatural a contraption. Felicity got into the car and pulled, then got out again and pushed, but he was immovable.

"Now what?" she asked. "You can't sleep in the caravan, the cat would never forgive me. And if I tie you up out here, you'll probably howl all night." The dog dashed a warm, slobbery tongue across the back of her hand in confirmation. "Do I really have to walk you home?"

Fluffy, who had been leaning his great weight against her leg in a state of bliss as she scratched his neck, stood up straight and growled, his ears cocked forwards. There was a rumble of stones being crunched under tyres from further up the drive towards the road, although no car headlights were visible. For the second time that night, Felicity set off to investigate, her heart thumping, with the dog tugging at his lead.

They passed through the belt of trees and emerged onto the exposed track that ran between the two fields that fronted Hope Cottage. Coming from the road, slowly, secretively, was a car without lights, carrying four dimly seen passengers. Felicity froze in her tracks, but not before some movement of hers had alerted the approaching driver to her presence. He flicked on his headlights and she was dazzled by their beam. She threw up a hand to shield her eyes and Fluffy bristled, uttering a deep, menacing growl. From the open window of the car, she heard a young man's voice say "She got that bloody dog of Chalky's."

"You wanna mind his teeth, boy," cautioned another voice. Suddenly the car accelerated past Felicity, who jumped into the ditch to give it clear passage, made a great skidding turn by the old pigsty and came hurtling back at a speed which endangered its suspension. Felicity watched its departing tail lights for two miles up the dead straight road, listening to the fading roar of its engine. Shaken, she picked herself out the ditch, requested Fluffy to stop barking threats at the now-vanished car, and set off to walk to Chalky's house.

At the end of the drive she turned left onto the road towards Orfton-Saint-Scabious. The verges, which had been sprayed, were devoid of wild flowers, but Fluffy, tugging at his lead, ranging here and there, found fascinating smells in the ditches and culverts. In the moonlight everything assumed a different shade of grey, with more or less depth. Felicity trod up the centre of the road, shivering, wishing that she had put on a jacket in her hasty dressing. When he could be dragged away from the pursuit of small animals, Fluffy trotted beside her, his claws rattling on the tarmac. They had covered a quarter of a mile together, when Felicity became aware of footsteps on the road behind them, the soft tread of a man wearing rubber boots.

She turned and found herself facing Farmer Bruton, shotgun nestling in the crook of his arm.

"Good evening," she said, with a feeling of unreality.

"Is it?" he growled, coming closer and peering into her face. "You taken up poachin'?"

"What?" she goggled at him.

"What else'd you be doin' with a lurcher then? You been takin' birds off of my land?"

"This is a public road."

"And where you come from, before I was watchin' you? Out my field, I daresay. Got that bloody animal huntin' my pheasants."

"This is Chalky's dog, I'm taking him back."

"Ah, Chalky White," said Bruton, knowingly. "He's an old poacher. I've had to turn him off my farm before now. Teachin' you the tricks of the trade, is he?"

"I don't know what you're talking about."

"And I say, you're a trespasser and a poacher."

"I've never set foot on your land," said Felicity, hotly.

"What about my wife?"

180

"What about her?"

"You're set on turnin' her against me. I call that poachin'."

"I've never even discussed you with her."

"Up there, all hours," he continued, ignoring her denial. "Says she's workin' on that house of yours. Why should a woman wanna turn herself into a navvy? You should get a builder in and I should get my tea, and my kids looked after proper, 's what I say."

"Perhaps you should mention it to Shirley."

"Shirley is it?" he sneered. "Very matey. All girls together up there. You and my wife and that fat cow, Elspeth Maybe. Well, Elspeth may be, and you may be, but my wife won't be, I can tell you that for nothin'."

"I'm really not sure that I get your drift."

Bruton slipped a pair of cartridges into the breech of his gun, which was broken open over his arm, and snapped the barrel towards the stock. "I don't like you," he said, conversationally, pointing the gun at Felicity's stomach.

"I don't much care for you," she replied, feeling as though everything was moving very slowly. "But I'm not threatening your life."

"I've had one wife bunk off," he continued in the same light tone, which was belied by the pointed shotgun, "I won't stand for that again."

At Felicity's side, the dog stood quivering, every hackle raised, and a continuous growl rumbling in his throat. Although she could not believe that her own life was seriously endangered, she did not imagine that Bruton would hesitate to shoot the dog, should Fluffy spring to her defence. She patted the hairy head beneath her hand, and kept a tight grip on the lead.

"That dog'd have my throat out," said Bruton, reading her thoughts. "Maybe I should shoot him now, as a lesson to poachers."

"If you don't stop playing cowboys, I'll report you to the police, and you'll loose your shotgun licence."

Bruton laughed, "Go on then, there's a policehouse 'bout a mile down the road. You trot along and make your report. Daresay my brother-in-law'll be right interested. 'Course, when I tell him you was poachin', it'll be a different story."

"Nobody's going to believe I'm a poacher. I don't even eat meat."

"They'd believe anything about incomers, round here. There's enough townies takin' up old country ways. Corn dollies, poachin', it's all the same. We're just extras in a rural theme park to you lot."

"I'm not going to stand here all night listening to your paranoid delusions," said Felicity more calmly than she felt. "I'm going to leave now, and if you shoot me, I daresay the dog will kill you and if you shoot the dog, I shall certainly take the matter up with the police, whatever you may say about family influence."

"That's a brave speech," said Bruton, coming nearer with a grin of singular unpleasantness on his face. "Are you so brave?"

As though in a dream, Felicity observed the farmer take another step towards her, his gun going before him, heard the sudden commotion of two dogs barking furiously at each other and saw a giant of a man, six and a half feet tall, and broad in proportion, loom out of the darkness and clap a hairy hand on Bruton's shoulder. Her adversary spun round and looked up into the eyes of the man who towered over him, greasy hair brushing across his forehead and right fist clenched and raised under Bruton's nose. The new-comer's dog, another lurcher, hurled insults at his rival, Fluffy. From the capacious pockets of the stranger's old tweed jacket protruded the hind paws of two dead rabbits and a partridge's head, flopping on a broken neck.

The big man plucked the shot-gun from Bruton's unresisting grasp, ejected the cartridges and wedged the barrel in the fork between the trunk and branch of an oak tree which grew by the road. With three great wrenches, using the tree as a vice, he bent the barrel and returned the useless gun to its owner. Felicity recognised a variation on her own approach to Bruton junior in similar circumstances, and wondered that the farmer did not protest. The dogs were still clamouring at each other when the stranger, resuming his grip on Bruton's shoulder, spun him around to face in the direction of his farm gate and gave him a shove to get him moving.

"Bugger you, Randolph, they should never have let you out," cursed Bruton, but went obediently home.

Randolph extracted a tobacco tin from his waist-coat pocket and rolled a cigarette with one hand, controlling his agitated dog with the other. With a grunt, he offered the tin to Felicity, and although she didn't normally smoke, she felt that these were exceptional circumstances, and she didn't want to give offence by refusing. Surmising that this must be Bruton's peculiar cousin, she hoped that she had not leaped from the frying pan to the fire in the personal safety stakes.

Without much further conversation, her enormous companion began walking towards the village, indicating that he would accompany her on her journey. The dogs were more or less quiet, but had to be kept apart, so the two of them walked on either side of the road. Randolph hummed to himself, a melody that Felicity was surprised to recognise as coming from the Trout Quintet. They reached the bend in the road where Chalky's cottage was situated and Randolph vanished into his own adjoining house, without saying good-night. Breathing a sigh of relief, Felicity set about trying to rouse Chalky from his drunken slumbers by banging on the door.

****

After shopping in Norwich, Shirley Bruton and Elspeth Maybe repaired to a tea-shop for a reviving drink. Their purchases were safely stowed in the boot of Shirley's car in the multi-storey and there were forty minutes still on the ticket. Although it was a blazing summer day outside on the crowded and dusty pavements, the interior of the tea-shop was air-conditioned and sheltered from the sunlight. Despite the dimness, Shirley seemed reluctant to remove her sun-glasses. Elspeth chattered enthusiastically about the recently restored Dragon Hall, which she thought they ought to visit, but Shirley would not be tempted.

"I can't be doin' with the past," she said. "All that history's a waste of time."

"But it's our heritage!" Elspeth was affronted.

"Merchant's hall, innit?"

"Thirteenth century," affirmed Elspeth.

"Then it ain't my heritage, 'cos six hundred years ago, I'm sure my people was peasants, not merchants. And yours was probably serfs, if they had serfs in Ealing."

"It's still our common inheritance, no matter what individual owned it at the time. After all, it's the labour of the poor workers which made places like that beautiful, as much as the wealth of the great people who commissioned the building."

"'sloada bollocks," muttered Shirley. "My gramps was the boot boy up at the big house th'other side of Scabious. They woulda set the dogs on him, if he ever showed his face at the front door. Not that he would, 'cos he knew his place. And now, I can walk in the front way, tread on the great staircase, even if the have got a drugget over the good carpet, and bounce on the bed that old Queen Elizabeth slept in, if no one's looking. And what for?"

"Because times have changed."

"For one pound fifty, because they need my money so they can go on living there. We paid with our sweat to build the place, and now we got to pay an entrance fee to keep 'em in the style to which our grandparents accustomed them."

"But they aren't living in that style at all," protested Elspeth. "I believe the young couple who have Crampton Hall now treat it very much as a job of work, displaying the place. You should think of them as resident caretakers."

"So why didn't they get the grandson of the housekeeper, or the stable boy to live in the place then? They'd know more about caretaking."

"Oh dear, we do seem to be on difficult ground. I've always thought it rather added to the interest of the place, if the descendants of the original family still lived in the house."

"That's because you never thought about it properly at all." Shirley slammed down her cup on her saucer and sent a small tidal wave of tea slopping over the side. There was a hurt silence across the tablecloth.

"I'm sorry if I've outraged your feelings on the subject," said Elspeth eventually, in a small, tight voice. "But I do think that was uncalled for."

"Don't be so prissy," snarled her companion.

"Shirley, what on earth is the matter? You've been strange all afternoon."

"So, I'm in a foul mood. So what?"

"It's not like you."

"Shows how much you know about anything."

"I know that you aren't usually gratuitously unpleasant. What's the matter?"

"Nothin'."

"I do wish you would take those sun-glasses off. I can't see anything except my own reflection in them."

Shirley growled. With great daring, Elspeth reached across the table and removed the offending shades.

"Spot the difference," Shirley remarked. "Two lovely black eyes." They were indeed dark purple and puffy, one completely closed, and the other swollen but half open. The visible eyeball was full of blood, and broken veins trickled down each cheekbone. A sticky yellow gum oozed from the tear ducts, encrusting the eyelashes.

"My god!" Elspeth was aghast. "What happened?"

"Walked into a door," Shirley shrugged, putting her sun glasses back on.

"Do I know the name of the door?"

"You have been introduced,"

"It looks terrible."

"Thanks."

"I mean it looks painful. Does it hurt a lot?"

"There has been days in my life when I felt better," admitted Shirley.

"You must think I'm very stupid, not to have realised before. I thought you weren't yourself today. Do you mind me asking why this happened?"

Shirley shrugged again and played with the sugar in

the bowl. "He come in late, after midnight, in a wicked mood. I made the mistake of asking him what he been doin'. You can see what happened then."

"Is that it?"

"I didn't expect too much of an explanation, really."

"Has this happened before?" Elspeth asked. Shirley made a non-committal gesture. "Don't you have any idea why?"

"Jealousy, I s'pose. Fear of losing what's his. The first wife, she tried to divorce him for cruelty, but he got a better lawyer, and divorced her for adultery. That's how he got custody of the kids."

"I thought she ran off and left the kids."

"That's his story. And the kids believe it. Chalky saw him drive her off the place at gunpoint, though, with the kids asleep with half a bottle of rum in their bedtime milk. She had her fancy man in Lowestoft, alright, but she weren' plannin' on leavin' Donny and Phoebe behind when she done her flit."

"I never knew."

"Her mistake was in thinkin' that he didn't know what she was about. He's a watchful bugger though, and he's got friends, god knows how. He saw what she was at and beat her to the drop."

"He sounds like a monster, I had no idea."

"He's no worse'n many others. Least there's no way you could call him a wimp."

"Is that so important?"

"I've no time for those men always leaning on their wives. Great big overgrown toddlers. I'd rather one with a bit of a temper than a long drink of water in trousers."

"But why should your husband be jealous?" Elspeth was puzzled. "You don't have a fancy man, do you. Oh," she blushed, "I didn't mean to be nosey."

"Don't worry, Elspeth," Shirley patted her hand, "you'd know if I did, and I ain't."

"So why should he hit you?"

"Partly 'cos he don't approve of me goin' over to Hope Cottage to help Felicity with her buildin'. He don't think a woman should have interests outside her home and kids. Reckons it might give her dangerous ideas."

"I knew that had been an issue between you. But

why now, when you've stopped spending so much time there?"

"Any time at all's too much for his taste. But also, he was provoked last night, and I just happened to be in the way."

"Provoked by what? Or whom? You're not blaming yourself, surely?"

"I'm not so soft. Listen," she lowered her voice conspiratorially, although no one in the busy tea shop was taking any notice, "I heard him talkin' with Jimmy Sturgess this morning in the yard."

"That obnoxious young man with the medallions who drives your tractors?"

"That's him. He said him and some of his mates went down Hope Cottage last night, after the pub shut. God knows what they was thinkin' of doin'. But they met Felicity comin' up the drive with Chalky's dog, and so they took themselves off."

"Oh dear, how worrying."

"Then Bruton says, yes he's seen Felicity after they left, walkin' along the road. He must of known they was goin' down hers, 'cos he was in the pub last night, and why else would he have been wandering about the road in the middle of the night?"

"I hope there wasn't any unpleasantness."

"He tells Jimmy Sturgess he give Felicity a proper fright, they was gigglin' over it like a pair of boys with a skin mag. Then Randolph, that's his mad cousin, comes buttin' in, and he has to let Felicity go. That's what made him furious, so he come in and thumps me, straight after. There's no love lost between those two."

"But why should he be trying to frighten Felicity? I don't understand."

"She's a stranger, she's a woman, she's doin' up her house without givin' the local lads any work," Shirley built a little wall of sugar cubes and knocked it down with a swipe of her teaspoon.

"Why should it bother your husband, or Jimmy Sturgess. They wouldn't have wanted the work anyway?"

"Solidarity. Anyway, I learned another reason, why he wants her out."

"What's that?"

"He told Jimmy that he made an offer on the cottage, through the old woman's solicitor, before Felicity had come down. I didn't know, of course, he don't tell me about the business."

"What would he do with a cottage?"

"She's doin' it up to live in, he would've bought it cheap, slapped it into shape cheap and flogged it off as a holiday cottage, or a commuter house."

"But," Elspeth protested, "I thought the bottom had fallen out of the housing market? I thought where we live is too ugly and inconvenient for holiday makers and commuters?"

"So it would've been a bargain. You may not be able to sell a sheep pen for fifty thousand and more these days, but he would've found someone who'd take a nice little modernised cottage, secluded, rural setting, undiscovered part of Norfolk. They'd think they were getting the jump on the rest of the crowd, and even if it didn't get what it would if it was in the Broads, he'd still clear thousands on the deal. He never could resist quick bulk cash, didn't you know?"

"It must be obvious to him by now that Felicity won't sell."

"He hates her though," sighed Shirley. "He's mixing business and resentment. There's a lot of his father in him, by all accounts. He'd want her out, even if there was no profit in it for him, and he also blames her for losing the money he would've made on the sale, same as if she'd broken into his safe and taken the cash from him."

"That's very unreasonable," protested Elspeth.

"I didn't know he had his eye on Hope Cottage since the old woman died, though I should've guessed. It's bad enough Felicity wouldn't sell, but with me over there, helping to settle her in, that was like addin' injury to insult."

"He should have explained his objection to you from the outset," said Elspeth, indignantly. "If you had known it was for business reasons, surely you would have been more compliant?"

"I don't know as I would," Shirley rubbed her aching head. "Anyway, he wanted it kept secret, that it was him making the offer. Perhaps he didn't trust me not to go gossiping with Felicity. He knows she'd never sell to him, not if she knew."

"If he's so concerned about secrecy, I'm surprised he should chat about the business with one of his farmhands."

"Oh, him and Jimmy's thick as thieves," Shirley said, carelessly. "You got any painkillers on you? My head's thumpin'."

"Poor Shirley," Elspeth rummaged in her bag and produced two foil wrapped tablets. "Should I take you to the doctor? You might be concussed. I'm sure you should be resting."

"I'll be alright."

"You certainly shouldn't be driving. Really, it can't have been safe, you driving us in with only half a bleary eye to look out of and a head like a jackhammer. You must let me drive us home."

"It's a good thing I didn't tell you sooner, or you would never've let me come at all."

"No, I wouldn't. You should be asleep in a darkened room with an ice pack, or a pound of raw steak on your face."

"Ugh," Shirley shuddered. "I feel too much like tenderised beef to look a real dead cow in the eye. And headache or no, I needed to get out of the house."

"You could always have come round to me and had a lie down on the sofa. Archibald wouldn't mind."

"Bruton would've. I'm afraid he don't hold with you much more'n he do with Felicity."

"Why on earth not?" Elspeth puffed up, affronted, like a pigeon about to croon. "I've never offended his dignity or thwarted his business interests."

"I think," said Shirley, watching the pain-killers dissolve in a glass of water, "and it's a strange thing for a woman to have to say of her own husband, but I think that he don't like women. On the whole."

"You know you can always come and stay with me, if you want a break," said Elspeth. Shirley smiled gratefully, but shook her head. "What should we do about Felicity? Is she in danger? Perhaps the police should be asked to keep an eye out for her."

"The police round there's my useless brother Vincent. He don't know his dick from his truncheon. You'll find him in the White Stag, havin' afters any night you care to look, 'cept it'd be closing time to the likes of you. Bruton gets on better with Vincent than I do, so I don't think he'd be a lot of help to Felicity, poor love."

"We must do something, surely."

"She'll be alright," Shirley said, offhandedly. "They're just trying to scare her away. You got to be married to a woman to get away with hitting her."

"I'm sorry, I didn't mean to seem insensitive."

"Don't worry. We better be goin' now, or there'll be another hour to pay on the car park. Shirley drained her tea-cup, checked her appearance in the mirror of a powder compact and stood up.

SIXTEEN

Felicity remained unaware of the reason for the nocturnal disturbances which she had suffered, even when Elspeth returned to Hope Cottage, the day after her trip to Norwich. She had been sworn to silence by Shirley about Bruton's interest in the property. Elspeth was torn, for the information would surely have eased some of Felicity's fears, by making them more explicable, but a promise was a promise. She kept quiet, but she was worried. Archibald would say she was interfering, no doubt, and between man and wife at that, a heinous offence, but she didn't want either of her friends to be threatened or hurt.

Unaware of Elspeth's dilemma, Felicity made no mention of the events of the night before last. She had not been able to rouse Chalky, who was comatose when she returned the dog, so she had simply shut Fluffy in the kitchen and walked home. The solitary journey back along the dark lanes had terrified her, but nothing more alarming than stepping in the remains of a run-over rabbit had befallen her, although that sickening skid on spread-out intestines had surprised a small scream from her overstretched nerves.

By daylight, her fears seemed absurd. As she dug up the kitchen floor, aware of the muscles bunching in her back and the solid weight of the pick in her hands, she was able to feel quite capable of defending herself. She dug out the kitchen floor, where she would lay a proper concrete replacement, with damp proof membrane and an even screed, while Elspeth pottered distractedly amongst her petunias. On a blazing hot June day, the cool damp darkness of the inside of the house made a pleasant workplace. At lunch time, she emerged from the interior, blinking in the sunshine, like a crab at low tide.

Elspeth tried to drop hints about the hostility of the local lads, in such a way as to elicit from Felicity the story of her midnight ramble, but Felicity was resolutely refusing to be drawn on an episode which she was determined to relegate to the trivial in her own mind. The hints, in any event, were so constricted by Elspeth's duty of confidentiality to Shirley, as to be completely obscure.

By the beginning of the next week, Felicity had completely excavated the ground floor, and was ready to pour concrete into the resulting cavity. She had designed, with great ingenuity, and no practical help from the Bible according to G.P. Turvey, a run of pipes from a back boiler which could be worked off the Rayburn to the bathroom and scullery. The hot water would not be plentiful but at least, some time in the future, she might be able to wash in the winter months without risking her life to pneumonia.

"This is going to be a two woman job, at least," she told Elspeth, as they sat on the lawn, she calculating cubic metres of concrete on the back of an envelope, and her friend lost in a seed catalogue.

"Is it, dear?" said Elspeth absently.

"Yes, it is. Do you think Shirley might be persuaded to help?"

Elspeth suddenly began to attend to the conversation. "I'm sure she's very busy," she said, repressively.

"Still having trouble with her husband?"

"She can't spend all her time over here."

"I haven't seen her for ages."

"I'm sure she'd come if she wanted to," Elspeth tried to close the subject. Although she longed to discuss Shirley's predicament, Elspeth was an honourable woman.

"Speak of the devil," said Felicity, unaware of the moral struggle being waged in Elspeth's breast. Shirley drove up, jumped out of her car and came round to open the passenger door.

"I went to take Chalky his library books, and the old fool says he wants to come up here on a visit," she called cheerfully across the garden hedge. "So here we both are." She wore sun-glasses still, but on a hot day this was not remarkable. Chalky clambered out of the car, accompanied by Fluffy. The cat fled screeching up a tree.

"Why wouldn't you go in a car with me, you old rascal?" asked Felicity, pulling the dog's ears.

"He sit on my lap," explained Chalky, subsiding into the deckchair which Elspeth set out for him.

"But he's bigger than you. Why don't you sit on his lap?"

Chalky chortled, and Elspeth covertly observed her friend, whom she had not seen since their shopping trip. Shirley smiled at her reassuringly and Elspeth was glad that she had maintained her confidence, tempted though she had been to tell Felicity.

"Shirley, you're just in time," Felicity was saying, "I need to do a concrete pour, and I can't manage on my own. One load would be set before I could mix another one, if I don't have some help. Can I interest you?"

"I could do tha'" wheezed Chalky.

"No you couldn't," said Felicity, firmly. "I'm not burying you in the foundations for a good luck charm."

"This house int go' no foundations," said Chalky, scornfully.

"Yes, we have no foundations," sang Felicity, who was in high spirits, "We have no foundations today. Anyway, Shirley, would you be so kind?"

"Don't see why not," said Shirley, with a trace of hesitation that was not lost on Elspeth.

"You shouldn't force her, Felicity" she remonstrated. "Shirley can't just drop everything to play on your building site you know."

"It's alright, " Shirley asserted, "I'd like to. I'll come tomorrow mornin' after the kids're off."

"Great," Felicity, thinking of nothing but her cottage, beamed upon Shirley. It is hard to be sensitive to the feelings of others when in the grip of an obsession, and Shirley did really seem quite willing. "Let me show you the layout."

* * * * * * * * * *

She is prone to happiness, this one. It bursts upon her, and she basks in it, forgetting that life was ever other than joyful. Tomorrow may be another story, for she is up and down in her feelings, like the sun in the sky, although not so well regulated. Why are happy people described as having a sunny disposition? It is in the nature of the sun to give way to darkness, that is the one thing you may safely predict. Are good-natured people merely waiting to fall into the night time of their own displeasure?

Felicity is happy today, despite the frights of the other night. She suspects, but is not sure, that she is in danger. There are a number of interpretations that may be put upon the visit of the lads in the car, and the behaviour of Bruton, none of them sanguine, but perhaps they were isolated incidents, not to be repeated.

Shirley knows there is danger, and has shared with Elspeth her fears for Felicity's safety. Shirley knows best of all how real is the threat, but she has instigated this conspiracy of silence. In this way, she protects herself from the knowledge of the harms that might come to her. I have no illusions, myself. When enemies become so bold as to show their faces, as they did the other night, it is only a matter of time. Does she realise that she will have to fight for this home which she is building? I think not. She believes that ownership is secured on paper, rather than in the flesh.

Chalky may also be aware of what has occurred. It is possible that he knows the farmer's mad cousin rather well, they have lived one thin wall apart for half a lifetime at least. I naturally suspect one who has survived so long, with a lame leg and no powerful friends, of being possessed of a very acute instinct for danger. How else does one account for the survival of fieldmice, when the mammoth, with all his strength, is long since failed?

Danger gathered about us, like gnats around a tallow dip, that winter after the ship returned. Soft Axe had been number one cheese among his people for so long by then, that he believed himself above censure. Or he loved to court danger, for the boredom of being chief executive of a rapidly expanding business was lowering his spirits. Maybe he was simply too bent on having a good time to consider the risks.

The first night, when, as I have admitted, I was slightly fuddled, he could persuade me to go to Green Eyes' hut. Not that there was anything very remarkable in me stumbling about the camp trailing my blankets behind me and winding up in the wrong hut, for half the village was rat-arsed that night, and doing much the same themselves. She wasn't particularly pleased to see me, being caught fast in a sober sleep. Not being a drinker, she had little patience with my whirling head and foul breath. Nor was she keen to share her living space, even for the night. I have never known a woman who has to have all her bits and pieces just so, and looks on another body in her bed as a disarrangement of the proper order of things. Green Eyes was never going to sacrifice her comfort for passion. I should have realised, but I was alone in a strange land and half way to being in love by then.

I was permitted to stay that night, and having been admitted, however begrudgingly, to her bed, I hoped to make the best of it. Green Eyes wouldn't hear of such a thing. Apart from the fact that she had been woken up, and was cross, and I was drunk and smelly, she didn't want the neighbours to know. Well, I thought that was taking discretion a bit far. Wild though our loving was, I doubt if it would have shaken the hut down, and anything less would not have been noticed on a night like that. Still, she was adamant, and I soon passed out.

When I awoke in the morning, with a head like the bottom of a cesspit, and an atmosphere in the hut as unpleasant as the one in my mouth, Green Eyes was already up, and had been out. She was also furious. I would have pretended to be still asleep, but if I didn't have a pitcher of cold water to pour down my parching throat straight away, I thought I would die. Stealthily, I reached a hand out from under the covers for the water jug on the floor. Green Eyes spotted the movement and pounced.

"Why didn't you tell me what Soft Axe was up to last night?" she demanded, her splendid emerald eyes flashing.

"Didn't I mention it?" I said evasively, burying my

face in the jug. Water dripped down my chin and splashed onto my naked stomach as I drained the container.

"No you didn't. And if you had I would have been straight over there and told him not to be so stupid. He'll get us all killed."

Was this a justified fear, I asked myself? Green Eyes' fortunes were closely tied to those of Soft Axe, as were mine. Although I knew that theirs was a strange and barbaric people, with unnatural customs and odd attitudes to couplings, I had never taken the need for secrecy as seriously as Green Eyes. While I assumed that all the women in the fort had lovers, but that convention demanded they pretend to be attached to men, Green Eyes had a genuine horror of the truth being known. I wondered if this distaste extended to our encounters, although she gave every sign of being an enthusiast for those. A woman so divided, I thought sadly, would be a ripe candidate for conversion to the dreary new religion, which seemed to thrive on self-hatred and denial of womanly joys. Then she kissed me, admittedly a distracted peck on the cheek, but I pulled her into bed with me and forgot my doubts.

"What are we to do?" she asked, disentangling herself from my embrace. "Soft Axe may think he can indulge his every whim, but he can't."

"Is this a whim?"

"He's always had the hots for Gull," she said, bitterly. "People would have started to talk, if the wretched boy hadn't been sent off on that stupid adventure."

"From which he wasn't, I take it, supposed to return."

"I wish he hadn't," she said savagely. "Oh, he's pretty enough, I'll grant you that, but nothing in his head at all. Look at the way he managed that trip, losing half his company, and bumbling about from shore to shore, like a chicken in a ring."

"Aren't you being a little hard on him?" I asked.

"He could ruin everything."

"I did try and talk Soft Axe out of it," I said in my

defence, although I could not remember whether or not I had.

"You must go back to his hut and get rid of Gull."

"Now?" I protested, "I've only just woken up."

"Then you must do it before everybody else is astir."

"Come and have a cuddle first."

"No, I must get to work."

"Oh go on, Greenie," I enticed, "the corn can wait. No one's going to be working today, surely?"

"The women will," she said snappishly, "you can bet on that. Go and sort my brother out. He listens to you."

"Not that I'd ever noticed. What if they're busy?"

"Interrupt them."

"No wonder you're sending me to do this."

"Just get on with it." She bundled me out of the hut, head athrob and dignity rather frayed. There were few signs of life around the camp, although the fires were smoking, and I could smell cooking. My stomach rose protestingly.

Soft Axe and Gull were, I was glad to find, asleep. I shook Soft Axe, who was lying on his back wearing a fatuous grin, by the shoulder to wake him.

"What is it?" he grunted blearily, opening one eye.

"Time to wake up and act normal," I said, with a joviality I was far from feeling.

"What?" he sat up, rubbing his head. Gull snored on at his side.

"Green Eyes says you've got to stop this nonsense and send Gull away."

"Oh, she does, does she?" he eyed me wrathfully. "Why doesn't she come and tell me this herself?"

"Because she has more sense," I said. "Why risk getting her own head broken, when she can volunteer mine instead?"

"She's got a nerve," grumbled Soft Axe. "And so have you come to that. Where did you spend last night, I'd like to ask?"

"Where you sent me. In a depressingly chaste bed, as it happens."

"Talk about the goat calling the dung heap smelly,"

he grumbled. "Wake up, Gull," he nudged his sleeping companion in his protuberant ribs. "There's someone here come to see about your morals."

"It is time he went," I said, seriously. "Some of the people are up and about already, and the rest won't be insensible for ever."

"Oh alright," said Soft Axe, crossly. "Out you go, bonny lad."

"Where am I supposed to go?" enquired Gull, sleepily.

"Go down to the river and have a swim. That should wake you up."

"I can't swim."

"Fine sailor you are," said Soft Axe. "Go and get some food in your skinny belly then." Gull crawled out of bed and departed, with a slap on the rump from Soft Axe to hurry him into his clothes. I sat myself down on the bed in his place, hugging my knees to my chest and trying to persuade my fuddled brain to work.

"What are you going to do?" I asked.

"After two seasons of celibacy, what do you think?"

"Your sister is worried."

"She's so hidebound."

"This is a very hidebound community. And apart from me, she's the only one around who wouldn't have you and Gull put to death for this carry-on."

"It would be worth it," he grinned, stretching out luxuriously in his bed, "for one night with him."

"Don't be silly, nothing is worth getting killed for."

"Such a pragmatist," he sighed. "Don't you get a thrill from danger?"

"Nothing compared to the one I get from safety."

"I don't believe you, but never mind. What do you and my cautious sister suggest?"

"That you don't get caught."

"How?"

"Can't you take him off on a hunting trip," I suggested. "Then you can rut all round the forest without being seen."

"Fine," he said, "and then what? We can't stay out in the forest forever, it's nearly mid-winter. I have ceremonies to conduct, a business to run. It's hard, being the head man."

"Don't make me cry. Wouldn't you be satisfied with a fling?"

"No," he said, decidedly.

"Oh dear. We'll have to think of something."

We sat half the morning, trying to make plans. One of the children brought us a bowl of stew, grinning all over her face as she left it by the door. I gathered that the wild cries of the troublesome Gull had been mistaken for mine, an idea which I found excessively distasteful. At length, Soft Axe decided that Gull would have to be paired up with Green Eyes, to allay suspicion, and she was summoned to the hut to confer with us.

I had thought that she would reject her brother's suggestion out of hand, but to my surprise she announced that it offered protection to them both, and that she would go along with it. I think there ought to be limits as to how far concealment should go, but she was happy to pretend. I did not mention to her that Soft Axe's original idea had been that I should assume a connection with Gull, so that he might have an excuse to stay in Soft Axe's hut, an idea which I had vetoed immediately. The plan was agreed. Gull would move into Green Eyes' hut and Soft Axe would be able to slip down there at night, no-one would think it odd if he were to visit within his own family. Green Eyes might, on these occasions, exchange places with her brother and come to me in Soft Axe's hut. She might, but I doubted if she would, one risk at a time was more than enough for her. How she could tolerate the notion of accommodating a man in the jealously guarded solitude of her home was beyond me, but she accepted even this, in the interest of deceiving the people of the fort. I thought the whole business was crazy, and said so.

Gull was called, and naturally agreed to the plan. I say 'naturally' because I could not envisage him disputing any suggestion made by Soft Axe. He was indeed rather empty-headed, although swelled with the importance of his role as hero of the hour.

Remembering Green Eyes scathing assessment of his character, I wondered that she thought herself capable of dissimulating her contempt for him.

We then embarked upon a dangerous charade, whose dangers grew with the proportions of the deception. I have never felt as close to madness as I did that winter. Green Eyes worried, but felt her position enhanced by her newly acquired man. Gull went along with the game, rather noxiously pleased with himself to think that he was pulling a fast one on the stupid metal-workers, whose beefy orthodoxy he seemed to find both fascinating and repulsive. I stayed, because it was winter and I could not leave, and maintained the pretence, because to do otherwise was to forfeit all our lives. It was Soft Axe who loved the pretence for its own sake. The more convoluted and precarious grew the drama, the more his eyes shone and his appetite for acting grew. He was like one possesed, rushing on to his fate. I wondered if he would have stayed with Gull above two nights, if there had not been so strong a prohibition against it. I began to carve charms for my own safety, and visit the caves alone to address the Goddess on the subject of survival.

Green Eyes and Gull paraded about the place, the simulacrum of a happy young couple. It turned my stomach, but the people did not detect the counterfeit. I heard more than one man say behind his hand that Green Eyes had always been a tight-arsed, superior bitch, and it was time she took a tumble. Gull's already high popularity increased even further for having tamed a lass who had thought herself too good for any man.

Winter had a grip on the country, snow fell. If the river hadn't been so full of salt from the sea, it might have frozen. The people hung about the camp, with little employment, moaning about the weather. What did they know about cold? In my country, where the Easterly wind tears across the flat landscape, bearing shards of ice to pierce your heart and withering the cattle where they stand, huddled with their rumps to the gale, there is a real winter. Here, in the soft

Western hills, there was still green grass under the snow.

My aim at the time was to be unobtrusive, as a long-staying visitor should, especially when she is part of a conspiracy to make fools of her hosts. I spent less time watching the metal-workers. There was always a crowd of idlers hanging about down at the furnace, cadging warmth. Green Eyes, having won the approval of all and sundry, by her apparent pairing with Gull, I hardly ever saw alone. She stopped her visits to the cave in the hills, saying it was too cold, and the days too short, to be frolicking about in the back country with me. Sometimes she sneaked into my bed, when Soft Axe was in hers, with Gull, but so tense and anxious was she on these visits, so fearful of discovery, that I began to wish she would stay away.

SEVENTEEN

I roamed the country more widely than ever, keeping a wary eye out for bands of the Beaker People, either the domesticated variety who lived with Soft Axe's people, or the wild sort. In the cave, where Green Eyes and I had been used to worship the Goddess, and each other, I began to accumulate a store of food and other necessities, like a mouse after harvest. The cave was set high up in the hillside, its mouth overhung by concealing rock, approached by a scree slope in whose broken snow footsteps did not show. At the back of the cave was a natural cistern made by the dripping of water from above. Every time I set off for one of my solitary rambles, I took something, a bag of cornmeal, or salt, small enough to be hidden about my person. On my way to the cave, I collected a stick here and there, slowly building a store of firewood. The people of the fort were so used to my wanderings, they took no notice.

Apart, that is, from Little Moon, child of the daughter of the last medicine woman, now displaced by one of Soft Axe's overweening priestlings. By some ill-chance during her carrying or birth, Little Moon had emerged into the world without all her wits. She had her name from her face, which was round and smooth, with heavily lidded, bulging eyes. Her stomach also bulged, with the belly button pushed outwards, for one of Little Moon's deficiencies was that she never knew when her gut was full, and always wanted more food. Although five summers old, and sturdy with it, she had never learned to speak, and her nature was that of an overgrown baby.

Poor Little Moon, always hungry and not entitled to a share of the common pot. The elders had decreed it a waste to feed her, as she would not live past ten. Having made their decree, the elders more or less forgot about the child, or they might have wondered how she grew so stout on no rations. Her mother fed her, of course, sharing her own portion, and happily sated adults might sometimes throw her their leavings, as she scurried about the fire, her big round eyes blank, but her nose twitching. Mainly she survived by being an accomplished sneak thief. I don't know how she did it, for her movements were uncoordinated, and her peculiar face, with its loose, drooling mouth was instantly recognisable, but if anything edible was left unwatched for more than an instant, Little Moon would have it.

I didn't notice her attach herself to me, but she began to follow me on my trips away from the hill fort. I tried to discourage her, for I would not go to the cave when anyone might see, even if only a brainless child, but she was determined. If I sent her away, she followed five paces behind me, or out of stone's throw, if I was really angry. Little Moon was used to dodging flying stones and fists, being chased with blows whenever she was caught thieving. She must have reckoned it worth the risk, if she was capable of calculating such things, because she had always swallowed her booty before the outraged victim could recover it. No-one could eat a rabbit as fast as Little Moon.

She appeared one day, as I was leaving the hill fort, trotting at my heels and smiling all over her well-fleshed face. It was not a day on which I had planned to visit the cave, so I tolerated her company, chatting away to her, unsure whether she understood a single word. I began on my repertoire of bird calls and animal noises, for I had always been a good mimic. She greeted this performance with gurgles of delight, and it shows you how lonely I was at the time, that even such appreciation as hers could gratify me.

I was hunting hedgehogs that day, a delicacy where I come from, but Soft Axe's people would no more eat one than they would consume a toasted rat. Despite Little Moon's help, which was of the bumbling and obstructive kind, I unearthed two fat hedgehogs from their winter slumber in the forest litter. I kindled a fire and set Little Moon to feed it with dry branches, while I dug a pit. When there were sufficient glowing embers to line the pit, I put the hedgehogs in to cook, and covered the whole with earth.

Little Moon was fascinated by the construction of the oven, and when we broke it open that afternoon, digging out the baked contents, she indicated her willingness to help me eat the hedgehogs. I had not imagined it would be otherwise. We passed a pleasant day, and I almost forgot the feeling of impending disaster which hung over me during every waking hour and invaded my sleep with anxious dreams.

The child began to follow me every time I left the village. Sometimes I wished she would leave me alone, but I had no way of making her. She refused to understand instructions, and I knew her to be careless of blows. When I wanted to visit the cave, without her observation, I left her in a coppice at the foot of the hills, bribed with a honeycomb to stay still. There she would be, her face covered in sticky mess, waiting for me on my return, and if I had qualms about leaving her in the forest, she did not share them, for she seemed to bear a charmed life.

If there was one thing Little Moon loved more than food, it was cuddling. Perhaps that is why we found each other such good company. She had the strength of a girl twice her age, and would fasten her arms around my neck like a bear wrestling for its life. She was the most affectionate child I have ever known, and the rough treatment with which she met from most of her neighbours had not soured her nature. I tried to dodge her kisses, which were extremely sticky, but her hugs were welcome. Often, as we walked around, searching for berries or nuts, I would carry her on my back, pausing only to save myself from strangulation, as she gripped me enthusiastically around the throat.

The truth is that I had as much need for comfort as she did. If I was in love with Green Eyes, it was not reciprocated, and I began to wonder whether her pretence of being Gull's woman had not warped her perspective. On the infrequent visits which she made to my bed, whether or not she took her pleasure with me, she would sleep away from me, her knees and elbows thrown out like barricades to keep me at bay. I missed the warmth of the lover I had left behind in my own village, a great, sprawling luxury of a woman. I missed my own people, who touched and held and patted each other as part of conversation. This Western lot were as hard to hold as the great wet clouds that drifted in from the sea every day. When a child was old enough to run about, in their way of thinking, it was old enough to stop it's babylike clinging and snuggling. No wonder they were such a joyless lot.

Little Moon's mother would have made an exception to this rule for her damaged child, but she went in fear of the man with whom she lived. If ever Little Moon was seen tumbling into the ditch, pursued by a shower of stones, his would most likely be the arm which had hurled them.

Despite the hardships of her life, Little Moon was happier than most of her fellows, and more willing to be pleased. In this strange company, I passed many days, wandering the countryside, her small grubby hand tucked into mine, telling her stories of my own home. She may not have understood, but it comforted me. Soft Axe, I had begun to avoid, not trusting the wild glitter in his eyes, nor the delight he took in pushing his dangerous game to the frontiers at which he might be caught out. Gull had become such a big noise in the village he disdained to notice one who was not only female and foreign, but also a stone-trader to boot. That just shows you how nice was his grasp of tactics, for I had it in my power to ruin him. Green Eyes, who could not understand why I should cavil at the presence of Gull in her bed, became ever more of a stranger to me.

It was Little Moon, idiot though she was supposed to be, who saw the difference between pretence and reality. She could not speak, but she could draw, with a pointed stick in the soft earth. Her symbol for me was a spiky creature, like a hedgehog, and for herself a small circle atop a larger one. Her mother was represented by a bowl of food, her father by a flying stone. In this way she told me stories, as we sat by our fire in the woods.

One day, she began drawing the shape of two eyes,

on each of which she placed a holly leaf. Green Eyes, I supposed. Next to that, she drew a flying bird, with waves underneath its outstretched wings. Looking at my face, to make sure I understood the story, she drew a circle around the two. I nodded, and drew the hut they shared. It was, after all, common knowledge. Little Moon shook her head and rubbed out the drawing. Once again she depicted Green Eyes, and this time drew Gull much closer, almost on top, the bird poised to swoop on the holly leaves. The circle which she drew around them was small, tight and emphatic. She then drew another circle containing a Gull and a drawing of the ornate brooch worn by the chief, which was her way of describing Soft Axe. I rubbed both drawings out with my heel, grasped Little Moon by the hand and set off for the hill fort. Whatever had got into her murky mind, I did not want to encourage it.

A suspicion, once planted, even by a five year old child who does not know her own mother's name, will take root and flourish. I began to watch Green Eyes more closely. She was a model wife, following Gull two paces behind, waiting on him at the fireside, listening with downcast eyes to his endless braggart plans for next summer's expedition to the goldfields. On a night when Soft Axe was not visiting Gull, I crept to their hut and sat shivering in the shadows outside it, with my ear to the door, which was closed only by a hanging skin. No wonder Gull had such a reputation among the men, for the shrill squeals that emanated from his hut every night were a great testimony to his prowess. They weren't to know that half the time the high pitched cries were his, when Soft Axe was visiting, but then I had not known that Green Eyes supplied the same evidence of sexual activity on the nights when he made do with her in her brother's absence. I wondered if Soft Axe knew.

As I crouched in the darkness, sickened, I suddenly felt warm breath on the back of my neck, and found Little Moon's strong arms across my back. She laid her head against my shoulder and stroked my face, as though trying to comfort me. In the cold night, I was glad of her presence, but I soon sent her back to her home and returned, sadly, to my own bed.

Now the four of us, actors in the deception, slipped faster and faster towards the climax of the play. Gull and Green Eyes began to strut and preen like a new royal family, and it became obvious that Gull supposed that he would succeed to the headship when Soft Axe, who was some ten summers older than him, was dead. If Soft Axe suspected that his lover and his sister were forming a dangerous combination to challenge his power, he gave no sign of it, but his recklessness was undiminished. Gull had so firmly established his popularity with the people, that I suspect only fear of a stronger character kept him from trying to oust Soft Axe immediately. Green Eyes had obviously thrown her lot in with his, and was wholeheartedly involved in building a dynasty.

When, on one of the rare nights we were together she left the bed at first light to be sick, I was sure of it. Gull still admitted Soft Axe to his bed, but I was sure it was only the awkwardness of explaining the presence of a dead and naked chieftain in his sleeping quarters that saved Soft Axe from being greeted with a dagger. The transition from love-object to rival had been swift, but it was almost complete. I tried to drop hints to Soft Axe of the changes in the air, but he was obdurate in refusing to understand. I don't know whether he was besotted with Gull, or simply believed that the power struggle between them was a new and exciting element in the game of chance, but he seemed unconvinced of his own vulnerability.

One full moon after mid-winter, it was the custom in that place to have a small supplementary feast, when spring seemed farthest away, and everything was cold and wet and rather drab. For a couple of nights the fires blazed higher, rowdy games were played and everyone got drunk in an effort to lift their spirits. Soft Axe presided over some quasi-religious rigmarole, which he had devised for the event, after which the men buried their faces in their drinking flasks and the women prepared a meal that would have pacified a dragon.

On the second night of this revel, I enjoyed the rare honour of Green Eyes gracing my bed. Foolishly I confronted her with her ambitions to do away with her brother and put Gull in his place, with herself at his side. I don't know why I felt impelled to discuss the matter with her, perhaps my judgement was a little fuddled by the feasting, but I knew my mistake the instant it was done. She denied it vehemently, but looked me such daggers I realised I should have held my tongue. When she told Gull my suspicions, I doubted even Soft Axe would be able to save my life. To my surprise, Green Eyes then began to stroke my body in a way that suggested a warmth of feeling which I knew no longer to exist between us. Perhaps it was her farewell gesture to one who was about to die.

Afterwards, she slept, and not wanting to be found poisoned in my bed in the morning, I slipped on my clothes and crept away. There was still a great deal of noise, and the serious drinkers had not quit the fire. The old bard was singing one of his interminable salacious songs, in which Gull was compared to a stag at the rut, and all the metal-workers bawled out the chorus. Slipping through the shadows beyond the fire, I saw a gang of the Beaker People toughs making their way back to their settlement. Even when invited to accept the hospitality of their paymasters, they had come fully armed; above the drunken singing, I could hear the chink of metal at their belts. With some thought of making Soft Axe see the danger of Gull and Green Eyes' ambitions, I made my way towards the hut where he and Gull where consorting.

The Beaker People were before me, passing on their way to the gate. They stopped as they passed the hut, their attention caught by a squeal which sounded like a pig being gutted, but which was in fact Gull in the throes of his lover's embrace. I melted into the shadows and waited, thanking every minor deity that Gull's ecstasy emerged in such a high-pitched voice. The leader of the gang of Beaker People made some ribald remark, and they all laughed, like a pack of wolves. One of the youngest, for a joke, and to curry favour with his elders, put his eye to a crack in the wall of the hut the better to report on the progress of the inhabitants. What news he gave I did not hear, but I could guess, for the lad was roughly pushed aside by his seniors, who all peered into the hut as best they could through the rough hurdle wall. The angry guttural voices muttered together for a few moments about the outrage, then the youth who had first peeped through the wall was sent running to fetch a torch. He returned, breathless; the brand was seized from him by the leader of the men, who thrust the torch into the dry thatch to fire the roof of the hut. The drunks from around the fire staggered up, protesting at the arson but they were easily pushed aside by the mercenaries. As the fire took hold, and flames leaped into the night sky, the whole fort turned out to watch, huddled in their bed wrappings, or swaying in a drunken fog.

First Gull, and then Soft Axe were smoked out of the burning hut. The faces of the Beaker People were red and wolfish in the reflected firelight, and the crowd behind them peered through the smoke. Gull had tumbled naked from the inferno, but Soft Axe had stayed to wrap his cloak around him and snatch up a dagger. I waited only to see the leader throw a cord around Gull's neck, and begin to tighten it with a stick, before I fled. I could hear Gull's voice behind me, pleading with his people, his former admirers and drinking companions, but not one of them braved the closed ranks of the armed men to come to his aid. An animal choking in a trap does not make such a foul noise as a man being garrotted slowly before the eyes of those who could save him but will not, and I ran from the sound, out of the gate and into the night.

EIGHTEEN

It was lucky for me that all the warriors were busy with their public executions, for they normally guarded the gate at night, and would not have let me out. Lucky also that a heavy fall of snow began as I was running for the hills, covering my tracks. At the time, I cursed the cold drifts, through which I waded, for slowing me down. I was expecting the assassins to set off in pursuit when they noticed my absence. Once or twice, I missed my path in the dark and featureless landscape, but I came eventually to the scree at the foot of the hill, and scrambled up it with dangerous haste, not seeing the ground underfoot and trusting to luck that I would not slip on the wet rubble and fall to my death.

From the cave I could see across to the much smaller hill on which Soft Axe had built his fortified camp. The hut where the two men had been trapped was a small glow; Soft Axe's own hut, where I had been lying not long before was a larger, brighter conflagration. I hoped that Green Eyes had got out before they torched it. Even at this distance, I could see figures, silhouetted by the flames, swarming round the burning hut. No doubt wishing they had thought to loot it before they set it alight.

My shelter was cold, but secure for the moment. The pictures on the wall, drawn by Green Eyes, or some previous worshipper, smiled down at me. The Goddess statue which I had carved for her nestled in a niche of the rock, belly flopping contentedly onto thighs, pendant breasts dripping with comfort. I wrapped myself in my cloak, damp though it was, and lay down on the bed of dried bracken, shut my eyes and went to sleep with my fears.

In my dreams, I saw Gull, as I had seen him dying. I hadn't liked the man, but I didn't welcome his eyes bursting from their sockets and the tongue forced from his mouth by a grinning barbarian with a twisted necklace. I saw Soft Axe, my difficult friend, with his vision of trading empires, facing his enemies in the firelight, outnumbered, certain of death and armed only with a dagger and his pride, determined to the last, I suspected, to be a better man than his worthless father. I didn't see Green Eyes, whom I had left sleeping in a hut that was now reduced to cinders.

You may imagine the sort of night I spent, shivering in my cave. If I had gone back to warn Green Eyes, would she have fled with me to safety? If I had roused the drunkards by the fire when I saw the mercenaries close in on Soft Axe and Gull, would they have stayed the killer's hand? Could I have saved anyone, including myself, if I had not run away? Although I suspected that the answer to all these questions was no, they crowded my head all night, nagging away like the pain of a rotten tooth.

In the morning, very little rested, I crawled out of the cave and looked across to the hill fort. At that distance it looked like an ants' nest that has been trampled by cattle; tiny creatures milling about in furious agitation. I watched until the snow came down again and blotted out the view, then retreated to the furthest recesses of the cave and lit a small fire, the smoke from which was sucked away into invisible cracks in the rock and dispersed on the far side of the hill. I boiled up some cornmeal, using one of the sacramental vessels which Green Eyes had left there. I was sure that the Goddess wouldn't mind, she isn't finicky about these things.

The sun set and rose again twice, while I scrabbled a living in that cave, like a rodent in its burrow. Which was more dangerous, I asked myself, a hundred times a day, to stay here, within reach of the Beaker People, who might well be searching for me, or to try and journey home through the winter storms? If I stayed where I was, I confess it was because I lacked the resolution necessary to go. I can tell you, perhaps you already know, I was frightened. Also cold and lonely and bored, but those were minor miseries. I had food and water, enough firewood for cooking and I had a shelter that was hidden from my enemies. It was tempting to stay put, immobilised by fear, and pretend it was a rational decision.

The cave was dank and chilly, the overhang admitting little sunlight. Most of the day I lay wrapped in my cloak, shivering on the bed. By the third day, my shivering was continuous, as the fever which had lived in my blood since my journey in the autumn caught me in its sweaty grip. Alternately freezing and sweltering, I lay miserably wondering if, after all the dangers I had survived, I was going to die of a chill like an old rabbit in its hole, with nobody to notice my passing. Tears of self pity streamed down my heated face, adding to the general dampness of the bedding.

Towards nightfall, as the fever rose, I made my way to the water-filled rock, parched with thirst. The water, cold as the end of the world, struck my throat like fear and lay in my stomach like a stone. When I had forced down as much as I could drink, I turned back to my bed, and there, standing in the mouth of the cave, was the ghost of Soft Axe.

It was a horrible sight, reddened by flame, blackened with soot, the hair gone from his face and head, only a few singed whisps remaining. Without his beard or eyebrows, I barely recognised the apparition. Great lengths of blistered skin were sloughing off from his face and hands, revealing raw and weeping flesh beneath. No feverish hallucination of mine had conjured this appearance. "Why bother me?" I asked the ghost bitterly, "I know I ran away and didn't try to save you, but what could I do? Shouldn't you properly be haunting your killers?"

Soft Axe laughed, a horrible sound, like bare feet scraping over live coals. Then the smell hit me. Now, I may not have had much to do with spirits, leaving that sort of thing to my mother, but I know that ghosts may be seen and heard, but not smelt. Soft Axe stank like a slaughtered pig, when the bristles are singed off its skin by the butcher. This ghost was alive, although not for long, by the look of him.

"What are you doing here?" I asked, not very hospitably, but I was amazed. He took a couple of painful, teetering steps into the cave and collapsed on my bed.

212

"A drink," he croaked. Pulling myself together, I fetched him some water and held him up to sip at it. In the ruin of his face, only his eyes were recognisable, foxy and watchful as ever. With a damp cloth I bathed his wounds as best I could, and though I burst more than one bloated blister in the process, he seemed to find some relief in the cold water. As he was too weak to eat, I wrapped him up again and told him to try and sleep. Feeling fairly wretched myself, with a spinning head and exploding stars of colour before my eyes, I lay down beside him. It was with little expectation of either of us waking alive that I closed my eyes.

In the morning, the aching of my limbs and foul taste in my mouth informed me that I was still in the mortal world, and so, to my surprise, was Soft Axe. He was obviously in agony, but he had slept, however fitfully. I had with me a small supply of herbs which I had gathered and dried before the winter killed their growth, valerian and skull-cap amongst them. The previous night I had seen no point in wasting them on a dying man. They were all I had, until I reached my own home, or spring came again, and who knows what might befall me in the meantime. Think me callous if you like, but I had not intended to waste their precious anodyne qualities on the burnt man. Such was my resolution, and had he wheedled or pleaded, I would have maintained it, but he didn't, just lay there looking at me with his speaking eyes, with half a twisted smile on his charred face. Crossly, I brewed up a handful of the precious herbs in boiling water and gave him the infusion, drop by grudging drop.

The mix was powerful, and he fell into a deep and groan-free sleep, from which he did not wake until the sun was going down. I felt ill enough myself not to want to be nursing someone else. My own fever was receding, as an illness sometimes will, when a greater emergency requires the body's attention. Apparently, the claims of friendship could reduce a temperature.

Soft Axe was a contrary man, for he should have been dead of half a dozen different causes, yet here he was, clinging onto his life as though it were the only one he would get. His vanity would not permit him to look at the devastation of his body, so he stared at the roof of the cave, or lay with his eyes shut, telling me, in short and painful bursts of speech, the story of his escape.

When I had last seen him, emerging from the burning hut, confronted by a solid line of attackers and with Gull's last breath being choked out of him, Soft Axe had looked at the faces of his fellows beyond the wall of Beaker People. In them, he saw only arousal and scorn. They were men he had made rich, to whom he had given a trade which would secure their dominance in their own country and far beyond it, whom he had rescued from the arbitrary tyrannies of his own father. Yet he could see, in that one glance, not only would they not save him from the barbarians, they would watch his death as a splendid entertainment, and fight amongst themselves as to who would take his place.

Before the fighters could finish with Gull and turn on him, he stepped back into the burning hut. The lads took this as a gesture of self-immolation, and howled with delight. The roof collapsed at that moment, and the watchers stepped back a pace to avoid the flying sparks. Fortunately none of them was bright enough, or sober enough, to think of going around to the back of the hut, where Soft Axe, having crossed the heart of the blaze, was fighting his way out through the far wall, which was collapsing in flames. With his cloak on fire, he cut away the burning material to save his brooch (the things people think of in emergencies!), put the precious clasp in the charm bag that hung at his throat and ran, naked and half blinded by the smoke, through the dark to his own hut, where Green Eyes was sleeping.

"Was she pleased to see you?" I asked, unable to keep the bitterness from my voice. "Did she want to save your life? She and Gull were planning to do away with you and make him chief instead, you know."

He sighed, and looked at me, with great sadness in his smoke-reddened eyes. "She is my sister," he said, simply. "Whatever she had planned, she was in danger."

He had dragged the sleepy Green Eyes out of bed and, snatching up a long knife from his collection of weapons, had led the way out into the night. All the people were by this time gathered around the burnt-out remains of Green Eyes' own hut, although whether they expected Soft Axe to rise from the ashes, or whether they were entertaining themselves with Gull's body he did not say. Unnoticed by the crowd, the two of them slipped out of the gate and across the ditch. Once they had a head start, in case they should have to run for it, Soft Axe thrust the long knife into Green Eyes' hand and instructed her to call out to the people to watch her execute her wicked brother. She then marched him off towards the river, as he had told her, with the slow-witted populace streaming out of the fort, a hundred paces behind.

At the edge of the river, Green Eyes continued the performance, and I wondered how hard she had to pretend. Holding Soft Axe at knife point, she shouted that she was personally going to root out the evil in her family, either by running Soft Axe through, or forcing him to jump in the river. Before the mob could reach him, Soft Axe leapt into the dark and icy waters, bobbed under the surface a few times, with convincing gasps and was, as far as the watchers were concerned, swept out to sea. Green Eyes, who might otherwise have been put to death, as the wife of one pervert, and the sister of another, escaped reproach.

Because few of the people could swim, it did not occur to them that Soft Axe might, let alone under-water. Because everybody knows that the river flows out to sea, they forgot that the tide, which laps up the estuary at that point, was sweeping Soft Axe inland. They failed to sea his head break the surface, and begin working its way upstream. Soft Axe had played in that river all his neglected childhood, and swam like an otter. Even so, I was surprised he survived the immersion in the icy water, or the exhaustion of swimming upstream. Let alone the stinging of the salt water on his burnt skin.

215

Good swimmer though he was, he was half drowned before he could haul himself out of the black and snow-laden water. He lay, dripping naked, in a marshy field, until dawn was almost broken. Tempting though it was to lie by the river and slip into insensibility, when at least the pain of his burns might stop, Soft Axe had hauled himself to his feet and set off in search of cover. He had reached the shelter of the trees as the false dawn began, and by the time the sun came up, was hidden under a pile of dead leaves, unable to move any further.

During the day he hid, emerging at nightfall to resume his journey through the wood and away from his enemies. As you can imagine, his progress was slow. His judgement overset by pain, he spent half the night walking in a large circle. He was heading for the hills, but his sense of direction betrayed him. By the second dawn, he was only as far from his former home as you or I might have travelled in a leisurely stroll. Once again, he went to earth as the sun rose, this time in the hollow of a tree that had been struck by lightning. It was there that Little Moon found him.

He had come, by chance, to the clearing where I had left the child when, on our walks, I was heading for the cave where she was not allowed to follow. "She had come to wait for you," Soft Axe said.

"How do you know?" I asked.

"She drew me a hedgehog with a flint in its paw. Who else could that be but you?"

She also drew an eye with a holly leaf placed on it, with a tear coming from one corner, so I deduced that Green Eyes, although she had saved her own life, was unhappily circumstanced. Soft Axe persuaded Little Moon to run home and steal him a blanket and some food. She returned that afternoon with the blanket. She had actually filched some cold meat, left over from the feasting, too, but on the way back, she ate it. Then she sat down again to wait for me, in the place to which I always returned when I had been away.

When Soft Axe asked where it was that I went on my solitary rambles, Little Moon pointed to the hills, indicating with surprising accuracy the path which I always took. I had not thought her capable of sustained attention, but she must have watched me every time I walked away and left her.

At dusk, Soft Axe crawled out of his hiding place, and tried to persuade Little Moon to go home. As he set off uneasily on his way, she was still sitting there, still waiting.

"How," I asked, "did you find your way to this cave, even with Little Moon to point out the path?"

He looked at me pityingly. "Did you think this was Green Eyes' special place alone? I have known this cave since I was a boy." He reached up a livid hand and stroked one of the wall-paintings, a stag leaping across a stream. "In a better age I would have been an artist instead of a businessman."

On his way up the hillside his bare feet, torn by sharp stones and thorns, had become numb with the cold. He had slipped on the scree, started a rockslide, and fallen heavily to the bottom of the slope. A boulder, tumbling after him, crushed his shoulder. With agonizing slowness, he had crawled back up the hill. Weak and pain-racked, in a time stolen from death, he crawled towards the cave which had sheltered him as a persecuted child, like a baby missing the womb.

I tried to set the bone, but the shoulder blade was shattered and past my skill to repair. We talked of trust and disappointment, the things that people will do for power and wealth. He seemed remarkably philosophical about the betrayal which Green Eyes had plotted with Gull. Perhaps he blamed himself for introducing them to the idea of riches that are not grown in a field or shared with ones kin. For the prurient metalworkers, who had regarded the murders as a splendid spectacle (once the Beaker People had informed them of the nature of his and Gull's offence) he had nothing but contempt, but then he had never been one of them. We both agreed that the hired muscle, having disposed of the head man and his heir apparent without hindrance, would not be sent tamely back to their camp to take orders again. The metal-workers would find that they had a new and more brutal set of masters now. Soft Axe's former people would become the slave-labour in their own foundry.

We considered the old ways, and the dying man struggled to convince himself that the spirit world had not been modernised. Perhaps I should rather call him the living man, for no-one I know had met their death so often and escaped it. He had no right to the breaths which he stole from the air, but still he took them. I did what I could to ease his sufferings but it was little enough, his body was shattered, only his obstinate will outlived it.

"What will you do now?" he croaked suddenly, after a lull in which I thought he had drifted into unconsciousness.

"Go home," I said, making the decision on impulse. "I'll start the journey as soon as you are well enough to take care of yourself, you lazy bastard."

He smiled. "My mother used to call me her runt," he said, dreamily. "The little runt of her litter."

"You haven't done badly for a runt."

"Will you start working metal? When you get home?"

"Does it matter so much?"

"Yes," he said, "If I must leave the world, I want to know that I have changed it."

"Still building empires?"

"Even on my death bed," he joked.

"A modern man to the last. Who is also hoping for an ancient spirit world in which to rest his ghost?"

"Consistency is another word for dullness." He gripped my hand with his remaining strength. His burnt flesh was hot and slimy to the touch, but I could not pull away. "Go home, build a foundry," he commanded. You can seize the future that has slipped out of my grasp."

"The future isn't an eel," I protested.

"That's exactly what it is," he insisted. "You must trap it and hold it tight." I said nothing. "Go back to your silly rocks then," he said petulantly. "Be a primitive. Be forgotten."

"Don't take on so," I soothed. "Alright, if it makes you happy, I'll go home, and introduce my people to a new craft. Only because I think it inevitable. I won't have such grand ideas as you do."

He released my hand. "Good," he said. I walked across to the embers of the small fire and built it up to boil water. As I reached for the pot, I smelt the palm of my hand, where Soft Axe had been holding me. The sickly rotten smell of gangrene assaulted my nostrils. His body was dying before him. Sadly I boiled up the last of my powerful sleeping herbs in a strong draught. When it was made, I took it to Soft Axe.

"Drink this," I said, "and stop worrying about immortality."

He pulled a face at the strength of the brew, giving me a knowing look. Why must he be so aware of everything?

"I'm glad," he said gently, "that you accept the inevitability of progress." I snorted. He fumbled with the charm bag, which hung by a cord from his neck, but his fingers would not obey his will. I helped him, undoing the leather pouch.

"Here," he said, handing me his precious brooch. It glinted wickedly in the firelight. "Take this with you when you go."

I held the ornament in my hand, feeling its weight. "Shouldn't this be buried with you?" I asked, not looking at him.

"No, I'd rather you had it."

"Thank you."

"Thank you," he said, without irony, draining the last of his medicine. I should have known he would smell the poison berries, even in so pungent a brew. One must do what one can for a friend. His eyes closed and he slipped away from me. As I watched, his already shallow breathing eased to a sigh and stopped. With a last spasm of failed breath rattling in his throat, he was gone.

NINETEEN

I shan't tell you the story of how I walked home across the deepest part of the winter, the whole width of the land, from West to East. I don't know how I survived the journey. However, I made it, accompanied only by my sense of loss, and going in peril of my life every day, but thinking little of it. I don't care to recall the painful details and so you shall be spared them.

It was still some way off the turning of the season when I staggered into my own village, safe home at last. Do you think me naive to have expected a welcome? Even my own mother, although glad that I was alive, wished me elsewhere. She took me into her hut and gave me shelter. If she had not, I must have slept in the open, for my own home had been appropriated by Little Stone-Dealer, my erstwhile apprentice, and her loutish miner. She showed no inclination to quit the premises. Although she welcomed me with a smile, it was as false as a new god, and the look in her eyes told me all I needed to know. The swelling of her stomach when I left had now burgeoned into a child almost ready to be dropped. She waddled around the village giving herself queenly airs, while her mate, who no longer worked in the pit, swaggered about, cracking the heads of any who displeased him.

For the first few days, I recovered from the exertions of my journey, and took little interest in anything. As my strength returned, and I began to go about, I noticed more. The flint-knappers, that fine and raucous body of women, were cowed. The miners had somehow become convinced that theirs was the greater labour of our trade, and that the women on the surface, whose skills had been honed over generations, added little to the value of the flints we produced. Such a reversal of the truth! It had not been easily brought about, I was sure. My mother told, in a lowered voice, of the days of rioting, in which all the statues of the Goddess were smashed and many of the women fled to the forest, to avoid the new order that was sweeping in. For this change was not caused by some great philosophical leap on the part of the miners, but by the intervention of a tribe of the Beaker People, who, failing to return across the sea after their summer of pillaging in the West, had noticed our prosperous village and settled nearby. They had brought their warlike male gods, their barbaric notions of social organisation, and a calculating eye to the value of the flint trade.

Deciding that they would rather stay here and secure a monopoly on our produce than go home, they installed a clique of the most thuggish miners, led by Little Stone-Dealer's man, as their proxies and retired to a camp by the sea. From this stronghold, they regularly came to inspect their new fiefdom, taking what they wanted and treating my people like milch cows. The puppet rulers, grovelling when their masters were present, bullied the rest savagely when they were gone.

I could see the appeal, for the Beaker People, of controlling a major local industry. Like their fellow countrymen, who had settled in the South and West, they were tired of commuting across the North Sea for a season of plunder. If they were determined to settle, what better place than the greatest flint mine, on the major trading route from the East Coast to the Southlands? I doubted whether they had a plan, since their settling seemed to depend on the whim of the headman of the band.

I was in a delicate position. Former friends hardly dared talk to me, for fear of the displeasure of the woman who had usurped my place and the local tyrant with whom she consorted. I found myself as much of an outsider in my own village as I had been in Soft Axe's, and with as little employment. I would not turn my hand to flint-knapping for Little Stone-Dealer, especially now it had become a degraded art. Once more I was forced to spend my days hunting and watching and staying out of the way of the Beaker People.

Spring arrived with its first wet flourish, and our customers began to trail up to the village to barter for a new load of flints. As I had expected, their goods were taken from them, flints were exchanged, and no sooner had they regained the path homewards than a band of Beaker People fell upon them and robbed them. The forest began to stink with the bodies of murdered traders.

For a while, the villagers were happy. They received the benefit of the goods inwards, and the flints which they traded were never gone for more than a day before the Beaker People brought them back. Of course, the warriors took the bulk of the spoils, but still the miners had enough. The trouble with this system was that it did not encourage productivity. Why bother about new flints, when the same ones might be traded again and again, always returning? The miners and flint-knappers became very loth to do any work, drunkenness was their major occupation. The poor flint-knappers were not long free to enjoy their newfound leisure. Following the male gods encouraged the miners to act like them, and they began to demand that their food was cooked and houses mended by the women.

I had not been in charge of our trading all this time for nothing, and I could see that the season, which had begun well, was becoming a very slack one for business. Rumours of the dangers of a visit to our mines were obviously spreading. You can't keep anything secret in this country, people love to gossip. It infuriated me that what had taken generations to build should be destroyed by gangsters in one season. This fury gave me the courage to call a village meeting.

We used to have these often, in the old days, but the necessity for them had passed with the arrival of the Beaker People's appointed junta. However, the memory of the tradition was strong enough for the villagers to gather at the arranged time, keeping a wary eye out for our armed protectors. We had never been a warlike people and even the miners were cowed by the superior savagery of the invaders.

I spoke to them of the future of our trade, of the starvation that would visit us if the parasites who were feeding off our good name continued to rob our customers, with our connivance. I talked of the changes in the West, where metal was replacing stone in people's values, and how our flints would be disregarded in turn. I didn't remind them of Soft Axe's visit, or the derision with which they had driven him away, but I let them know that I had the secret of good metal weapons in my head, and that if they would agree we could be the first metal workers in the East and capture a new market. Even the brutal invaders who had settled on our peaceful village, like ticks on a sheep, would surely permit such a development. As a final clincher, I showed them the splendid ornament which Soft Axe had given me, promising them that such treasures as this were freely available to metal-workers.

They listened in silence, with eyes downcast, which was not like the argumentative people I had left. No-one even shouted 'Blasphemy!', as they should have done, at the suggestion that humans could replicate the functions of Mother Earth, in melting rock. How could I blaspheme against a religion in which no one dared believe any longer? As I finished, and resumed my place in the seated circle, those either side of me edged away, like ripples on a pond.

Little Stone-Dealer rose, her great belly sticking out like a reproach. She knew, if we were to begin metal-working, who would be in charge, and that was the sole consideration for her. She may be a big noise in the village now, I thought sourly, listening to her rubbishing my schemes as the ravings of a mad-woman, but if she puts spite before strategy, she won't last long.

My poor people, how glad they were to be convinced that change was dangerous and not for them. I suppose they had had too much change thrust upon them recently. As I listened to Little Stone-Dealer pouring vitriol on my name, and saw the relief on faces that had been disturbed by the vision of the future which I painted, I knew that I would be fleeing for my life once again. An idea whose time has not quite come is never forgiven. Or at least, the one who voices it prematurely may not be forgiven, while the idea itself lies waiting for another day. As my former pupil and betrayer lashed up a storm of contempt for the idea of non-stone weapons, I slipped away.

What was Little Stone-Dealer thinking of, to let me go? She had barely reached her peroration as I slunk out of the circle, but her conclusion was inevitable. Dangerous lunatics with revolutionary ideas were not customarily let off with a caution, and she had every reason to order my killing. She knew I would undermine her authority, and that of her oafish companion, as long as I could draw breath. Perhaps her child was ready to drop, and the pains were distracting her. She certainly looked rather clenched about the mouth, shifting from foot to foot as she spoke. Her face was both drained of blood and bathed with sweat, although it was not a warm day. She had to make the speech herself though, in whatever extremity of discomfort she might be, for she could not trust her bone-headed lover to sway the people with arguments. With his fists, perhaps, but that would hardly answer the case. Little Stone-Dealer could have had me put away quietly in the night, but she did not know how many of the villagers I might have won over with my wild talk. As it happened, I had not tried to build a faction of converts before the meeting. She was still speaking as I quit the village and dived into the forest.

I ran until my sides ached with lack of breath, then slowed to a walk until I could run again. The scythe of winter had cleared the entangling undergrowth, which spring was beginning to replace with young green snares that snagged my legs as I hurried through the trees. I hoped I might meet some of the flint-knappers who had fled the village after the riots, but they were well hidden or far distant. Before the meeting, suspecting the outcome, I had taken the precaution of hiding, at the edge of the trees, a small pack of essential supplies which now bumped against my back.

When I reached the great road I sat down to make

my choice. If I turned left along the road, I would reach the sea, if I turned right, I would be retracing my steps of the previous autumn. To the North lay invaders, and the boats of the Beaker People, making their spring landings in the tradition of their grandfathers. To the South and West, the way would take me back to the rich countries, where metal-craft was an opportunity, not a threat. Which way would my pursuers believe me to have gone, when they came on my trail? Picking myself up, I followed my right hand, back towards the country from which I had fled only that winter. Taking no care to obscure my footprints, I continued down the middle of the track until it crossed a stream. Instead of fording it and regaining the path, I turned along its stony bed and walked downstream until I was out of sight of the road. Then I scrambled from the water and ran once again, North by East across an unknown country, away from my village and away from the path which my enemies would suppose me to have taken.

I hurried across the unfamiliar, flat and scrubby country until sundown, when I lay, unsleeping, wrapped in my cloak. Every badger shuffling through the underbrush sounded like the footsteps of an army, and every twig that poked into my back as I lay on the relentless ground was as sharp as an assassin's dagger. In the morning, I continued, past a lake-village and through bogs, following the power lines until I came to a place that could have modelled for a painting of nowhere. There were trees, but not a forest, land cleared by lightning-strike fires, but no crops, and most of all, no people, nor sign that any had ever been there. I built a temporary shelter of branches, intending to rest a few days and then press on to the sea. I never left.

Three thousand seven hundred and forty summers is a long time to spend somewhere which had nothing much to recommend it in the first place, apart from an absence of neighbours. That's how it is, you go somewhere not intending to stay, thinking your life is before you and the world your own, and then there you are, still there come the millennium, and the one after that. Such is the illusion of choice. Shall I tell you how this unlikely spot came to be my home? You have the rest of the story, after all.

I scraped myself a small hollow in the ground and roofed it over with branches, as I have said. Although not the most comfortable dwelling I had ever built, being rather damp, it was hardly noticeable, which I counted a great virtue. I took care not to signal my presence with my cooking fires, avoiding the use of wet wood on clear days and watching with all my senses for the approach of danger.

Why did I stay? No sickness or injury confined me to the place, no enemies came and struck me down on the spot. I was neither over-run by Beaker People, although the whole country soon became as good as theirs, nor did I find myself to have been trespassing on some sacred tribal territory. Nothing happened. No enchantment was worked upon me, the charm of the place did not seduce me into staying, for its charms were few. It simply became my home.

On the fourth day, I dug over a patch of soil and planted the vegetable seeds which I had brought in my pack. It would have been a waste not to plant them, and my future plans were still unclear. Then I enlarged my shelter, because it really wasn't very comfortable. I dug a little deeper and built a raised wooden floor and covered the roof with turves from the vegetable patch. When the seeds had germinated, of course, I had a reason for staying at least until the summer, for then I would have a supply of fresh food ready to hand, which it seemed a shame to waste. Thus one day merged into the next, without me ever deciding to stay, or managing to leave.

I think it was disappointment that kept me in my place. I knew two crafts and could practice neither. The flints I had worked and traded all my life were closed to me because my own village had turned against me. Metal-work was the craft of the new religion, in which a woman, however skilled, would never be more than a drone. If I had had any idea of venturing to the South-West and setting up my own foundry, in a land where its output might be appreciated, the dream was, I knew, idle. Soft Axe's people had been ready to surrender their futures to him, because he arrived in the guise of a god, fire flashing from his sword and novelties in every bag. They were prepared to accept a god-in-human-form, because they had made gods who looked like men. Miracles never happen in unexpected ways. If the Goddess herself had leapt out of that boat with Soft Axe, with a tidal wave in one hand and the motion of the planets in the other, they would probably have thought she was his cook.

Whatever promise I had made to Soft Axe was discharged. I had tried to persuade my people to embrace the future and perpetuate his imported craft, but they had turned up their noses at the idea. There might be another tribe, somewhere, which both revered the old ways and would welcome me, but gradually, my willingness to go out and find them drained away. I realised that I had done with building empires when I ceased looking forward to the barely revealed future, and began instead to re-live the past.

I harvested my vegetables that summer, and the small patch of corn which I had sown, carefully collecting seed for next year's crops. By then, perhaps, I was beginning to realise that my temporary refuge was becoming home, that this was, in fact, the rest of my life. You might have thought me mad, for I talked to myself, and I was often lonely, but in the uneventful procession of days, there was great tranquillity. For this, after all the rushing about and adventures of my recent past, I was grateful. By degrees I was becoming the kind of crazy crone who lives alone in an inhospitable spot, attending to her garden. I had been at the top of one profession, as a flint-dealer, and would have been mistress of another, if my people had accepted the progression to the metal-age. That's more than most people can say of their lives, so you needn't pity my early retirement from the competitive fray.

Like many another solitary spinster, I was a religious conservative. I carved myself a Goddess figure, like the one I had made for Green Eyes, and promoted her worship in a congregation of one. I would have amused myself with casting spells upon the treacherous Little Stone-Dealer and the bullies with whom she held power, except that I felt sure that the Beaker People, true overlords of the village, would eliminate her when her overweening ambitions became apparent even to their strategically limited imaginations.

I missed the company of women. For the first three seasons, I saw nobody at all. Then spring came round again and, convinced that no pursuit from my own village had found trace of me, I began to scour my new countryside for other inhabitants. I found a few, half a day's walk away, subsisting in miserable ignorance. Although our mistrust was mutual and permanent, I looked forward to the society of these people, with whom I came to trade on a regular, but infrequent basis. I had lost none of my old skill at making a deal. Every autumn I came to their village to barter my carvings and produce for their dried meat and skins. Thus I ended my life a stoneworker, as I had begun it, which was a nice irony.

In the end, there was no rush of invaders across my land, no probing swords of Beaker People, nor flying stones of outraged villagers. I never again fled with what I could carry, or was hunted for my life. No wild animal rent me limb from limb, nor riot or civil commotion attended my passing. Nothing more dramatic than a fever, which I could not cure with herbs, in a winter of exceptional severity, at the end of a life of reasonable length and great variety. What better place to die, than in one's own bed, in a home built by one's own hand, under the roof on which the grass was already growing?

TWENTY

Elspeth, with her gardener's muscles, flung a spadeful of sand into the mouth of the cement mixer as it ground round in hungry circles on its stand. Shirley Bruton, who was strong enough to carry two protesting children, one under each arm, stood waiting with a wheelbarrow to receive the sloppy mixture. It was the Fourth of July. The clatter of the mixer's motor was drowned out by the roar of a Liberator grinding overhead, down towards the airfield, its four props thrashing the hot air as menacingly as ever, but its belly barren of bombs. From the control tower, the garbled voice of the airshow announcer floated, tinny through a tannoy. A reconstructed Mustang came hurtling out of the sun towards the landing strip. The crowd cheered. Across the field, Archibald Maybe gave a welcoming hoot on the whistle of his steam engine.

Felicity emerged from the cottage, blinking like a cat as her eyes adjusted to the bright light.

"What's all the racket?" she asked, "The poor cement mixer can hardly hear itself think."

"It's the Yankee Doodle Airshow," explained Shirley.

"I wish they'd stop shaking my roof," grumbled Felicity. "Don't they know its brand new?"

"They seem so slow," said Elspeth, shading her eyes with her hand to watch the progress of the Mustang, "compared with the modern planes. I remember going to Heathrow with Archibald, on our tenth wedding anniversary, to watch Concord take off, for a treat. The speed of it! I've always wanted to go on an aeroplane," she said, with regret.

"There'll be a fly-past of F1-11s from Mildenhall, at the end of the afternoon," said Shirley, "if it's speed and noise you want."

"Shall I deal out the ear protectors now?" asked Felicity.

"You know what the F stands for, don' you?" joked Shirley. She tipped the load of freshly mixed concrete into the wheelbarrow, hefted the handles and trundled her burden into the house, to tip it on the floor. Elspeth followed her in to draw water from the pump for the next load. Felicity took her place at the mixer, shovelling in powdered cement, which flew back in her face and choked her. The hands of all three were dry and wrinkled, leached of oils by the concrete. They raced to fill the floor space, before the first wheelbarrow-full set hard. Planes buzzed the house, and the cheers of the crowd floated across the fields as the three women worked on. When the last load had been splattered onto the damp-proof membrane, and the last smoothing line been drawn across the hardening surface with wooden straight edge, they turned off the mixer and luxuriated in the sudden silence.

Elspeth produced a picnic box, loaded with chill-packs and containing three perfectly cooled cans of beer; they fell on them like carrion crows upon a new born lamb. Even Elspeth drank straight from the can, not bothering with the paper cups she had brought. The three of them stood on the lawn, heads tipped back, pouring the fizzy liquid down their dust-caked throats. Felicity paused, burped and wiped the still-cold can across her heated forehead, leaving a trail of condensation. They grinned at each other, like con-spiratorial school girls.

"Elspeth, you devil," she teased, "and the sun not even near the yardarm."

"I've never really liked lager," said Elspeth, wiping a moustache of froth from her upper lip. "But you see men drinking it on hot days, and they look so.."

"Rapacious?" suggested Felicity.

"Smug?" said Shirley.

"They look just the way I felt drinking that can. It's absolutely the right thing for a day like this, when you've been working hard."

"It doesn't taste the same in a pub, out of a warm glass," agreed Shirley.

"I bought six cans as an experiment," confessed Elspeth. "I didn't expect that it would be so deli-cious."

"Does that mean there's more in your magic ice box?" asked Felicity, splashing her freckled face with water from the bucket.

"One more each." Elspeth dealt out a second can all round, and carefully collected the ring-pulls, posting them into one of the empty cans. "Anyway, we should celebrate, getting the floor done."

"Comin' along, isn't it?" observed Shirley.

"Put the screed down, replace the upstairs floorboards, finish off the wiring and connect up the plumbing, and I reckon I could move in, bar a bit of painting and plastering," said Felicity. "The doors and windows need replacing, but this old building is pretty sound now," she slapped the outside wall affectionately.

"There'll always be somethin' more to do," cautioned Shirley. "Old houses are like that."

"You've done so well to get this far," said Elspeth.

"Thanks to you two," Felicity toasted them with her beer can. "I don't know how I would have managed without you."

The three women stood, basking in a glow of satisfaction, outside the house that they had made. The threatened flight of F1-11s screamed past and overflew the airfield. If the crowd applauded, it was inaudible. Felicity shook her fist at the bombers as they made another pass overhead and roared back to base.

Shirley's husband, whose arrival had gone unnoticed amidst the fly-past, opened the garden gate and walked up the path. He stopped in front of his wife. He looked her up and down, in a way that suggested he did not see before him the women whose strength and ingenuity had rescued a house from dereliction. He looked like Judge Jefferies at a witches' sabbath.

"Well, look at you," he sneered, taking in Shirley's clothes and skin, spattered with grey globules of hardening cement, her flushed face and filthy boots. "Pretty as a picture."

Elspeth patted her curls, suddenly aware that she must look a fright. Felicity stopped leaning on the wall and straightened up.

"Having a good time with the girls?" he asked, indicating the beer can in his wife's hand. "Bit early for that, I woulda thought."

"It's only lager," Elspeth offered, placatingly. Shirley silenced her with a look.

"Should've known I'd find you here," he continued. "Gettin' tipsy with your girlfriends, when the kids needs you."

"Don' be silly," she said, "the kids is at school."

"School rang up," he shook his head, sorrowfully, "poor li'l Donny fell off the climbin' ropes in the gym. Broke his arm, they reckon. Needs fetchin' home from the hospital."

"What're you doin' here then?" she demanded angrily. "Why didn't you go and fetch him?"

"I've got a farm to run," he snapped, glaring at them all in turn. "I had to leave Jimmy short-handed as it was, to come here and find you. It's only lucky I was there to take the 'phone call, otherwise my son could have been left there all night, and who's to know?"

"Surely the school have sent someone with him?" said Elspeth.

"Isn't the same. Boy needs his mother at a time like that. I'm not surprised at you, bein' so irresponsible," he advanced his face to within inches of Shirley's. "You always put your own pleasure first. Women do."

"You're enjoyin' this," Shirley accused. "If you cared about Donny, youd've got down that hospital soon as they rung. He's your son, after all."

"And he isn't yours," shouted Bruton, suddenly exploding with rage. "You never cared about him, poor kid. You made a favourite of his sister, but you never cared for my son like a mother should. You only married me for my money."

"Really, Mr Bruton," expostulated Elspeth, acutely embarrassed.

"Shut your fat mouth," he screamed at her. "Meddling cow."

"Married you for your money? That's good," Shirley was also shouting. "Then a bloody bad bargain I got. You're a worse bastard than your dad, and he was a miserable ol' skin flint. Anyway, you only married me 'cos it was cheaper'n hiring a nanny."

"If you don't get down that hospital right away, and fetch my son, you needn't bother coming home tonight," he threatened.

"I should be so lucky," said Shirley, scornfully.

"Go," he screamed, his face purple, "now."

"Who's goin' to pick up Phoebe from the bus?" Shirley stopped shouting and her voice became cold and level, but a muscle in her face twitched, and she flinched away from Bruton every time he moved.

"I'll fetch her," offered Elspeth.

"You will not," bellowed the farmer. "I won't have you near my kids, you great lump of lard. You're a trouble maker, like all of your kind. The spoilt brat can walk home, it'll do her good."

Shirley, as white about the mouth as her husband was puce, spun on her heel, jumped into her car and drove off, the wheels spinning on the loose stones in the drive.

"And she won't be comin' back here," he continued to the remaining women. "I'll see to that. You won't be able to meddle in my family no more, the pair of you. Try and turn my wife away from her duty."

"You needn't threaten us," said Elspeth, bravely. "You may be able to bully Shirley, but neither of us has to live with you."

He looked as though he would spit in Elspeth's anxious face. The tendons on his neck were knotted with anger. Felicity stepped forward from the shadow of the house, where she had been standing.

"Elspeth is right," she said, trying to keep her voice steady. "Your wife may choose to let you play the petty tyrant, but you needn't come here and expect to repeat the performance. It's time you went."

"I've warned you before. . ." he began, pointing a stubby finger in her face.

"Don't be melodramatic," she said, coolly. "Get off my land."

"You want to act like a man," he shouted, his voice rising again, "'cept when it comes to a fight. Then you'll hide behind your skirts."

"Don't be ridiculous," Felicity advanced another step into the sunlight, twirling the straight edge nonchalantly in one hand. Bruton, although a bulky man, was no taller than Felicity, and didn't look as though he fancied his chances.

"You ain't heard the last of this," he snarled.

Felicity tutted gently between her teeth. "Will you stop rehearsing the text of a Victorian penny dreadful and get out of here?"

Bruton stood, with his fists clenched and his lips drawn back in a snarl. Despite his manner, he had never been a fighter himself. To everybody's great relief, he backed away, jumped into his Land-Rover and retreated in a cloud of ill-feeling. Felicity propped the length of wood very carefully against the timber-stack. Her hand was shaking.

"You were very calm," admired Elspeth.

"Was I? I was trembling like a leaf, really. Did you see my calves wobble?"

"No, and I'm sure he didn't."

"It's the fight or flight mechanism. A rush of adrenalin makes the poor old muscles flap about like that."

"I hope Shirley will be alright tonight."

"I suppose he hits her?" Elspeth was silent. "You're not going to say, are you? Did she swear you to secrecy? I admire your loyalty."

"He is a horrible man," said Elspeth, vehemently.

"This is a bit of a change from a few weeks ago, when you were giving me the 'marriage is made of compromise' line."

"How can you compromise with a monster?"

"Is he so unusual?" mused Felicity. "He's very crude, of course. But are degrees of coarseness really important?"

"Archibald would never dream of talking to me or my friends like that," said Elspeth, defensively.

"Does a man who takes you on a tour of vintage tractor rallies for your honeymoon ever need to raise his voice?"

"There's no need for you to be snide."

234

Felicity was suddenly desperately tired of navigating the shoal waters of rural life. She craved the metropolis and the society of other thirty year old women who didn't feel that placating an unreasonable man was their life's work. She wanted to sit in a pretentious cafe drinking pastis, while contemplating a choice of restaurants wider than the one Indian takeaway in Dereham, or the nearby country house hotel (English cooking at its most ordinary).

"If I drive very fast, and pay no attention to the highway code," she announced, coming out of this reverie, "I can be in London in time for the rush hour."

"Why should you want to do that?" said Elspeth, puzzled.

"Don't you ever get sick of the countryside? The smallness of it."

Elspeth looked around at the great open fields, and the huge sky, crisscrossed with the exhaust trails of the departed jets. She looked at her friend, bafflement on every inch of her round and open face.

"I want crowds," said Felicity, stripping off her shirt and shorts and pouring the remains of the bucket of water over herself. Elspeth looked away, shocked, but not before she had noticed that all of Felicity' hair was red and springy. "I want variety and anonymity," she continued, returning from the house with another bucket of water and a bar of soap. "I want to go to a cinema that isn't showing Nightmare on Elm Street part one hundred and three'." She lathered her armpits busily, splashing Elspeth with soap suds. Her eyes gleamed. "I want to go to a bar where the collecting box on the counter is for Frontliners, not the Royal British Legion. Somewhere that the people talk about the Serbian/Albanian crisis in Yugoslavia, not their entry for the fatstock show." She dipped her head in the bucket and shook her hair dry.

"I thought you had left all that in disgust?"

"I want to go and be reminded of what I'm running away from."

"How impetuous."

"Come with me if you like."

"What would Archibald say?"

"Aha! The sixty four million european currency unit question."

"But I can't drop everything and race up to London."

"Do you want to?"

"I don't know. Such an idea. . ."

"Now is your chance, dear Elspeth," Felicity ran to the caravan and emerged two minutes later in clean clothes, dragging a comb through her still damp curls.

"Are you really going?"

"Yes. The smoke is calling me."

"Perhaps I'll come next time, if you give me a bit more warning. I haven't even got anything in the freezer to give Archibald for his tea."

"Carpe Diem, Elspeth. If you plan to come next time, it's an arrangement, not an impulse. You must seize the moment. There is more to life than watching concrete harden." She flung her jacket and cheque book into the car and blew Elspeth a kiss. "See you tomorrow," she cried, slamming the door behind her. Elspeth, feeling rather breathless, waved, as Felicity rocketed up the drive in a cloud of dust.

TWENTY-ONE

As Elspeth settled down that evening in her living room, with a tray of shepherd's pie on her lap and Archibald's favourite nature programme on the television, Felicity was luxuriating her way through Pizza Napoletano, no anchovies, extra garlic, at Marine Ices, and contemplating an open sundae and cappucino to follow. In his cottage, Chalky White confronted the heel of a bloomer loaf with gladiatorial determination, hacking off its crusts, which were a challenge to his dentures, and sucking whole pickled onions from a jar, one at a time.

Adonis Bruton, his arm not broken, it transpired, but badly bruised, sat up in bed, his injured limb in a sling, crowing over Phoebe, who had not missed an afternoon of school, or had the treat of seeing the bones of her own arm in an x-ray photograph. Downstairs, their parents sat in tense and fulminating silence in their respective armchairs, Bruton pretending to read a farming magazine, and Shirley affecting interest in her needlepoint.

Chalky White and Felicity were the only ones who looked forward to the night with any enthusiasm. Although Jean at the Post Office would not disburse his pension until Thursday, Chalky had picked an unfancied winner and a second at long odds on an each way bet, and flushed with the profits of the day's racing, was going to treat himself to a good night at the White Stag. Felicity was simply spoiled for choice. However much she had fallen in love with Hope Cottage, it was a demanding relationship. The building programme had improved her health, self-confidence and mental composure, but had not offered a riot of entertainments. As she finished her salad, she flicked through her address book, trying to remind herself which of her London friends she had genuinely missed, these past few months, and wondering if any of them would be amenable to a wild night on the town.

Fluffy the lurcher neither anticipated the future,

nor worried about the past. He lay on the damp tiles of Chalky's kitchen floor, his nose on his paws, fast asleep, with a well-gnawed shin bone in easy reach. Instructing his pet to be a good boy, Chalky let himself out of the back door. Fluffy's ears twitched at the sound of the latch, but he slumbered on.

In the cluttered sitting room of her ugly bungalow, Elspeth wished that she too could find an excuse to go to sleep, although it would not be bed-time for an hour at least. Archibald was watching the news, which was mainly of strikes and environmental disasters, at home and abroad. Since he adduced both phenomena as evidence of a global communist conspiracy, he was kept busy answering back to the television.

"Why don't they tell us where these unions get their money from, for their so-called secret ballots? I don't believe they really post out votes to all their members, it stands to reason, the ordinary working man has no time for this sort of nonsense."

"I thought they got money for ballots from the government, dear," said Elspeth.

"Hah! Which one. Ours or the Russian's? But the news is rubbish. What can you expect, its written by a bunch of pinko fairies? Journalists! They're on strike half the time themselves, of course they're all sympathy for their union brothers."

"We could turn over, if it's annoying you."

"Same load of codswallop on the other side," snorted Archibald, as he did every night.

"I think I'll go to bed, when I've done the washing up. I've got a bit of a headache."

"You should take something for that. Shall I get you an aspirin?"

"No thank you. They don't agree with me. I'll make a pot of tea." She collected the tray of supper things from the floor by his feet.

"Leave that," he said, without taking his eyes from the screen. "I'll do it later."

"Yes, dear," she said, carrying out the tray, knowing that he never would. "I'll say good night then."

Elspeth undressed and lay on top of the bed covers

with the window open. The day, which had been scorching hot, had ended sultry. She felt stifled by the clammy humidity. Great black clouds blotted out any stars that might be emerging, and hordes of thunder-bugs, driven down to earth by the air pressure, brushed against her in the muggy darkness. She slapped at a mosquito on her thigh, and it exploded, full of her own blood. Her head thumped, and the sweat which gathered wherever her skin touched skin, or the nylon of her bedspread, did not evaporate.

Elspeth worried about Felicity and wondered at the agitation of spirit that produced her mad dash to town. She wondered at herself, that she should have been tempted, even for a moment, to go too. Technically, she was old enough to be Felicity's mother, and she certainly belonged to another generation. They had lived such different lives, she could not imagine Felicity would have been glad of her company amongst her smart London friends.

She worried too, and more seriously, about Shirley. Felicity, she was sure, only considered her a friend because society was so limited, here in Norfolk. Shirley, on the other hand, she could imagine being on good terms with in any circumstances, had they been neighbours in Acton, for instance. They had more in common. They both understood what it was to have responsibilities and commitments, not being able to dash off to the big city for the evening on a whim. She remembered Shirley's blackened eye, and the towering rage in which Bruton had been that afternoon, and shivered, despite the heat. She had never precisely believed that battered women asked for it, more that men were fundamentally uncivilised, and that a woman whose husband beat her had failed in her basic duty to ameliorate his animal nature. Now, for the first time in her life, she considered that there might be worse things than a marriage break up. Despite her horror of loneliness and poverty, Elspeth wondered if Shirley, middle-aged and unskilled though she was, wouldn't be better off without her husband.

She tried to picture where her friend might go, or how she would support herself if she were to leave him. A bedsit in Norwich, perhaps, and a job stacking supermarket shelves? It was too gloomy. And what about the children? The murderous hatred on Bruton's empurpled face that day haunted her dreams when she finally drifted off to sleep.

The man in question sat in a cold rage in his own sitting room, debating whether he might forbid his wife to visit Hope Cottage again, or to see that crone Elspeth Maybe. He had tried before, and she had defied him, even at the expense of a beating. He could not, in cold blood, strike her again, and she had wisely driven off that afternoon at the very moment when he felt his self-control give way, and his fists bunch irresistibly into clubs with which to batter her smooth, disobedient face. He did not dare to issue another ultimatum which might be flouted, for then how would she feel about him? Contemptuous? She had a look sometimes which made him cringe. The labourer's daughter had become the farmer's wife, and seemed in danger of forgetting what she owed him.

He sneaked a glance across at her, as she sat staring at her canvas, stretched on its frame. She had not set a stitch for half and hour. He hated the patterns she worked, complicated, geometric things, in pinks and mauves and greys. He blamed Elspeth and the public library in Dereham, between them, for introducing his wife to this sort of nonsense. The stag at bay had been good enough for his mother, he had no desire for a house that looked like a Mexican craft museum. Every finished cushion cover was banished to the children's bedrooms, where it was soon obliterated by spilt orange juice and pillow fights.

He was not proud of hitting her, he wouldn't boast of it to his mates, unless very drunk, but he regarded it as a necessity, like mulesing the sheep, painful and messy, but productive. She must respect him. He stole another glance at her, under his sandy lashes. The problem was, he hit her because she didn't respect him, and in the aftermath she despised him even more, which made him want to chastise her again. He sighed. He wished one of the F1-11s had crashed into Hope Cottage that afternoon, obliterating the building, its owner, and poisonous, polite, Elspeth Maybe. He could see no other way of successfully asserting his will that Shirley should no longer consort with those harridans.

Shirley, matching yarns with eyes that barely focused on the thread, knew exactly what he was thinking. She sat, rigidly, determined not to be driven from the room by the force of his silent anger. Her patience was rewarded, when he eventually surrendered his right to sit in his own chair, even in miserable discomfort, and took himself off to the pub.

By the time Bruton arrived at the White Stag, Chalky was in a state of happy, and largely incomprehensible, garrulity. He had given the assembled company a stride by stride account of the races of his two astutely backed horses, and was now propped in his usual corner, clutching a glass of barley wine, and muttering to himself "knew 'ey'd come in" at frequent intervals. A merchant banker, who had bought the old vicarage, affably stood him a drink, because he was a local character, then beat a retreat to the other end of the bar. Chalky did smell rather pungently of pickled onion, old boots and strong tobacco. Bruton got a drink and ignored his former cowman. Although it was late, he had no fear of the bar closing before he might get soused. The landlord of the White Stag considered licensing laws to be something which should be applied only to tourists and other townies. His regulars were never troubled by closing time.

In the big city, Felicity put the 'phone down, after her tenth encounter with an answering machine. Her smart London friends were not at home to callers. Reminding herself that she had vowed never to speak to any of those friends again, after the way they had cut her dead when she lost her job, she cast about for solitary entertainments. It was too late for the theatres, and anyway, she was so out of touch, she didn't know which was the play of the moment. Her favourite cinema was showing a Swedish art-house movie that she had already seen at the festival in Norwich. Dinner had been good, but a full stomach, and her lifestyle of healthy outdoor labour combined to make

241

her sleepy, although it was barely half past nine. Fighting against provincialism, she took herself to a club, across the road from King's Cross station, and resolved to dance.

The club was swelteringly hot, and already crowded. Despite the heat, everyone but her seemed to be wearing a black leather jacket, which she presumed too valuable to be taken off and slung over the back of a chair. The air was heavy with sweat, smoke and after-shave. A few women looked at her, as she tried in vain to reach the bar, but their eyes held no interest. The men looked exclusively at themselves, in mirrors, reflected in their partner's sun glasses. One youth drooped at the bar, like Narcissus, admiring his image caught in a spilled puddle of wine.

Felicity, in her jeans and polo-shirt (her very smartest) felt like a hick. With her calloused hands and hairy armpits, her face free of lipstick and her hair unstyled, she realised that she was just not making it. She also suspected that she was five or ten years older than most of the patrons of the bar, and, despite her secret addiction to pop-radio, she had not yet recognised a single one of the dance tracks being played. When a peroxided teenage butch took pity on her and made a space for her at the bar, she ordered tequila and drank it in one gulp, wondering why she felt like a mammoth, thawed back to life after a ten thousand year sleep in the Siberian permafrost, and wishing it wasn't so nearly her bedtime. Smothering a yawn, she tried to feel some of the energy which noise, heat, crowds and alcohol are supposed to engender in club-goers.

After an uncomfortable hour, in which not the slightest frisson had tingled her spine, she was, although incapable of passing a breathalyser test, in her car once more and starting the journey home. No sooner had she passed Redbridge and turned onto the motorway, than the first fat raindrops exploded onto her windscreen out of the heavy air. With her foot flat on the floorboards, she drove the old car recklessly into the storm.

Felicity hammered down the M11, pursued by a

thunder-cloud. The storm in which she drove had not yet reached Orfton-Saint-Scabious. There, the muggy night sucked the breath from the lungs of the mildly befuddled merchant banker, as he left the White Stag at closing time, wondering why the other customers where being so tardy about drinking up. The group around the red-faced farmer who was holding forth about a woman's place, had shown no sign of breaking up, despite the landlords repeated calls of 'lessave your glasses now, gents, please!"

Shirley Bruton, summoned upstairs by the sound of small feet thumping along the landing, climbed tiredly out of her chair and went upstairs to chase Phoebe out of Adonis's bedroom for the umpteenth time. The children were too hot to sleep, and as she made Phoebe's bed once more, smoothing the warm sheets and the soon to be thrown-off duvet, she couldn't really blame them.

"Goin' to be a storm," observed Phoebe

"I reckon."

"Donny's frightened of storms."

"So are you," said Shirley.

"I am not. Can I come in with you if it thunders?"

"No, your dad don't like to be disturbed. You stay here and go to sleep."

"My jamas're too hot," complained Phoebe.

"I'll fetch you a nightie."

"Mum," called Adonis, from his room, "I wanna drink of water." Shirley sighed. It was going to be a long night.

At Maybe Halt, Elspeth woke up and heard Archibald turn off the television and walk down the corridor to the bathroom. She wondered why, after all these years of living on one floor, they still spoke of going up to bed. As he entered the bedroom, shuffling in his slippers, she pretended to be asleep. He went directly to his own bed, turned back the sheets in exactly the same way he had done every night of his life, one fold, and then another on top, and set his glasses down on the bedside table. Anxious not to disturb him, she forced herself to stop tossing and turning, looking for a cool spot in the bed, where there was none. The effort of keeping still brought her even wider awake, although her head felt thick and her mouth was scummy. Archibald heard the drone of mosquitoes, rose from his bed and firmly shut the window. He had heard that blood-drawing insects could transmit Aids, and wished to take no chances. The air in the bedroom ceased to move, and the temperature rose.

In Chalky's cottage, Fluffy snapped out of his canine slumbers and leapt to his feet barking. An answering bark from next door was muffled, as Randolph clapped his giant paw around the muzzle of his own lurcher, who was in fact Fluffy's half brother. Silently Randolph slipped through the garden gate and across the dark fields, his dog at his heels and his poacher's pockets emptied in readiness.

Shirley lay, listening to the grandfather clock strike midnight. She was apprehensive, awaiting the return of her husband who might be brave enough, drunk, to do what he had been wanting to all day; give her a good pasting. She heard his car bouncing over the cattle grid, which they had never removed after the cows were sold, and braced herself, feigning sleep like Elspeth. The car door slammed and she heard unsteady footsteps on the concrete of the yard, but he did not come into the house. It sounded as though he were looking for something in the tractor shed. Metal clanged on concrete and the petrol pump whirred. If she wondered why he should be filling a jerry can at this time of night, it was only for a moment, as she waited for the banging of the front door and the footsteps on the stairs. They did not come. As five, then ten minutes passed, she began to be sure that he had left the farm and got up to look out of the window.

Chalky reeled unsteadily down the lane towards his house, his money, and the patience of the other regulars, having finally run out. He could have got a lift with Bruton, but the farmer had left in a foul mood, fighting drunk, not offering a seat in his car. Chalky, inebriated, was not too proud to have asked, but something in the man's wild and bloodshot gaze stopped him. Leaning heavily on his stick, he stumbled along the crown of the lane, sweating profusely. When a car came up behind him, driving fast, he turned and waved his stick to flag it down, not thinking to move from the middle of the road. The headlights rushed towards him unswervingly. At the last minute, the driver saw the small dark figure of the man waving a stick, and stamped on the brakes, screeching to a halt within inches of Chalky's feet.

"You old fool!" shouted Felicity, frightened almost sober. "I nearly didn't see you."

"'s no fool like an' ol' fool," Chalky hiccuped amiably, unaware of his narrow escape. "Gisa lif' then."

"Oh, get in," Felicity opened the door and pulled him roughly into the passenger seat.

"Where you been?" he asked.

"London."

"Ah."

"For the evening."

"'snice."

"Not really."

"I been there once," he confided. "Seen the Tower."

"That's nice."

"No it we'nt. Horrible place. Fulla tourists."

They drove on in silence to Chalky's house. Felicity stopped and helped him out. He opened the kitchen door, and Fluffy came bursting out, pleased to see them both, and eager for a run.

"Wha's 'at?" asked Chalky, peering into the darkness of the field behind his house. "Tha' pink ligh' over there?"

"Delirium Tremens, probably,"

"Can' you see?" he pointed a gnarled and shaking finger.

"No."

"Somethin' up, over your house," he said, firmly. "Me 'n Fluff'l come home with you."

"Oh, for god's sake!" Felicity protested in vain. Chalky and the dog got into the car and sat waiting for her. "I shall only have to bring you home again. There's nothing there." She looked across the fields, in the direction of Hope Cottage, but her eyes, strained by the glare of headlights on the motorway, could see nothing amiss. Reluctantly, she got back into the car and drove the stubborn, drunken old man, and his uncontrollable dog towards her house.

Elspeth, abandoning sleep, had risen from her bed as soon as Archibald's snores filled the sultry air. Slipping on gardening shoes and a coat over her night dress, she sat on the porch, ready to catch any stray cooling breeze that might be about. She was rewarded by a sudden rush of wind, which swept across the garden and then died again. Thunder rumbled menacingly, but the storm was still more promised than real. She sat, lost in thought, hot and uncomfortable. Her nose twitched. She wondered if she had left the oven on. There was a foul, singed smell coming from somewhere close. She rose and went indoors to check the kitchen. Everything was in order, as always. Returning to the verandah, she smelt the acrid drift of smoke once more. Perhaps Archibald had failed to douse the firebox of his engine, after running it up and down the track all day? She walked through the garden and let herself out into the field. The engine stood, black and massive, smelling only of oil and soot. With difficulty, she hauled herself up onto the footplate and gingerly touched the metal door through which coal was shovelled. It was cool.

As Elspeth was about to get down from her vantage point, she glanced across to Hope Cottage, and caught a flash of light. Felicity must have come back from London early. She was used to seeing the dancing light of candles and torches from her neighbour, for Felicity was not yet on the mains. She climbed down from the engine, and was about to return to the house, when something about the quality of the light struck her. It was too bright for a candle, and in the wrong place. She looked again. It was not the caravan window that was illuminated, but the empty upper storey of Hope Cottage itself. The light flickered again, from what would be the bedroom window, now empty of glass. Felicity might be exploring her house at night, or there might be intruders.

Elspeth began to walk across the field, between the rustling stalks of ripening wheat. As she walked, the dancing light appeared again at the window, and grew steadier. She saw that it was not light, but flame, and the explanation for the smoke which stung her eyes occurred to her. She began to run, hampered by her loosely tied shoes and the growing grain. Across the field she raced, her coat flapping, her nightdress catching around her legs. Halfway across the field, she stopped to think. Felicity had no telephone. Turning on her heels, she fled back to her own house to ring the fire brigade. Having given breathless directions to the operator, she rushed once more into the night, banging the door behind her, but not thinking to wake Archibald.

Shirley lay in her darkened room, waiting for her husband to return from whatever drunken errand he was on, her nerves stretched by the expectation of a beating when he got home. The creak of a settling floorboard or thump of the plumbing made her start, tense in every muscle. When she felt, at screaming point, that she could stand it no more, she got up and dressed quickly. Nothing, she thought, could be worth this. No amount of security or comfort. Dressing the children, who were still fretfully awake, she bundled all three of them down to her car, terrified lest her husband return as she was leaving.

"Where're we going?" asked Phoebe, suspiciously.

"For a drive. None of us can sleep."

"You running away from Dad?" asked Adonis, nursing his arm in its sling. "Mum tried to take us with her, when she done a bunk, but Dad soon stopped that."

"Shut up and get in the car, Donny. We're just going for a drive." Looking over her shoulder, and jumping at every shadow, she piled in, locking the doors on the inside.

"Why you doin' that?" Donny eyed her curiously.

"Safety. It's for safety," she said, knowing that if she stopped to think, the courage of her impulse would desert her. With her heart in her mouth, she drove down the farm track as fast as she dared and turned onto the road.

"Look mum," said Phoebe, her nose pressed to the window. "There's a fire."

"Where?" Shirley did not look round, concentrating on the road ahead. Bruton had not taken his car, or the Land-Rover.

"Hope Cottage," said Phoebe. "It's on fire."

Shirley braked hard and looked out of her window. Sure enough, beyond the belt of trees that stood back from the road, a glow of flames could be seen. She was in a quandary, her need to escape tugging her one way, and her desire to help her friend pulling the other. Car headlights approached from the village, and she had an irrational fear that it was Bruton, in some other vehicle.

"We'll go and take a look," she announced, driving onto the track that led to Hope Cottage. "You kids must stay in the car."

Ahead of them, the cottage was thoroughly ablaze, flames licking out of the empty windows and under the eaves of the new roof. Behind them, the headlights of the following car turned onto the track. Shirley stopped, feeling trapped, not knowing what to do. Elspeth emerged from the night and rapped on the window.

"You must pull your car off the track," she said. "you and Felicity both. I've called the fire brigade, but they won't be able to get down here if your cars are blocking the path."

"Felicity?" said Shirley, dazed.

"She's right behind you," Elspeth almost danced with impatience. "Do get off the track."

Shirley drove obediently into the field of wheat, bumping her chassis on the headland of the plough. Felicity followed suit. She ran, with Elspeth and Shirley, towards the house. with Chalky hobbling slowly behind, and the children, for the moment, staying where they were.

Elspeth grabbed a bucket, with some idea of making a human chain, filled it from the pond and dashed the water against the dully glowing corrugated iron which covered the front door. The heat was fierce and drove her back. The flames, fed by the draught from the empty windows, were roaring up through the house and licking around the new tiles.

"Help me pull the caravan clear," shouted Felicity, "It's too late to save the house." She ran to the side of the burning building, with Shirley at her heels, and kicked away the blocks on which her temporary home rested. The two of them, soon joined by Elspeth, tugged fruitlessly at the tow bar, as huge, glowing embers rained dangerously down on them. The caravan, immobile for twenty years, its tyres flat and perished, sunk in the soft earth and grown about with clinging weeds, resisted their efforts. Chalky limped over to the back end of the vehicle and leant his meagre weight to the effort. The caravan would not move.

Their lungs scorching in the super-heated air, they strained and gasped, pulling and pushing, trying to rock the wheels out of their ruts.

"Get your things out of it," yelled Shirley, "We can't move it." As she spoke, the caravan lurched forwards, as though it had been struck from behind by a runaway train. Another great impact shuddered through the old tourer, and the wheels disengaged from the ruts in which they had been held fast.

Randolph appeared, his face, illuminated by the blaze, wearing an expansive grin. Having shoulder-charged the caravan free from behind, he picked up the tow bar and began to pull it clear of the fire. The women hurriedly took the strain again. With sweat pouring down their faces, their heels slipping as they tried to dig in for purchase, they dragged the caravan over to the garden fence, as far from the licking tongues of flame and showering sparks as they could take it.

"Where's Chalky?" screamed Elspeth suddenly, over the noise of the conflagration. Everyone looked blank. Randolph, who was humming to himself, a great musical booming from deep in his chest, ran back towards the house and scooped up his drunken neighbour, who had fallen flat when the caravan against which he was pushing had lurched forward. As a child carries a teddy, Randolph bore the unconscious Chalky over to the patch of waste ground by the pond, and fanned his face with his cap. Felicity, kneeling by the old man's body, felt inside his jacket for a heartbeat, and to her relief, found a strong and regular thumping. Chalky's clothes were singed on the side that had lain nearest the fire, but his face was the pale green colour of a faint, not the livid red of a burns case. As they watched, and Randolph fanned, still humming cheerfully, Chalky groaned and sat up.

"Randolph, you silly ol' bugger, why d'you go an' shove tha' bloody caravan so sudden as all that? You're subtle as a tank," he complained, peevishly. Randolph merely smiled, and helped Chalky to his unsteady feet.

The crackle of roof timbers starting to burn turned their attention back to the disaster. They stood by the pond, reduced to helpless spectators. As they watched, the roof began to sag, and a slate popped off, like a cork from a shaken champagne bottle. A siren wailed towards them, still some miles distant. Retreating step by step, until their backs were against the trees around the pond, they watched the roof go up. Felicity had her hands clapped over her ears, to shut out the roar of flames and loud cracking from the broken roof.

"You know wha'?" asked Chalky, of no one in particular. "'s a terrible smell of petrol round here."

Shirley looked at him sharply, an expression of horrified conviction on her face. Elspeth, not understanding the look, took her hand, soothingly. A fire engine arrived, crashing down the drive, and the scene was suddenly transformed from the ruin of a home to an orderly place of work. Running their hoses from the pond to the house, they sucked cool green water up and spat it onto the inferno. The last part of the roof collapsed inwards with a crash as the stream of water began to play on it. The brickwork glowed, and the whole house became a chimney for the roaring fire.

Men in helmets stamped about shouting, watched with fascination by the children, who had crept from the car to see the fun, and with indifference by the adults, shocked into immobility. When there was nothing left to burn, the fire died down, helped on its way by the last drop of water from the meagre pond. A stinking outline of charred walls and smoking rubble sank back into the darkness. As the last flame died into glowing ashes, the storm which had rumbled overhead as the fire-fighters worked to save the house, crashed into life and hurled down on them a torrent of useless water.

"I think," said Elspeth, when Felicity had finished talking to the leading fireman, who announced that they would stay for a while, in case of a flare-up, "that we should all go back to my house and have a cup of tea." Miserable, soaking and stunned, they trailed after her.

TWENTY-TWO

Archibald Maybe stood in the hallway of his home, open mouthed, his hair tousled and his pyjamas gaping at the fly, watching the procession that was making its way across his threshold. It looked like the aftermath of an earthquake. Chalky, wrapped in a car rug, soaked and shivering, his face blackened by smoke, was helped through the door by Elspeth, solicitous at his elbow.

"Go and put the kettle on, Archibald," she commanded. "And, she added, with an uninterested glance at his dishevellement, "put a dressing gown on will you?" She was followed by the two Bruton children, wide-eyed, their hair plastered to their heads by the lashing rain. Shirley entered next, tightlipped and pale, saying nothing, lost in some private horror. Behind her, Randolph ducked his head, which the door lintel menaced, nodded to Archibald and followed the rest of the party into the living room. His face, strangely unlined for a man in his sixties, was suffused with a glow of exhilaration even more marked than that worn by the children. He was still humming quietly to himself, but Archibald, who was no fan of Faure's, did not recognise the tune. Finally, Felicity limped in, the sole of one of her shoes melted through by contact with a molten roofing nail which had fallen from the ruin. The streaks on her dirty face could have been caused by the rain, or by tears. At her heels slunk a bedraggled and frightened Fluffy, tail down, ears flattened. To Archibald, he seemed to be all teeth and legs.

"The kettle, dear," reminded Elspeth, rather sharply, and Archibald pulled himself together. He had slept through the sirens, and the great crashing thunderstorm which still raged overhead; he had not been disturbed by the drumming of torrential rain on the roof. Only the slamming of car doors outside his house had woken him, and he failed entirely to comprehend what all these disreputable people were doing in his living room.

Shirley was rubbing the children dry with more vigour than gentleness. The airing cupboard was rifled for the rest of the next week's supply of clean towels, so that the other refugees, even the filthy dog, might be dried. Chalky, who confessed that he was still not quite feeling himself, was laid tenderly on the settee. Randolph kindly unlaced his neighbour's boots, and put the offending articles on the hearth, by the ornamental fire irons. Felicity, without waiting to be asked, had raided the drinks cabinet, and was pouring reviving tots of Archibald's Christmas whisky all round.

Archibald himself returned from the kitchen, bearing a tea-pot and determined to demand an explanation for the invasion. Shirley, having got the children dry, was equally determined to get them into bed, and Elspeth had gone to make up the spare room. Felicity, taking a cup of tea with a shaking hand, and tipping her whisky into it, to fortify the pale brown brew, became aware of Archibald's puzzlement, if not his outrage, at the intrusion.

"My house burned down," she explained helpfully.

"Oh."

"Nobody was hurt," she continued, "except Chalky, a bit."

"I'm a'righ'," slurred Chalky, gallantly, from the settee, his outlook much improved by a shot of spirits. Elspeth bustled back into the room with an armful of blankets, eager to wrap up any potential victims of shock.

"Archibald, fetch the sugar bowl please," she commanded. "People need sweet tea at times like this." Unused to being so ordered about in his own home, he went off grumpily to do as he was bid.

Randolph produced a dead hare from his pocket and proffered it silently to Elspeth. The outstretched hand in which he held it was smeared with blood. The hare's beautiful limpid eyes had not yet clouded over. Elspeth, with an audible gulp, managed to take the morbid offering in her stride.

"Oh, dear, yes," she said politely, "I quite see you don't want to leave that in your pocket on a warm night. Should I hang it up." Randolph made a gesture with his thumb, indicative of gutting, and dangled the hare by its hind legs. Elspeth took it from him cautiously. "Too kind," she murmured. She whisked out to the kitchen, colliding on the way with Archibald.

"What's that?" he asked, eyeing the hare with distaste.

"A present from that strange cousin of the Bruton's, isn't it thoughtful of him?"

"What are all these people doing in my house?" demanded Archibald, pettishly.

"There's been a fire."

"So I gather. I don't see why we should be turned into a casualty clearing station and general doss house. And," he eyed her unusual garb, "don't tell me you've been running about the countryside in your nightdress?"

"It was an emergency," said Elspeth, defensively, blushing under his critical gaze.

"Well send them home, I want to get some sleep tonight."

"Felicity hasn't got a home any more," pointed out Elspeth, preparing for battle.

"I suppose she'll have to stay," Archibald conceded grudgingly. "But that Bruton woman's got a perfectly good home of her own. Unless you're going to tell me that's burned down too?"

"Shirley's staying here tonight," said Elspeth, firmly. She had had a quiet word with her friend as they were putting the children to bed.

"Why?"

"She isn't going home."

"Elspeth, I forbid you to interfere between man and wife."

"I'm not," said Elspeth, guiltily. "She's not going home, so she can either sleep here or in a ditch, if you insist on making her leave."

"I'm going to ring Bruton," he fumed, "and tell him where his wife and children are."

"You can't," protested Elspeth, aghast.

"It's my duty," said Archibald, terribly. "As you

should realise. He has a right to be told. I don't supposed you've considered how he must feel, not knowing where they are? Out of his mind with worry I shouldn't wonder." He picked up the telephone, looked up the number and dialled. Elspeth wrung her hands. "No answer," he announced, testily. "I suppose he's out looking for them. Really, you women are so selfish."

"He hits her, you know," Elspeth blurted out, forced to reveal what she had promised to keep secret. Archibald considered the revelation gravely.

"I don't imagine," he pronounced, "that he would do such a thing unless he was provoked. It isn't for us to meddle, anyway. I'm glad," he added, "that I left teaching before this fad against corporal punishment came in."

"I don't understand how you can be so cruel."

"I'm doing what I know to be right. You must tell your friend that she has to go home where she belongs. And while you are about it, you can clear out the village idiot and that smelly old tramp and his mongrel."

"Archibald," Elspeth drew herself up to her full height and looked him straight in the eye, "Shirley and her children are staying here tonight, because I've offered them our hospitality, and I don't intend to deny it. Chalky and Randolph and Felicity are staying too, if they want to. We've all had a great shock, and what's needed is rest, peace and quiet. I'm sorry if you don't like it, but there it is." Her husband goggled at her. Soothingly she said, "the dog can sleep outside if you insist, although I imagine he might howl."

"Entertain your guests as you see fit," stormed Archibald, turning on his heel, "I'm going to bed. Unless you want my bed for someone else, that is?" he added, with awful sarcasm.

"That's probably best," agreed Elspeth, "will you leave the sugar bowl, or are you taking that with you?"

Archibald glared at the decorated bowl which he still clutched, and put it down with a snap on the telephone table. To his horror, before he could reach the safety of his bedroom, the door of the sitting room opened, and Randolph emerged. He stared at Archibald with an unblinking gaze which caused the other man to scuttle into his bedroom, shook Elspeth politely by the hand and ambled off into the night.

"Randolph's gone," announced Elspeth, walking into the sitting room. Chalky was snoring on the settee, neatly rolled in a blanket, and Felicity was crying silently into her teacup. "Oh, dear," said Elspeth perching on the edge of the chair and putting her arm round Felicity's shoulders. "What a terrible business. It could have been worse, at least no-one was there to get hurt."

"Maybe it wouldn't have happened, if I'd been there," sobbed Felicity.

"There's no need to blame yourself. I'm sure it's just one of those accidents."

"No it isn't," said Shirley, coming silently back into the room. "That wasn't an accident."

"How do you know?" demanded Felicity, sceptically.

"Bruton took a can of petrol and went off somewhere, just after midnight. I heard him."

"That doesn't prove anything," said Elspeth, anxiously.

"Why?" asked Felicity.

Shirley looked at her with compassion. "He hates you," she said, "and he wants to punish me. And 'cos no Bruton never done nothing without a profit in mind, I s'pose I thought you'd be more likely to sell to him, if he burnt you out."

"What good is a burnt-down house to a property speculator?" asked Felicity, not wishing to believe what her instincts told her must be true.

"He'd have to rebuild, anyway. Buyin' a write-off might be cheaper."

"I won't sell to him."

"You sell to anyone else, chances are they're actin' for him," pointed out Shirley.

"Are you sure about this?" asked Elspeth.

"You all smelt the petrol," Shirley shrugged.

"That was from the concrete mixer," Felicity protested, blowing her nose messily.

"That didn't go up till after we got there." Shirley was right, the fuel tank of the concrete mixer had exploded in a dramatic fireball, minutes before the arrival of the first tender.

"The bastard!" exclaimed Felicity, conviction dawning. "No wonder you daren't go home."

"I'll have to," said Shirley, disconsolately, "don't know what I was thinkin' of, runnin' away. We've nowhere to go."

"You mustn't go back there," said Elspeth vehemently. "You can stay here as long as you like."

Shirley shook her head sadly. "I heard you and Mr Maybe arguin' in the hall," she said, "I know we can't stay here. Thanks anyway."

"Archibald will have to be told. He's had his own way all his life, now it's somebody else's turn. And if he doesn't like it, I'm afraid he will just have to lump it. Now I think it's time we all went to sleep while there's still any of the night left." She marshalled them to their sleeping quarters, Shirley to the spare room to share a bed with the children, and Felicity, snivelling quietly for her lost home, onto some cushions on the sitting room floor, beside the dog.

In the morning, the mundane necessities of finding a breakfast cereal that the children would accept, and queuing for the bathroom eased the awkwardness of the situation. Archibald kept to his bed with a sore throat. Elspeth took him a hot lemon drink, but she was obviously distracted. Felicity and Chalky, their heads thickened by smoke inhalation and alcohol, coughed their way into the kitchen, a pair of bleary, red-eyed derelicts. It was agreed that they would walk over to Hope Cottage and view the ruins.

"Dad never lets us walk through the crops," said Phoebe, apparently perfectly rested by four hours sleep, as she trampled her way through the wheat field.

"Don't make a habit of it," said Shirley, automatically.

"This is a public footpath, actually," Elspeth informed them, "it gets ploughed over every year."

It was a beautiful morning, once again, clear, warm and fresh-smelling after the storm. Fluffy bounded through the wheat in erratic circles, chasing scents, and Chalky consented to lean on Felicity's arm for support. The little procession wound its way across the field.

Hope Cottage rested, like the stump of a rotten tooth in an inflamed gum, a blot on the clean loveliness of the morning. A sour smell of wet cinders and smoke-clogged rubble assailed their nostrils as they approached. A red car, bearing the crest of the Norfolk fire service, was parked in the drive and as they trailed up, the officer leading the investigation introduced himself, looking curiously at the motley crowd which had accompanied Felicity. 'I wonder if he assumes that I did it myself,' she thought. A shout from his assistant called the investigator's attention to the rear of the building, and with a brief apology he left them.

The old deck chair stood incongruously intact under one of the apple trees, and Chalky settled himself in it, as though on a normal visit. Fluffy roamed the garden, and began digging holes, aroused by the smell of mole-tunnels under the lawn. The children went to investigate the pond, sucked dry by the firemen's pumps. In the green and slimy depression all that was left was a small pool of rain-water and, sticking up in the middle of the muddy bottom, Adonis's air-rifle, which Felicity had hurled into the pond on their first meeting. The ducks had fled.

The fire investigator returned to his car and began speaking quietly into the radio in the sort of code-language affected by emergency services, in which numbers substitute for nouns. Bees trundled through the air, fat with pollen, buzzing contentedly. The same thrush which had carolled for Felicity the previous morning, sang in the same willow tree. Hoping to slake her thirst, she picked a green apple off the tree under which she stood and bit into it. The fruit was hard and bitter, so she threw it away. The blank face of the house stared at them from the smoke-blackened eye-sockets of its empty windows. The honeysuckle, burnt off the walls, lay shrivelled on the ground. The brickwork was cracked and bulging in several places, and the end gable, which Felicity had so painstakingly rebuilt, displayed an ominous gaping rift.

"Was it insured?" asked Chalky conversationally, cocking a shrewd eye at the wreckage.

"Yes," said Felicity. "Suspiciously enough, it was. Bricks and mortar cover."

"But what about your time and effort?" asked Elspeth, "You can't insure those."

"Five months' work up in smoke," agreed Felicity bitterly.

"Will you rebuild?" asked Shirley.

"I don't know," Felicity looked at the sorry jumble of dirty bricks and charred timbers. "I don't know if it's possible to repair. I don't know if I have the energy to start again."

"But it's your home!" protested Elspeth.

"It's only a house," answered Felicity, rubbing her bleary eyes. "Was a house, rather. I never even lived in it."

"But you put so much of yourself into it," insisted Elspeth.

"That's gone now," said Felicity. "Anyway, who knows, we might have done it wrong," she joked feebly. "Maybe the roof was going to fall in of its own accord."

A second official car drew up, and a police inspector got out, accompanied by two constables. The fire investigator, who had come to meet them, conducted the new arrivals around to the back of the house, which seemed to be a source of great interest.

"I wonder if they'll find out how it started?" asked Shirley, nervously.

"Boun' to," said Chalky.

"If I did rebuild," said Felicity, suddenly, awaking from her reverie, "I'd do it from scratch. There's no point hanging on to these four walls, which is all that's left. I'd raze the lot and start again, properly, with foundations and drainage and a damp proof course. History is all very well, but it can be damned inconvenient"

"That's the spirit," encouraged Elspeth.

"I only said if," cautioned Felicity.

The police inspector walked over to them. "Miss Rouse?" he asked.

"Ms," corrected Felicity. "Can I help you."

"If you would come with me please." He led the way across the garden. Felicity followed, with a wink from Chalky to speed her on her way.

"I wish you'd stop your dog from digging up my lawn," she called back to him.

Around the corner of the house, and a little behind it, a temporary screen had been erected about something on the ground at which the fire investigators and the constables were peering with professional stolidity. The inspector ushered Felicity up to the spot, and the constables stood respectfully aside.

"Do you know this man?" he asked, coolly.

Felicity looked down at the wildly staring eyes of Farmer Bruton, as malevolent in death as they had been in life. A pulse pounded noisily in her ears and she wiped her suddenly clammy hands on her trouser legs. It was the first time she had seen a dead body. He appeared to have shrunk, the broken veins on his face faintly traced in the pallor of death. There was no particular shape to his body, as if his limbs had lost their purpose. His hair and clothes were singed, but his face was unmarked.

She cleared her throat and tried to speak as calmly as the policeman. "His name is Bruton," she said, her voice croaking uncontrollably. "He has the farm over the road. Had," she corrected herself.

"Was he a friend of yours?" she was asked. The blank faces of the men in uniform were carefully schooled to show no interest.

"No," she said.

"Any idea what he might have been doing here, with a jerry can full of petrol?" She realised he was asking her these questions when she was still shocked at the sight of the body, hoping she would be too shaken to guard her tongue.

"No," she said again.

"The doctor will be here soon, to examine the

body. If you wouldn't mind not leaving the vicinity for a while. There will be more questions."

"Shirley Bruton's here," said Felicity, feeling as if her words came from a million miles away.

"Would that be the lady with the children?"

"Yes. You mustn't let them see." Felicity had a sudden, horrifying vision of Phoebe and Adonis stumbling upon the body of their dead father.

"We won't," the inspector reassured. "I'll have a word with Mrs Bruton myself." He walked back the way he had come, and Felicity followed in a daze. The policeman took Shirley to one side, and spoke to her in the clipped and measured tones in which officials announce the deaths of those they have never met in life. Eventually the two of them retired to the screened-off area, where Shirley identified her husband's body.

"Bruton's lying dead outside my back door," said Felicity quietly to Chalky and Elspeth. The children were still playing by the pond.

"My god!" Elspeth's little round eyes widened in her perfectly circular face. She clasped her hands to her mouth. There was no time for her to say anything else, before Shirley returned, walking slowly, looking straight ahead.

"Perhaps you'd be so kind as to take Mrs Bruton home," said the very proper inspector of police to Elspeth, Mrs. . .?"

"Maybe," said Elspeth.

"I really think you should," he insisted.

"No, Maybe is my name. Of course I'll take her home. Come on Shirley," she grasped her friend by the arm, "you come home with me."

"No," said Shirley, calmly, "I'm going to my own home. I hope you'll come too. Phoebe! Donny!" she called the children. "Come on now, we're goin' home."

"One of my men will drive you," offered the inspector.

"No need," said Shirley, in the same emotionless tone of voice.

"If Archibald should come looking for me," said

Elspeth, hurriedly to Felicity, "tell him where I've gone. He may not like it, but I'm going to be staying with Shirley."

"I'll tell him," promised Felicity.

Shirley, with Elspeth still holding her arm, set off towards home. The inspector returned to his business.

The morning passed. A doctor arrived, and a scene-of-crime officer, closely followed by the photographer. Men stood around, talking in normal voices about their summer holidays, and drinking coffee out of thermos flasks. The radios in their cars chattered to the empty air. Felicity overheard one bored constable say to the other that the doctor had given it as his opinion that Bruton had died of the effects of smoke inhalation, sometime between midnight and two am.

Chalky sat contentedly in the deck-chair, watching the comings and goings, and nursing his hangover. Felicity sprawled beside him, waiting for them all to go away. She found herself humming a tune that had been stuck in the back of her mind all day. Fluffy scrabbled in the bottom of his deep exploration punctuating his digging with sneezes, as the flying earth got up his nose. Pawing at something in the bottom of the hole, he scraped it from side to side, until he could get his teeth around the object.

"Fluff!," shouted Chalky, "Come 'ere boy." The dog trotted over and dropped the object he had been carrying in his mouth into Felicity's lap, the better to slobber over his master. "I tol' you to stop diggin' up the lawn, din' I?" Chalky asked sternly, holding the dog by his muzzle.

Felicity had been about to throw the object away, expecting some disgusting anatomical relic, but the gleam of metal caught her eye. With the edge of her shirt, she cleaned off some of the encrusted mud, and revealed a crude, heavy ornament, in dull shining metal. Empty sockets showed where stones had been set. The design was ornate, but primitive.

"Wha'sat you got?" asked Chalky.

"I don't know. An ornament of some sort. Here, have a look." She passed it over.

Chalky buffed the metal vigorously on his sleeve,

held it up to the light, peered at it, and tried to sink his teeth into it. "Damn these dentures," he said, "they don' bite through nothin'. 's gold, though, you can tell tha'."

"I wonder how old it is?"

"Goes back a fair way, I reckon. Someone as lived here musta hidden it. Or lost it."

"Treasure trove?"

"'a's righ'"

"It's quite fetching, in an ugly sort of way," Felicity cleaned the last of the dirt off the find. "I think it used to be a brooch. There's a catch for a pin at the back."

"'s yours now. Found on your land."

"Thank you, Fluff," she thumped the dog affectionately. "What a strange day it's been."

"Nothin' strange about Bruton comin' to a bad end," snorted Chalky.

"I'm prepared to believe that he set fire to my house," said Felicity, puzzling, "but why should he lie down in the garden for a nice lungfull of smoke and asphyxiate himself?"

"I don' s'pose he did tha'," said Chalky, slyly.

"What then?"

"Who d'you know a's got a hand big enough to put over a man's face an' stop him breathing. Jus' long enough so he was unconscious, perhaps? So as you could leave him in the path of the fire he set, knowing he'd either fry or choke?"

She looked at him strangely. "What are you saying?"

"I'm not sayin' nothin'," he pursed his lips. "There's plenty with reason to want the ol' bastard dead, an' if one of them happens to be hangin' aroun' where they foun' his body. . ."

"Randolph?"

"He's a big strong lad, Randolph."

"But he was so cheerful, last night," she protested.

"Ah, 's what I thought," agreed Chalky, tapping the side of his nose sapiently. "He may be mad, but he i'n't stupid."

Felicity sat with her arms wrapped around her drawn-up legs, hugging herself. She hummed again the tune which had been going round her head. The half remembered words of the Libera Me came back to her, one phrase in particular repeating itself in tremendous bass chords in her head. "Dies illa, dies irae," she sang, absently, humming the rest of the line.

Fluffy's ears twitched, as he lay at her feet, and Chalky raised an eyebrow. "Wha'sat you're singing?" he asked.

"It's from Faure's Requiem," she said, "I don't know why, but I can't stop humming it."

"Soun's like one a Randolph's tunes," he said, casually. "Sings'em in Latin too. Use ter be in the choir, 'fore he got too ugly-tempered to be let near a church. Still knows 'is Latin though. 'e's clever, for a loony."

Felicity fell silent, and the bright morning sun faded from her eyes. She saw, once again, Randolph, emerging from the darkness in which Bruton had died, singing to himself of the Day of Wrath, his face illuminated by the savage flames and a beautiful angelic smile.

Onlywomen Press publishes fiction, poetry and theory to express and illuminate a developing Radical Lesbian Feminism. To ensure that development and recognise the radical lesbians upon whom it depends, Onlywomen has established the U.K.'s first annual award for lesbian feminist poetry, the MARGOT JANE MEMORIAL POETRY PRIZE. Our books may be purchased from good bookshops everywhere or by mail-order directly from Onlywomen. For a free catalogue detailing all our publications, send S.A.E. to: ONLYWOMEN PRESS, 71 Great Russell Street, London WC1B 3BN.

Some of Onlywomen's prose fiction titles are listed on the following pages.

THE REACH: lesbian feminist fiction
ed. Lilian Mohin & Sheila Shulman
The first 'out' lesbian anthology in Britain (1984), reprinted for its gripping writing and wide range of subjects. 17 stories including: family connections and confrontations, exhilarating love stories, struggles with anti-lesbianism and futuristic fantasies.
ISBN 0–906500–15–X

THE PIED PIPER: lesbian feminist fiction
ed. Anna Livia & Lilian Mohin
Stories by 19 authors in this 1989 selection. Here the settings range from medieval Britain to 19th century Jamaica and contemporary dyke bars in North America and Europe. A timely essay on the state of U.K. lesbian feminism forms the editors' introduction.
ISBN 0–906500–29–X

IN AND OUT OF TIME: lesbian feminist fiction
ed. Patricia Duncker
The 18 stories in this 1990 selection include new work
from renowned Irish poet, Mary Dorcey, as well as
stories from Asian prose writers such as Shameem
Kabir and Daljit Kaur. The editor's afterword discusses
the lesbian feminist literary tradition.
ISBN 0–906500–37–0

PERFECT PITCH: lesbian feminist fiction
ed. J. E. Hardy
Blurring the distinction between fantasy and reality,
the 1991 selection emphasizes the supernatural as a
facet of everyday lesbian life. 15 stories, contributors'
notes and details of editor's intent.
ISBN 0–906500–41–9

HATCHING STONES
Anna Wilson
A mordantly witty novel set in the near future when
easy, successful cloning brings the issues of gender and
male supremacy into everyone's consciousness.
ISBN 0–906500–39–7

STEALING TIME
Nicky Edwards
A novel about corporate fraud and urban lesbian
feminism with a rascally 14 year old anti-hero at its
centre.
ISBN 0–906500–31–1

CACTUS
Anna Wilson
A novel about 2 lesbian couples, one modern and
managing to live in our hostile society and one which
broke up through social pressures some twenty years
earlier.
ISBN 0–906500–04–4

ALTOGETHER ELSEWHERE
Anna Wilson

Futuristic novel about women as vigilantes against male violence. Writing that hums with sinister and playful energy.
ISBN 0–906500–18–4

RELATIVELY NORMA
Anna Livia

Humorous novel set (mostly) in Australia where a London feminist 'comes out' to her family. Written with panache and linguistic invention.
ISBN 0–906500–10–9

BULLDOZER RISING
Anna Livia

Science fiction gleefully detailing a 'secret' congress of old women who plot their own survival and, incidentally, the downfall of male supremacy. An invigorating satire.
ISBN 0–906500–27–3

INCIDENTS INVOLVING WARMTH:
Lesbian Feminist Love Stories
Anna Livia

Friendship, long-term relationships, involvement with straight women, mobilizations against rapists, passion where you least expect it. Astute inventions from an author know for the precision of her prose.
ISBN 0–906500–21–4

SACCHARIN CYANIDE
Anna Livia

Livia's snappy language is perfect for this collection of sexy thrillers and lyrical feminist fables.
ISBN 0–906500–35–4

THE NEEDLE ON FULL:
Lesbian Feminist Science Fiction
Caroline Forbes
Short stories and a novella about female astronauts.
Forbes' plots include: evidence free revenge, friendly
little green aliens, freedom in unexpected guises. An
invigorating first collection.
ISBN 0–906500–19–2

A NOISE FROM THE WOODSHED
Mary Dorcey
Short stories from the pen of Ireland's foremost
lesbian feminist poet. Rich, powerful, lyric imagery
infuses these exuberant, often hilarious, definitely
lesbian feminist stories.
ISBN 0–906500–30–3

WATER WINGS
Caroline Natzler
Elegantly written short stories about: brave, impetuous
children, sensible elderly women, fanciful middle-
aged feminists.
ISBN 0–906500–38–9

STRANGER THAN FISH
J. E. Hardy
Realistic stories about: the turbulence of 'coming out',
world-weary experience with heretofore heterosexuals,
family ties across time and nationality. Brilliantly
written tales of hard-won self knowledge.
ISBN 0–906500–32–X